# NOBLE STORM

WILLIAM MILLER

D1738127

LITERARY REBEL, LLC

NOBLE STORM

Copyright © 2022 by William Miller

Book and Cover design by www.LiteraryRebel.com

First Edition: July 2022

# NOTE TO THE READER

I started this novel in December of 2020, before Russia's invasion into Ukraine and the reader would do well to imagine the story taking place before the invasion as well.

Careful reading will reveal that I suspected Russia would move on Ukraine even then (December 2020), however I didn't think it would happen so soon. After the invasion I toyed with idea of changing locations so as to avoid the conflict altogether, but in the end, this is the story I wanted to tell.

In addition, you'll note that some characters refer to it as *the* Ukraine and others simply as Ukraine. That is intentional. Some people still use the definite article in front of Ukraine while others do not. And while I understand Ukrainians prefer the latter, it doesn't change the fact that many still use the former.

With that out of the way, let's get on with the show....

*Dedication and special thanks:*

*This one is for the fans.*

# CHAPTER ONE

Arkady Alexandrovich Lukyanenko backed his Skoda into a vacant spot at the curb, shifted into park and switched off the engine. The aging sedan died with a series of soft ticking sounds. He gathered a battered leather briefcase from the passenger seat, a Styrofoam cup of lukewarm coffee from the center console and threw open the driver's side door. A delivery truck honked and swerved. The driver yelled something, but it was lost beneath the shriek of rubber on asphalt.

Arkady took a minute to let his heart migrate back down into his chest. He had nearly spilled his coffee. The lid was half off and tepid dark liquid ran down over his knuckles. He held out the cup so none of it got on his slacks, checked for any more traffic and climbed out.

Arkady was on the wrong side of fifty, with thinning hair and a pot belly that hung over his belt. His overcoat was rumpled and fraying and his shoes were scuffed. He had to bump the door closed with his hip and only then realized his keys were still in the ignition. He muttered a curse, slung his briefcase on the roof of the car and grabbed for the handle, afraid he'd locked it. Ludmilla, Arkady's wife, claimed he would forget his head if it weren't screwed on. Maybe she was right.

By some stroke of luck, the car was unlocked and Arkady was able to retrieve his keys. He pocketed the fob, started up the sidewalk toward his apartment block and had to backtrack when he remembered the briefcase, still on the roof of the car. He finally made it up the steps to his building, let himself into the lobby and climbed the stairs.

Home was a two-bedroom suite on the third floor of an apartment block in the heart of Kiev. Arkady reached the landing, juggled the coffee and briefcase in one hand while rummaging in his pocket for his keys, then noticed the front door was open. His bushy brows made a V on his forehead as he let himself inside.

"Ludmilla?" he called. "Why is the door open?"

The television was on and Arkady smelled smoke. His belly filled with the first warm runny sense of danger. He hurried to the kitchen, where he found a cast iron pan of charred meat turning to blackened leather. Oily black tendrils curled up from the pan. Another few minutes and it would have set the smoke detector shrieking. Arkady dropped his briefcase and coffee on the counter; he really did spill the coffee this time, but paid no attention to the spreading puddle as he twisted knobs and snatched the pan from the stove top.

Exquisite pain raced up his arm. The flesh of his palm sizzled against the scalding cast iron. Arkady screamed, let go and the pan cartwheeled across the linoleum, spilling strips of burnt meat and hot oil. Arkady bent over double, clutching his scorched hand to his chest and mewling in pain. Now he knew why Ludmilla always used the pot holder for the cast iron. The skin of his palm was an angry red. Blisters were already forming. It was a second-degree burn, maybe third. He'd need a hospital.

"Ludmilla?" He went to the sink, avoiding splatters of oil on the floor and turned on the cold tap. He thrust his wounded hand under the running water and clamped his teeth around a groan. Shockwaves of searing pain radiated out from his palm, causing his arm to shake and his knees nearly buckled. "Ludmilla? Where are you?"

When she didn't answer, Arkady turned off the faucet, wiped tears from his eyes with the back of hand and checked the rest of the apartment. Their bedroom was empty. The second bedroom, the one Ludmilla used as her craft room, was a disaster zone. Several cabinets had been turned over; glitter, ribbon, buttons and stickers were everywhere. A pair of scissors lay on the floor. One side of the open blade was flecked with dried blood.

Arkady stood in the doorframe, staring at the mess. His heart beat out a gentle warning. He could still smell her perfume, hanging in the air like a snatch of song on the edge of memory. Who had taken her? And why? Arkady went to the bathroom, grabbed a bandage from the medicine cabinet and did his best to wrap his burned hand as he went back to the kitchen. A cordless phone hung on the wall. He tied the bandage in place with his teeth, dialed 02 and dropped the handset on the counter. He could hear the operator asking about his emergency as he rummaged through the kitchen cabinets for a bottle of aspirin. He found what he was looking for, dry swallowed several tablets, grabbed his brief-case and walked out the door. He didn't stop, and didn't look around as he made his way back downstairs. He went directly to his Skoda, slid behind the wheel and keyed the ignition.

## CHAPTER TWO

OLD EBBITT GRILL STANDS ON THE CORNER OF G Street and 15th, across from the Treasury Department, within walking distance of the White House. It's a DC mainstay, where Washington's movers and shakers like to meet up for a drink and discuss business. Originally constructed in the ground floor of the Ebbitt Hotel in the nineteenth century, the bar has changed locations and owners several times throughout the years. Albert Dulles, the CIA's director of operations, remembered when it was called simply the Ebbitt Grill and was located at 1427 F Street. Back in those days he had been more concerned about communist Russians than Middle Eastern extremists. He'd passed many a secret with West German intelligence officers sitting at the mahogany bar top. At the time, the Cold War had seemed so complicated, but it had been downright cut and dried. It had been us versus them, West versus East, freedom and capitalism versus an oppressive socialist regime hell-bent on world domination. Those had been the good old days, when Americans knew the stakes and were ready to do whatever it takes to win. Now the lines had blurred. The Russians were no longer seen as enemies and new threats had emerged to replace the specter of communism. September 11th had caused Americans to forget all about their adversaries in Eastern Europe. Instead, they had found a new enemy in Islamic extremism. But Dulles knew better. Middle Eastern terrorists, in Dulles's opinion, were merely an ugly blot on the long scroll of history, an inconvenient problem more to be endured than dealt with. Tin-pot dictators in the Middle East could rattle their sabers so far as Dulles was concerned. Sure, they had managed to give America a black eye, but that was all and nothing more. They could threaten and they could posture, and they might even blow up a few buildings, but in the end their days were numbered. Soon the oil would run dry and then the Middle East would go back to being a bankrupt scrubland in a corner of the globe where people rode donkeys to work and crapped in holes.

While his cohorts in the CIA had been hyper focused on the Middle East, communism had come creeping back, making inroads into the West, taking over countries and institutions, until the proverbial Huns were literally at the gates. Hell, they were inside the gates. They'd taken over American education and politics. And Wizard had watched it happen. He'd tried to raise the alarm, tried to warn Presidents and CIA directors alike, but no one would listen. So he'd kept a silent vigil, marking all the places communism had taken root, waiting for the day when he would once again be called on to do battle. Which is why Dulles wasn't surprised when an old friend from Ukrainian

Intelligence had asked for a meet on a chilly afternoon in early October.

Wizard tossed a butt as he pulled open the heavy brass door. He wore a Navy peacoat with the collar turned up. His grey hair was slicked straight back from a high forehead with enough castor oil to keep the blustery winds from making crazy patterns. He had a face carved from stone, deeply lined, with a gash where his mouth should be. He stepped into the warmth of the Old Ebbitt, shook off the chill and scanned the faces.

Andrei Popov sat in a corner booth, a large man in a tweed suit with a wide face and small, watery eyes that darted around the darkened interior, watching everything at once. He lifted one hand in greeting then cradled a tumbler of bourbon.

Wizard cut his way between tables, working the button on his coat with one arthritic claw and wedged himself into the booth. "Andrei. You're looking well."

In truth he looked as if he'd put on weight and his nose was a collection of busted blood vessels, but his dark little eyes were sharp as ever. Popov had been Wizard's line inside Ukraine during the bad old days of the Cold War. He and Popov had traded info when they weren't running ops against each other. It had been a confusing time when allegiances shifted with the weather.

Popov shrugged, lifted his glass and said, "My doctor tells me I have to lay off the drink for the sake of my kidneys."

"My doctor keeps telling me to give up cigarettes." Wizard flagged down a waiter and ordered a dry martini with olives.

"When did we get old?" Popov asked.

"Sneaks up on you." Wizard patted his pockets, found a pack of smokes and popped one into his mouth but didn't light it. Just having a butt clamped between his lips sometimes helped him think and Popov hadn't called him to reminisce. Wizard said, "It's this line of work. Makes you old before your time."

"You ever think about retiring?"

"You kidding?" Wizard said. "And give up tax payer-funded lunches at the Old Ebbitt with Ukrainian spies?"

"Spies." Popov shook his head. "You can no longer call it spy work. I sit around all day reading reports and getting fat."

"Longing for a return to the days of field work?"

"Longing for actual human intel. Everything comes from computer and satellite surveillance now days."

"The nature of the game has changed, but the mission remains the same."

"I didn't take you for an optimist."

Wizard lifted one boney shoulder. "A realist."

"Still," said Popov, "you must miss it?"

"The Cold War?"

Popov nodded.

"How can I miss what never ended?"

The waiter brought Wizard's drink and Popov lifted his glass. "To old times."

Wizard scooped up his martini and sipped.

"I've got a little problem," Popov said.

"I figured you might."

Popov glanced around the busy dining room, then took

his phone from his coat pocket and queued up a song. He set the volume low and placed the phone against the window. The music was too soft to be heard more than a few inches away, but the vibration against the glass would prevent anyone outside from picking up their conversation. Computers could turn the vibration from the glass into a transcript, a technology perfected by the CIA.

Popov folded his huge hands around his glass and lowered his voice. "Two weeks ago, a scientist working for our defense department disappeared. His name is Arkady Lukyanenko. He is a physicist who specializes in electro-magnets. He was working on an experimental EMP when he vanished. My superiors are trying to hush the whole thing up."

"Defection?" Wizard asked.

Andrei shook his big head and frowned. "This man, Lukyanenko, he is not the type to defect. He is a family man, content, no outstanding debt. He left work Tuesday evening and forty minutes later someone dialed emergency services from his apartment in the city."

"Which city?"

"Kiev," Popov clarified.

"And?"

"And emergency services show up twelve minutes later to find the place empty."

"Signs of a struggle?" Wizard guessed.

Popov nodded.

"And your people aren't interested?"

Popov shrugged one massive shoulder. "They came to the same conclusion as you, defection."

"It's been done before," Wizard said. "A man decides to defect and stages an abduction to cover his tracks."

"There were no early warning signs." Popov drained the last of his drink and signaled the waiter for another. "Usually, if it's going to rain, there are storm clouds."

"Anyone seen or heard from the wife?" Wizard asked.

Popov shook his head.

"When our people go missing we usually look into it," Wizard said.

"We are looking into it," Popov said, "but my paymasters don't want anyone to know about Lukyanenko's disappearance. I've got a bad feeling."

"What do you want from me?" Wizard asked.

Popov sucked his teeth, sipped his drink, thought it over and said, "Maybe you put one of your people on it?"

"That bad?" Wizard asked.

Popov hitched up his giant shoulders and let them sag. "Like I said, I've got a bad feeling."

Wizard picked up his martini and swirled it. "In this business you learn to trust your gut."

Popov's head went up and down in a slow nod.

"Give me everything you've got on this guy."

Popov produced a thick manila folder which he passed over the table.

Wizard took the file, put it on his lap without opening it, and said, "One more thing, Andrei. Is this you asking a favor of an old friend, or your country asking a favor?"

Popov emptied his glass. "If my people find out I brought this to you, I'll spend my retirement in a cell. I trust they won't find out about it?"

"I was never here and this never happened," Wizard said as he climbed out of the booth.

"Дякую," Popov said and then motioned to the drinks. "Eh... Any chance Uncle Sam could see his way to paying for the drinks?"

Wizard waved a hand in the air. "It's on the tax payer."

# CHAPTER THREE

"Next question," Ben Jameson said. He was a heavyset man in a garish sweater and he reeked of cologne. He was reading from a thick page of notes. "First team to call out the answer gets the point. What discovery earned Einstein his first Nobel prize?"

"Photoelectric effect!" Gwen shouted.

The denizens of CIA's third floor basement had gathered in the Town Tavern for their annual trivia competition. This year's topic revolved around physics. Ben Jameson was the moderator for the evening and promised everyone that he had come up with some devilishly wicked brain teasers. The computer ninjas were crammed in a booth near the back of the crowded bar. Ezra Cook was on Gwendolyn Witwicky's team and the two were generally considered unstoppable.

"Next question," said Ben. "How long does it take light to travel from the sun to the earth?"

"Approximately eight minutes," Gwen blurted out. Mousy brown curls were pulled back in a ponytail and coke-bottle glasses were slipping down her nose. She pushed them back in place with an impatient stab of her fingers.

"Correct." Ben marked another point for their team. "On your pads, what are the five main laws of physics?"

"Newton's Law of motion," Ezra whispered as he scribbled the answer on a yellow legal pad with a stub of pencil. He was shoulder to shoulder with Gwen, breathing in the intoxicating aroma of vanilla and lavender. Their thighs gently brushed under the table, making it hard for him to think.

Gwen counted the others off on her fingers. "Stefan's law, Coulomb's law, Ohm's law and Avogadro's law."

Ezra showed their pad and Ben scored them another point. Two other teams got it right as well.

"First to answer: what's the antimatter equivalent of an electron?" Ben asked.

Gwen practically came out of her seat. "Positron."

"Correct," Ben said and the other teams groaned.

Ezra held up a fist and Gwen bumped it.

The competition went well into the night. While the rest of the bar cheered the exploits of a local sports team on the flatscreens, Ezra and Gwen managed to keep a safe lead over their fellow coworkers.

Tonight was especially important because Ezra had finally decided to ask Gwen out. He had rehearsed his line countless times in his head. He was ready.

The last two months had brought them closer than ever. A big lunk by the name of Derek had shattered Gwen's heart and Ezra had been there to pick up the pieces. And just last week, Gwen had sworn off guys like Derek, the tall

WILLIAM MILLER

good looking guys with the easy smiles. Through puffy red eyes she had promised to only date guys in her league. Guys, she had said, more like Ezra.

If that wasn't an opening, Ezra didn't know what was.

Only he hadn't made a move that night. He had hesitated, like always, not sure if she was giving him the signal or not. It wasn't until later, lying in bed, staring up at the dark ceiling and replaying the interaction over and over, that Ezra had decided, yes, she'd definitely been giving him the green light. He wanted to kick himself for missing it, but reasoned that it wasn't too late. After all, if she had given him the green light once, surely it would come again. And Ezra had bided his time. But tonight, he decided, was the night. He was going for broke. Tonight he'd find out once and for all if he had a future with Gwen.

He was wearing his best sport coat and had a splash of expensive cologne on each wrist. He planned to brush a strand of Gwen's hair back at some point in the evening. It was a tip he'd picked up from a 1.99 ebook on how to attract women, called *Learn to Score!*

The first flaw in his plan came in the form of neuromuscular. His guts had turned runny at the first sight of Gwen. Suddenly his plan had seemed foolish and rash. What if she said no? What if she laughed in his face? It would humiliate him in front of the whole third-floor crew. It was an effort just to get a deep breath. His tongue had swollen up until it barely fit inside his mouth and his fingers had turned to blocks of wood. His body did not seem to be cooperating with him this evening. He had dropped his pencil on his way to the booth, had to bend over and scoop it up, and

14

nearly dropped it a second time. Gwen had giggled and Ezra felt his ears burning.

It had taken several minutes just to get his mouth working, but now that they were into the game, and winning, Ezra was feeling more relaxed. He even found an excuse to push back a lock of her hair when a curl came loose.

By the end of the evening, Ezra and Gwen were clutching a cheap trophy made from a circuit board glued to a magnifying glass and covered in imitation brass while Ben Jameson snapped a picture. Ezra leaned in until their heads were almost touching.

"This is going on the corkboard," Jameson said.

The other teams slapped them on the back and congratulated them. The night was going well and Ezra was feeling great. He was certain he could end the night with a kiss. Maybe even a hot and heavy make-out session.

But the second major flaw in his plan came in the form of three large frat boys with popped collars. They were coming in as Ezra and his group were leaving, and the two groups tangled in the entryway. The frat boys stumbled through the door, bringing with them the ripe smell of beer.

"Whatcha got there?" one of them asked in a drunken slur.

"Win sommat?" another one said and Ezra couldn't tell if it was a question or a statement.

"It's the annual trivia trophy," Ben Jameson informed them. "It's kind of a big deal."

The frat boys fell all over themselves laughing. One wiped a tear and said, "That so? Let's have a look then."

He reached for the trophy but Gwen pulled it away.

"Look with your eyes, not with your hands," she said.

Ezra cringed. He wished she hadn't spoken. Thus far she had escaped their notice. They were too inebriated to see much of anything, but as soon as she spoke up, the ring leader's dilated pupils found her through the soupy haze inside his brain and he formulated a sloppy grin on his face. "Hey, sweetie, it's all good. We're just having some fun."

"Yeah," another said, eyeing Gwen. "Fun."

Gwen narrowed her eyes. "Go have fun someplace else."

"Take it easy." The ring leader draped an arm over her shoulder, pulling her into a sideways hug. "We just want to be friends."

Gwen tried to shrug him off but he held on tight.

Growing up skinny and weak, Ezra had plenty of experience with bullies. Once they locked on a target they didn't let up. He had to do something to defuse the situation. He swallowed a cold hard knot in his throat and said, "Let her go."

"Oh, this your girlfriend?" He hugged Gwen a little tighter.

*Where was the staff?* Ezra wondered. *Why didn't someone step in and do something?*

Ben Jameson said, "Why don't you leave us alone?"

"Why don't you mind your own business, fat boy."

Ben's shoulders slumped and his face turned fire engine red.

Everyone one in the third floor basement knew Ben's weight was a bit of a sore spot. He'd tried and failed just about every kind of diet in existence and still couldn't lose the weight. Ben was fat, no denying it. He was also awkward, and he wore too much cologne and he was a hopeless geek, but he didn't deserve to be made fun of.

"You're mean," Gwen said. "Take your hands off me."

"What's the matter, honey? Don't you want to have a good time? I got a game we can play."

"Yeah," his friends guffawed. "We got a game to play. Want to play with us?"

"You heard her," Ezra said and started forward. "Take your hands off."

# CHAPTER FOUR

ONE OF THE FRAT BOYS STUCK HIS FOOT OUT AND THE other gave Ezra a shove. He yelped and went sprawling. He banged into a table, made a loud clatter, went to the floor and beer soaked through his sport coat.

The frat boys laughed like the audience at a Laurel and Hardy routine. One of them bent double, clutching his belly, pointing and hiccupping. Ezra sat there in a pool of beer, head swimming and ears burning. He tried to get up, slipped and went back down hard on his butt, which made the three bullies laugh even harder.

Gwen turned and brought her knee up in one smooth motion.

The ring leader let out a loud *oof* and doubled over. His friends stopped laughing. One of them called Gwen a dirty name and the other balled up his fists.

The commotion had finally got the attention of the bartender. He lifted his head to see above the crowd and hollered, "What's going on over there?"

The inebriated frat boys looked around at the over-turned table and broken glasses and decided to head for the door. The ringleader had to be helped. He was still bent over, hacking and coughing, and promising to make the slut pay.

Gwen crouched next to Ezra, concern bunching the pretty lines of her face. She put a hand out and asked, "You okay? Did they hurt you?"

Hot with shame, Ezra scrambled off the floor and headed for the bathroom. He turned on a faucet, splashed water on his face and inspected himself in a mirror. His sport coat was soaked and his face was pink. Tears mounted but Ezra managed to hold them back until a guy at the urinal finished and exited. The door opened, letting in a wave of noise, then clomped shut again. Ezra was finally alone and he let the tears flow.

Suddenly he was fourteen again, hiding in the school bathroom from the class bullies. He decided to stay until everyone left. No way could he go out there and face his friends. He would just stay here until they went home. But of course, that wasn't really a plan. At some point he'd have to go back out there and face the proverbial music or they'd come in looking for him.

He gripped the sink, hot tears pouring down his cheeks, wishing he wasn't such a coward. Two years of karate classes, and he'd been knocked down with no more effort than a child kicking over a sandcastle.

"What a wimp," he told the reflection.

The man in the mirror agreed.

Ezra stood there, hating himself, wondering how long

he could hide out in here when the door opened and Gwen poked her head in. She peeked to be sure he was alone, then let herself in. Her expression was one of concern, the kind of concern you have for a little boy who'd fallen and scraped his knee. She said, "You okay?"

Ezra scrubbed his face dry with his sleeves. He cycled through a series of emotions; love, shame, hope, fear, and finally settled on humiliation. He muttered, "Fine."

"Sorry about what happened."

Ezra shrugged.

"Those guys were complete jerks," she said and shook her head. "So immature. Did you hurt your head?"

She tried to touch his throbbing skull, but Ezra pulled away.

"I'm fine."

"I'm just trying to help."

"I don't need help."

"Are you mad at me?"

Ezra started to shake his head but that hurt. Tomorrow his neck would be stiff and sore. He said, "I'm mad at myself."

"Don't be so macho." Gwen took hold of him and bent his head towards her. "Let me have a look."

Ezra stood there, feeling like a little boy being tended by an over-protective mother. She prodded the goose egg forming on his skull and he winced. "I'm fine," he said. "Really."

"Don't be ridiculous."

He pulled away and Gwen said, "What is your problem?"

"This is not the way tonight was supposed to go," Ezra complained. "I wanted tonight to be…"

"What?"

"Special," Ezra said.

She nodded in quiet understanding, took a paper towel from the dispenser, wet it under the tap, and dabbed it against his aching skull. She said, "And the goon squad showed up to ruin it."

"I should have handled those guys," Ezra said.

"There were three of them and one of you."

"Doesn't matter."

"And they were all bigger," Gwen pointed out.

Ezra silently fumed. "I should be the one saving you, not the other way around."

"You think beating up a couple of bullies is going to impress me?"

His chin trembled and he could feel another wave of tears piling up behind his eyes. "Those are the kind of guys you like," he said. "Cocky guys with popped collars."

"That's not true," she said. "I like confident guys. There's a difference."

She hit a particularly sore spot and Ezra hissed. "Guess that leaves me out."

"Ez…" she wrung the paper towel out in the sink and stared at him in the bathroom mirror. "We've been over this."

He nodded and felt a lead anchor inside his chest hauling him down to the grimy bathroom tiles. "You could never go for someone like me," he said and a strange, choked half chuckle worked up from his throat. "Someone short and weak. A loser."

"You're not a loser, Ez."

"Then why won't you go out with me?"

The expression on her face was one you normally reserve for the family dog just before you haul the poor thing off to the vet for the last time to be put to sleep. She said, "Ez, you're a really nice guy, but I need someone who makes me feel..."

It was the part she didn't say that hurt the worst. She had been about to say she needed someone who made her feel safe. She had caught herself before she could finish. If she had jammed her thumb into the knot on his skull and pressed, it wouldn't have hurt nearly so bad. The anchor in Ezra's chest turned radioactive, burning through his heart and stomach, filling him with an ache that went deeper than anything the frat boys could do to him. He cleared his throat in an effort to swallow the hurt, nodded and said, "I get it. You want a guy who can stand up for himself."

"I didn't say that."

"You were about to."

She didn't try to deny it. Her face worked into a pitying smile and she said the five words every man hates the most. "Can't we just be friends?"

"Sure," Ezra heard himself say. "Of course."

"You're one of my best friends and I don't want to lose that."

She gave him a big hug that flattened his heart with the efficiency of a steam roller. When she let him go, Ezra said, "You have to get out of here now."

"Why?" she asked. "So you can be mad and fume?"

"Cause it's the men's room and I have to pee."

She laughed. "Right. Of course. Sorry."

When she'd left, Ezra turned and put his fist through the bathroom mirror. It cracked, showing him a fractured image of himself. Blood oozed up from his knuckles. He ran his fist under the faucet. There were no more tears, just a deep, hollow ache where his heart should have been.

# CHAPTER FIVE

"And you think it's your fault," Susan Sokol asked. She sat in an overstuffed chair, a silver ballpoint in one hand and a black leather notepad balanced on one knee. Sokol was a Georgetown graduate with dishwater blonde hair who wore just enough makeup to let people know she was a professional, and not interested in appearances. She was wearing a dark blue pantsuit today, along with beige heels that brought her a little closer to Jake's height.

Her office was clean and sparsely decorated with a soft beige carpet underfoot and a dozen accolades hanging on the walls.

"I'm the only one left to blame," Noble told her. He perched on the edge of a settee, his elbows on his knees with his fingers laced together. He had made it clear from day one he would not be laying down and talking about his relationship with his father.

"Why do you feel someone must be to blame?" Susan asked.

After his disastrous mission in Iran, the CIA had mandated Noble see a Company psychiatrist. Jaqueline Armstrong, director of CIA, had made it abundantly clear that if Noble ever wanted to work in the field again, he needed a clean bill of mental health. Since then, Doctor Sokol had been Noble's standing Wednesday evening date for the last two months.

"Seven guys went out and only one came back."

"And one little girl," Sokol said. "Don't forget her. You saved her life."

When Noble didn't reply she said, "And since you're the only member of the team who survived, that makes it your fault?"

"I was team leader." Noble stared at his scuffed boaters. "My decisions got them killed."

"Do you believe that if someone else had been in charge, they would have made better decisions?"

"Maybe," Noble said, but deep down he didn't believe it. Reyes may have made different choices along the way—he'd been opposed to the plan from the start—but that didn't mean the outcome would have been any different.

Susan leaned forward and cocked her head to one side. "Is that what you really believe?"

"Like I said"—Noble spread his hands—"I'm the only one left."

"You still haven't told me why anyone has to bear the blame," Sokol said. She leaned back, recrossed her legs, moving the notepad from one knee to the other, and waited. She had a habit of cutting through Noble's bull, getting right to the heart of the issue. He liked that and at the same time hated it. The way he both liked and hated her.

He stood up, went to the window and looked out over downtown Saint Petersburg. Sokol's office was on the seventh floor of a high-rise on Central Avenue, facing east. From here Noble could see the marina where his boat was docked. He watched toy cars motor along the roadway below and tried to think of an answer that didn't include survivor's guilt.

Susan joined him at the window, putting her notepad down on her desk and she asked, "Are the answers out there somewhere?"

Noble gave a half chuckle. "If they are, I haven't found them."

She put a hand on his forearm, gently turning him to face her. "Why does someone have to take the blame, Jake?"

A knot formed in his throat. "Because my friends are dead."

"Why not blame Madani?"

As a Company psychiatrist, Sokol had clearance and had seen all the relevant details of the mission in Tehran. Madani had been the Iranian commander who chased Noble and his team halfway across Iran. Noble laid awake nights thinking of ways to get Madani. He'd even cooked up a plan to infiltrate the country with a team of private operators and assassinate Madani, but couldn't bring himself to go through with it. There was no way he could pull off the mission without the CIA getting wise, and that would be the end of his career. Besides, taking a team into Iran on a revenge mission would only end up getting more guys killed. More corpses stacked directly at his feet. Noble scowled and chewed the inside of one cheek.

"Jake?" Sokol said. "Why not blame Madani?"

"He's just another cog in the wheel," Noble told her and went back to the settee.

"Then blame the wheel," Sokol said. Instead of going to her leather chair, she sat down beside him on the settee. "Why not blame the government of Iran?"

Noble didn't have an answer.

"Because the Iranian government is a faceless entity on the other side of the planet," she answered for him. "And you need someone to hate. Someone you can see every day. Someone who stares back at you from the mirror. He's always there, easy to blame. Easy to hate."

"Is this where you give me another lecture on survivor's guilt," he asked. "Tell me to stop the blame game so I can start on the road to recovery?"

"I see you read the book," she said.

"I read it," he assured her. "Some of it anyway. A lot of it was gobbledygook."

She grinned. "One of the world's leading psychiatrists wrote that gobbledygook, as you so eloquently put it. He's a very smart man."

"He ever lead men into battle?" Noble asked.

"You're very intelligent, Jake. You already know that you're beating yourself up out of a misguided sense of blame and smart enough to know that beating yourself up won't get you anywhere. So why not let it go? Why not admit that bad things happen in war, things that no one can control, and move on with your life?"

Noble sat in silence for several seconds. "Because I don't want any more bodies stacked at my door."

"You're worried that if you go back into the field, you'll lose more people," she said, a statement not a question.

He nodded.

She hesitated and he could tell she was choosing her words carefully. "Maybe the field isn't the right place for you, Jake."

Noble leaned away and questioned her with his eyes.

Sokol got up and crossed back over to her leather office chair. She took up her notebook, scribbled a note and then said, "Are you sure that's what you want?"

"That's why I'm here."

"Let's not kid ourselves," she said. "You're here because Armstrong ordered you to be here."

Noble shrugged. "You're going to suggest she reinstate me, right?"

Sokol looked down at her notes. "I'm not sure I can do that, Jake."

He leaned forward, coming halfway off the settee. "What are you talking about?"

She took a breath. "You've been through a lot, Jake. You've suffered traumas most other people couldn't even imagine. Perhaps it's time for you to leave the field. You'd make an excellent op commander and I'm sure if I put in a word with Armstrong I could get you a desk at Langley. Wouldn't it be nice to know where you're going to wake up every morning? I'm sure your mother would like to know that you're not jetting off to a dangerous country every couple of months to risk life and limb."

Noble leaned back and gripped the edge of the settee in his hands. "I can't believe I'm hearing this. I did what you asked, I read the books and processed through my feelings."

"That's part of the problem, Jake. You did what I asked, not because you wanted too, but because you want to get back in the fight. At this point I think you're addicted to the rush you get on a mission."

"I'm not a combat junkie," Noble told her.

"Be that as it may," she said, clearly unconvinced, "I'm not sure I can, in good faith, recommend you for field work. I don't think you'll ever be ready for field work again, Jake. I think it's time for you to transition into a normal life, make some friends, maybe even get married and start a family."

Noble sat there, her words ringing in his ears, feeling like he'd just been hit by a runaway bus. It was hard to get a deep breath. He finally said, "We're done here."

He stood up to leave.

"Jake," Sokol said, "I expect you here next Wednesday at the same time."

Noble jerked open the door and said, "What for? If you aren't going to clear me for field duty then there's no sense in me coming here."

"Jake... wait," Sokol said, coming up out of her seat and tossing the leather notepad onto her desk, but he was already out the door.

# CHAPTER SIX

Home was a forty-foot wooden sailboat with brass accoutrements christened *The Yeoman*, harbored in the Central Yacht Basin across from Straub Park. The ship rocked gently on a swell. Polished wood rubbed against the pylons and hawser lines creaked. The sun was a burnished copper disk in the west, throwing long shadows across the parking lot of bright white fiberglass hulls. October may be an autumn month for the rest of the country but Saint Pete Florida is still locked in summer's sweltering grip.

Noble sat in a lounger on the deck, his feet propped on the gunwale and a rod in his hand, trying to catch dinner. A breeze ruffled his long hair, bringing with it the smell of exhaust from Bayshore Drive. Noble was dressed in a green linen shirt, khaki shorts and deck shoes. At his feet lay a Czechoslovakian wolf-dog, his muzzle between his front paws and his eyebrows twitching. The wolf-dog had a thick leather collar around his neck with a tag that said his name was '*Gadsden*'. Noble had come up with the name on the spot when he'd taken the dog to a local veterinarian for a checkup. The college girl behind the counter had asked for a name and Noble gave the first that popped into his head.

His line danced, then tugged. Noble gave the rod a sharp jerk and started reeling but the line suddenly went slack. Whatever had taken a bite had absconded with his bait and left him with a mostly empty hook.

"We might be eating rice and beans again tonight," Noble told Gadsden.

His mother lived at the Wyndham Arms, *a thriving community for active seniors,* and most of Noble's money went to the exorbitant fees. The rest went into *The Yeoman.* There was nothing left over for things like food so Noble caught dinner most nights.

Noble reached into a red Igloo cooler beside his deck chair for more bait. A Jimmy Buffet tune floated across the harbor. Noble's neighbor three boats down was having a party. Several knockouts in string bikinis lay tanning on the deck. When *Son of a Sailor* ended the disk jockey came on to update Floridians on the hurricane taking shape in the Atlantic. The storm was tracking west, aiming for the Gulf of Mexico. Where it went from there was anybody's guess.

The dog let out a low growl and came to his feet. A moment later Noble felt the tell-tale shift as someone stepped on deck. He dropped the bait and pulled out a .45 caliber 1911 pistol instead. The nickel-plated semiautomatic winked in the setting sun. Noble slipped the fishing rod in a holder, rested the handgun alongside his thigh and swiveled around in the deck chair. It might be a neighbor popping by to say hello and Noble didn't want to scare them. Sticking a loaded .45 in your neighbor's face is the kind of thing that can get you evicted from the harbor.

Albert Dulles, AKA the Wizard, shuffled around the pilothouse to the back deck. He was dressed in a somber black suit with a slim black tie. Iron gray hair was slicked straight back from a high forehead. He clutched a brown paper sack filled with takeout in one arthritic claw. In the other, he carried a slim manila folder. He spotted the dog and stopped. "That mutt going to chew my leg off?"

"Depends," Noble told him.

"On?"

"Why you're here," Noble said.

Gadsden watched Wizard with steely blue eyes. One hundred and seventy pounds of muscle and fur, ready to pounce.

Wizard held up the takeout sack. "I brought tacos."

Noble turned to the dog. "Down boy."

Gadsden sat back on his haunches.

"To what do I owe the pleasure?" Noble returned the pistol to the cooler and closed the lid.

"Mind if we get out of this heat?" Wizard motioned to the galley.

"Not much cooler in there," Noble told him, "but at least we'll be out of the sun."

They stepped inside and the dog followed. Noble fetched two bottles of water from the fridge. Wizard eased himself into the galley table with a tired groan. Naugahyde creaked. He opened the sack. Inside were tacos from The Grumpy Gringo, a Mexican joint next door to Noble's favorite jazz bar.

He eased into the bench across from Wizard, opened the box and said, "You even got my order right."

One side of Wizard's mouth twitched with the ghost of

a smile. It was such a small movement others might miss it, but Noble had learned to read the taciturn Director of Operations.

"They remembered you," Wizard said as he lit up a cigarette. "Bad tradecraft for a field officer, having a regular haunt. That kind of routine could get a guy killed."

"I'm not a field officer," Noble said as he bit into a taco. He spoke around a mouthful of food. "Not anymore. You and Armstrong saw to that."

Wizard blew smoke up at the ceiling. "The shrink was Armstrong's idea."

"You went along with it."

Wizard hitched up one boney shoulder. "Had to be done. You know that."

Noble chewed his taco in silence.

Wizard said, "How's it going with Doctor Sokol?"

"Like you don't already know?"

Wizard drew on his cigarette and studied Noble with cold blue eyes. After a minute he tapped the manila folder with one nicotine-stained fingertip. "I've got something you might be interested in."

Noble worked a bit of tortilla shell from between his teeth with his tongue and said, "I'm not cleared for field duty and, according to Susan, I may never be."

"Susan?" Wizard turned up a brow. For the taciturn old spymaster it was tantamount to a shout. "You two are on a first-name basis?"

Noble didn't bother to respond.

"This is low risk." Wizard slid the folder across the galley table. "Strictly investigative work. You do this for me and I'll make sure you get a clean bill of mental health."

Noble studied the folder a moment before reaching for it. There was a red slash across the cover, meaning it was classified EYES ONLY. Inside was a brief dossier on a Ukrainian experimental physicist named Arkady Lukyanenko.

"What am I looking at?" Noble questioned.

"Lukyanenko went missing two weeks ago. He went home after work, dialed emergency services and left the phone off the hook. No one has seen him since. His wife is missing too."

"What was he working on?"

"Something to do with electro-magnets. That's all I know."

"When did you find out he was missing?"

"Yesterday."

"There's not much here," Noble said, paging through the file.

"Until today he was just a low-level physicist working out complicated maths for Ukraine."

"We thinking abduction?"

"Maybe." Wizard blew smoke. "There's a chance it's a defection."

"What makes you say that?"

Wizard put the cigarette to his lips, took a slow drag and said, "I've seen this type thing before. Hell, we used this play ourselves in the Cold War when Russian scientists wanted out of the Soviet Union. Pack a bag, wreck the house, then call the police on your way out the door. The other side thinks their person got rolled up by the opposition, meanwhile he and the family are setting up a new life as a mom and pop dry-cleaning operation in Juarez or

Buenos Aires. No one ever finds out what happened and the other side can only speculate."

"How did we get wind of it?"

"I've got friends inside Ukrainian intelligence. They asked us to take a peek."

Noble's eyebrows crept up his forehead. "The Ukrainians want our help finding their missing scientist?"

Wizard nodded.

"Any idea why?"

"Several. None of them good," Wizard said. "One thing is certain; this guy wasn't working on improved cell reception."

"Where do we even start?"

"You in?"

"If it means you'll reinstate me."

"He has a remote cabin in the mountains outside Kiev," said Wizard. "If he was keeping secrets that's where we'll probably find them. Got someone who can take care of the mutt?"

"Might take me a few days to arrange."

"What about that cute little number who sings at the club?"

"Ruby," Noble told him and shook his head. "She watched Gadsden for me while I was in Iran but I have a feeling that's no longer an option."

"I'll make sure the dog is taken care of," Wizard said. "Pack a bag. We'll fly back to Langley together and you can meet your team."

Noble was halfway out of his seat when he stopped. He sat back down and said, "No way. I don't need a team."

Wizard blew smoke and shook his head. "No dice, Jake."

"I can do this on my own."

"You know that's not going to happen," Wizard said. "Your last mission went to hell. You watched six friends get butchered and you've spent the last two months on a psychiatrist's couch. No way is Armstrong sending you out alone."

"More people means more risk," Noble argued. "More chance someone will screw up. I don't need any more bodies."

"You go with a team or you don't go at all," said Wizard. "What's it going to be?"

Noble thought about it and said, "You'll get me off the hook with Su... Doctor Sokol?"

Wizard inclined his head. "But only if you take a team."

# CHAPTER SEVEN

Arkady Lukyanenko had a rough woolen sack over his head that smelled of sawdust and mold. They'd cuffed his hands together behind his back and his fingers were going numb. He was in a plane—felt like a small Cessna, definitely not a commercial airliner—travelling through rough weather.

They had been waiting for him at the cabin. He never should have gone back, but he needed his papers. The place had been ransacked. That was the last Arkady remembered. Someone had socked him over the head and stuck a needle in his arm. When he woke, Arkady thought he'd gone blind. It was a moment before he'd realized he had a bag on his head. Then he heard the rumble of jet engines. No one spoke but Arkady knew they were close. He asked who they were and what they wanted. They refused to answer. Arkady had no idea how long they'd been in the air. He was beyond terrified, to the point that fear and exhaustion had mingled into a kind of numb shock.

His throat felt like it had been scrubbed with steel wool

and his bladder was about to pop. He never knew it was possible to be so badly in need of water and desperate for a toilet at the same time. It seemed it should be one or the other.

The aircraft hit a pocket of turbulence and Arkady's teeth came together on his tongue. He tasted the hot coppery taint of blood and spat against the inside of the hood. He had given up hope of rescue. He was a dead man. The people who abducted him were professional and had left nothing to chance. Arkady had to wonder if it was his own government. Had Ukrainian authorities learned of the research secrets Arkady had sold to the Russians over the years? It was possible. Arkady wasn't above the occasional bribe and most of the research he did was not all that sensitive. He had made minor alterations to the documents before passing them to the Russians. It was a victimless crime. The Russians never got enough to reverse engineer whatever Arkady's department was working on and Arkady was able to enjoy the little things, like a new pair of rabbit fur slippers to soothe his aching feet at the end of a long day, or a pretty pearl necklace for Ludmilla. His wife got pearls. His mistress got lacy black thongs and a monthly allowance. And Arkady got his needs met. But now he wondered if all the excess had come back to haunt him?

No, Arkady thought. If Ukraine had learned of his double dealing, he would be in a cell right now, not the back of a twin-engine Cessna. Why bother with all the cloak and dagger? Ukrainian authorities would have simply arrested him. This was something else. Russians? It was possible. That would explain the plane ride.

"Where are we going?" he asked through the hood.

He got no answer. He knew there was a man sitting next to him; Arkady could hear the soft rustle of fabric and feel the man's weight on the seat.

"Are we in Russia?" Arkady asked.

Still no answer.

The plane slammed through another pocket of turbulence but this time Arkady avoided biting his tongue. He didn't bother asking any more questions. It was useless and talking only made his throat hurt. He tried to ease the weight off his hands, but the metal cuffs dug into the small of his back so he let his fingers turn to dead stumps and wondered where they were taking him. He thought about Ludmilla. Was she okay? Did they have her too? Had they hurt her? Not knowing only made his fear worse.

The plane eventually slowed and started a descent. The weather turned rough, the small craft hitched and bucked on choppy currents. Someone muttered a curse. Arkady could hear rain lashing against the fuselage. The engines climbed to a throaty roar and then tires touched down with a shriek. The craft taxied over bumpy terrain and finally came to a stop.

When the hatch opened, Arkady felt a wave of tropical heat, like the breath from an open oven, and knew they were not in Russia. Fingers like iron bands dug into the soft flesh of his arm and dragged him from the plane into a steady downpour. He stumbled through muck and almost fell but the man holding his arm pulled him back up.

"Doctor Lukyanenko," a deep Arabic voice said. The sack was jerked off Arkady's head, leaving him momentarily blinded by the driving rain. "Welcome to Cuba."

# CHAPTER EIGHT

WIZARD STOOD WITH HIS HIPS AGAINST THE SHARP edge of his desk, his arms folded over his boney chest and a Chesterfield spooling out thin ribbons of sweet blue smoke which formed halos around buzzing fluorescents. His office was a madhouse of folders, leaning stacks of papers and sticky notes covered in Wizard's tiny scrawl. One entire wall was hidden beneath newspaper clippings, surveillance photographs, operation reports, and red string. The ceiling tiles were stained a sickly yellow and ashtrays full of butts nestled between tottering piles of paper. Wizard took a drag, let out a stream of smoke and squinted at the collection of information.

There was a knock and before Wizard could open his mouth, his secretary stuck her head in. "Irate psychologist on Zoom."

"You know I don't know how to make that work."

His secretary crossed around his desk, woke his computer and opened a new window. Susan Sokol was on screen, demanding to know why Noble was gearing up for an operation.

"With all due respect, Director, I haven't cleared Jake Noble for field duty," Sokol said.

"Good to see you too Ms. Sokol." Wizard blew smoke.

Her dishwater blonde hair was cut in a no-nonsense, shoulder-length style. She was thin and good looking in an academic sort of way, but her face was a little too narrow to be a stunner. A little extra makeup wouldn't hurt either, but Wizard had the impression Sokol was the type of woman who went with minimal face paint in a misguided attempt to prove she was a serious professional. She was the type woman who would tell you looks don't matter, but still spent an hour in the mirror every day trying to carefully construct just the right balance between pretty and low maintenance.

Wizard lowered himself into his office chair with a grunt. "I take it you've been informed about Jake's impending operation." He made a mental note to find out who had let that detail slip and detail them to a radar dish in Alaska.

"There's not going to be any operation," Sokol said. "Not for Jake anyway. He's not cleared for field duty."

"Calling it an operation might be an overstatement," Wizard said. "We just need him to hop a plane to the Ukraine and check up on some personnel for us."

Sokol shook her head, tossing her dishwater bangs. "Out of the question."

"Look, Ms. Sokol, I like you. You're a professional," Wizard said, telling her the things she wanted to hear. "We both have jobs to do. All I'm asking for is a little cooperation."

She crossed her arms. "You're asking me to send a mentally unfit man into a potentially dangerous situation. I won't do it."

"Mentally unfit might be a little hyperbolic."

"I wasn't aware you held a degree in psychology."

"My understanding of human psychology was earned the hard way," Wizard told her. "Through experience."

Sokol huffed and shook her head. "I forgot, you old-school types know everything there is to know about human behavior because you've lived it."

"Experience is the best teacher."

"If you put Jake Noble into a dangerous situation, I don't know how he's going to react."

"No one knows how they'll react under pressure until it happens," Wizard said. "Surely they taught you that at Georgetown. Don't forget, Jake has a lot of training and experience to fall back on. I think you underestimate him."

"And I think you overestimate him," Sokol said. "I don't think you appreciate the kind of psychological damage he's been through. His entire team was wiped out. Jake watched them die. You don't just get over that. It's not the type of trauma you shrug off."

"Unfortunately, in the spy business we often have to do just that," Wizard told her. "Comes with the territory."

"I can't believe I'm hearing this."

Director Armstrong rapped her knuckles on the open doorframe and stuck her head in. "What's all the fuss?"

"Who is that?" Sokol wanted to know. She couldn't see the door from her angle.

"Director Armstrong," Wizard said. "I've got doctor Sokol on the line."

Sokol said, "The deputy director has activated Jake Noble for a mission to Ukraine."

Armstrong's eyebrows went up. She stepped inside the crowded office and said, "I wasn't aware you had an operation on."

"Nothing to bother the Director over," Wizard said. His face was a careful mask. "I just need an extra set of eyes."

Sokol said, "You can't let him go through with this, Mrs. Armstrong. Jake's got no business being in the field."

Armstrong stuffed her hands in the pockets of her fitted pinstripe blazer and fixed Wizard with a questioning look. "What have you got brewing, Al?"

Wizard leaned back in his seat and shot smoke up at the ceiling. He was trapped. He had to give the Director some excuse for sending Jake Noble into the field so he told her about the missing scientist.

"And you chose Jake of all people," Sokol said.

"Best job for the man," Wizard said.

"What do you mean by that?" Armstrong asked.

"I mean the best thing for Jake is to get back on the horse," Wizard told her. "The kid is tough as nails. He'll bounce back. He always does. Sitting on a sofa talking about his relationship with his father isn't going to get him there. He needs to get his head back in the game."

"That's not your decision to make," Sokol said. "I'm the psychologist assigned to this patient. Any field assignments have to be cleared by me, and Jake Noble is not cleared for field duty."

Wizard sniffed. "Help me out here Director."

"I'm inclined to agree with Doctor Sokol. What's your reasoning for sending Noble?"

Wizard tapped ash. "I told you already. I believe the best thing for Noble is to be back in the field and this mission is very low risk."

"How low?" Armstrong asked.

"Minimal."

"But there is risk," Sokol pointed out.

"There's always risk," Wizard said.

"I'm not willing to clear Jake for field duty based on the folksy wisdom of a Cold War warrior," Sokol said. "No offense, Mr. Dulles."

"Because Noble is not fit for field duty or because you're developing romantic feelings for him?" Wizard shot back.

Sokol's eyes got big. She covered her surprise with a scoff of indignation. "That's preposterous."

"Is it?" Wizard asked. "I checked the logs. Noble has been on your couch two months now. None of my other field officers have seen you more than four sessions."

"None of the rest have suffered nearly as much Trauma as Jake."

"None of them quite so rakishly good looking either," Wizard added. "He's about your age too. A guy like Noble would make a better than average husband if only you could keep him out of the field. Maybe get him a nice job teaching trainees on the Farm while he comes to terms with the fact that his days as a field officer are over?"

Sokol let out a breath, shook her head, ran a hand through her hair and then turned her eyes to Armstrong.

"This is preposterous. Director, I've been nothing but professional in my dealings with agency people."

"I'm not suggesting you've been anything less," Wizard said. "I'm only suggesting that your feelings for Jake, as you keep calling him, are coloring your perception."

Armstrong leaned her back against the wall and studied Sokol. "Any truth to this, Doctor?"

"I've never set a foot out of line."

"That's not what I asked," Armstrong said. "Are you developing feelings for Jake Noble?"

Sokol wet her lips with her tongue. "It's true that I'm attracted to Ja... Noble, but I would never let it affect my professional opinion of his mental health. He's not ready to be back in the field and he probably never will be."

Armstrong nodded. "Thank you for your assessment, Doctor. For now, I'm going to give Noble temporary clearance for limited field duty. Dulles, I'm assuming he's not travelling alone?"

Wizard shook his head. "He'll be part of a team."

"Part of a team?" Sokol asked, "Or the leader?"

"An integral part," Wizard admitted.

Sokol shook her head. "I'm lodging a formal complaint. This is all going into my report. I want it noted that I was against this from the start."

"Duly noted," Armstrong said.

"Don't say I didn't warn you," Sokol said.

Armstrong nodded. "You're not under scrutiny here, Susan."

"Why did you even hire me if you aren't going to take my advice?"

"I take your objections very seriously," Armstrong said.

Sokol let out a hysterical little laugh. "So that's it then? You two are just going to override me? What happens when Jake goes completely off the rails?"

"He won't," Wizard said.

"You don't know that," Sokol said.

"And you can't be sure he'll crack up," Wizard countered.

"Fine but you're going ahead with this against the recommendation of a trained psychologist."

Armstrong said, "You've made your point, Doctor."

Sokol stared at Armstrong as if she couldn't believe what she was hearing, then shook her head and mashed a button on her keyboard. The screen went blank and a notice popped up informing Wizard that his meeting had ended.

Armstrong turned to Wizard. "I hope you're right about this, Al. I just took a big risk backing your play. Are you sure Noble is up to this?"

"He'll be fine," Wizard assured her. "This job is just what he needs."

"You keep saying that." Armstrong had to move a stack of papers so she could sit. "I hope you're right. What if this turns out to be more than a simple affair?"

"Then we'll be glad Noble is running the show."

Wizard's eyes went to the wall and Armstrong followed his gaze. "You chasing ghosts again?"

"It might be more than just a missing scientist," Wizard told her.

Armstrong took in some air and let it out through pursed lips. "This is an unhealthy obsession. You know that, right?"

Wizard pulled on his cigarette.

"What if the good doctor is right?" Armstrong asked. "We can't have an agent going off the rails. How are you planning to keep Noble in line?"

"I've got a pair of babysitters," Wizard told her.

# CHAPTER NINE

THERE WAS A STICKY NOTE ON GWEN'S COMPUTER when she got to work the next morning. She plucked the yellow square from her monitor and squinted. An untidy scrawl that looked like it belonged to Duc Hwang read; *Armstrong's office. 9AM sharp!* Which meant... Gwen checked the time on her computer.... she was already two minutes late. She pocketed the note and hurried across campus toward the Old Building, wondering why the Director of the CIA wanted to speak with her so early in the morning. There must be a mission brewing. Or Gwen had screwed up. CIA had three thick binders full of rules and regulations they expected every employee to memorize. It was hard to keep all the different rules straight and, even though Gwen had read all three binders cover to cover making notes along the way, she still occasionally committed minor infractions. Twice she had been verbally warned by the CIA's internal security division. Once she had received a written warning. But she had been squeaky clean since and as she crossed the quad between buildings, she decided it must be a mission. Unless of course the Director had gotten wind of last night's dust up. Physical altercations with civilians were strictly prohibited. Had Armstrong somehow found out? And if so, Gwen wondered just how much trouble she was in. She had nailed one of the smart alecks in the balls, sure, but it was self-defense. And he deserved it. But that excuse wouldn't cut muster with Armstrong.

Gwen shook her head, tossing mousy brown curls, and walked a little faster.

Last night had been a complete disaster. Ezra had been humiliated in front of the entire bar and gone off to the bathroom to sulk. Then he went and made things even more awkward by asking Gwen out. He was sweet, and incredibly genuine, but he had the world's worse timing. Over the last few weeks, Gwen had started warming up to the idea. Derek had broken her heart and the thought of settling into a relationship with someone who liked the same things, someone like Ezra, really appealed to her. But seeing him pushed around by a couple of frat boys had put an end to that. On paper they were a perfect pair, both bona fide members of the geek community. They both liked video games, superhero movies, and roleplaying games, but Ezra just didn't do it for Gwen. She had spent long hours asking herself why and finally come to the conclusion that Ezra didn't make her feel safe. He was sweet, well-mannered, and intelligent, but he wasn't someone who could change a tire. He certainly couldn't protect her from bad guys. And Gwen knew better than most that the world was full of bad guys. It was unfortunate too. They'd make a good team if Ezra would only man up.

She shelved all that emotional drama as she stepped out of the elevator onto the seventh floor and passed a sea of cubicles lit by anemic fluorescents. Armstrong's secretary, a stodgy old librarian with halfmoon spectacles riding low on a thin nose, motioned Gwen to the door. "Go right in. They're waiting."

"Who's they?" Gwen asked.

But Farnham had turned back to her desk and was peering down her nose at a stack of reports.

Gwen knocked once and pushed through the door into the director's office. Track lighting illuminated a bookshelf full of thick operations binders and leather-bound volumes. There was a plush blue carpet underfoot emblazoned with the CIA emblem in gold, and a pair of sofas flanking a low coffee table. Albert Dulles, deputy director of operations, was there along with Ezra. Dulles clutched an unlit cigarette in one mangled claw and watched Gwen with cold blue eyes that seemed to peer right down into her soul, as if he could read her thoughts.

Armstrong was behind her desk, her blonde hair up in a French twist and held in place by a plastic clip. She was a no-nonsense woman who wore pinstripe business suits and just enough makeup to cover the worry lines. She motioned Gwen to a seat on one of the sofas.

"You wanted to see me?" Gwen said.

Wizard consulted his watch. "You're late, Ms. Witwicky."

"I uh... had a rough night. Got a late start today," Gwen said. "It won't happen again."

"So we heard," Wizard croaked.

Ezra had a goose egg on the side of his head, half hidden

by untidy shocks of black hair. His eyes flicked to Gwen and then back to his scuffed Converse tennis shoes. He looked like a schoolboy called to the headmaster's office. His ears were bright pink and his prominent Adam's apple kept bobbing up and down.

Armstrong stood, crossed around her desk and leaned her hips against the edge. "Mr. Cook tells me you two had a bit of an incident last night at a local drinking establishment."

"Is that what this is about?" Gwen asked. "It wasn't our fault really. Three jerks singled us out because of our trophy."

Wizard had his lighter out and was about to touch flame to his cigarette. He paused. "Your trophy?"

Gwen nodded. "A science trophy."

"Is that some sort of hipster slang, Ms. Witwicky?"

"No, sir," Gwen said in a small voice. "It was an actual trophy."

Wizard lit up and blew smoke. "You won a trophy?"

"For the third floor annual trivia night," Gwen said and her voice seemed to be shrinking down to a squeak. "Every year the entire third floor basement has a trivia night. This year the topic was physics. Ezra and I won."

Armstrong turned to Ezra. "You forgot to mention that part, Mr. Cook."

Ezra sank a little lower in his seat.

Wizard said, "Let me see if I understand; every year the entire third-floor crew gathers in a public drinking house to quiz each other on advance scientific principles?"

"It's nothing you couldn't get from google," Gwen said but her voice was a broken whisper now.

"And these three men picked your group out of the crowd?" Armstrong asked.

Gwen nodded and Ezra said, "They saw the trophy and started making fun of us."

"Did it occur to either of you that they might be a foreign intelligence outfit?" Wizard asked through a cloud of smoke.

Ezra's mouth hung open. Gwen shook her head. "They were just frat boys."

"That's what agents would want you to think," said Wizard.

Armstrong said, "So a couple of frat boys, or foreign intelligence officers, made fun of your trophy and you decided to pick a fight."

"That's not what happened," Ezra said.

"They picked a fight with us," Gwen said.

"And you kicked one of them between the legs." Armstrong crossed her arms and studied Gwen.

"I didn't really kick him. I just kneed him."

"And you know that drunken altercations are a fireable offence," Wizard said.

Gwen came halfway off the sofa. "We were just defending ourselves. They pushed Ezra down and one of them tried to accost me. Ask anybody."

"We will," Armstrong assured her.

"How much trouble are we in?" Ezra asked.

"Depends." Wizard leaned forward and tapped ash into a brass dish on the coffee table. "If we find out it's like you say, you'll be reprimanded and get a ding on your service record. If we find out you were the instigators, you could be facing possible termination."

Gwen felt a frosty finger working its way into her guts. "What happens to us in the meantime?"

"We've got a little assignment for you," Armstrong said.

Ezra sat up straight. "We're not suspended?"

Wizard shook his head. It was just a small back and forth motion, barely noticeable unless you looked for it. "As punishment for your indiscretions, you two will be part of a team headed to the Ukraine."

Gwen couldn't quite believe what she was hearing. Instead of a reprimand, they were being sent on an overseas assignment. Something didn't add up. She said, "We're computer ninjas, sir. Our only field experience was Mexico City."

"A standout performance," Wizard said with a perfectly straight face.

"Yes, I read about your exploits in Mexico," Armstrong said. It was before her time as Director but she had access to the case files. Gwen and Ezra had been disarmed and stranded in the middle of nowhere. "I'm sure you'll both do fine. You handled yourselves pretty well last night."

Gwen's eyes narrowed behind her coke-bottle glasses. "Why us?"

Wizard explained to them about the missing scientist and finished with, "Jake Noble will do most of the heavy lifting, but he might need a pair of brains to help with the science. As I understand it, you minored in physics at university, Ms. Witwicky."

Armstrong said, "And you both won a trophy last night for science."

The icy finger in Gwen's belly gave a wiggle. "What

exactly are we dealing with here? What was Lukyanenko working on?"

"We don't know," Wizard said. "Maybe something. Maybe nothing. Maybe he and the wife ran off to Acapulco. We won't know until we investigate."

"And we're working with Noble," Ezra said.

"Is that a problem?"

"No problem," Gwen said. "It's just that..."

"Trouble has a way of finding Noble," Ezra finished for her.

"And his last mission..." Gwen said.

"Didn't go so well," Ezra added. "Word around the water cooler..."

Gwen shrugged. "People say he's cracked up."

"That's why we want you two on board," Wizard told them. "You are going keep an eye on Jake for me. If he starts to come apart, you can pull the plug."

"So we'd technically be in charge," Ezra said.

Armstrong nodded. "That's right, Mr. Cook. You and Witwicky are going to be the team leaders, but Jake's got all the experience, so you'll need to rely on his judgement."

"Get down to the Office of Technical Services," Wizard said. "They've got luggage, phones, cover legends and pocket litter for you both. You're on a seven thirty flight to Kiev."

# CHAPTER TEN

ARKADY LUKYANENKO STOOD IN THE CARGO HOLD OF A large plane. Big wet beads of sweat gathered on his forehead, trailed down his face and formed fat drops on his unshaven chin. All of his research was laid out on a series of worktables made from particleboard and held up by sawhorses, along with the various parts and tools needed. Work lamps hung from the roof of the cargo bay, throwing off heat, turning the plane into a sweatbox. The floor was covered in rubber to protect against static discharge and thick electric cables pulled juice from a large generator sitting at the base of the ramp.

Beyond the open cargo door was a small airstrip of hard packed earth with two rusting Quonset huts and a crude fuel locker surrounded by miles of fetid jungle. Banyan trees made an impenetrable wall in every direction.

Arkady, who had never been to the tropics before, was layered in sweat. His shirt was pasted to his back and his underwear was a soggy rag. He had a hard time getting a deep breath. It felt like his lungs were full of water and his heartbeat was a low thrumming in his own ears. He had barely slept, tossing and turning on a low canvas cot in the back of the cargo plane. He mopped a slick of sweat from his forehead and gazed out at the jungle.

Fifty or sixty meters of open ground separated the plane from the thick tangle of vegetation.

*And then what?* Arkady thought.

What would he do then? Where would he go? He had no idea where he was, or in which direction the nearest town lay. He would probably end up wandering the jungle until he dropped dead of dehydration. Or until his captors found him and dragged him back.

He was looking at the trees, gathering up his courage to run, when the Translator started up the ramp with a plate of food in hand. He was a tall Arab with sloped shoulders and a neatly trimmed beard disfigured by a puckered scar on his right cheek. The guards, in their Cuban military fatigues, referred to him as simply The Translator. He spoke perfect English and was unfailingly polite but there was a cruel streak beneath his cultured façade.

"You'd never make it, Doctor. We're surrounded by forty kilometers of impenetrable jungle in every direction."

Arkady thrust his chin at the food. "For me?"

"Hope you like *huevos con frijoles*," he said. "It's pretty much all we get round here."

Arkady didn't speak Spanish but the translation wasn't difficult. The plate was swimming in runny eggs and black beans. He wondered which were the huevos and which were the frijoles. In the end he decided it didn't matter. He reached for the plate and started gobbling beans with his bare hands before the Translator passed him a slightly warped spoon of rusting metal.

"Just because we're in the tropics doesn't mean we can't be civilized," he said.

"Kidnapping is your idea of civilized?" Arkady asked around a mouthful of food.

"Think of it rather as an opportunity for unbroken concentration," the Translator said.

Arkady put the plate down, wiped his chin with the back of one hand, then ran his gaze over the collection of parts and shook his head. "I won't do it."

"You haven't any choice," The Translator said. "We have your wife. If you don't want to her suffer, you'll do as we ask."

"Why are you doing this?"

"You are a married man," The Translator said. "Wouldn't you do anything to protect your wife?"

"Of course but..."

"And if your family was killed," The Translator asked, his voice low and dangerous, "would you not avenge them?"

Arkady had no answer.

"Get to work, Doctor. Your wife is counting on you."

"I want to see her," Arkady said. "I need to know she's okay."

"When the work is finished, you and your wife will be reunited and my associates will escort you both anywhere in the world you wish to go."

Arkady said, "I don't believe you. She's dead, isn't she?"

The words should have choked coming out, should have brought tears to his eyes, but he was numb to the horror. Instead he sounded like a man commenting on stock prices.

"If she was still alive, you'd have shown me video. You'd have her here, now, where you could use her to control me." He shook his head. "You killed her, didn't you? What happened? Did she put up too much fight?"

The Translator gave a rueful grin. "I'm afraid you're right. Your wife is dead. It was an unfortunate accident, I assure you."

"Then you've got nothing," Arkady told him. "Kill me now because there's no way I'm going to do what you ask."

"You'll finish the work, Doctor Lukyanenko." The Translator stepped forward and Arkady retreated. "You're going to do *exactly* as I say."

"And why would I do that?"

"What about Ms. Anastasia Rudenko?" The Translator asked with a polite smile. "We can get to her as well. She's very pretty. It would be a shame if anything bad were to happen to her. And there is your sister. She's living in Odessa, correct? We can get to her too. In fact, we can get to anybody and everybody you care about, my friend."

The Translator kept advancing, backing Arkady into a corner. He laid a hand on Arkady's shoulder and squeezed. "Please, don't make this harder than it has to be. Do what you are told, finish the work, and you can go home. Won't that be nice? You can go on back to your comfy cabin on the lake, sit down by the fire and forget all about this."

"And the device?" Arkady asked. "Where are you going to use it?"

"Do not worry yourself about that, friend. You just need to focus on finishing the task at hand."

Arkady felt himself nodding. What else could he do? This man, and his thugs, had snatched Arkady right out of the heart of Kiev. They'd have no trouble getting to Anastasia. He swallowed a lump in his throat and heard himself say, "Okay. I'll do it."

"Very good," The Translator said and started back down the ramp. "And please don't take long. We have something of a schedule to keep."

## CHAPTER ELEVEN

Noble was cramped next to the window, his forehead riding against the fuselage, rattling slightly with the turbulence. He was sleeping, or trying to. Cook kept muttering under his breath and it was intruding on Noble's sleep. They were flying coach aboard a direct flight to Kiev. The big jumbo commuter had lifted off from Dulles international just after eight in the evening. Kiev was seven hours ahead of DC which meant they'd be landing close to three in the afternoon. Noble peeled open one eye for a peek at his watch to confirm his math. He had replaced his broken Tag Heuer with a much less expensive Citizen Nighthawk. His math was good and he reset his watch to local time as the pilot came over the intercom to inform them, first in English then Ukrainian, that they would be landing in fifteen minutes. "Please fasten seat belts and return all seats to the full and upright position."

Noble rubbed sleep from his eyes and cleared his throat. "What are you muttering about?"

"How do you keep it all straight?" Cook asked.

"Keep what straight?"

"Cover legends," Cook said under his breath.

"You went to the Farm," Noble said. "You had the same training I did."

"I'm a computer jockey. I never thought I'd be going on..."—he glanced once around the compartment and dropped his voice to a whisper—"on classified operations. First time I was in the field I had diplomatic cover. I didn't need a legend. How do you do it? How do you keep all this stuff straight?"

"You want the secret?" Noble asked as the big commuter jet started down through the clouds with a whine of over-taxed engines.

Cook nodded.

"Remind yourself that your life depends on it," Noble told him. "*My* life depends on it too. There's no room for amateurs in this line of work, so man up, buttercup."

Noble stared out the window at a scrim of slate-gray clouds that broke up to reveal the city of Kiev laid out below like a vast miniature. The metropolis was surrounded by lush rolling fields, dotted with trees dressed in fall foliage, giving color to the lifeless autumn landscape.

Cook glanced once at Witwicky who was pretending to sleep. "Just cause I'm not Joe macho doesn't make me a sissy," he said. "I have skills you don't. I'll bet you don't know a router from a hard drive."

Noble knew the difference but didn't bother to tell Cook. He said, "That's the *only* reason you're here."

A stewardess came down the aisle handing out customs

cards and collecting trash. The plane hit a pocket of turbulence and the overheads rattled. Noble said, "Stop pretending to sleep, Witwicky. We're landing."

"I'm not pretending," she said without opening her eyes. She was curled up in her seat with her arms wrapped around her knees and her head propped on a small travel pillow. Her thick glasses were askew. "I'm resting my eyelids."

Cook snatched his customs card from the stewardess and scribbled on it with the stub of a pencil while his ears turned bright red. Noble studied the pair for a moment, wondering which of them would die. He said, "Don't forget to use your cover legend."

Cook ripped his card into tiny pieces of confetti and flagged the stewardess down for another. Witwicky pushed her glasses into place and went about filling in the relevant details. The two analysts, normally thick as thieves, had barely spoken a word to each other the entire twelve-hour flight. Noble figured it was a lover's spat. Operations had gone to hell over far less. And when operations go bad, people die. Without looking up from his card, Noble said, "Is this going to be a problem?"

"What are you talking about?" they asked in unison.

"What's going on between you two?"

"There's nothing going on between us," Witwicky said.

Cook said, "I don't know what you're talking about."

"Long as it doesn't get in the way of the job," Noble told them.

They were traveling under false passports that listed them as two accountants and one operations manager working for a global conservation outfit based out of Seattle. The CIA's science and technology division, known within the halls of Langley as the Alibi Shop, had supplied IDs to them on short notice. Noble was traveling under the name Jacob Knight. Good cover identities are never more than a few degrees away from the truth and the guys in the Alibi Shop liked to have fun with synonyms of Noble's last name. Cook was Cochran and Witwicky was Warren. They all had business cards and phone numbers that, should anyone call, would be answered by a polite secretary who would confirm their employment at Green Solutions.

The plane touched down and passengers cheered for reasons Noble never understood. He waited for the jet to reach the terminal before standing up, stretching, and reaching for his single carry-on in the overhead. Both of the computer jockeys had their phones out already. Noble frowned and shook his head.

They followed the planeload of passengers to customs, where their fake IDs were stamped by a customs agent, then Noble led the nerds to the car rental where he used a Company card to secure a four-wheel-drive SUV.

"What's our first move?" Witwicky wanted to know as soon as they'd loaded into the faded blue Renault Duster. The sky was a gray overcast and little flakes of white gathered on the windshield.

Noble fiddled with the dials for the heat as he got them out of the parking lot, headed for the highway. He said, "Food. I'm starving."

Witwicky gave him a long-suffering look. "I meant about the mission."

Noble gripped the wheel a little tighter. His brow pinched. "Let me ask you something, *Warren*. How do you know this car isn't bugged?"

She opened her mouth, closed it, folded her arms over her chest and shrank down in the passenger seat.

Noble adjusted the rearview so he could level a silent warning at Cook. The geek mimicked zipping his mouth shut, locking it, and tossing the key. Noble returned his attention to the busy series of exchanges which led to the highway. He got them out of the airport and onto an express lane headed toward the heart of Kiev.

"Give me your phones," Noble said as he pulled off the highway toward downtown. The sidewalks and rooftops were laced with ice and steam piped up from manhole covers in cracked asphalt. The sky was a dull, leaden gray, promising more cold. Noble took a right-hand turn at random and watched the rearview to see if he recognized any vehicles. He thought a black Skoda might have been following them back on the freeway, but the hatchback had kept going as he took the exit. That didn't mean it wasn't a tail, only that the followers were sophisticated enough to have more than one car. A good surveillance team would have cars in front and behind, and they'd switch out the tail often to keep from being spotted.

Witwicky was consulting Google maps and pointed left. "The hotel is that way."

"I know where the hotel is," Noble assured her. "Give me your phones."

"What for?" Cook asked.

"Because I said please."

"You didn't actually say please," Witwicky said but handed hers over. Cook had his out snapping pictures of the buildings. He passed it up between the seats.

Noble buzzed his window down and tossed both units out into the cold.

# CHAPTER TWELVE

"The agency gave us those phones!" Witwicky cried. "We're responsible for them."

"Don't worry," Noble said. "They'll take it out of your paycheck."

"*That's* what I'm afraid of," Witwicky said.

"Why the hell did you do that?" Cook wanted to know.

"Because your phones were compromised."

"How could you possibly know that?" Cook asked.

"Because both of you knuckleheads turned your phones on as soon as the plane landed," Noble said, as if he were explaining simple math to a particularly dull pair of students.

"So?" Cook said. "So what?"

"Ever heard of the man in the middle?"

Cook shook his head and Witwicky's brow knotted.

"Of course not," Noble said. "Neither of you are field operatives."

"What's the man in the middle?" Witwicky asked.

"Foreign intelligence services know people turn their

phones on as soon as a plane lands and they install annex relays in or near airports to tap all incoming phones," Noble told them. "Your phone starts looking for the nearest signal and instead of a tower, it finds the relay. They can hack your phone, listen in, track you, even install a virus and you'd never even know."

Witwicky sat back in her seat and raked a hand through her brown curls. Cook looked like a fish out of water, gulping air. He said, "How do you know?"

"Field work," Noble told him. "It's one of those things you won't learn sitting behind a desk in an air-conditioned office."

"Excuse me," Cook said, "I never signed up for field work."

"You're here now," Noble told them. "And you had better get your act together or we're all going to die. Between your phones and your chatter, you blew our cover. We have to assume the Ukrainians know we're in country and because you looked up the hotel on Google maps, they know where we're staying. We haven't got diplomatic cover. We're non-official, traveling on fake passports. The Ukrainians could arrest us for espionage. You know what the penalty for espionage is in Ukraine?"

Cook gulped.

Witwicky turned for a look out the back window. "That's why you're doing a surveillance detection route."

"You *always* do a surveillance detection route," Noble said. "Always."

"Are we even safe to talk in the car?" Witwicky whispered. "You said it might be bugged."

Noble took out his cell, the one issued to him by the

Alibi Shop, and turned it on. He drove with one hand, watching the road and trying to navigate the menus with his thumb.

"Truck," Cook said. "Truck!"

Noble looked up in time to mash the brakes and avoid rear-ending a delivery van stopped in the middle of the street. He cut the wheel, edged around the back of the truck, and took a narrow alley between buildings, stopping long enough to download a Benny Goodman album. He linked the phone to the car stereo, turned the volume up, and said, "We should be safe to talk now."

Witwicky's face scrunched up at the rattle of bass through the amped speakers. "What about the hotel?"

"We'll find another. We shouldn't have too much trouble..." Noble fell quiet. A black sedan had turned down the alley.

"What is it?" Witwicky asked and turned for a look. "Oh no."

Cook twisted around and said, "That's not good."

Noble shifted into gear, stamped the gas and roared out into traffic. Horns blared and tires shrieked. A small green Skoda cut the wheel and hit the front end of a truck with a plastic crunch. Noble wrenched the wheel, first one way, then the other as he slipped through the mass of cars. His head was on a swivel. He was looking for some way to shake the tail while Benny Goodman and his crew ripped their way through *Sing, Sing, Sing*.

The black sedan was keeping pace, weaving in and out of traffic.

"Who are they?" Witwicky wanted to know. She was turned around in her seat, one hand on the dash.

"Want me to stop and ask?" Noble said.

She shook her head.

"Get your hand off that dash," Noble ordered and Witwicky snatched her hand away as if the dashboard was suddenly electrified.

"They're either Ukrainian intelligence, which is bad," Noble said, "or another outfit, which is worse."

Noble sped down the avenue, foot inching closer to the floor and the speedometer climbing. He didn't want to be in a high-speed chase through the heart of Kiev. That would only end in disaster, but he had to lose the tail.

Behind him, the black sedan kept pace.

Noble took a turn at random, jumping a red light and the sedan slewed through the intersection a moment later with a loud blast from the horn, narrowly avoiding a head-on collision with an antique VW bug.

"Oh man," Cook moaned. He kept looking out the back window. "This is bad."

"What're we going to do?" Witwicky wanted to know.

Noble opened his mouth to tell them both to shut up, that he needed to concentrate, when he spotted a farmer's market flash past. Vendors and pedestrians crammed the small side street. Noble mashed the brakes. The front end of the SUV dipped as the back end humped in the air. Tires hissed on asphalt, leaving a trail of black rubber. Before the Skoda had even come to a complete stop, Noble rammed the gear shift into reverse and put his foot down. The Renault leapt backwards.

# CHAPTER THIRTEEN

Arkady Lukyanenko made a notation in pencil on a large blueprint, tucked the stub of pencil behind one ear, then straightened up and groaned at a kink in his back. Sleeping on an army cot was doing him no good, and he wasn't sleeping much at all because of the heat. Ludmilla had always wanted to vacation in the tropics and Arkady had promised her one day they'd go, but he'd kept putting it off. And a good thing too. Who'd want to spend time in such wretched heat? Arkady palmed droplets from his face and went over his blueprints one more time.

His kidnappers had done their homework. They had everything he needed, including six large diameter rare earth magnets and the centrifuge needed to polarize them. All he had to do was put it together.

*And where would they use it?* Arkady wondered. *Ukraine? Russia? How many would die?*

The unrelenting heat wasn't the only thing that had kept Arkady awake. He had laid on the cot, his burned hand throbbing, thinking about the cost in human life. How many people would die if Arkady did what they wanted? Millions? Hundreds of millions? Arkady was between the proverbial rock and hard place. There were no clear answers. Only terrible choices. The Translator had made it clear Arkady would suffer, exquisitely, if he refused. He stood looking at the blueprints and his sleep-deprived brain stumbled onto a solution.

He reached for a flathead screwdriver in an open toolbox at his feet. He gazed at the sharp end, gripping the tool in his fist, his knuckles turning white, and imagined jamming the sharp end through his eye socket, into his brain. One quick thrust was all it would take.

*Do it*, Arkady told himself.

His tongue darted out over cracked lips. He poised the screwdriver beneath his eye. His hand started to shake. *One hard thrust.* But he couldn't do it. He put the tool down with a sob, reached for a spanner and started to build.

# CHAPTER FOURTEEN

WITWICKY SQUEAKED LIKE A FIELD MOUSE AND COOK shouted, "Are you crazy?"

"This is a bad idea," Witwicky said.

"They won't follow us through the farmer's market if they're Ukrainian intelligence," Noble said. "They'll be afraid of civilian casualties."

"And if they *do* follow?" Cook wanted to know.

"Then we've got major problems," Noble said.

"Shouldn't *we* be afraid of civilian casualties?" Witwicky asked.

"Don't distract me," Noble ordered. It was hard enough driving backwards. He was twisted around in his seat, one hand on the wheel, the other slung over the passenger seat. Cook ducked down, giving him a clear field of view as he reversed toward the market.

"Work the horn," Noble barked at Witwicky.

She reached over and started mashing the button.

People looked up, saw the oncoming SUV and scattered, dropping pumpkins, lettuce, squash and jars of home-made butters that smashed in the street. The rear bumper clipped the first cart, knocking the table over and sending strawberries in all directions. The vendor leapt back, threw his hands in the air and shouted. His screams were lost beneath the strained notes of Benny Goodman's clarinet. Noble chewed the inside of one cheek as he made a micro adjustment to the wheel, trying to keep the Renault steady. The SUV zipped along at thirty kilometers per hour, slow enough for people to get out of the way and fast enough to make the threat real.

The crowd was running and screaming. Tires bumped over carrots and mashed turnips. One of the vendors lobbed a loaf of bread at the back windshield.

The black sedan slowed and then stopped as it reached the first overturned cart. Noble could just make out the face of the driver. He was a broad-shouldered man with a crew cut, probably state security, and his face was fixed in a frown. His partner was urging him forward but the driver shook his head, shifted into reverse and started to back up.

They'd go around and try to catch Noble as he emerged on the other side but they'd be too late. Noble kept his speed steady as the Renault reversed through the farmer's market, past crowds of gawking onlookers, reached the end of the lane and swung back out into traffic. By now the crowd had recovered from their shock. Instead of scared, they were angry and they chased the Renault with a hailstorm of vegetables. A bag of turnips impacted Noble's door and an avocado smashed against the back windshield. Onions bounded off the hood. Someone grabbed at the door handle but the locks were engaged.

Noble pushed the pedal down, took the next right, and

then another. In a matter of moments they were safely away from the chaos of the market and had merged back into the flow of traffic.

"Ohmigod." Witwicky buried her face in both hands and said, "Ohmigod. That was crazy. You are totally out of control. You could have killed somebody."

"I know what I'm doing," Noble assured her.

"Do you?" Cook questioned.

"Who's in charge here?" Noble said. He missed the look exchanged by Cook and Witwicky. He navigated unfamiliar neighborhoods until he found a busy shopping district and pulled into the first available parking spot.

"Grab your bags," Noble told them as he climbed out.

The trees lining the busy shopping district were a vibrant orange and dry leaves decorated the sidewalks. Ukrainians in coats and scarves made their way along the row of stores.

"What are we doing here?" Cook asked.

"Every cop in the city is going to be looking for this rental," Noble said. "It's not going to take them long to track it down."

The computer nerds grabbed their luggage and piled out. They had to jog to keep up with Noble.

"This is a disaster," Witwicky was saying. "I think we need to call Wizard and tell him..."

"We're not calling anybody," Noble told her.

"They tailed us from the moment we left the airport," she said. "We lost our cellphones and our rental car. And the police are looking for us. We can't possibly complete our mission now."

"Minor setbacks." Noble steered them to a coffee shop with an outdoor dining area.

"What're we doing here?" Cook asked, looking through the window of the shop.

Noble said, "Three coffees and try not to screw it up."

"How can I screw up coffee?"

Noble made a face that said *you've screwed up everything else, why not coffee?*

"What kind does everyone want?"

"Mocha cappuccino for me," Witwicky said. "Extra foam."

Cook turned to Noble. "You?"

His face would have curdled milk.

"Black?" Cook guessed.

Noble nodded.

"Cream or sugar?"

Noble stared at him.

"Black," Cook said and reached for the door.

Noble watched him go, shook his head and parked himself at an empty table.

Witwicky sat down across from him. "We're new at this."

"I'm aware," Noble told her.

She settled back in her seat, looked at the crowds and said, "Watching for watchers?"

Noble tapped his nose.

"How long?"

"Long as it takes."

Cook returned five minutes later with three large cups of coffee. "One black, one mocha extra foam," he said. "I'm not sure which is which."

Noble sniffed, peeled the lid up, and passed the cup to Witwicky. She traded him and he sipped. Caffeine hit his system like a jolt of electric. Noble knew it was more psychosomatic than chemical—it would take another thirty minutes for the caffeine to work—but it still brought his brain to attention. He sat, sipping strong black coffee and watching the crowds. After a minute he said, "Did you use cash?"

"Um..." Cook said. "We haven't been to an exchange. I didn't have any local currency. I had to use a card."

Noble stood up, slung his carry on over his shoulder and picked up his cup. Cook and Witwicky hurried after him. He spent the next hour touring the city, turning down random roads and doubling back to throw off pursuit. As they walked, Noble brought out his cellphone and found a vacation rental app.

Cook was peering over his shoulder. "Is that some sort of secret navigation app cooked up by the Alibi Shop?"

"No."

"A secret communication app?" Witwicky guessed.

"It's SkyBnB," Noble said.

"What are you using it for?"

"Same thing everybody else uses it for," Noble told them. "A place to sleep."

He found a rental less than three blocks away, but took his time getting there, prowling the back streets until he was certain they had not been followed.

"Aren't you going to book it," Cook asked. It was a three-story building set back off the main road with an iron gate over the front entry and a lockbox fixed to the wall. The rental was on the second floor and the key for visitors was in the lockbox.

Noble scowled at him, then shook his head and turned his attention to the box.

"How are you going to get the key without the code?" Witwicky asked.

"These boxes are not as secure as you might think," Noble told them. "There are only ten digits and they can't repeat. For instance, you can't have 1111 or 9999 or 1231. Each number can only be used once and it doesn't matter which order you enter the code. So if the combination is 3246, 6423 would work as well."

Witwicky was nodding her head.

Cook said, "That only leaves us with..."

"Two hundred and ten combinations," Witwicky said.

"Assuming it's a four-digit code," said Cook. "Two hundred and fifty-two if it's five-digit."

"That's a lot of different combinations to try," Witwicky said. "We could be here all afternoon."

Noble bent over the box, pushed his thumb down on the release catch and started pressing buttons. He had the box open in a matter of seconds. "Presto."

"How did you do that?" Cook asked.

"Not everything is math and science," Noble said. "And computers don't always have the answers."

The analysts stood there with blank stares. Witwicky said, "I don't understand. How did you guess the combination so quickly?"

"It's mechanical," Noble explained. "The buttons which are a part of the combination have a different feel than the buttons that aren't. You can feel and even hear the differ-ence when you press down hard on the release. And like I said; it doesn't matter which order you press the buttons."

Witwicky said, "So you just hold down the release and press all the buttons until you've got the code."

Noble held up the key. "Exactly."

# CHAPTER FIFTEEN

"YOU COULD HAVE AT LEAST BROKEN INTO A PLACE with two bedrooms," Witwicky said as she slung her bag onto a low sofa parked against the wall. The apartment was a one bedroom, one bath, with a small kitchen, not much bigger than most budget hotel rooms. The bed was set off from the rest of the space with a folding screen, and the door to the bathroom was frosted glass. A pair of arched patio doors opened onto a balcony the size of a postage stamp.

"Next time I'll ask for connecting suites," Noble told her. He pulled the gauzy white curtains closed, blocking the view from across the street.

"What are the sleeping arrangements?" Cook asked.

"I'm going to be sleeping on the bed," Witwicky said in a matter-of-fact tone. "You two decide who gets the couch."

"Flip you for it?" Cook said.

"You take the couch," Noble told him. "I'll be on the floor in front of the door."

Cook's eyes went to the door. "If someone tries to come in it will wake you."

Noble nodded.

"I still think we should call Wizard," Witwicky said. She had to nudge the coke-bottle glasses up the bridge of her nose. "Let him know what's going on."

"We aren't calling until we have something to report," Noble said.

"What if he tries to reach us at the hotel and finds out we never checked in?" Cook said. "He might think something went wrong."

"Something did go wrong," Witwicky said.

"Would you two relax?" Noble dropped his only carry-on on the low table in front of the sofa and said, "This sort of thing happens in field work. You improvise, adapt and overcome."

"Fine," said Cook. "What's our next move?"

"Lukyanenko had a cabin outside Kiev where he liked to work," Noble told them. "I'm going to secure us a set of wheels and go check it out."

"You mean steal a set of wheels," Cook said.

"Credit cards are out so we can't rent another."

"Shouldn't we go with you?" Witwicky asked.

Noble shook his head. "I'll collect up anything I find and bring it back here for you to analyze."

Witwicky had her hands together in front of her, torturing her fingers. "I still think we should go with you."

Noble sat down on the edge of the coffee table. "Ukrainian police are going to be looking for the three people who rented a car from the airport and drove it through a farmer's market."

"Then take one of us at least," Witwicky said.

Noble shook his head. "Out of the question. You two will only get in my way. Stay here, set up your laptops and do what you do best."

Witwicky started to protest but Noble was already up and moving for the door.

Cook said, "What's your ETA? How long do we wait?"

"If I'm not back by eight mount a rescue party," Noble told him as he let himself out.

# CHAPTER SIXTEEN

Noble followed an old logging road down the side of a wooded hill, through a small town with one traffic light and a petrol station, then along a gravel lane between towering pines to a cabin with a wraparound deck that looked out over the crystal-clear waters of Bucha River as it wound its way west away from Kiev. He was behind the wheel of a stolen ZAZ Slavuta which he had picked up in a parking lot less than a mile from the SkyBnB. He stepped on the brake and eased the gray hatchback to a stop alongside a shallow ditch. Rubber crunched on gravel.

He had already been to the missing man's house and seen the chaos. There was a pan on the kitchen floor and crafting supplies scattered all over the bedroom. Noble doubted Lukyanenko was into crafting, so the wife had either been rolled up along with the scientist, or got caught in the middle and killed. Or someone was using her as leverage. A hundred other possibilities presented themselves and Noble didn't care to speculate on any of them.

He set the parking brake and disabled the overhead

dome out of habit. The sun was still high overhead, helping to melt some of the cold, and a soft light filtered down through the pines. Noble threw open the driver's side door, stepped out and stood with his arms on the roof of the SUV while he waited for his senses to acclimate to his surroundings. A blackbird gave an indignant croak before taking wing, and a squirrel capered in the underbrush. Beyond that the forest was quiet. A stillness pressed in on Noble, causing gooseflesh to march up his arms in ranks. He watched the cabin and listened. His breath made little silver clouds before breaking apart on a gentle breeze.

Several minutes passed before he was satisfied. He left the car door open and made his way between trees toward the side of the house. He took his time, going from tree to tree, taking care where he placed his feet. It was hard to be quiet with dry leaves all over the ground, but Noble managed. He reached the corner and had to stand on his toes for a peek through a side window. He had intentionally chosen the side away from the sun so that he could see in without a mirror effect on the glass.

He saw overstuffed armchairs flanking a log fireplace and stacks of papers everywhere. Noble circled around to the backdoor, tried the knob and found it unlocked. He let the door swing open and peered into a tidy little kitchen. Pine scented cleaner filled his nostrils.

Noble eased around the doorframe into the building, taking in the cool, slightly musty air and straining to hear any sounds that were out of place. When he was sure the house was empty, he went from room to room.

Someone had been here. They hadn't ransacked the place, not exactly, but there were little things out of place, like a chest of drawers left open and a stack of books over-turned. Noble's brow pinched. He chewed the inside of one cheek while he studied the evidence. The farther he went down the rabbit hole, the more convinced he was that Lukyanenko had been rolled up by a rival intelligence agency. The question became who and why? Russia was the most obvious culprit. Had the Russians learned what Lukyanenko was working on?

Noble made his way through the cabin, searching for clues, and heard a small click followed by a soft electronic beep when his foot pressed down on the polished floorboards.

# CHAPTER SEVENTEEN

Every muscle in Noble's body turned to spring steel. His heart clawed up into his throat where it got stuck. He stood still, a statue carved from granite, afraid to even draw a deep breath. His right foot was on a pressure switch and the slightest movement might set it off.

Mines come in a number of different varieties; some explode when the weight was lifted off, some were on a timer, others went off the moment the switch was triggered. Lucky for Noble it wasn't the later, or he'd already be dead.

That left two possibilities; either it would explode when he picked his foot up, or it was on a timer. Noble suspected both. That's what he would have done. Set a pressure switch and backstop it with a timer. The victim is caught standing there waiting for rescue and anyone who tries to help will likely be caught by the timer. Two for one special.

In Iraq and Afghanistan, Noble had seen guys blown to bits. The Taliban spread landmines around like candy. The results were never pretty. Glen Buehlman had been thrown fifteen feet in the air. He lived an agonizing twenty minutes without his legs while Noble and two other guys tried in vain to stop the bleeding, waiting for a helicopter that would never make it in time. Everybody knew it was a losing battle, including Glen, who made Noble promise to call his wife. It was the hardest phone call Noble ever had to make. Missy Buehlman shrieked into the phone when she heard Noble's voice and then dissolved into tears. Six months later, she swallowed a bottle of tranquilizers along with half a bottle of tequila and never woke up. Two for one special.

Large beads of sweat were forming on Noble's forehead, despite the cold, and ran down his chest in greasy rivulets. He concentrated on his breathing, telling himself to stay calm and trying not to shift the weight on his foot.

How long?

If it was just a simple pressure switch, he'd live until he could no longer stand up, or until he fell asleep on his feet. If there was a timer, there was no telling.

He looked around the cabin for anything that might help, but the mug who'd planted the bomb had done a good job, leaving nothing to chance. The pressure switch was right smack in the middle of the floor. Noble leaned over as far as he dared, reaching for the arm of the sofa in the hopes of dragging it onto the floorboard, but it was just out of reach and nothing else in the rustic log home would approximate Noble's weight, even if he could reach it. He was alone, stranded, with no way of dismantling the bomb.

His only hope was a pair of computer jockeys so green around the gills they didn't know to do a surveillance detection route. He was due back at the SkyBnB by eight. Noble checked his watch. It was a little after five-thirty. The sun was already sinking. It would take Cook and Witwicky a little over an hour to get here. Then they'd have to call a bomb squad. The bomb squad would be another hour and change.

Five hours was a long time to play statue. His muscles would start to tremble and his nerves would fray. Sooner or later he'd have to take a leak. His mind would start to wander. Fatigue would set in. Noble figured his chances were slim.

He slid one hand slowly into his jacket and brought out his phone. He couldn't risk making a call. The cellular signal might activate the bomb, but that didn't stop him from using other functions. First he disabled the auto-lock function and passcode. He didn't want Cook and Witwicky to have any trouble getting the phone open. Next he turned on the camera, switched to video and pressed record.

He fought to keep the tremor out of his voice. "I'm inside Lukyanenko's cabin," Noble narrated. "I've stepped on a pressure switch. It was a stupid mistake. I'm not sure how much time I've got."

He played the camera around the room as best he could without moving his feet, trying to record all the details. "The place has been searched and someone didn't want anybody else snooping around. This is looking more and more like a kidnapping and less like Lukyanenko split town. Whoever rolled him up was professional. My first guess would be the Russians. I hope you get this video and it does some good. Jake Noble, signing off."

He ended that recording and started another. This time he pointed the camera at himself and forced a smile. "Hi Mom. It's me. Just wanted you to know how much I love you. And er... I wanted you to know that I believe now.

You've been telling me for years and I never wanted to listen. Never put any stock in it. But I believe now." He paused and took a deep breath, not sure how to go on. He could feel tears building up behind his eyes and didn't want his mother to see him cry. He didn't want that to be her final memory. He put the waterworks in check through sheer force of will and grinned. "Take care of the dog for me and I'll see you on the other side."

The tears had forced their way out in the end. Noble's eyes were wet when he pressed the stop button. No way to fix that.

Now came the hard part. From where he stood, he could see into the kitchen. The door was open. He leaned forward as far as possible, careful to keep his right foot flat on the floorboards, and lobbed the phone underhand toward the open door.

He thought for sure the motion would trigger the bomb, but the phone sailed through the doorframe, bounced off the refrigerator and clattered over the tiles without Noble's world erupting into light and sound. Noble let out a breath he didn't know he was holding and palmed sweat from his forehead. Now all he had to do was wait. Wait and hope. After a minute he started to pray.

# CHAPTER EIGHTEEN

Cook and Witwicky had set up a temporary op center in the SkyBnB. A pair of ruggedized laptops were on the credenza where the television had been before they moved it, and a small portable booster allowed them to jack into the Wi-Fi signal from a pastry shop across the street. Half-eaten pastries and cups of coffee littered the makeshift desktop. Both laptops were logged into a dummy website for Green Solutions which acted as a backdoor to the Langley database. From here, the pair of analysts could do almost everything they could do sitting at their desks in the third floor basement. But thus far they had nothing to do.

Cook kept flicking the tip of a ballpoint pen against a rubber band, making an annoying twang, and swiveling in his seat. Gwen nibbled the corner of a pastry, trying to think of something that would break the ice. Everything had happened so fast, she never got a chance to mend fences before climbing aboard the plane to Kiev, and she couldn't very well hash out their relationship with Noble sitting one seat over, so she'd spent eighteen hours pretending to sleep.

Now they were finally alone and she couldn't think of anything to say.

The incident at the bar had really crushed Ezra's spirits. It was written all over the lines of his face and Gwen wanted to make her friend feel better. She just didn't know how to do that without giving him false hope. She felt trapped. She was, after all, at least partly the reason he felt so down. Her, and a couple of idiot frat boys.

And why did he love her so much anyway? It was a question Gwen kept asking herself. She wasn't particularly pretty and she didn't have much personality, unless you like girls with an encyclopedic knowledge of Star Trek. Still, Ezra had fallen hard for her and no matter how much she tried, Gwen couldn't find the same feelings for him. And she had tried.

They wiled away the hours in uncomfortable silence, speaking only when necessary. His rubber band was getting annoying. Gwen wanted to tell him to stop. Instead she picked up her cup and sipped stone-cold coffee.

Time marched on with interminable slowness. Gwen watched the digital clock on her laptop. Six o'clock became seven and as seven got steadily closer to eight a bundle of nerves in her belly started to tighten. She said, "You don't think anything happened?"

Ezra shook his head. "He probably stopped for food on his way back."

Gwen nodded as if that made perfect sense, but eight o'clock came and went, and still no Jake. She took off her glasses, cleaned them on her sweater and stuck them back on. "That's the deadline," she said. "We have to go after him."

"Give him a little more time," Ezra said. "He might be on his way here right now."

"He might be in trouble," she countered.

"Try calling," Ezra said.

They hadn't bothered replacing their phones yet and Gwen had to make the call from her laptop. She plugged in Noble's number and it went straight to voice mail.

"He's not answering."

"Try again," Ezra told her.

"He's not answering."

"Just try."

Gwen sighed, shook her head, and dialed again with the same result. She dropped her head into her hands and thought of Mexico City. "It's happening again, isn't it?"

"Why is it, every time we get in trouble, Noble is at the center of the controversy?" Ezra asked.

Gwen stood up. "Wish we had guns."

"Like they'd do us any good," Ezra said.

Gwen admitted that with a shrug. "So how are we going to do this?"

"We need a car," Ezra said. "You remember how to steal one?"

"I think so."

"We need a blood pressure cuff," Ezra said.

"I'll find a pharmacy." She turned to her computer.

Forty minutes later they were in a mostly full lot across from a large shopping center. Gwen was trying to wedge the inflatable cuff into the door of a lime green Toyota Prius while Ezra kept a lookout. It was a lot harder than she remembered. She pushed at the fabric with both hands, causing the Prius to rock on its springs.

Ezra gave a loud fake cough.

Gwen looked up and saw an elderly couple walking arm in arm. The blood pressure cuff was stuck fast in the door frame, no way to get it out without making a lot of noise, and Gwen didn't want to have to put it back. Instead she put her back against the car door and tried to look casual.

Ezra leaned up against the car as well, bopping his head to an imaginary beat.

The old couple hardly glanced in their direction as they made their way along the line of cars. Gwen waited until they were out of sight, then went back to work.

"Will you hurry up?" Ezra said.

"You want to do this?" Gwen growled through clenched teeth. She finally got most of it wedged under the doorframe and started squeezing the rubber bubble. The door popped open with a loud clunk and Gwen waited to see if an alarm would sound. When nothing happened, she hopped into the driver's seat and reached across to unlock the passenger side.

Ezra slid in beside her, leaned down and felt around under the dash for the bundle of wires. He was still sorting when a gaggle of teenagers with punk rock hairdos happened through the lot.

Gwen cleared her throat and Ezra popped up just as the group of kids turned in their direction. She grabbed Ezra's head, pushed it back down into her lap, closed her eyes and gave a long moan. "Yes!" she cried. "Yes! Yes! Yes! Just like that!" She tossed her head side to side and raked fingers through her hair.

The boys gawked and the girls giggled, then the group was hurrying past.

Ezra lay on his side, his head pressed against her thighs and his heart thundering in his chest. His ears felt like they would burst into flame. He asked, "They gone?"

"They're gone."

He split wires with a small pocket knife and a minute later the Prius hummed to life. Gwen shifted into gear and pulled out of the parking lot with her cheeks still flush from her performance.

# CHAPTER NINETEEN

NOBLE'S HEAD LOLLED ON HIS CHEST AND HIS EYELIDS drooped. He wasn't asleep, far from it, just conserving energy. It was getting late. His Citizen Nighthawk told him it was close to nine thirty. Cook and Witwicky should have been here by now. Noble cupped his hands together and blew hot air into his palms, then rubbed them together and stuffed them into his pockets. The temperature had dropped with the setting sun and Noble could see his breath misting up before him in silent little clouds. Cold made him shiver and standing still only made it worse. His back muscles screamed with the effort of remaining motionless for so long. His right heel felt like it had fused to the floorboards. Toes had become pins and needles. Who knew standing still could be so exhausting?

A wave of dizziness washed over him and Noble put his hands out for balance, like a surfer trying to stay on his board in an upswell. His body was coming unraveled like a spool of thread, his muscles begging for release, but his mind was racing. He was thinking of all the things he should have said to his mother. It was the last time he'd ever get to speak to her. He should have told her how much she meant to him. But it was too late now. The phone was well out of reach. Hopefully it was far enough away to survive the explosion.

Noble knew this was the end. He glanced again at his watch. Where were Cook and Witwicky? Probably lost. Noble imagined them driving in circles on the far side of Bucha River in search of the address. Sooner or later his legs would buckle and that would be all. He closed his eyes and cursed.

*Just lift your foot and end it,* Noble told himself. Cook and Witwicky might be a hundred miles away. There was no telling when they would get here and even when they did, there was no way they could deal with the landmine. They'd have to call in a local bomb squad. That would take even longer. Even then, there was no guarantee they would be able to dismantle the explosive. If the bomb maker was even halfway decent, he'd have anti-tamper devices in place.

But another part of Noble's brain told him to hold on. He had survived worse. *All you have to do is stand still, after all.* But standing still is a whole lot harder than most people think. Especially when you know there's enough explosive under your foot to turn you into pulp.

Another wave of dizziness hit and Noble's upper body started to pitch forward. He felt it happening but couldn't do anything to stop it. The weight came off his legs. The balance of his right foot was shifting from his heel to his toes. The floorboard actually creaked before Noble managed to lever himself upright through sheer force of will.

Sweat ran down his cheeks and dampened his collar. His hands shook and the air came trembling out of his lungs. While he stood there, doing his best to remain motionless and upright, he thought of all the ways he could have died over the years and decided stepping on a land-mine was the least glorious.

*Careless,* Noble told himself. *That's what it was.*

He shook his head and looked out the large picture window. A flimsy set of diaphanous curtains gave the living room some privacy, but would also help protect Noble's body if he jumped through the glass. He was thinking of making a run for it. Throw himself at the picture window and hope beyond hope he was fast enough to at least hit the glass before the bomb went off. Maybe the explosion would throw him onto the front porch instead of turning him inside out.

*Fat chance,* Noble thought. He wouldn't so much as lift his foot before the bomb would plaster him all over the ceiling. *Forget the window,* Noble thought. *Never make it.*

Still, he had to try something. He couldn't just stand here and wait to die. His only other option was to dive behind the sofa. Maybe the heavy old piece of furniture would absorb enough of the explosion to save Noble's life.

He shook his head. That would never work either. He turned back toward the window. It was probably his best chance, slim though it was. He was working up his courage when he spied headlights pulling up the drive.

His heart leapt and then faltered. His first thought was Cook and Witwicky. Then a darker, more terrible prospect came to mind. Maybe whoever had planted the bomb had come back.

Tires crunched in the gravel and the car—it looked like a lime green Prius through the curtains—stopped in front of the house and the doors cranked open. Noble cast about for something to use as a weapon. There was nothing within reach. His hands curled into fists and he set his teeth. If anyone other than Cook or Witwicky came through the door, Noble was going to lift his foot and catch them with the blast.

Two figures emerged from the car. One of them crossed in front of the headlights, their shadow splashed across the big picture window, and they mounted the porch.

"Has to be the right place," Cook whispered.

"Think he's in there?" Witwicky asked in hushed tones.

"Stop," Noble shouted. "Do not open the door!"

# CHAPTER TWENTY

ARKADY LUKYANENKO HAD A BUNDLE OF WIRES IN ONE hand, brandishing them at The Translator. The Arab stood with his arms folded over his broad chest and a frown on his scarred face. Arkady held the wires up for his inspection. "I can't use these. These are rubber insulated. They won't work, not for our purposes. I need high tensile copper insulated in thermoplastic."

"I believe you're stalling," The Translator said without so much as a glance at the bundle of wires. "Perhaps I should have my men motivate you."

With The Translator, the threat of physical violence was ever present. When Lukyanenko had told him he needed a larger power supply, the Arab had accused Arkady of stalling and threatened to smash his toes with a hammer. He was right, of course, Arkady was using any excuse he could to delay the work, but he also needed more voltage if he was going to generate the kind of charge necessary to complete the device. He was able, through a lot of technical speak, to convince The Translator they needed more voltage and another generator had been installed.

"I'm not stalling," Arkady told him. "Without the right wiring the device won't work."

"My employer grows impatient," The Translator said. "He thinks you would be better motivated if you had company. Ms. Anastasia, perhaps. I could have my men bring her here."

Arkady's hand fell to his side, the bundle of wires flapping against his thigh. So they knew about his mistress. His throat clutched and then released. He found it difficult to swallow. It took him a moment to work some moisture back into his mouth. "Please, I'm trying to do what you asked of me. But I can't work without the right tools."

The Translator's nostrils flared.

"Why would I lie?" Arkady said. "Do you think I want to put Anastasia in danger? I'm trying to do what you ask, but I can't do it without the proper wiring."

The Translator snatched the bundle from Arkady's hand. "Write out what you need. And I had better not find out you are lying."

Arkady snagged a stub of pencil and a yellow legal pad from his work bench. Sweat was pasting his shirt to his chest and he'd taken off his shoes, preferring to work barefoot in the oppressive humidity. He scribbled out the necessary wiring, specifying coils of expensive materials which he knew would be hard to come by. If he had made a request like this in his laboratory back in Kiev it would be four or five months before he received the spools. First his request would have to go through the proper channels and it would take several weeks just to get the right approvals. Then a few months would go by before his department managed to free up the extra cash. It would be another few months before the parts were actually delivered.

It all came down to time. Arkady knew he was a dead man and at this point he was just playing for time. As an afterthought, Arkady wrote down sandals and clean underwear on his shopping list before handing it over.

The Arab scanned the sheet. His eyes reached the bottom. He stepped forward and delivered a devastating backhand that rocked Arkady's head to one side. There was a flat, hard smack and Arkady felt his world tip on end. He stumbled and the ground came up to greet him. Fairy lights capered in his vision.

The Translator waved the paper under Arkady's nose. "You don't make demands of me. Do you understand?"

Arkady nodded and heard the muscles in his neck creak like rusty hinges. His vision was still swimming as he tried to lever himself off the floor. His heart was working overtime, like an engine struggling to produce the necessary RPMs. He managed to sit up with effort. He was expecting another blow, but The Translator turned on his heel and stalked from the cargo plane.

Arkady's cheek was hot to the touch, as if someone had burned him with a hot iron. He gently probed with his fingers, wincing. He'd have a large welt tomorrow and he'd cut the inside of his cheek on his teeth. Leaning forward, he spat blood onto the bare floor, then massaged his chest, trying to calm his racing heart.

# CHAPTER TWENTY-ONE

GWEN FROZE MID-STEP. HER EYES GOT WIDE. SHE looked to Ezra. He had one hand on the doorknob and his eyebrows crept up toward his hairline. His hand slowly let go of the knob and he called out, "Noble? Is that you?"

"It's me." His voice was muffled by the door and haggard, like a man who'd just woken up from a long sleep. He said, "I'm standing on a landmine and I don't know if there are any other boobytraps. Go around to the backdoor."

Gwen felt a rising tide of panic. Her feet wanted to run and her chest felt like someone had pumped her full of helium. She took two shambling steps backwards off the porch and nearly tripped. She would have gone down on her bottom but she managed to grab hold of the porch rail. Ezra was right beside her.

"You just said there might be boobytraps," Ezra called out. "What if the backdoor is wired?"

"How do you think I got in?" Noble growled.

"You want us to come inside?" Gwen said.

"I need you to collect my phone," Noble told her. "It's got information on it that you'll need."

Gwen and Ezra exchanged a look, then started around the cabin, going slow. Ezra was in the lead and Gwen took care to walk in his footsteps. Thankfully he was about the same size and had a similar stride. Gwen stayed close on his heels and when they got to the back porch, they stepped up together. The wood groaned under their combined weight and Gwen nearly screamed. The sound started up her throat and was nearly out before she managed to check it.

The backdoor was open and she could see into the kitchen. She crowded up to the frame, not yet ready to set foot inside. The lights were out and the kitchen was steeped in shadow.

"You're sure it's safe?" Gwen called out.

"Sure?" Noble said. "No. But I walked through it once already. You should be fine."

Gwen turned to Ezra. His face was waxy pale in the moonlight, but he put on a determined frown, stepped forward and felt for a light switch. Gwen let out a breath, licked her lips, gave herself a little shake and took a step inside.

Ezra found the switch and the lights blazed on. Modern appliances gleamed under stark white overheads. The linoleum was covered in a riot of muddy boot prints.

From the living room Noble said, "Did you just turn on a light?"

"Yeah," Ezra said and then, "Sorry."

Gwen imagined the expression on Noble's face. He had a way of saying a lot without saying anything at all.

"My phone is in the kitchen somewhere," Noble told them. "Look around."

Gwen spotted the device lying next to a chair leg. The screen was cracked, but other than that it was okay. "Got it."

"Great," Noble said. "I took video of the room for you to analyze. I don't know what this guy was working on, but somebody was very interested in his research. And there's a video on there for my mother. I'd appreciate it if you didn't watch it. Just make sure she gets it, okay?"

Gwen pocketed the cellphone and stepped to the adjoining door. Now that she was inside the house, and nothing had exploded, some of the fear had drained away. She stuck her head around the frame and saw Noble standing in the middle of the room, sweat forming a dark bib on the front of his sweater and his surfer hair hanging in limp tangles. His face was pale and his hands twitched. There was a puddle on the floor two feet directly in front of him.

Ezra said, "Did you take a leak?"

Noble shrugged. It was just a small up and down movement of one shoulder. His eyes swiveled in their direction and he hitched an awkward smile on his face. "Had to go," he said. "Didn't want to die with a full bladder."

"You're not going to die," Gwen said automatically, but the words sounded false on her lips.

"We're going to get you out of this," Ezra agreed.

Noble said, "Call a bomb squad and then take that phone and get the hell out of here."

Gwen shook her head. "That will blow your cover. Even if they get here and manage to dismantle the bomb, how will you explain what you're doing here?"

"That's my problem," Noble told them. "Take the phone and go."

Gwen couldn't walk away and leave Noble to die. She turned to Ezra and knew he was thinking the same. She said, "We're going to get you out of here."

Noble frowned. "I'm in charge of this operation and I'm ordering you to leave."

"Gwen was the best in our class at explosives," Ezra said.

Noble shook his head slowly. "You need to go. There's no reason for all three of us to die."

"We're not going to die," Gwen said with more conviction this time.

"It must be underneath the house," Ezra said. "I'll pull the car up and turn on the brights."

"I'll see if I can find a flashlight," Gwen said, though she didn't know how she was going to make a search of the house with the possibility of more bombs. She would have to settle for searching the kitchen.

Noble said, "The phone has a flashlight on it."

"Oh yeah!" Gwen dug the phone out of her pocket and turned on the light.

Ezra was already outside, headed for the car. Gwen was still in the kitchen and Noble said, "Witwicky, you don't have to do this. Take the phone and go."

"We're a team," she said. "We don't leave anyone behind. Isn't that what you Special Forces guys always say? No one left behind?"

Noble closed his eyes a moment and then said, "You really think you can do this?"

"I know I can," Gwen lied.

Five minutes later she and Ezra were crawling under the house for a look at the bomb. Cold seeped through her coat, turning her boobs into hunks of ice. Her nipples were hard enough to cut glass. She slithered through decades of dead leaves, dirt and mud, knocked her head once on a low hanging pipe, but managed to get close enough to reach out and touch the device. It was a small stack of powder and ball-bearings wrapped in plastic and wired to a pressure switch attached to the floor. Lights from the Prius turned the crawlspace into an alien landscape of shifting shadows and glowing cobwebs. Gwen thought she felt something skitter inside her shirt and said, "Does Ukraine have poisonous spiders?"

"Don't know," Ezra said as he dragged himself along on his forearms. "I'm more worried about snakes."

Gwen shined the light from the phone on the bundle of wires and studied the device while clouds of white mist burst from her open mouth. She had to push her glasses up and left a muddy smudge on one lens that partially blocked her vision. Any more mud would leave her blind. She made a mental note not to touch her glasses. A sheen of sweat was forming on her back and her toes felt like little chips of frozen wood. Her fingers were turning numb and her hands were shaking.

"Sure you can do this?" Ezra whispered.

"No," Gwen said. "Why did you go and tell him I could?"

"I didn't say you could. I said you were the top in our class at explosives." Ezra shifted around on his belly for a better angle on the device. "And that's true."

"That was training," Gwen said. "Doesn't mean I can do it in real life."

"You can," Ezra told her.

"What makes you so sure?"

"You have to," he said.

"Great," Gwen said. "No pressure."

"Just take your time," Ezra said. "See if you can figure this out. If not we can always back out and call the local police."

Gwen licked her lips, used her coat sleeve to push her glasses back into place without getting any more mud on them, and went to work examining the wires. Her heart was slamming at the wall of her chest, like an angry beast that wanted out, and her bladder was about to pop. She had lost all feeling in her toes and her fingertips were tingly. Her nose was six inches from enough explosive to rearrange all her internal organs and, if she screwed up, the locals would be picking up what was left of her in little Tupperware containers.

# CHAPTER TWENTY-TWO

WITWICKY MOVED THE CELLPHONE FLASHLIGHT around, studying the device from every angle as she tried desperately to remember her training. The Farm teaches recruits a basic overview of explosives and bomb diffusion, but mostly focuses on how to minimize damage. "Avoiding a boobytrap is a lot easier than trying to dismantle a bomb," their grizzled old instructor Peters would always tell the class. He was a heavily scarred veteran of the Cold War with one limp arm who had spent most of his time showing recruits how to spot an improvised explosive device. An ounce of prevention, in his words, was worth a pound of cure.

Gwen studied each wire, where it originated and where it connected. She made a thorough examination of the pressure switch and the actual explosive. By the time she was relatively certain she knew how the bomb operated, her entire body was lathered in sweat. Beads rolled down her cheeks, gathered on her chin and fell in large, heavy droplets. One fat drop of perspiration rolled along the rim of her tortoiseshell glasses, reminding her of a silly spy movie she had seen where a secret agent catches a drop of sweat in his palm, all while hanging from wires. Gwen would need a bucket to catch all the sweat. She took two quick breaths, forcing oxygen into her brain, licked her lips, then reached for what she thought was the link between the pressure switch and the accelerant.

"Are you sure?" Ezra whispered.

"Why are you whispering?"

"I don't know," he whispered.

Their voices sounded incredibly loud in the cramped crawlspace. Silver clouds burst from Gwen's lungs, obscuring her vision and fogging her lenses. She scolded herself for not making the switch to contacts. Her fingers touched the wire and she pulled back, second guessing herself.

"Maybe you should get out of here," she told Ezra.

He shook his head. "No way."

"Seriously Ez. This might not work. Probably *won't* work. There's no need for all of us to die."

He dug a small folding knife from his pocket. "Tell me which wire to cut and you go."

Gwen shook her head. "I'm not going either."

She held out her hand. Ezra passed over the pocket knife. She looped the wire around the blade and called out so Noble could hear. "You ready?"

"Get on with it!"

Gwen screwed her eyes shut tight and jerked the knife. The wire separated. The whole thing was anticlimactic and that was a good thing. Gwen opened her eyes and Ezra let out a breath.

"Almost done," Gwen called. She cut the wire connecting the accelerant to the pressure switch, severing the last connection between the device and the trigger, then she was scooching backwards through the leaves. She cleared the porch, climbed to her knees and brushed herself off.

"Noble," Ezra called. "We think we got it. Give us a minute before you step off."

"Roger that," Noble shouted back.

They hurried around to the back of the Prius and Gwen shouted, "Now!"

A moment later the front door opened and Noble appeared.

Ezra shouted. "You did it! That was amazing!"

Gwen let out a trembling breath and had to focus on keeping her legs locked or her knees would have let go. She gripped the back of the car to stay on her feet. She suddenly realized how badly she needed to pee, but Ezra was trying to wrap her up in a hug.

"Gotta go," Gwen told him. "Gotta go right now."

She disentangled herself and sprang into the woods, like a deer trying to escape a hunter. She stopped behind the first big pine, pushed her pants down around her knees and squatted in time to avoid wetting herself. Her hands were shaking and her heart fluttered, but she was alive. She let out a jerking, hysterical little laugh that turned into a sob and then back to a laugh.

When she was empty, Gwen pulled up her pants and picked her way through the trees toward the house. Noble was sitting on the porch, his back against the doorframe, lit by the headlights. Ezra was bent over him, asking how he felt.

"I need a good stiff drink." Noble closed his eyes and scrubbed his face with both hands. He looked like a man who had just run a marathon. His sweater was soaked through with sweat and his hair was tangled. He had dark circles under both eyes. His face was white in the glare of the high beams. He looked up at the sound of Gwen's feet in the gravel and scowled at her. "That was incredibly stupid. You both could have been killed."

Gwen stopped, put her hands in her pockets and stared at her scuffed sneakers. "I... I just..."

"I'm going to put you in for a commendation," Noble said.

Gwen's chin came up, her eyes wide.

Noble turned to Ezra. "Both of you."

"What did I do?" Ezra asked.

"You stayed when you could have gone." Noble clapped a hand on Ezra's shoulder, nearly buckling the smaller man's knees. "That was above and beyond. You did good."

Ezra smiled.

Noble cocked a thumb at the front door. "There's a lot of research in there that might be helpful, but be careful. I'll be inside in a minute. I need a few."

"Take all the time you need," Gwen told him.

He caught her wrist as she started past. "Give me that cellphone."

Gwen passed it over and watched him delete a video before she stepped through the door into the dim interior. She and Ezra set to work gathering papers while Noble collected himself.

# CHAPTER TWENTY-THREE

Noble stood with his back against the wall of the cabin, filling his lungs with the clean scent of pine, letting the cold drive the fatigue from his exhausted brain. His legs felt like spaghetti noodles and his hands were spastic butterflies, dancing and flapping. He had erased the video to his mother and now he scolded himself for being so careless. He was a seasoned field officer. He should have been more careful. He'd put himself and his team in danger. He shook his head and whispered, "Stupid and careless."

Maybe Sokol was right, maybe he was too old for field duty. He'd rolled those dice one too many times. Sooner or later, he'd roll snake eyes. Game over. Lights out. It was bad enough he'd nearly gotten himself killed, but he could have gotten the geeks killed as well. That was unacceptable. It was one thing to risk his own neck, it was another thing to put the other members of his team in jeopardy.

Sokol had talked about acceptable risks and losses. It was her opinion that Noble should take a desk job. He'd put in his time, both in the Army and in the CIA. He could ask for a desk at Langley, he'd been around long enough to be promoted to case officer. In Susan's opinion, he'd make an excellent chief of station somewhere, but that meant giving up the boat and moving away from mom. Two things Noble knew in his heart he could never do. Besides, he didn't want to be trapped behind a desk reading field reports from younger officers, trying to make judgement calls about missions unfolding on the other side of the globe. He'd end up a chain-smoking, hard-drinking, sharp-eyed hawk, like Wizard. Noble had a lot of respect for the old man, but he didn't want to *be* the old man.

"You're rattled," Noble told himself. *And talking to yourself,* he added internally.

He concentrated on breathing deep, clearing his mind. He'd had a close call, but he'd come through. Another minute was enough to shake off the creeping dread that tried to take hold of him. He offered up a quick prayer, thanking God for pulling his bacon from the fire one more time, and then went inside to help the geeks with their search.

Ezra and Gwen were busy gathering armloads of paper, staying well clear of the pressure switch in the middle of the floor, and Noble took the opportunity to make a careful examination of the rest of the house. He started in the kitchen, moved into the bathroom and then checked the master bedroom, picking out clues about Lukyanenko as he went.

You can learn a lot about someone from a thorough search of their living space. Lukyanenko had been a bit of an absent-minded genius. There were books in the bathroom and winter gloves on top of the fridge. A toothbrush sat on a table next to the sofa.

Noble found a metal box at the back of the closet secured with a cheap lock. He took a set of picks from his wallet, scrubbed the lock and threw open the lid. Inside was a collection of photographs of Lukyanenko with a much younger woman.

Noble let out a low whistle. The scientist had been a bit of an amateur photographer and the redhead in the pictures wasn't shy. He gathered the photos and closed the lid, returning to the living room.

The geeks were in the door, stacks of paper in their arms, waiting for him.

Noble held up the photographs. "Lukyanenko had a mistress."

Gwen's eyebrows went up and Ezra's jaw dropped.

"We shouldn't have too much trouble finding out who she is," Noble said. "Got everything you need?"

Gwen nodded.

"Then let's get out of here," Noble told them.

None of them wanted to hang around any longer than necessary. They were still standing on top of a nasty explosive. They hurried down the drive and Noble asked, "Where'd you get the Prius?"

"Stole it," Ezra announced with a note of pride in his voice.

"Wipe it down," Noble ordered.

Ezra handed his stack of papers to Gwen and ducked in the car to clean away any fingerprints. When that was done, they piled into the ZAZ. Noble hot-wired the engine and got them headed back to the highway while the geeks went through Lukyanenko's research. Noble was more interested in the girl. Hot young redheads did not normally go for paunchy middle-aged men with receding hair.

## CHAPTER TWENTY-FOUR

"This is bad," Gwen was saying. She was in the passenger seat, a stack of papers in her lap and her glasses slipping down her nose. She kept having to tuck an unruly strand of curls behind one ear.

High beams pushed back the darkness and the tires hummed on the blacktop. The stolen ZAZ sailed around gentle curves along a lane cutting between towering pines.

"What's bad?" Noble wanted to know. He had one hand on the wheel. The other kept going to his face. He pushed shaggy locks back from his forehead and blinked hard in an effort to clear his thoughts. He'd come close that time. Very close. He could practically hear Susan whispering in his ear. *You've done enough. You've paid your dues. You've done your bit for God and Country. Time to let someone else do the heavy lifting.*

Noble shook his head. *No time to think about that now,* he told himself. He had a job to do.

Gwen motioned to a page. "If I'm reading this right, Lukyanenko was working on a high yield EMP."

Ezra said, "EMP stands for..."

"Electromagnetic pulse," Noble finished for him. He didn't need the geeks to explain an EMP. Pop off a nuke at high altitudes and it creates an electronic pulse, killing anything with an electrical circuit. During the Cold War the Soviet Union had experimented with EMPs as a way to bring down American infrastructure without destroying crops. An EMP doesn't damage buildings or farmland, it just takes down the electrical grid. And modern people rely entirely on the electrical grid.

"I know what an EMP is," Noble told them. "You mean this guy was working on a nuke?"

Gwen shook her head. "No, that's the scary part. These plans are for a wholly unique device. It's not nuclear. It's electromagnetic. You could take this device through any port in the world and it would never ping a Giger meter."

Ezra reached for the paper and his brow pinched. "So he managed to come up with a design for a non-nuclear EMP?"

"Looks like," Gwen said. "And if my calculations are correct it would be pretty small."

Noble let out a low whistle. "How small? Suitcase?"

Suitcase nukes are the stuff of nightmares for intelligence agencies the world over. There's almost no way to stop one from coming into your country and they can be detonated anywhere.

"Not that small," Gwen said.

"Thank God," Ezra muttered.

"But it could easily be built into a container the size of a small truck," Gwen said. "Maybe even a hatchback."

"That's bad," Noble said.

"What are we going to do?" Gwen asked.

Noble said, "Time to contact Langley."

"And run this up the flagpole?" Gwen asked. "What if I'm wrong?"

"What if you're right?" Noble was already dialing.

"Jake." Wizard's sandpaper voice came on the line and they heard him exhale. "What have you got for me, kid?"

"I don't think Lukyanenko took a powder," Noble said. "We've just been to his cabin. The place was searched and someone left a parting gift."

"Boobytrapped?" Wizard asked.

"A nasty pressure mine attached to the floorboards in the middle of the living room," Noble said. "Witwicky disabled it. Cook assisted."

"Why in the hell would they take that kind of risk?"

"I was standing on it at the time."

There was a pause while Wizard let that information sink in and then, "They in the car with you now?"

"Yes," Noble said. "You're on speaker."

"Good work you two," Wizard said. "Any idea who might have taken Lukyanenko or why?"

Gwen explained to him about the experimental EMP and Wizard cursed.

"Witwicky, in your professional opinion, how hard would it be to actually build the bomb?"

Gwen let out a helpless little breath of air. "Deputy Director, this is way over my head. I can barely even..."

"I'm asking you to take your best guess."

Gwen pushed the glasses up her nose and said, "If they have access to a large pair of rare earth magnets and an electrogyroscope, it wouldn't be that hard at all."

Wizard said, "Jake, I need you to find who took Lukyanenko, figure out how much they know, and stop them before they can build an EMP."

"There was a mistress," Noble said. "I found pictures of her in Lukyanenko's cabin. We should start with her."

"Suspiciously good looking?" Wizard asked.

"Way too good looking for a scientist." Noble turned to the pair of computer cowboys and said, "No offense."

They both shrugged.

"Look into the girl," Wizard said. "I've got to take this to Armstrong."

"That's going to turn into a circus," Noble said.

"I know."

"We might lose control of the situation," Noble continued.

"I've got no choice," Wizard said. "The sooner you find Lukyanenko the better."

Wizard hung up and Ezra said, "This is serious, huh?"

"As bad as it gets," Noble said.

Gwen reached for the pile of photos in the center console. "So we investigate the girl next."

Noble shook his head. "Next we pick up a pair of burner phones."

He took the off ramp headed into downtown. It was getting late, but the stores were still open and if they hurried, they could buy a pair of pay as you go mobiles. Noble had made a mistake by not replacing their phones right away. It was a mistake he wouldn't make again. He kept his eyes peeled for an electronics store and found what he was looking for six blocks from the SkyBnB. He gave

Witwicky a wad of cash and instructed her to get a pair of phones with internet capabilities.

She popped open the passenger side door and darted across the sidewalk, frizzy brown curls dancing in the wind.

Cook watched her go.

Noble studied the younger man in the rearview. It didn't take a genius to fit the puzzle pieces together. Ezra was crushing hard on Gwen but she didn't feel the same. He was short and skinny with an oversized beak and a video gamer's complexion. Gwen was a geek too, but she was a cute geek. If she traded out the glasses for contacts and did something with the wild mass of mousy brown curls, she'd be pretty. She obviously thought she could do better than Ezra and that was a shame, because they'd make a good couple.

She was back fifteen minutes later with two phones in clear plastic clamshell cases. She held up the loot like she'd just pulled a bank heist. "Got 'em. Now all we need to do is find the mistress."

# CHAPTER TWENTY-FIVE

Wizard lit a Chesterfield as he crossed the large reception area to Armstrong's office. Her door was closed. Wizard knocked, stuck his head in without waiting for an answer and said, "Got a minute?"

She was in a meeting with a group of freshman senators and she didn't look happy at the interruption, but Armstrong knew when Wizard wanted to talk it was important. She gave the newly-elected representatives a tight-lipped smile and said, "Be sure to read your briefing package and don't be afraid to reach out if you have any questions."

The senators spent the next five minutes shaking hands. Armstrong promised they would all meet up for drinks just as soon as she had a break in her busy schedule. Several of the younger senators scowled at Wizard and the cigarette stuck to his bottom lip. One muttered something about the legality of smoking in the workplace. No doubt the little weeny would be drafting new legislation the minute he got back to the Hill. When they were finally alone, Armstrong closed the door and said, "What's so important you had to interrupt me?"

Wizard shot smoke at the ceiling. "Just heard from Noble."

"And?" Armstrong said and moved behind her desk, a clear sign she was unhappy and asserting her dominance.

"Lukyanenko was working on a new kind of EMP." Wizard related to her, in layman's terms, what Witwicky had done her best to explain. He ended with, "Because it's non-nuclear it won't show up on any scanners."

Armstrong reached for the box of cigars on her desk, snipped the end off one and got it lit, then dropped down in her chair. "So we have a missing Ukrainian who may or may not be in possession of a doomsday device."

"That's about the gist of it." Wizard took a seat across from her.

Armstrong sat in silence for a minute and puffed on the cigar. Her eyes were distant, unfocused. Wizard smoked his cigarette, lighting one off the end of another, and let her think. He didn't rush. He liked to take his time with his thinking and respected Armstrong for doing the same. Fast thinking was usually lazy thinking.

The director leaned back in her chair and chewed her bottom lip while the cigar sent curlicues of smoke up toward the ceiling. "That's a lot to take in."

Wizard nodded.

"Did you know the Ukrainians had someone working on a new kind of EMP?"

He sniffed and flicked ash into a cut-glass tray on her desk. "It's not a new idea. Lot of people are working on non-nuclear EMPs. I didn't know the Ukrainians were this close to making it a reality."

"So much for American intelligence," Armstrong muttered. Her cigar had gone out and she relit it. "Has Noble got any leads?"

"He's got a line on the mistress," Wizard told her. "The kid thinks she has something to do with Lukyanenko's disappearance."

"Why's he think that?"

"Lukyanenko is old and balding. She's young and pretty. Do the math."

Armstrong nodded. "Tell Noble to keep digging. We have to find this guy."

"Jake is like a dog with a bone," Wizard said. "He won't stop until he's got Lukyanenko in his sights."

"Good."

"The question is; what are we going to do?" Wizard said. "If this guy is in possession of an EMP, we have a duty to alert the president. This is a national security issue."

Armstrong winced. "I'd hate to raise a red flag and find out we're wrong. There's still a chance this guy took a powder."

Wizard cocked one eyebrow. "A scientist working on a doomsday device decides to run off to Bora Bora? Not likely. If you ask me, he either built it and decided to use it, or he built it and someone else is about to use it."

Armstrong closed her eyes. "I liked this Lukyanenko guy better when we thought he and the wife had run off to a sandy beach somewhere."

Wizard didn't bother to respond to that. It wasn't productive. This was the situation and they had to deal with it. Armstrong knew what the next move was, but Wizard had to let her get there on her own. He smoked in silence while she weighed her options.

She finally stubbed out the cigar, buzzed her secretary and said, "Call a meeting with the President, the DNI and the Secretary of Defense."

"The President is in Puerto Rico," Ginny Farnsworth told them.

Armstrong cursed.

The islands had recently been hit by a category two storm that wrecked most of Puerto Rico's infrastructure, and the President was touring the damage, calling for a disaster relief bill to support the commonwealth. It was a busy storm season. According to the news networks, another storm was barreling toward the Gulf.

"And the DNI is vacationing in the Poconos," Wizard added.

Armstrong waved a hand in the air. "No big loss there."

The hint of a smile tugged at Wizard's lips. There was no love lost between the Director of CIA and the Director of National Intelligence. The position had been created after September 11th as a way to facilitate communication between America's various intelligence communities. In reality all it did was add another layer of bureaucracy. As Wizard liked to say, *politicians can screw up a one-man parade.*

Armstrong jabbed the intercom button and said, "I want the Secretary of Defense in my office in one hour, priority alpha, and get the president on speaker."

"What about the DNI?" Farnsworth asked.

"I don't have the number for the Poconos," Armstrong said.

"Understood."

"What do you want me to do?" Wizard asked.

"Put together a doomsday team."

Wizard inspected the end of his cigarette. A doomsday team is a group of experts in various fields who could strategize responses to various emergency scenarios like nuclear attacks. Wizard had been on his share of doomsday teams during the sixties when the whole world had been certain the Reds were about to start lobbing missiles. Wizard took a drag and said, "Like the Cold War all over again."

# CHAPTER TWENTY-SIX

Noble had showered and changed and the after-effects of almost being blown up were starting to wear off. His hands were no longer shaking and the iron band around his intestines was starting to let go. He could hear the water running from the bathroom. While Ezra went in search of food, Gwen had hopped in the shower, leaving Noble a few minutes to collect himself. He was sitting on the corner of the bed, a picture of Lukyanenko's mistress in hand, but Noble was staring off into space. He was thinking about Ezra and Gwen—he no longer referred to them as simply the Geeks. When they had landed in Kiev, he'd been certain one or both of them would die. That was just the breaks. Intelligence work is dangerous and people get killed. Now he was determined to see both of them through. They were young, inexperienced, and way out of their depth. They should be back at Virginia, safe behind their computers. Instead they were in the field, risking life and limb. Noble shook his head. He didn't want to see their stars carved into the wall at Langley.

The shower shut off with a squeal of rusting pipes and a few minutes later Gwen emerged from the bathroom wrapped in a fluffy bathrobe, smelling of lilac, her hair pulled back in a bun and her glasses sliding down her nose. It reminded Noble of his mission to the Philippines where he'd met Sam Gunn, and a painful shard of ice pierced his chest.

Gwen thrust her chin at the picture in his hand. "Any luck?"

"I haven't even started yet." Noble tossed the picture aside and stood. "I wanted to thank you."

She shrugged and had to hold the towel to make sure it didn't slip. "We're a team. That's what teammates do."

"Not many people would have been able to do that," Noble told her. "You really went above and beyond."

An awkward smile turned up the corners of her mouth and she wrapped her arms around him. Noble felt her body pressed against his and her damp hair soaked through his shirt. The soft scent of her shampoo crowded his senses, making it hard to think.

Ezra chose that moment to return with a sack full of takeout. Noble and Gwen came apart like a pair of teenagers when Dad walks into the room. There was a flash of suspicious jealousy in Ezra's eyes, but he didn't say anything, playing dumb instead.

The three of them gorged themselves on pirogis and when they'd finished, they turned their attention back to the task at hand. Ezra and Gwen spread Lukyanenko's research out on the floor while Noble went to work uncovering the name of the mistress.

Social media is a wonderful thing. Noble didn't have

any social media accounts and never would. It was a waste of time and social media companies trampled the rights of individuals, but it was, however, a quick and convenient way of identifying people.

Five minutes was all it took to set up a Spacebook account on Noble's burner phone. He snapped a picture of the redhead in the photographs, uploaded one to the network and within seconds the amateur intelligence company's algorithms put a name to the face, asking Noble if he wanted to tag Anastasia Rudenko.

"Got a name," Noble told the pair of computer cowboys.

Ezra and Gwen looked up from their labors.

"Anastasia Rudenko," Noble said. "See what you can dig up on her."

Ezra nodded and reached for his laptop while Gwen stretched out on her belly. She was in the middle of the floor, ankles crossed in the air, reading a flimsy sheet of foolscap covered in Lukyanenko's blocky letters, and her bathrobe shifted, revealing a generous amount of thigh. Noble noticed and so did Ezra. And Ezra noticed Noble noticing.

Ezra scowled and Noble pulled his eyes away, focusing his attention on Anastasia Rudenko's Spacebook page. She was a knockout with legs that went on for days.

"She's clean," Ezra said, by which he meant she wasn't connected to any known intelligence, military, or law enforcement networks. "She's a bit of a wild child. She's got a handful of unpaid speeding tickets and she's been busted on drunk and disorderly, but she's not wired in."

"How does she earn a living?" Noble wanted to know.

Her page showed a few pics taken in a club called The Neon Circus where she had worked as a dancer six months ago, but nothing recent.

Ezra shook his head. "Her last official employment record is from four years ago when she was waitressing at a bar in downtown Kiev. Nothing since then."

"Home address?" Noble asked.

"Nada," Ezra said. "She had an apartment downtown, but that was also a few years ago. Her phone is still connected to that address, but she hasn't been paying rent there for at least three years. Looks like she's a drifter."

"Not from what I'm seeing." Noble showed him a recent selfie of Anastasia, clad in a slinky white dress, in an upscale boutique with half a dozen shopping bags slung over one shoulder. She looked like the cat who ate the canary. Her shoes, a pair of white stiletto heels, probably cost more than Noble's entire wardrobe. The caption said, YOLO #shopping #highlife #spendingspree.

Gwen rolled her eyes. "Hashtag vapid."

"Where's a gogo dancer get that kind of cash," Noble said. "That's what I'd like to know."

"Did you just call her a gogo dancer?" Gwen asked.

"Is that no longer politically correct?"

Gwen giggled. "It's fine as long as you're eighty-seven."

"Ring ring." Ezra put his thumb and pinkie to his ear like a telephone and then held it out to Noble. "It's the forties calling. They want their slang back."

Gwen cracked up laughing.

"Hilarious," said Noble. "Can you get a location on her phone?"

"Not from here," Ezra said, indicating his laptop. "Not with this equipment."

"There are other ways to find people," Noble told them.

"How?" Gwen inquired.

"Field work," Noble said. "Computers don't have all the answers."

"Says the guy who just used Spacebook to find a *gogo* dancer," Gwen said.

Ezra did a bad Humphrey Bogart impression. "I'm hip to it, doll face."

Noble ignored their jabs and said, "I'll start at the club. They might know where to find her."

Gwen sat up and adjusted the hem of her bathrobe. "Do you want one of us to come with you?"

Ezra stopped what he was doing and looked up expectantly.

"Afraid I'll step on another landmine?"

They exchanged a glance. Ezra said, "I think we'd both feel a lot better if one of us went with you."

"Right," Gwen nodded.

Diffusing the bomb had turned this mission into something real, something dangerous. Before that, it had just been a simple field assignment to Kiev, a cool story they could tell their friends back in the intelligence directorate. The computer cowboys at Langley generally got a kick out of being selected for a field assignment. It was a chance to get out of the basement and experience the life of a spy without having to take any of the risks. Most of the time, the intelligence geeks were along for the ride. They spent their time in embassies or hotel rooms while the Operations people did all the leg work. But Ezra and Gwen had gotten a taste of the real thing. Now they understood the danger. They were operating in the black and one small mistake could end their lives, or the life of the person next to them. They were starting to take this seriously, thinking through every move, and that was the first step to being good in the field.

Noble weighed his options. Whoever he picked might be going home in a body bag. It was a rotten choice to make, but he pointed at Ezra. "I'll take geek number one."

"Yes!" Ezra pumped his fist like he'd just won a prize, while Gwen pouted.

# CHAPTER TWENTY-SEVEN

NOBLE SAT BEHIND THE WHEEL OF THE STOLEN ZAZ Slavuta, watching little bits of ice collect on the wipers and slowly melt. It wasn't snowing, it wasn't quite cold enough, but small icy pellets were falling down from a slate-black sky. The heater was blowing. Noble rubbed his hands, cupped them together and blew. Cars rumbled past, going slow, tires humming on the blacktop.

The Neon Circus was situated in a row of nightclubs. Baselines pounded all along the boulevard and drunken Kievites staggered along the sidewalks, dressed in party clothes. The guys wore the latest hip-hop style and the girls wore short, tight dresses that left gooseflesh on their exposed skin. No price is too high to pay for fashion. The Neon Circus was one of the better clubs. The door was uphol-stered in red leather and the sign flashed green and blue electric. There was a bouncer, but no line. None of the partiers seemed to stay in any club longer than thirty or forty minutes. Then it was on to the next spot, the next baseline, the next drink.

Noble glanced in the side mirrors. It's hard to spot surveillance in a street crowded with pedestrians. He had the windows cracked so he could hear as well as see, but it was letting in the cold air and he put his hands up to the vents for warmth.

Fifteen minutes later Cook emerged from the front door of The Neon Circus, crossed against traffic and made his way along the sidewalk to the stolen Slavuta. He climbed in the passenger side, bringing with him the acrid stench of cigarette smoke and cheap vodka. He dug a small allergy bottle out of his pocket and squeezed a shot into each nostril. His voice was thick, like a man just getting over a long bout with the flu. "Hope you don't have allergies."

"None that I know of," Noble told him. "What's the layout."

"Pretty basic." Ezra produced a tissue, blew his nose, peeked at the results and then wadded the used tissue and stuffed it in his pocket. "Mostly one big room with a dance floor in the center, and a balcony around the upper floor with private booths. There's a small entryway, a beaded curtain, and the bar is on your left when you enter. The bathrooms are straight across the dance floor, at the back of the building. There's a stairway marked private that goes up to what I suspect is an office on the second floor. The fire exit is near the bathrooms."

"Good job." Noble reached for his door handle

"She's not there," Cook said.

Noble let go of the latch and turned back. "What?"

"I asked around," Cook told him. "None of the other girls have seen her in months."

"You were just supposed to scope the place out."

Cook shrugged. "I looked around, Anastasia clearly wasn't there, so I asked a few of the girls about her. It's cool. I acted like a customer."

Noble closed his eyes. The muscles at the corner of his jaw bunched and released.

"What's the big deal?" Ezra asked.

"Now I'm going to be the second guy tonight asking about Anastasia," Noble told him. "It looks suspicious."

Ezra's face fell. He mumbled an apology. "I was just trying to help."

"From now on, do what you're told." Noble threw open the door and stepped out. "Keep the motor running and the doors locked. If you see anything suspicious, you circle the block and find a new parking space. If you're in a different spot when I come out, I'll find my own way back to the SkyBnB and you do the same. Understood?"

Cook nodded. "Got it."

Noble threw the door shut with more force than necessary, turned his collar up against the cold and crossed the street. Icy pellets attacked his face and the wind put spots of color in his cheeks. He didn't know how the Kievites walked around without coats in this cold but, growing up here, they were probably used to it.

The bouncer, a small mountain in a cheap black suit with an earpiece, looked Noble over before nodding.

Noble hauled open the red upholstered door and passed through the small entry hall into a pulsing kaleidoscope of smoke and flashing neon. The center stage was a long catwalk where the girls slithered around brass poles. There were three dancers at the moment. Two were dangerously underweight. One was dangerously overweight. Other girls cruised the tables like hungry sharks.

The music was turning Noble's brain to spaghetti, a sure sign that he was leaving youth behind and entering into what some would call middle age. He set his teeth against the powerful electronic drumbeat and made his way to the bar. With a beer in hand, he found an empty table, watched the dancers and waited for one of the girls to make her move. He didn't have to wait long.

"Hi, sweetie." She spoke Ukrainian and planted her boney bottom on Noble's thigh. "What's your name?"

Noble could understand Ukrainian, mostly, but wasn't versed enough to speak it. He spoke German instead, the closest thing to a universal language in Eastern Europe. "I'm Jacobin."

"German? Ya?"

"Ya." Noble looped one arm around her narrow waist and rested his hand on her thigh.

"You're cute." She obliged by using German. "What brings you to Kiev, Jacobin?"

"I'm in town on business."

"Then you should probably go back to your hotel room." She tapped his nose with the tip of one finger and gave a playful pout. "Get a good night's sleep so you can wake up early tomorrow."

Noble grinned, sipped his beer and told her, "Tomorrow is my day off, fräulein."

"Then I can keep you up all night and not feel bad about it."

Noble looked her up and down. "I hope so. But maybe you are not enough woman for me."

"Oh?" Her eyebrows went up.

"Sometimes one is just not enough," Noble said. "Know what I mean?"

She put on a smile but Noble could feel her skin crawl. She said, "I can invite a friend along and we can party."

"Guten," Noble said. "I was here last year and met a girl I really liked. I think her name was Annalise, or maybe it was Anastasia. You know her?"

The dancer's face changed with the speed of a political candidate flip-flopping on campaign issues. The smile vanished, replaced by a marble mask. She got up from his knee and walked away.

"Must have been something I said," Noble told the empty space.

Her sudden departure spoke volumes. Someone had warned the girls to clam up and Noble was betting it was management. The fact that Ezra had been here minutes before asking after the same girl definitely hadn't helped. It was time to go. He took a swallow of beer, peeled off a few bills and dropped them on the table before getting up.

The big mountain from the entrance was inside now and the girl whispered something in his ear. She turned and pointed at Noble. The mountain started weaving between tables.

Noble waited. He couldn't reach the exit without going past the bouncer and making a break for the fire exit would be suspicious. He wanted to keep his cover legend intact as long as possible.

The bouncer planted himself in front of Noble, drawing up to his full height and flexing massive shoulders. He spoke in a baritone that was hard to hear over the crashing baseline. "Why are you asking about Anastasia?"

"I like her," Noble shrugged. "I met her last year while I was in town. I was hoping she still worked here."

The mountain narrowed his eyes and cocked his head to one side. His big paw went to his earpiece and he listened a moment then said, "Come with me."

"I don't want any trouble." Noble put his hands up and said, "I'll just go."

He tried to move past, but the bouncer's hand darted out and caught Noble by the elbow. He moved faster than a man his size had any right to and his fingers sank into Noble's bicep with bone crushing strength.

"I said come with me."

Noble allowed himself to be dragged across the club floor, through a beaded curtain and a door marked БАНКЕТНИЙ.

# CHAPTER TWENTY-EIGHT

Armstrong's office, normally spacious, felt cramped with the joint chiefs, the Secretary of Defense, the head of homeland security and the acting Secretary of State all crowded around a pair of sofas flanking a low table. Harold Trasker, an expert in Electromagnetic Pulse Science and head of Wizard's doomsday team, was there as well. A dozen mugs of coffee, emblazoned with the CIA logo, had turned room temperature and smoke made slow eddies around the ceiling. Armstrong stood in front of her desk, a slim cigar in hand. Silent blue ribbons unfurled from the glowing embers.

A Marine Corp General named Doug Moench said, "This is my worst nightmare come true. How long have we known this guy was missing?"

"Four days now." Wizard waved away a cloud of smoke. "We moved on the information as soon as we learned Lukyanenko was MIA."

"Four days." Moench shook his head. He reached for a

cup of coffee, couldn't decide which mug was his, and took one at random. "That's a lifetime in a case like this."

The acting Secretary of State, a woman named Ogden, took off her glasses, cleaned them on her sweater and pushed them back into place. She was a fish out of water and it showed. She had only been at her post for a week. The president had unceremoniously fired her boss and Ogden was standing in until a replacement could be found. Her face was a pale moon surrounded by bottle blonde hair. She said, "I'm not even sure I understand what you're all so worried about. What's the big deal? What's an EMP?"

Armstrong looked to Harold Trasker. The analyst had an armload of books and paperwork which he spread out on the coffee table after clearing a space in the forest of mugs. He was a bulky man in his late fifties, with a droopy mustache and wide hips. He smelled like mothballs. "An EMP, or an electromagnetic pulse, is a high-altitude nuclear yield which sends out an invisible surge that fries anything with an electronic circuit."

"Did you say nuclear?"

Trasker bobbed his head. "But it's not a nuclear blast in the way you're probably thinking. It's a high-altitude nuclear explosion. It doesn't destroy anything on the ground. There won't be any fire or heat. In fact, if you were taking a walk in the park you might not notice anything had happened at first."

"Then why all the fuss?" Ogden asked.

"Because an EMP destroys all electronics."

"Like my watch?" She lifted her slim gold Rolex as an example.

"Anything that runs on electricity," Trasker told her.

"Cars, TVs, radios, computers, microwaves, refrigerators, the whole enchilada."

Ogden shook her head. "I'm still not sure what everyone is so excited about. So the power goes out for a few minutes? That's not the end of the world."

"Actually," Wizard rasped, "it *is* the end of the world."

Trasker nodded enthusiastically. "The end of the world as we know it."

"How's that?"

"In the event of an EMP the power doesn't go out for a few minutes or even a few days," Trasker said. "The power goes out and it doesn't come back."

"Ever?"

"We'd have to rebuild the entire national power grid," Trasker told her. "An EMP would knock out the power stations. America's network of power is basically separated into five large grids. An EMP attack, detonated in the right spot, could knock out all five simultaneously and those machines can't be fixed overnight. They can't even be fixed locally."

"We can't repair our own power grid?" One of the joint chiefs spoke up. He was a gray-haired Admiral from the Navy named Cutter.

"The replacement parts are only made in Japan," Trasker told him. "And it's a six month lead time."

Admiral Cutter leaned back in the sofa and scrubbed his face with both hands. "We're reliant on Japan for our national power grid? How in the world did we let that happen?"

"That's not important right now, Admiral," Wizard said.

"How much damage are we talking?" Doug Moench asked.

Trasker indicated a file folder marked CLASSIFIED/EYES ONLY on the coffee table. "This report is from a red team that war gamed this vary scenario a few years ago. Keep in mind, it's a little old, some things have changed, but they estimate a million deaths within the first few hours of an EMP strike."

"A million dead people," Ogden blurted. "A million people are going to die because the lights go out?"

"You still don't quite grasp the situation," Trasker said.

She bristled but Trasker didn't seem to notice. "Think of all the people in hospitals around the country at any given moment. If the power goes out, everybody on life support, everyone in the middle of a life-saving surgery, and a lot of people having minor surgery, will die."

"Don't hospitals have emergency generators?"

"An EMP will knock out the backup generators," Trasker told her. "Hospitals will go dark and anyone reliant on electricity will die. Anyone with a pacemaker will die. Cars will lose power, trains will grind to a halt, and planes will fall out of the sky. Like Deputy Director Dulles said, our way of life would suddenly end. We'd effectively be living in the Stone Age."

"What does the report have to say about long term casualties?" Wizard asked.

Trasker rocked his head side to side. "That's where things get really bad."

"It gets worse?" Ogden said, a small tremor in her voice.

"Much worse," Trasker told the gathering. "America gets most of our food from Mexico and Canada. Without a continuous supply of trains coming in, we'll run out of food in about three days. After that people will be fighting in the streets for cans of tuna. The east and west coast will be the hardest hit with another wave of casualties about two weeks into the catastrophe. There is another wave of death after thirty to sixty days. People on life saving medication usually only have a month's worth. All in all, experts predict two thirds of the population of the United States would be dead within six months of an EMP strike."

"Ohmigod!" Ogden put a hand over her mouth.

"Let's everybody take a beat," Armstrong said. "We don't even know for sure there is a bomb, not yet."

"And if there is," said Wizard, "it might not be aimed at the United States."

Armstrong said, "All we know is that a scientist was working on the plans for a device and he's now missing."

"Along with his research," Wizard added.

Armstrong conceded that point.

"What are we doing to track this guy?" General Moench asked.

"We have a team on the ground in Kiev," Wizard said. "They're walking back the cat on the scientist."

Ogden turned to him, the question evident on her face.

"It means to retrace someone's footsteps, find out where they've been so you can figure out where they're going."

"Have they made any progress?"

"Some," Wizard said.

"What's that supposed to mean?" General Moench asked.

Wizard pulled at his Chesterfield and studied the

Marine Corps General with icy blue eyes. "It means they've made some progress."

"Can you be more specific?"

Wizard shook his head.

Moench leaned forward. "This is a matter of national security, Dulles. I know you want to keep your people safe, but we have a right to know what's happening on the ground. It might affect our decision making."

"If they kick over anything of value, I'll be sure to let you know, but for now, my people and their activities remain in house."

"Unacceptable." Moench shook his head. "I know you spy types like to keep your little secrets, but that's not going to fly in this instance. We need a complete picture of everything going on."

"You've got a complete picture," Wizard told him.

"I want to know what your people know," Moench said.

The acting Secretary of State nodded. "I'd also like more information about your team and their progress. Have they any clue as to the whereabouts of this scientist?"

"I'm not giving out any information that could put my people in jeopardy."

Moench turned to Director Armstrong. "As head of the joint chiefs, I demand you bring us into the loop on your ground team and their activities."

"She hasn't got the authority." Wizard blew smoke and stared hard at the general.

Moench turned an alarming shade of red. "This is a bunch of bull."

Armstrong opened her mouth to speak.

Wizard said, "I'm the director of operations for the

CIA, this operation and the people involved are under my command. I have final say in the dissemination of any and all classified information pertaining to the operation."

Moench turned to Armstrong. "Is that right?"

Armstrong glared at Al. "He's right. Technically speaking, I don't have the power to force him to turn over classified information."

"The president has the authority," Moench said.

"He's not here," Wizard pointed out.

"He will be soon."

"And when he gets here, he can give that order," Wizard said. "Until then, my people and their findings remain classified, eyes only."

Moench balled a fist and hammered his own thigh with it. "We're talking about the fate of a nation! Maybe our own!"

"I'm aware."

"And you still won't give us the information?"

"I've given you everything you need to know," Wizard said.

Armstrong held up her hands for peace. "Dulles has made his decision and for now we have to trust it's the right one."

"And if he's wrong?" Moench asked.

"He'll be asked to retire," Armstrong said with a flat look at the grizzled old director of operations.

Wizard lit one cigarette off the end of the other, as if they were discussing the Red Sox's chances at taking home the pennant.

Admiral Cutter broke in. "I wouldn't give up my people either. The question is, what are we going to do now?"

"I'll tell you what we're going to do," the acting Secretary of State said. "We're going to shut down all the airports and shipping lanes and we're going to call out the national guard."

"Hold on just a second," said Moench. "We do that and we'll cause a panic."

"People should be panicked. From what I've learned this EMP is a nightmare scenario."

Armstrong shook her head. "Causing a panic will only lead to more casualties."

Wizard said, "We don't even know if America is the target. Lukyanenko is Ukrainian. Maybe he's decided to use his invention against Russia."

Admiral Cutter said, "It could be a Middle Eastern terror group planning to use it against Israel."

"There are a thousand possibilities." Wizard nodded.

"Still," Ogden said, "Americans have a right to know."

Armstrong shook her head again. "I disagree."

"I'm not sure I like the attitude of the CIA," Ogden said. "First you won't tell us what your people are up to and now you don't want to warn the citizens of the United States about a potential disaster? This sounds like the kind of thinking that led to September eleventh."

Armstrong bit back a scathing reply. "There are steps we can take without causing riots in major cities."

"She's right," Cutter said. "We should move to mitigate damage without sending people into a panic."

"What are you proposing?" Ogden asked.

"We beef up security and put military forces on high alert. We also need to workshop what we're going to do in the event an EMP is deployed here, or elsewhere. If Russia loses power they'll expect us to help."

"If Russia loses power," Wizard said, "they'll assume it was us and retaliate with a nuclear warhead."

"How can they do that without power?" Ogden wanted to know.

"Their silos are hardened to withstand an EMP attack," Wizard said. "The moment they lose power, they'll assume it's a first strike by America. It would start a full-scale exchange."

"You don't know that," Ogden said but the doubt was evident in her voice.

Wizard said, "I know the way Russians think."

Armstrong turned to Trasker. "I need your team to come up with a game plan for restoring order to the continental United States in the aftermath of an EMP attack. And communications should be at the top of your list."

He nodded, pulled out a small notepad and started scribbling.

General Moench faced Wizard. His mouth was a tight line. "Our best bet is to find this scientist and his device, and stop this thing before it starts."

Wizard scratched one scraggly brow with a nicotine-stained fingertip. Flakes of white dandruff floated down, like snow, to land on his lapel. "Agreed."

# CHAPTER TWENTY-NINE

NOBLE ALLOWED HIMSELF TO BE MARCHED THROUGH the door marked PRIVATE, along a narrow hall, dimly lit and smelling of urine. The passage was full of dented aluminum kegs stacked against the wall, forcing Noble to turn his shoulders. The mountain had to go sideways and still his girth barely fit. They climbed a set of steps and stopped in front of a door. The mountain knocked twice.

"Come!" The voice was muffled by the flimsy wood panel.

The bouncer turned the knob and gave Noble a push.

He stumbled into a small office filled with a massive cherry-wood desk, far too grandiose for the space, and a metal filing cabinet with a coffee maker on top. The aroma of strong black roast wafted from the pot. The walls were bare cinderblock and the only window was a plate of two-way glass that looked out over the dance floor. A Tom and Jerry cartoon was playing on the flatscreen. The cat was trying to keep up with the mouse's frantic rendition of Liszt's Hungarian Sonata.

The man behind the desk was tall and slender, with long thinning hair, just starting to go gray. His shirt was open to reveal a hairy chest. He had gold on every finger and a pair of half-moon spectacles dangled at the end of a gold chain. He watched the Tom and Jerry routine with a toothy grin and when the mouse bowed to riotous applause, the club manager reached for the remote and muted the sound. He looked up at Noble for the first time. "I hear you are asking about one of my girls?"

Noble shrugged. "I met her last time I was here."

The manager put his glasses on and studied Noble through half-moon lens. "You are German?"

"That's right," Noble said. "From Munich."

"Why are you asking about Anastasia?"

"I told your security man, I don't want any trouble. She's not here anymore," he shrugged. "I'll go."

"You didn't answer my question."

"Why else would I come to a club full of pretty girls?"

"I have plenty of those. You are looking for a specific girl, isn't that so? I want to know why?"

"Because I liked her look," Noble said. "That's all. Can I go now?"

"I can make you talk, you know?" The manager's eyes flicked to the bouncer behind Noble's right shoulder.

"There's nothing to say," Noble told him.

"We'll see." He gave the bouncer a meaningful look and the big man clapped a giant paw on the back of Noble's neck.

Noble lunged, grabbed the coffee pot and swung it over his shoulder. Glass shattered against the mountain's head and scalding liquid splashed his face. Shards of broken glass embedded themselves in the big man's forehead. He staggered back against the wall with a sonorous boom. Blood spurted from the cuts, making him look like something out of a horror movie. He opened his mouth to scream and Noble struck him in the throat with an open hand blow that choked the sound before it could escape.

The bouncer went down on his butt, his back against the wall. Both hands went to his throat and he made small wheezing sounds.

"Look what you did," the manager gasped. One hand went to his throat like a silver screen diva about to faint at her first sight of Frankenstein's monster. He reached for the phone on his desk.

Noble swatted the mobile out of his hand. It hit the wall and fell behind the filing cabinet. On the flatscreen, Wile-E Coyote chased the Roadrunner in silence.

The manager squeaked and retreated until his shoulders impacted the two-way glass.

Noble heard movement and turned in time to see the mountain reaching for his waistband. His girth made getting at the gun a chore and by the time he had it in hand, Noble was on him.

Noble locked up the man's hand with both of his own, slammed his knee into the bouncer's chest, and used his body weight to wrench the weapon out of the bigger man's grasp. The bouncer's finger stuck in the trigger guard and Noble heard a snap.

The Mountain let out a shriek.

Noble turned the pistol around and rapped the bouncer on the nose. The bone broke with a wet crunch. Blood pissed over the cheap carpet and the Mountain pitched over on his side, openly sobbing, trying to staunch the flow with both hands.

The pistol was an old soviet Makarov, chambered in 9mm. It hadn't been cleaned in ages. Noble doubted it would even work. Semiautomatic pistols need regular cleaning and plenty of oil. He took a moment to eject the mag. It was full of copper-plated full metal jackets.

Noble turned back to the manager. He was pressed against the glass, hands still clutching his throat, his face a mask of horror. His bodyguard had been reduced to a sobbing mass on the floor, and now Noble had the gun.

"What are you going to do?" he whispered.

"That depends." Noble stuffed the pistol in his waistband and crossed around behind the desk, crowding the manager against the two-way glass. "You going to tell me about Anastasia?"

"What do you want to know?"

"Everything."

The manager started to shake his head.

Noble grabbed him, spun him around and slammed him against the glass. The two-way sheet shuddered under the impact. The manager yelped. Noble whispered. "I'll kill you right here and now."

"She left a few months ago," the manager whined. "She met an egg head who worked for the government. He liked her. He was taking care of her. Gave her money and expensive gifts. She didn't need the job anymore so she left. That's all I know."

"Where is she now?"

"How should I know?"

Noble slammed him again. This time a fracture

appeared in the glass. Beyond the window the dubstep beat continued to pound and the crowd watched a brunette spinning around the pole. No one noticed the cracked mirror overhead.

"I'm losing my patience," Noble warned.

"She's got an apartment on Lesi Ukrainy Boulevard," the Manager moaned. "It's a big high rise right in the middle of the city. You can't miss it."

"See how easy that was?" Noble pulled him away from the window and forced him down into his plush office chair.

The manager went down so hard he bit his lip. Blood dribbled from his mouth. He reached a hand toward the desk and Noble brought his fist up.

"I'm just getting a tissue," he said and plucked one from the box to dab at the blood.

"Have you got a way to contact Anastasia?"

"I've got her number in my phone."

Noble moved around the desk and pushed the filing cabinet over. It fell with a loud crash. He picked up the manager's phone and pocketed it. "If she finds out I'm coming, I'll be back here. And I'll be in a very bad mood."

The manager crossed his heart and said, "On my mother's grave."

# CHAPTER THIRTY

ARKADY ALEXANDROVICH LUKYANENKO STOOD OVER the device, sweat trailing down his face and soaking through his shirt, a thin smile on his lips. He was happy, despite the circumstances. Well, maybe happy wasn't the right word. He was proud and satisfied. He might be a prisoner but at the very least he had proven his theory correct. It was nearly done. The work was almost complete. He'd constructed a non-nuclear EMP in a package the size of a small automobile. It wasn't nearly as small as Arkady would have liked, but considerably smaller than an ICBM.

He trailed his fingertips along the aluminum chassis, basking in the joy of a job well done. Ukrainian military intelligence would have seen the project through to completion eventually, but it would have taken years, maybe a decade or more. The wheels of government turn slowly. The Translator and his team of thugs had made it happen in days.

Arkady circled the large contraption, inspecting the wiring, and making sure the connections were secure. The sun was setting and a warm red glow filtered into the cargo bay, bathing the device in a rich light. Arkady wiped sweat from his forehead and cleaned his glasses on his dirt-streaked t-shirt. He had forgotten all about the heat. The oppressive humidity no longer bothered him. Once he'd actually started to work, he had become engrossed. That was always the way. Arkady was a tinker at heart. He enjoyed the theoretical side but when it came time to actually turn screws, he often lost himself in the work. He could go days without food or sleep.

Unfortunately for Arkady, he'd forgotten to drink water and, in the tropics, that can be deadly.

But water was the farthest thing from his mind. He was more interested in proving his theory correct. If it worked...

The thought gave him pause. He had a screwdriver in one hand and a bundle of diodes in the other. Work lamps attached to the aircraft bulkhead flickered in the constant drone from the twin generators. What would happen when he finished the device? Where would The Translator use it? Or would he sell it to the highest bidder? The thought left a hot ball of wax in Arkady's belly. How many people would die?

He put the screwdriver down and rubbed a stitch in his chest. Why had he invented it in the first place? To give Ukraine a technological edge on the world stage? He should have known others would eventually get the technology. But he'd done it to prove he could. Like all men of science, he was interested mostly in proving it was possible. And proving he was smart enough to do it.

*How smart are you?* asked a little voice inside his head. Smart enough to create a device that could end the world, but not smart enough to ask himself whether or not a weapon of such magnitude should exist. Arkady had always envisioned his weapon being used as a deterrent, never as a first strike option, but he should have known the EMP would eventually fall into the wrong hands. He should have known that someone would use it for evil. Mankind had proven over and over again that his thirst for blood knew no bounds.

Arkady went to the cot, dropped down on the damp canvas, and rubbed at the stitch in his chest. He never should have shown his idea to Ukrainian intelligence. Never should have done the math. Never should have written any of it down. It should have stayed safely locked away inside his head. Now it was out. It was out and God help the world.

*But you don't have to finish*, Arkady thought. His chest was burning and his arm felt numb. He winced. The only thing to do now was to make sure this device was never used. The Translator was smart, he knew a thing or two about bomb making, but he wasn't *that* smart. He wasn't smart enough to know how it worked, or he would never have kidnapped Arkady to begin with.

Sweat was running down his cheeks in rivers, gathering on his chin in large wet drops and forming a puddle on the floor between his feet. His hands were starting to shake. He would install the magno-gyroscope, but he wouldn't connect the output. Without the intrarelay, the EMP would be useless, one big paperweight. The Translator would never know, not until he tried to use it, and by that time Arkady would be dead. *They'll probably shoot me in the back of the head the moment I tell them it's done.* By the time The

Translator found out the EMP didn't work, the one man who could fix it would be dead. That was fine by Arkady. He didn't need to complete the weapon to know it would work, that it *could* work. He knew, and that was enough.

The pain in his chest felt like a load of cinderblocks, crushing the air from his lungs. His arm was pins and needles.

"Thirsty," Arkady told the empty workshop. "Haven't drank anything all day."

He got up and went for water. The pain doubled, then tripled.

# CHAPTER THIRTY-ONE

THE BOUNCER WAS BADLY INJURED. HE'D NEED A hospital, which meant cops. Noble didn't want security cameras tracking him back to the stolen Slavuta so he turned right as he exited the club, stuffed his hands in his pockets and circled the block. Small icy spears attacked his cheeks. He stripped off his gray windbreaker, handing the jacket to a homeless man as he passed. A breeze cut through his sweater but Noble ignored the chill as he made his way back onto the busy street.

The temperature was dropping fast and Noble shivered against the cold. He approached the ZAZ from the rear and reached for the door handle. He was in the passenger seat before Ezra realized what was happening.

The little guy nearly jumped right out of his skin. "You scared ten years off my life. What happened? Why did you circle the block?" He sniffed and added, "And why do you smell like a coffee bean plantation?"

"Start the car," Noble told him. "The bouncer hauled me into the manager's office and tried to question me."

Ezra winced. "Because of me?"

"One guy showing up asking about her is coincidence," Noble said. "Two guys in the span of fifteen minutes is suspicious."

"I screwed up," Ezra said. "I'm sorry."

"You want to know how to survive in this business?" Noble asked.

Ezra nodded.

"Never make the same mistake twice." Noble pointed to the road with a *hurry it up* motion.

"Where to?" Ezra asked as he edged out into traffic.

"Back to the room," Noble said. He pulled the Makarov pistol from his waistband and stuffed it in the glove box, then inspected the manager's phone. It was password protected and Noble said, "Think you can break into this?"

"Barely an inconvenience."

They drove in silence for a while and then Ezra said, "Look, Noble, I'm really sorry. It won't happen again."

"I believe you."

"I mean it," Ezra said.

Noble glanced over at him. The little guy was genuinely concerned. His eyes were big and his mouth was tight. Noble said, "We survived and you learned from it. More importantly, we've got a lead on the girl."

"Are you going to tell Gwen what happened?"

"She doesn't need to know," Noble said.

"Thanks."

"You really like her," Noble said. It was more a statement than a question.

Ezra bobbed his head up and down.

# CHAPTER THIRTY-TWO

WEXLER SAT ON THE BALCONY OVERLOOKING THE RED shingled roofs of Bern, a fork in one hand and a book in the other. Breakfast was a large rosti made of scrambled eggs and potatoes. The book was a paperback copy of Cal Dupont's best-seller *Deep Meditation.* Wexler was never a serious student in his youth but had learned to love the printed page in his early twenties. Now in his mid-thirties, He had devoured hundreds, maybe even thousands of books, mostly non-fiction, and prided himself on his learning. He had been a troubled young man without direction in life who joined the military because he had no better prospects, and because the idea of killing things appealed to the little boy inside him who enjoyed pulling the wings off flies. In the British Special Air Service Wexler had learned to kill but, more importantly, he had learned there were people willing to pay for his expertise, people other than governments. He had worked for various mercenary groups around the world, until he'd been recruited by the Old Man.

The Old Man had changed Wexler's life forever. The Old Man had taught Wexler that he could be something more than just a hired killer. He had shown Wexler that he could do anything he wanted, *be* anybody he wanted. The Old Man had introduced him to the printed page, giving Wexler a dog-eared copy of a book called *Think and Grow Rich*. He had taught Wexler how to invest, to make money work for him, and more importantly, he'd taught Wexler the truth about the world. He had introduced Wexler to books like *Rules for Radicals,* and *Pedagogy of the Oppressed.*

Wexler forked chicken and chewed with his mouth open while he read, his lips silently forming the words. Cal Dupont was proving a real eye opener. He talked about many of the things Wexler already knew, but had never put into words, about the power of focus and eliminating distractions, and about taking small steps every day to achieve your goals.

Wexler was a man who had started out with nothing. He'd been born on the wrong side of the proverbial tracks and worked his way up from a troubled youth to the second in command of an enterprise that was going to change the world.

He had a mouth full of potatoes when his phone began to vibrate. Wexler set the book aside and picked up the phone thinking it was the Old Man but it was their operation in Kiev. He swallowed and took a moment to activate the voice scrambler before answering. "Dobryj den."

"I've got a problem," the foppish club manager said in a rush. "Someone was here asking about the girl."

Wexler wiped his mouth with a napkin, something he never would have done just ten years ago. Instead, he'd have used his shirt sleeve. He said, "She's a whore. Surely this isn't the first time some love-sick pup has come in asking about her."

"This one smacked around one of my bouncers and trashed my office." His lisping English cracked as he recounted the details. "He threatened to kill me."

"Alright," Wexler said. "Don't panic."

"Don't panic?" He screeched into the phone. "You promised me this would be simple. You said no one would ever find out."

"You may have to eliminate the girl."

"I didn't sign on for murder."

"You were paid," Wexler told him. "Handsomely."

"And I did my part," he said. "I delivered the scientist. You never said anyone would get hurt."

Wexler signaled his butler, a balding Swiss man waiting patiently at the patio door, who obediently collected the plates, asked if Wexler required anything else and then withdrew. Wexler was no longer hungry; he was thinking about how to break this news to the Old Man. Like his father, Wexler both loved and feared the Old Man. There were rewards for success, but there were also punishments for failure. Best he never found out, Wexler decided. He said, "Do you have a picture of the man who came to see you?"

"Of course. I have the whole club covered in cameras."

"Send over a picture."

"Hold a moment."

Wexler sipped coffee while he waited. A moment later a grainy black and white image appeared on his phone. Breakfast turned sour in his belly. He sat there gripping the phone for a long minute and then said, "His name is Jacob Noble. He's with the American CIA."

The club owner gave a plaintive whine. "What are we going to do?"

"Do nothing until I arrive."

"You're coming here?"

Wexler checked his watch. "I'll be there in three hours."

## CHAPTER THIRTY-THREE

By noon the next day, Noble was parked across the street from a modern high-rise in the Pechersk district. Situated on the hills overlooking the Dnieper River, Pechersk is the historic center of Kiev and arguably the most popular tourist destination. It's full of shopping, fine dining, and historic cathedrals. It's also where young up-and-comers choose to live. The buildings are a mix of old-world European architecture and grim soviet-era monstrosities off set by the occasional glass and steel.

A warm yellow sun was baking off the worst of the cold but frost still lined the gutters and smoke wafted from every sewer grate. Gwen was in the passenger seat, her hands in front of the vents and pink spots in her cheeks. She leaned forward and peered though the windshield at the towering apartment block. "Nice place."

The geeks had plugged Anastasia's cellphone number into their computers and it pinged off this address every night, usually in the early morning hours. During the day she was all over the city; in shopping boutiques, movie theaters, bars, and casinos. But she ended up here sooner or later and, according to the cell towers, was here now. Or her cellphone was here anyway and girls don't go far without their phones.

"What now?" Gwen asked.

"Now we wait," Noble told her.

"I thought we were going to find out what she knows?"

"We are." Noble cranked the seat back and stretched out his legs, trying to get comfortable.

"Well, shouldn't we go up to her apartment?"

"Sure," Noble said. "Which number is it?"

Gwen opened her mouth, thought that through, and said, "Oh."

Cell towers are able to ping the location of the phone, but not the exact apartment and since Anastasia had no formal address, all they had was a street number.

"Maybe I could go in and act like I'm a friend," Gwen said. "I could ask for her apartment number at the front desk."

"Or we could wait."

"Why?"

"First of all," said Noble, "we don't know if she's renting this place under her legal name or an alias, or if she's just crashing on a friend's couch. Second, if you go to the front desk, they'll buzz up and ask if she knows you. They aren't going to give out someone's apartment number to a stranger. Then she'll know someone is looking for her."

Gwen pulled a face. "So we wait."

Noble nodded, took a few bills from his wallet and handed them to Gwen.

"Let me guess," she said. "Coffee?"

"Black, no sugar."

She got out and made her way up the block to a pastry shop on the corner. Noble watched her go and then returned his attention to the high rise. After the boobytrap in the cabin, the geeks had determined that one of them should be with him at all times. Today was Gwen's turn. Noble didn't mind the company. This mission had gone from a simple missing scientist to an international incident in the time it takes an F-18 hornet to rocket off the deck of an aircraft carrier. The people back in Washington were worried the bomb might be headed to the United States. Might already be there.

Noble didn't want to think about that. His mother was in a nursing home in Florida. If the power grid went down, the trains that bring food into the country would stop running and mom would be dead within weeks. That was best-case scenario. Depending on how much fresh bottled water the Wyndham Arms had on hand, she might die of dehydration in days. A lot of people would be dead no matter where that bomb went off. And that was something Noble didn't want on his conscience.

Gwen returned ten minutes later with two coffees and a sack filled with pastries. Noble took the coffee and shook his head at the pastries.

"Not even chocolate raspberry?" Gwen asked.

Noble waved it away.

"I'll save them for Ez."

"Ez?"

"Short for Ezra," Gwen explained, as if that should be obvious. "How did he do last night at the club?"

Noble almost told her how badly he screwed up and then remembered his promise. "He did real good. He's a standup guy. Very smart."

"He screwed up," Gwen said.

Noble shrugged. "Took the initiative when he was scoping out the club, asked about the girl and blew my cover."

"He means well."

"The road to hell is paved in good intentions," Noble told her. It was one of his mother's favorite sayings.

Gwen nibbled the corner of a cheese Danish. "He's a really good guy though."

Noble agreed with a shrug.

"He's just got no guts," Gwen said, talking more to herself than Noble and he had the feeling she was rehashing all the reasons she couldn't be with him. "He's so scared all the time," she said, "of everything. You know when we go to the movies he makes me order the tickets? He doesn't like talking to the teenagers behind the glass. And any time there's something wrong with his order, I'm the one who has to flag the waiter and send the dish back."

Noble sipped his coffee.

"I just wish he could be more like..." She trailed off.

"More like me?" Noble finished for her.

"I didn't mean it like that."

"You're lucky he's not more like me."

The hurt showed on her face. "What's that mean?"

"Ezra's smart. He's got a good job. He's the type of guy who probably has a 401K and a retirement plan. He's stable and he'll live to a ripe old age. That's more than I can say for myself. I've got less than a thousand bucks in the bank and probably won't live to see forty. Guys like me have short lives." Noble turned to face her. "Besides, how important is street tough in today's society? You two get in a lot of fist fights?"

"More often than you might think."

"Talking about the knot on the side of his head?"

"You don't miss much," Gwen asked. "Do you?"

"My life depends on details," Noble told her. "What happened? You hit him with a frying pan?"

"A bunch of frat boys picked a fight with us in a bar."

"Ezra's been in a drunken bar fight?" Noble's respect for the little computer nerd went up a few notches.

"It wasn't exactly a fight. We were in a science trivia competition."

That raised more questions than it answered, but before she could say any more Anastasia emerged from the front of the high rise dressed in a stylish fur coat and heels with Jackie-O sunglasses. She started up the sidewalk toward the shopping district with a bounce in her step.

"You'll have to finish this story later," Noble said. "That's our girl."

Gwen made a disgusted noise in her throat. "Of course she wears fur!"

Noble said, "You're on foot. I'll circle in the car. Don't get too close and stay in contact."

"Got it." Gwen took a deep breath and reached for the doorhandle. "Okay. I can do this."

"Hey," Noble said and grabbed her arm. "Just remember your training. You'll do fine."

She gave a jerky head nod and opened the door. She hopped out, crossed the busy street and fell in behind Anastasia. Noble shifted into drive and pulled out into traffic a minute later.

# CHAPTER THIRTY-FOUR

They spent the day tailing Anastasia. One would follow on foot while the other drove. They were careful, but it was a wasted effort. A man in a wheelchair breathing through a tuba could tail Anastasia and she would never notice. She wasn't interested in anything without a designer label. It was immediately apparent that she was suffering the first stage of sudden wealth; shopping. Her first stop was a little café where she lunched on a salad and then it was off to the malls. She went from store to store, trying on all kinds of clothing and spending money faster than a drunken congressman. By dinner time she had half a dozen bags slung over one shoulder and she strolled back to her apartment high rise with a pep in her step.

It was Noble's turn on foot. He was thirty paces back, wondering how anyone could be so oblivious as he followed her along the sidewalk. He took out his cell and texted Gwen. She pulled up at the curb a few minutes later and Noble climbed into the passenger side. "She's headed home."

Gwen took her foot off the brake, cruised past Anastasia and circled the block once before parking in front of the building. They were backing into a spot as Anastasia rounded the corner. Gwen asked, "You think she has *any* idea she's being followed?"

"None."

"Clueless," Gwen remarked with a shake of her head.

"That's one word for it."

"You were thinking vapid?"

"That's closer the mark," Noble said.

"How do you think a stripper got all that cash?"

"Not from anything legal." Noble reached in the glove box, took out the Makarov and stuffed it in his belt, making sure his sweater hung over the grip.

"What are you going to do?"

"I'm going to have a chat with our working girl."

"Why do you need the gun?"

"Relax," Noble told her. "I'm just going to talk."

"Do you want me to come with you?"

"No," he said. "I want you to stay here with the motor running in case I need to leave in a hurry."

Gwen took out her phone and dialed Noble's number. He frowned, answered the call and Gwen said, "I'll keep mine on speaker."

"Points for creativity." Noble slipped his phone in his pocket and said, "If there's someone up there waiting for me, hang up, dial zero-two, then get back to the room and regroup with Cook."

Gwen nodded and pushed the glasses a little higher on her nose. "Be careful, okay?"

"I'd rather be lucky," Noble told her and cranked open

the passenger side door.

He crossed the street and made it to the front door of the building at the same time as Anastasia. Noble grinned at her and opened the door. "Ladies first."

She flashed him a smile without a trace of recognition. Noble had passed her at least twice in the course of the afternoon and she had no idea. He shook his head, followed her through the lobby to the elevators, and stepped into the car along with her. She reached over, pushed the button for seven and said, "Which floor?"

"Seven," Noble told her.

They rode up in silence and Anastasia showed the first signs of nervousness. She took a step away from him and switched shoulders with her bags, placing the purchases between her and Noble like some kind of shield. The elevator dinged and the doors rolled open. Anastasia flashed a nervous smile at Noble as she slid past. He followed her down the hall. She glanced once over her shoulder and picked up the pace. Her hand darted into her patent leather purse for her keys but fumbled them.

Noble scooped them up.

"Thank you," Anastasia said but the words trembled from her lips.

Noble pointed at number 704. He spoke German. "This one?"

Anastasia shook her head and started to turn, she was about to point at 706, realized her mistake and turned back. The stress was all over her face. She licked her lips and her pretty brow crinkled. For a moment they stood facing each other in the empty hall. Noble watched her, letting her paranoia build. She said, "I didn't tell anybody."

"You're about to tell me." Noble grabbed her by the arm, hauled her over to 706, and slotted the key.

"Please," Anastasia said. "I did what you wanted."

Noble swung the door open, pushed her inside and stepped just far enough in to keep the door from swinging shut. Anastasia stumbled, dropped her bags on the floor and turned to face him. One hand went to her throat and her mouth hinged open for a scream.

"Don't," Noble warned her and lifted his sweater enough to show the pistol.

She choked back the sound and whispered, "What do you want?"

"Anyone else in the apartment?"

Anastasia looked around as if someone might jump out from behind the curtains. "No... I mean... I don't think so."

Noble came the rest of the way inside, let the door clomp shut and said, "Let's find out together."

He took her by the arm and steered her into the bedroom, then the bathroom. She stumbled along after him, wincing at his grip. The place was decorated in what passed for stripper vogue. There were satin sheets on the bed, a full-length mirror in every room and a closet full of dresses. Negligée littered the floor of the bedroom and the bathroom sink was buried under lotions, soaps, and perfume bottles. The whole place smelled like a Yankee Candle Store.

When Noble was sure the apartment was clear he herded the girl into a high-backed chair near the door to the balcony. Late afternoon sunlight filtered in through a pair of gauzy white curtains. Anastasia was already crying. Tears ran down her cheeks, streaking her mascara. She sniffed and said, "What are you going to do to me?"

"That depends," Noble said.

"On what?"

"On you." He seated himself on the corner of the glass coffee table, propped his elbows on his knees, laced his fingers together and leaned forward, invading her personal space. "Someone paid you to get close to Lukyanenko. Who?"

Confusion muscled out fear for control of her face. She said, "I thought you were one of them."

"You thought wrong," Noble told her. He dropped the German and switched to English. "Who paid you to sleep with Lukyanenko?"

She started to shake her head. "I don't know what you're..."

"Cut the act, sister. I had a talk with your old boss at The Neon Circus. He told me all about you and Lukyanenko. Told me Lukyanenko was taking care of you. We both know you didn't pick him at random. You targeted him. You knew he was working for Ukrainian intelligence because someone told you. Who was it?"

"You're wrong." Anastasia shook her head. "I didn't know until later. Much later."

"Someone told you to cozy up to Lukyanenko," Noble said. "I want to know who."

"He was a redhead." Anastasia looked like a little girl curled up in the chair with her hands in her lap and tears running down her cheeks.

"I'm going to need more than that."

"He runs a gang. They sell guns, girls, drugs. Whatever you need. I think he's British."

"Why do you think that?"

"He speaks in a British accent."

Noble made a twirling motion with his hand. "Keep going."

"That's all I know!"

Noble grabbed hold of her arm and gave her a shake. "Quit stalling. You seduced Lukyanenko on the redhead's orders. How did he contact you? What's he look like?"

She drew her knees up to her chest and wrapped her forearms around her legs, rocking back and forth. Her dress fell, showing Noble a wedge of purple lace. "He's a tall redhead with a pug nose. Likes to hurt girls."

"How did you meet?"

"He came to the club one night," Anastasia said. "At first he was nice, you know? I liked him. Then we got back to his hotel and everything changed. He turned mean. He hurt me."

She stuck out an arm, revealing an old cigarette burn.

She was hoping for sympathy and Noble had none to give. "Tell me what happened."

"He knew all about Arkady," she said, drawing her arm back. "He knew all about me, too. He knows everything. He said he'd pay me to sleep with Arkady. Make him think I really liked him. He said I'd get ten thousand a month and a bonus when it was over. All I had to do was take pictures."

"Pictures of what?"

She shrugged. "Papers. Arkady has a cabin in the woods. There are papers everywhere."

"You knew he was working on something top secret," Noble growled. "And you knew the redhead was trying to steal it."

She let out a sob. "I tried to stop. I tried. He threatened to hurt me if I told anybody about our arrangement."

"And of course there was money. You were getting an allowance from Arkady and from the Brit. You didn't have to strip anymore. You had enough for all this." Noble waved an arm at the luxury apartment.

Her face scrunched up and she wailed. "I didn't know they were going to hurt Arkady. He was sweet. I liked him."

"How did you think it was going to end?"

She shook her head and shrugged.

Noble's face was a grim mask. "Stop playing the victim. Arkady is missing. His wife is too. They're probably dead and his research is on the black market. You want to know what he was working on? A bomb. And not just any bomb, a special kind of bomb that could kill millions of people. Now someone else has that research, and all because of you."

The tears were coming hard and fast now, but that didn't stop Noble. He jabbed a finger at her. "You traded a man's life for money. Now you're going to help me make it right."

"How?"

"Where do I find the Brit?"

She shook her head and cried harder still. "I can't. He'll kill me."

Noble grabbed her, hauled her up out of the chair and pushed her against the wall. "If you don't talk, I'm turning you in. You know what the Ukrainian government will do when they find out? You know the price for selling top-secret information? Treason. You'll get the death penalty."

"I'm sorry," Anastasia said, whipping her head back and

forth. Her hair made a red cloud around her face. "I'm so sorry. I never meant for him to get hurt."

"He did get hurt," Noble said. "Now talk. How do I find the Brit?"

"Ask the owner of the car wash on Yevropeiska Street. They hang out together at the club."

Noble let her go and she sank down onto her bottom, her back against the wall and her face in her hands. "What's going to happen to me?"

"Enjoy your new life," Noble told her. "It was paid for in blood."

She gave a groan of despair and dissolved into a fresh wave of tears.

He left her sitting there, closing the door behind him and rode the elevator down. He could have given her some comfort. He could have lied and said she wasn't to blame, but Noble wanted her to live with the guilt. He wanted her to know she had condemned a man to death for the almighty dollar.

He stepped out of the elevator, crossed the lobby, and was making his way across the street when he heard a tremendous crash; buckling metal, followed by the jingle of broken glass. Cars laid on the brakes. Tires shrieked and people on the sidewalk shouted in surprise. Noble's shoulders pulled up around his ears as he turned.

Anastasia's broken body was on the buckled roof of a sports sedan parked in front of the building. Her arms and legs were flung out like someone making angels in the snow and her neck was bent at a wrong angle. Her eyes were open and staring. Bright red droplets painted the car and the cold wet asphalt.

# CHAPTER THIRTY-FIVE

"What did you do?" Gwen gripped the steering wheel hard, her eyes locked on the body. A crowd had gathered around the body. One man climbed right up onto the smashed sport sedan in an attempt to give first aid, but there wasn't much he could do. Anastasia was dead. The desk clerk had come out of the high rise to see what all the fuss was about, recognized Anastasia, and dialed emergency services.

"I didn't do anything," Noble told her. "She threw herself out the window. I was already on the street when she jumped."

"She jumped because of you."

"That's horse crap and you know it."

"You were too hard on her. You shouldn't have been so mean."

Noble reached over and put the car in drive. Gwen was forced to jerk the wheel to avoid hitting the bumper in front. She mashed the brake and said, "Are you nuts? You could have gotten us in a traffic accident."

"I'm trying to get us out of here before the police show up," Noble told her. "They're already on their way. They'll go through video surveillance and they'll see me follow Anastasia up to her apartment. They'll tie us to her death. You want to spend the rest of your life in a Ukrainian prison for espionage and murder?"

Gwen's mouth opened but no sound came out.

"Drive the car," Noble said.

She took her foot off the brake, eased out into traffic and navigated the throng of vehicles, using the horn, until they were clear. She did a surveillance detection route without having to be told. It took the better part of an hour and, when they were sure they weren't being followed, she started back to the SkyBnB. "You didn't need to be so hard on her."

"She's the reason Lukyanenko is missing," Noble said. "There might be an EMP on the open market and she's to blame."

"Still." She wiped tears from her eyes. "You could have been nicer."

Noble turned to face her. "I don't have time to be nice. There's a criminal organization out there with a nuclear scientist and his research. They might already have a working bomb."

"It's a bad situation," Gwen said. "I'm not denying that. I still think you went about it the wrong way."

"Fortunately, it doesn't matter what you think," Noble said. "I'm running this operation."

"Actually," Gwen said, "it does matter."

His brow pinched. "What's that mean?"

"Ez and I aren't here as support." Gwen hesitated, wet

her lips with her tongue and then said, "We're here to keep an eye on you."

Noble sat in silence. They had reached the SkyBnB and Gwen was circling the block, looking for a place to park. He chewed the inside of one cheek and said, "Wizard doesn't trust me?"

"Armstrong doesn't trust you." Gwen found an open space and it took her three tries to back in. She shifted into park and said, "You've been on edge ever since Iran."

Noble shook his head. Opened his mouth and shut it again.

Gwen reached over and took his hand. "It's not your fault, Jake. Nobody blames you for what happened."

"I blame me," Noble told her.

She gripped his hand in both of her own and her glasses magnified her eyes. "You did everything you could and you brought that little girl out. You can't control the rest."

"That's where you're wrong. A field officer is supposed to be in control of his environment at all times. I led those guys into battle," Noble said. "They're dead because of choices I made."

Gwen nodded. "I get that, but you don't have to be such a hard ass all the time."

"When I let my guard down, people die."

"You can't control who lives and who dies, Jake. Sometimes bad things happen."

"Not on my watch." He shook his head.

She reached up and placed a hand on his chest. "You aren't God, Jake."

"Sounds like something my mom would say."

"She sounds like a smart lady."

Noble felt a sharp pain in his chest that moved up into his throat and formed a lump. Sam Gunn had said the same exact thing during their first encounter. And she died following Noble's orders. Another in a long list of casualties. He closed his eyes and breathed through the pain.

"For what it's worth," Gwen said, "there's nobody I'd rather be in the field with. I'm sure Ezra feels the same."

"Do you know any other field officers?" Noble asked.

She shrugged. "Greg Hunt."

"I wouldn't put that clown in charge of a bowl of Jell-O."

"He's not that bad."

"A lot of girls feel that way about him."

Gwen blushed. "I don't know what you're talking about."

Noble snorted. "So what's our next move, *boss*?"

For a moment she looked like a lost duckling searching for its mother. One shoulder crept up. "I don't know."

"Guess I'm still running this show," Noble said and opened the passenger side door. "Let's check out the Crimean."

# CHAPTER THIRTY-SIX

AHMED SHÁH KHAN LAY ON A COT IN THE RUSTING Quonset hut. The metal roof ticked in the tropical heat and palm trees swayed in a gentle breeze. Ahmad had one hand tucked behind his head; the other was holding a small wallet-sized picture of his wife and little girl. The edges of the photo were creased and the color fading, but the pain never faded. The pain was a rusty knife in his belly, twisting, digging ever deeper. Ahmed ran his thumb over his wife's smile and swallowed a painful lump in his throat.

The clock on the wall was ticking toward six, with loud steady clicks from the cheap gears inside the plastic housing. The face was yellowed and fading, along with everything else in this squalid country. He watched as the minute hand slowly made its way to 12 and then let it go a few minutes past. It was time. He slipped the picture into his breast pocket, sat up and fetched a heavy sigh. It was almost over. Soon there would be a release. Soon he could sleep. He pushed himself up from the cot and made his way through the clutter of equipment and airplane parts crowding the hangar to the open door. A Taliban fighter, Kalashnikov rifle slung over his shoulder, stood sentry.

"How is our guest today?"

"He has been quiet," the young fighter said without taking his eyes off the fetid jungle. "I haven't seen him all day."

Ahmad made his way across the hardpacked runway to the cargo plane where he found Lukyanenko stretched out on the floor, face frozen in pain, eyes open and staring.

# CHAPTER THIRTY-SEVEN

"Got him," Ezra said. He was sitting cross-legged on the bed, his laptop on his thighs and a can of Redbull in one hand. Untidy shocks of black hair were standing up in places and mashed flat in others. He sipped, balanced his can on the mattress and said, "The guy who owns the carwash is named Umar Bekir, and he's on our radar."

Noble sat on the floor, an empty pillowcase spread on the carpet, cleaning the old Makarov pistol. He aimed the barrel at the overhead bulb and peeked through to be sure it was spotless before adding a dab of oil. He spoke without taking his eyes off his work. "Talk to me."

"Umar Bekir got himself noticed by Interpol when he was implicated in a prostitution ring a few years back. He was never convicted but they suspect he's got ties to the Bashmaki."

Gwen was slunk in a chair paging through Lukya-nenko's paperwork. "I've never heard of them."

"They're an organized crime outfit based out of Crimea," Noble told her while he reassembled the pistol.

"How do you know so much?" she asked.

"This ain't my first rodeo."

"Another one of your mother's sayings?" Gwen asked.

Noble nodded.

Ezra said, "Why would a guy involved in organized crime spend his days running a car wash?"

"Car washes and coin laundries are perfect for money laundering," Noble told him.

"He's Crimean," Gwen thought out loud. She took off her glasses and cleaned them on her sweater. "Think this has to do with the Russian annexation of Crimea?"

"It's a good bet." Noble had the pistol back together and started thumbing rounds into the magazine. "Tell me more about Umar Bekir."

Ezra returned his attention to the laptop. "He was an officer in the Black Sea Fleet."

"That explains his ties to organized crime," Noble said.

Gwen questioned him with a look.

"The Black Sea Fleet was notoriously corrupt," Noble explained. "They essentially ran their own smuggling operation in the nineties and when that avenue dried up, a lot of the sailors left the service to start their own black-market outfits."

Still reading from the computer, Ezra said, "After his time with the Black Sea Fleet, Bekir bounced around the continent. He was arrested half a dozen times on minor charges, never anything major. A few years ago, he started buying up property through a shell company and opening car washes. No one knows where he got the money."

"He wasn't selling girl scout cookies," Noble said.

"More like selling girl scouts," Ezra said. "The Bashmaki have a hand in a little bit of everything; arms dealing, money laundering, racketeering, prostitution, and a score of other illegal activities."

"This is serious business," Gwen said. "We've got a missing bomb maker and now an organized crime outfit."

Noble placed the loaded pistol on the pillowcase and took out his phone.

"Reporting in?" Gwen asked.

Noble held up a finger for her to wait. The phone was already ringing. Wizard picked up with a cough and cleared his throat. "What have you got for me, kid?"

Noble put the phone on speaker and brought him up to speed on Anastasia and Umar Bekir.

"Where's the girl now?" Wizard asked.

Gwen's mouth formed a tight line and Ezra suddenly became very interested in the pattern of the bedspread.

Noble hesitated before saying, "She's dead."

"You killed her?"

"She threw herself out a window," Noble said.

"Too bad." Wizard clicked his tongue as if he'd just learned his stock portfolio was down half a percent. He hacked out a cough and said, "We don't have time to play this subtle. The joint chiefs are ready to lay an egg. They want to know who I've got in Kiev and what you're up to. So far I've managed to stall them, but sooner or later I'll be forced to turn this operation over. Once the Secretary of Defense gets involved this will go sideways. Too many cooks in the kitchen always ruins the soup."

Noble said, "I'll need something if I'm going to approach Bekir. Have we got any large weapon stores nearby?"

"This outfit might already have an EMP," Wizard said. "You want to sell them a load of machine guns to go along with it? Out of the question. Use the girl."

Noble was about to ask which girl when he glanced up and saw Gwen. Her mousy brown curls were up in a pony-tail and the coke-bottle glasses were slipping down her nose. She was the type girl you normally find in a library carrel buried beneath a stack of books. She saw Noble staring. Her eyes opened wide and the color drained from her face.

"With all due respect, sir, I'm not sure that's such a good idea," Noble said.

"We're running out of time here, Jake," Wizard said. "The president is going to be back from Puerto Rico tomorrow and then this thing is going to be out of my hands. We need to find out who's got Lukyanenko and what they plan to do with his research before the SecDef gets control."

"Witwicky's not a field officer, sir."

"She's in the field, isn't she?"

Noble started to protest and Wizard said, "The joint chiefs are already talking first strike initiatives. You three may be our only shot at avoiding a full-scale nuclear exchange."

Gwen pushed the glasses up the bridge of her nose. "I'll do it."

Ezra blanched.

"Good girl," Wizard said. "I'll do what I can to keep this in house. Make contact with Bekir and work your way up to the Brit. Let me know as soon as you have something solid."

Wizard hung up.

Noble put the phone down next to the pistol. He was chewing the inside of one cheek. Ezra looked ready to choke someone. His pale face was splotched with red and his nostrils flared. Noble ignored him, turned his eyes on Gwen and said, "Sure you can do this?"

"No way," Ezra said. "She can't go undercover. It's out of the question."

But Gwen nodded and straightened up in her chair. "I'm ready."

"You can't go looking like that," Noble said. "We'll have to go shopping."

# CHAPTER THIRTY-EIGHT

AHMED SHAH KHAN STARED AT THE SPOT WHERE Lukyanenko had dropped dead of a heart attack. His hands curled into fists and he frowned, causing the white scar on his cheek to pucker. He wanted to take Lukyanenko's contraption apart with his bare hands, but losing his temper wouldn't solve anything. Khan rubbed his eyes with the heels of his palms, trying to drive out the fatigue, then turned to the device.

Unconnected wires coiled around the chassis and a circuit board lay to one side like a forgotten birthday present. A red light flashed on one of the diodes.

It was so near to completion. Khan picked up Lukyanenko's notes and studied them, but they were in Ukrainian. Even if he could read it, Khan knew, he wouldn't understand it. He would need a physicist to translate Lukyanenko's work and finish the device. He shook his head and threw the sheaf of papers down with a curse. They were of no use to him now.

He reached into his breast pocket and took out the snapshot of his wife and daughter. He had failed them again.

"It would appear our little enterprise is at an end." Saeed stood at the bottom of the ramp. He was a large Afghan with a wiry black beard dressed in faded green fatigues. One hand rested on a pistol holstered at his hip. His eyes were dangerous black slits. He was a survivor of countless battles against American troops in both Afghanistan and Iraq, and the leader of the Hamas fighters guarding the airfield.

Khan returned the picture to his pocket. "We are far from finished."

"Oh really? Do you intend to complete the device yourself, brother?" Saeed came up the ramp, picked up a piece of paper, and studied it a moment before letting it go with a dismissive wave.

Khan watched the paper float back to the floor. "Where there is life there is hope."

Saeed sneered. "Did you learn that bit of wisdom from the Americans?"

"We can still complete our mission," Khan assured him. "Let me use the satellite phone."

"Ah yes," said Saeed. "Your mysterious benefactor. Perhaps I should be the one to call him this time?"

Khan shook his head. "He'll not speak to you."

"And why not?" Saeed closed the distance between them until they were nose to nose. His breath smelled like strong Arabian coffee flavored with cardamon.

"He'll only speak with me," Khan said. "That is how his organization works."

"I'm not sure I trust this friend of yours," said Saeed. "Any more than I trust you."

"Then use your gun on me," Khan said.

The Hamas commander took his time thinking it over, then turned and shouted a command. Moments later one of his fighters hurried into the cargo plane with a satellite phone which he passed to his commander. Saeed handed the phone to Khan, but didn't let go of it right away. "I want to listen in."

"As you wish," Khan said.

Saeed released the phone and Khan dialed. It rang three times and there was a soft click on the other end before a scrambled voice came on the line.

"Status update."

# CHAPTER THIRTY-NINE

"THIS IS NEVER GOING TO WORK," GWEN'S VOICE CAME from the dressing room.

Noble leaned on a rack of closeout tops with Gwen's handbag slung over one shoulder and a bored expression painted on his face. He should have sent Ezra, but didn't think the geeks would pick out anything appropriately slutty. Besides, Ezra and Gwen would have spent the whole time making googly eyes and awkward conversation. Despite her claims to the contrary, Gwen had a little thing for Ezra and he was head over heels for her. So Noble had taken Gwen to find a dress while Ezra put together everything he could find on the Bashmaki syndicate in Ukraine.

"I look ridiculous," Gwen said.

They were in Ocean Plaza on Antanovycha Street, one of the largest malls in all of Kiev with three floors and over four hundred retailers where Ukrainian women could buy everything from designer labels to custom couture. Noble had wasted no time, picking out a slinky black dress with a low-cut top which Gwen immediately vetoed. This was only supposed to take an hour. It was now almost noon.

Noble consulted his watch. Scratch that, it was five minutes past noon. He shook his head, blew out his cheeks and caught sight of himself in a mirror. Standing there with a woman's handbag over one shoulder, he looked like your average domesticated man with a job and wife, the type of guy with a car that consumer report called a responsible mid-size family sedan. Noble wondered what his life might have been like if he'd left the military and taken work in the private sector. He had no idea what he'd do in the private sector—sell insurance or something equally boring—but he'd probably be married with a couple of kids by now and he'd spend his weekends following the wife around shopping malls, holding her purse while she tried on dresses. Maybe he'd drive the kids to baseball practice. A nice, safe, predictable life. The kind of life Susan Sokol was pressuring him into.

Noble spotted another man in the mirror's reflection, a little older, a little heavier, leaning on another rack, a purse clutched in his hands and a bored expression on his face. The man spotted Noble at the same time and gave a look that said, *Women, waddya gonna do?*

Noble returned the silent sentiment.

The man's wife emerged from the dressing room with an armload of clothes and started handing him the articles she had decided against before going off in search of more. He promised to put the clothes back where they belonged and the moment she turned her back he stuffed them all into the rack he was using to prop himself up.

"I don't think this one will work either," Gwen said.

"It's fine," Noble assured her. "Let's just get it and go."

"Come in here a minute, will you?"

He took a step toward the dressing room and lowered his voice. "It's the women's changing room."

"No one's going to say anything."

Noble glanced around the store, expecting to find a sour-faced employee silently daring him to go into the women's changing room, but his only company was the bored husband, and he was scrolling social media. Noble took another step toward the changing rooms and said, "What do you need?"

"I need you to come in here."

He let out a breath and strode forward like a man going to the gallows, mentally rehearsing what he would say if an employee stopped him, but no one did. No one seemed to care that a man with a purse had just entered the small area separating the women's dressing rooms from the rest of the boutique. It was a brave new world. Noble stopped just inside the alcove and said, "Which one are you in?"

Gwen's hand popped above one of the doors. "Right here."

Noble knocked and a second later the door popped open. Gwen's hand shot out, grabbed him by the lapel and pulled him inside. He crowded into the tiny space and Gwen closed them in.

"I look silly," she said. She was a in a short red number with a low cut back. The silky material clung to her curves, showing off slender white thighs.

Noble's eyebrows crept up. "Silly is not the adjective I'd choose."

They were pressed close together and Gwen's perfume,

a combination of rosehip and lavender, wrapped Noble up in a tempting embrace.

"Please, don't patronize me. I look like a clown. I could never pull off a dress like this."

She peeked over his shoulder for a look at herself in the mirror and then twisted for a rearview. The scooped material went all the way down her back, showcasing a pair of dimples.

Noble cleared his throat and said, "You look—"

"Stupid," she said. "I know. Maybe this is a bad idea. No one is going to believe me in this getup."

A half-smile turned up his lips. Noble dropped her purse on the floor, reached back and pulled the band from her hair, freeing her curls, then took her by the shoulders and turned her to face the mirror.

"You're a knock out."

She flushed a deep scarlet. "You think so?"

"If you dressed like this every day, Ezra wouldn't stand a chance," Noble told her. "Fellas would be knocking each other over to get a date with you."

She let out a little breath. "You're flattering me."

"Not at all. You look ravishing."

"No one's ever told me that before."

"No one's ever seen you in this dress before."

She turned to face him. "You really like it?"

He nodded. "Bekir won't hear a single word I say. He'll be too busy checking out your legs."

"Do you mean that?"

"They're great legs," Noble said.

She rolled her eyes. "I meant; do you think I'm pretty?"

"I do."

The flush in her cheeks crept right down into her chest. She went up on tiptoes, planted a kiss on Noble's lips and then took a step back. "Ohmigod, I'm so sorry. I don't know what I was thinking."

Noble gathered her up in his arms and kissed her. Their lips melted in a passionate press of eager breath, teeth gently scraping. She held his face in both hands. They stayed that way for several seconds and then she abruptly pushed him away. Her hand went to her mouth, like she wasn't quite sure what had just happened.

She said, "That was a mistake."

"Was it?" Noble's heart felt like a racehorse inside his chest and his hands were shaking.

"We shouldn't have done that."

"Why not?"

"Because you're... you," she said, as if that explained it. "And I'm me,"

"And because I've got a short shelf life," Noble said.

She shook her head. "I didn't say that."

"You were thinking it."

"No, I wasn't."

"It's okay," Noble said. "I get it."

"It's not you." Gwen laid a hand on his chest. "It's... It could never work between us. We both know that."

"Do we?"

She nodded.

"Is that the truth?" Noble asked. "Or is that what you're telling yourself."

Her face fell. She gave him another kiss, but all the eagerness was gone, replaced by sadness and loss. "That's what I'm telling myself," she said. "Because that's what's best."

"Best for who?" Noble still had his hands on her waist.

She turned around, inspecting herself in the mirror, pretending to smooth out the lines of the dress. "Best for you," she said. "Best for me. Best for Ezra."

"Do you love him?"

"I don't know."

Noble took in some air, let it out slow and his hands slipped away. "It's a good dress on you. Let's buy it and get out of here."

She latched onto his arm. "We can't tell Ezra about this."

"Hadn't planned to," Noble told her.

"Promise?"

"I promise."

He opened the door and let himself out of the changing room. His heart was still galloping along at breakneck speeds.

# CHAPTER FORTY

Wexler's private Cessna touched down in Kiev just after one o'clock. Technically it wasn't his plane, it belonged to the Old Man, but Wexler had exclusive use of it, which was kind of like having his own plane.

A bitter wind howled into the open hangar bay, tugging the lapels of Wexler's cashmere overcoat and blowing through his short red hair. A sleek black BMW was gassed up and waiting. The keys were in the passenger seat. Wexler settled himself behind the wheel and thumbed the starter before realizing his phone was buzzing. The call was from his team in Cuba.

He made sure the voice scrambler was on and said, "Status update."

"We have run into a problem," Khan said, always careful not to use names. Satellite communications were not secure. "The Ukrainian has had a heart attack."

"Is he dead?"

Khan hesitated only a moment. "Yes. He's dead."

"And the device?"

"Unfinished," Khan said.

"That is unfortunate," Wexler said, thinking it was disastrous.

"We have his notes," Khan said. "All we need is a physicist who can complete the work. Preferably one who speaks Ukrainian."

"Oh, is that all?" Wexler pinched the bridge of his nose between thumb and forefinger, thinking about how to break this news to the Old Man.

Wexler took a breath and steadied himself. It had been his plan and it would be his fault if things went bad, which they had, but how can you plan for a heart attack? Wexler decided to lead with that. Maybe it would reduce the fallout. One thing Wexler knew for sure: Muddy water runs down hill. Whatever punishment he suffered at the hands of the Old Man would be visited upon Khan and those backwards tribesmen.

"We're so close," Khan was saying. "We cannot give up now."

*Lukyanenko is dead,* Wexler wanted to scream, *and there is no one else in the world who can finish what he started.* If he could reach through the phone and strangle the Arab, he would have. He stared at the glowing green lights of the dash and thought, *All I need is someone who understands pulse electronics.* His mind turned to Jake Noble and a desperate plot hatched inside his brain. The CIA had sent a team to investigate the disappearance of Lukyanenko. Someone on that team would know about physics and electromagnets.

Wexler held his breath, thinking through his options, then said, "Do nothing until you hear back from me."

He hung up the phone and tossed it into the passenger seat. It was an effort to keep his emotions in check. He slammed the car into gear and shot out of the hangar with his foot pressed to the floor. The German engine screamed and the tires squeaked on the blacktop.

# CHAPTER FORTY-ONE

Noble was behind the wheel of a sleek red Alpha Romeo. He swung the rental into the parking lot of the car wash and revved the engine, letting out a powerful roar that echoed along the block as he eased up to the queue of cars waiting on suds. He wanted to make a scene, to draw attention, and gunning the engine in a parking lot is a classic used by insecure guys the world over. It says; look at me, I drive an expensive car and I want everyone to know it.

It was just after four in the afternoon. Noble was dressed in a shiny sharkskin sport coat with his collar turned up and his hair slicked back. Witwicky was in her red dress and a pair of matching stilettos. She had practiced walking in them, pacing the room, looking like a newborn filly at first, but an hour later she was doing the catwalk strut. By that time, Ezra's eyes were falling out of his head and his tongue dragged the floor. Noble couldn't blame him. Watching Witwicky in the tight-fitting dress and heels was like witnessing a caterpillar transform into a butterfly.

The memory of their kiss was still hot on his lips,

burning a hole in his belly, as he eased the hot rod up to the front of the line. The procession of cars was going beneath the suds, the big machines throwing soap and water while the owners strolled along the observation deck, watching through a thick plate of glass.

Gwen said, "I can't see a thing without my glasses."

"You don't need to see," Noble told her. "Just look hot and let me do the talking."

Ezra was parked down the block in the stolen Slavuta. Noble could just make out the front end from where he sat. He said, "How's your signal, E?"

The headlights flashed once.

Noble had his phone in his coat pocket with the speaker on so Ezra could listen in.

It was their turn for the wash. Noble left the engine running, stepped out of the car and let the attendant take it the rest of the way while he and Gwen went to the observation deck. The smell of detergent and warm sudsy water filled his lungs, along with Gwen's perfume. He slung an arm over her shoulders, pulling her close. They had rehearsed the act ahead of time. Noble watched the car for a minute, then turned his attention to a fat man with a head full of curly dark hair and one gold tooth, sitting behind a cheap desk with a dusty computer and a large stack of soccer magazines. Behind him were framed photographs from his younger days on the soccer pitch along with a few old trophies.

"I know you," Noble said in his best German accent. "You used to play for Slovyansk."

The fat man looked up from his paperwork. He cocked

a thumb over his shoulder at one of the pictures. "You can read."

Noble said, "I used to play myself."

The manager leaned back in his chair and laced his fingers together over his belly. "Is that right? Who did you play for?"

"I was a striker for Fortuna Düsseldorf," Noble told him. It was a second-rate football club out of Düsseldorf Germany with two cup wins, and that was about as far as Noble's knowledge of soccer went.

"Ya, good team. We played them in eighty-two."

"Before my time," Noble said.

"Why did you quit?"

"Blew out my ACL. Ended my career."

The manager nodded while Noble spoke, but kept looking at Witwicky. His eyes traveled up from her legs and back down again. He said, "So what have you been doing with yourself since?"

"I specialize in unique merchandise." Noble cupped Witwicky's bottom. "Hard to get stuff. Know what I mean?"

"I think I understand you."

Noble glanced over his shoulder at the big picture window. The rental was almost through. He lowered his voice. "I'm looking for the redhead. I hear he's in the market and I've got goods to sell."

The manager narrowed his eyes and leaned back, causing his chair to creak. "You must be mistaken. I don't know any redheads."

"No games, my friend. I'm in the business." Noble gave Gwen a good hard slap on the rump and she yelped. "You like what you see? She's got twenty sisters, look just as good. Maybe your boss is interested, ya?"

The manager probed a molar with his tongue. "Maybe I know someone who would be interested. Where can he reach you?"

"Only my mother and my girlfriends have my phone number," Noble said. "I'll be back later this evening, around eight. Tell your boss."

The manager shot another lusty glance at Gwen. "I'll pass the word along. See you this evening, Düsseldorf."

"So long, Slovyansk." Noble threw his arm around Gwen's neck and steered her toward the door. The rental, clean before it went in, was now spotless. Noble passed a grossly large tip to the attendant, settled behind the wheel and pressed down on the pedal. The engine growled. Gwen piled in next to him, her skirt riding up in the process. Soon as her door was closed, Noble tore out of the parking lot with a shriek of rubber.

# CHAPTER FORTY-TWO

WEXLER SAT IN THE BACK OFFICE OF THE CAR WASH, watching a small black and white closed-circuit security monitor. There was no sound, but he didn't need to hear what was said. He recognized the man on screen. Jake Noble had been responsible for sinking the *Maersk Minerva* off the coast of Rijeka, nearly bankrupting the Old Man. Wexler watched the silent interaction, then leaned back in the cheap metal folding chair and rubbed his chin with his fingertips in thought. Sorting out Noble for the Old Man would be icing on the cake, but only if he could resurrect the operation in Cuba. The girl was the key. She was no field operative. Wexler knew that just by looking. He brought out his cellphone and used a weather app to check on the storm. A category two hurricane was barreling up through the tropics on a collision course with the islands. That complicated things.

On screen, Noble and his girlfriend walked to a hotrod and peeled out of the parking lot with a shriek of rubber that Wexler heard through the cinderblock walls. A moment later Bekir appeared in the office. He closed the door and put his back against it.

"He claims to be a German with girls to sell."

Wexler snorted. "He's a professional liar."

"His accent is pretty convincing."

"Of course it is," Wexler said. "They don't send dullards into the field."

"What are we going to do about him?"

Wexler used the controls to roll the video back and watched the interaction again while he considered that question. As Noble and the girl were walking out to the car for the second time, he said, "Noble has to die but I need the girl alive."

"I'm uncomfortable killing American intelligence agents," Bekir said. "Kill a million whores if you want and nobody even knows they're gone. Kill one CIA officer and you'll have the United States government hounding your every step."

"You'll be paid," Wexler said. "Handsomely."

"This isn't about money," said Bekir. "The CIA is involved now and I want no part of it. If they connect Lukyanenko's disappearance to my organization, they'll ruin me."

Wexler grinned. "In a few short days the CIA will have much bigger things to worry about. They won't have the time or ability to hassle you."

"Lukyanenko's little toy?" Bekir guessed.

Wexler nodded.

"You promised me it would not be used in Ukraine," Bekir said. "I do business here."

"And I'm a man of my word," Wexler said. "How did you leave it with Noble?"

"He'll be back in a few hours," Bekir said. "He's expecting a meeting with you."

"Then we'd best not disappoint," Wexler said. "Arrange a welcoming committee and leave nothing to chance. This bloke is not one to mess around with."

# CHAPTER FORTY-THREE

"That was amazing!" Gwen's voice came through the speaker. She sounded tinny and far away. "What a rush! What an incredible rush!"

Ezra sat in the driver's seat of the Slavuta listening to the conversation. The hot rod pulled out of the car wash and went roaring up the boulevard toward the intersection but got caught by a red light, forcing Noble to brake. Gwen was giddy as a schoolgirl. Her voice was high and lilting, the way she got when they watched a particularly good sci-fi movie. Ezra could imagine her bouncing in the leather bucket seat.

"It can be exciting at times," Noble said in his usual drawl.

"It was just like a movie. My heart is beating out of my chest. I feel like a real spy."

"You are a real spy."

"You know what I mean," said Gwen. "I can see how people get addicted to this work. It's empowering."

"It's not all fun and games," Noble told her. "Remember

this is deadly serious business. This redhead is a dangerous customer."

"I know," Gwen said. "It's just... This was incredible." She let out a high-pitched whoop and said, "I feel alive."

There was a rustle of fabric followed by the unmistakable sound of a kiss. Ezra suddenly had trouble getting air into his lungs. His stomach clenched. Had she kissed him on the cheek? On the mouth? Had he returned the kiss? Ezra's mind insisted on the worst-case scenario. He saw Gwen lean across the seats and smother Noble in a deep kiss. Saw Noble's hand on her bare thigh. Saw the flush in her cheeks. It felt like a rusty iron spike in his belly.

His knuckles turned white on the steering wheel and a sudden, intense dislike for Noble took shape like a dark cloud in Ezra's brain. He had known there was something going on between them when they came back from shopping. Gwen had come into the room with a bag over one shoulder and a faraway look in her eyes, like a girl who'd just met the man of her dreams. And the dress... the dress was a knockout. With her hair down and her glasses off, she was achingly beautiful, the kind of girl who would literally stop traffic. And that wasn't hyperbole. As they were leaving the SkyBnB, she had crossed the street in her new dress and nearly caused a pile up. That's hard to do in the Ukraine where every other girl is a catwalk model with legs that go on for days.

Ezra's brow knotted and he reached over to turn off the phone, but he couldn't do it. He listened while that iron spike twisted deep inside his belly.

Up ahead, the light turned green and the rental roared through the intersection. Noble's voice came over the speaker, "Ez, give yourself another five minutes then do a surveillance detection route and we'll meet you back at home base."

Ezra didn't bother to respond. It was a long, slow drive back. Ezra did a half-hearted surveillance detection route and was back in the room less than an hour later. He was sitting on the bed, staring at the wallpaper, feeling like something you find on the side of the road, guts mashed flat and body mangled. An hour crept by, then two, and the whole time Ezra's imagination was working overtime. He saw Noble and Gwen pull into a deserted parking deck somewhere. In the movie theater of his mind, Gwen sat on top of Noble, cramped between him and the steering wheel, her dress hiked up around her hips, their lips locked together.

He stood up, went into the bathroom and splashed cold water on his face, but the images refused to go. He was toweling off when the door opened.

Gwen came in positively bursting with excitement.

"Where the hell have you two been?" Ezra demanded. "I was starting to worry."

Gwen ignored him, did a turn in her dress and then plopped down on the mattress and kicked off her heels.

"I think we had a tail," Noble said. "We had to look natural, so we stopped for a bite to eat."

Ezra fists clenched. "You stopped for food?"

"We needed to look like a pimp and a prostitute," Noble said. "If we immediately shook the tail, Bekir's people would be suspicious, so we did what anyone would expect and stopped at a restaurant."

"Sure you did," Ezra said. He was picturing them locked in a passionate embrace.

Gwen was massaging the ball of one foot and said, "What has gotten into you, Ez?"

Noble said, "You're acting a little weird, bub."

"I'm not acting weird," Ezra told them. "I was just worried, that's all."

"You can stop worrying." Noble chucked him on the shoulder. Ezra wanted to belt him in the face.

Noble said, "We're back and we've got a hook in the organization. Let's get a hold of Wizard and let him know."

# CHAPTER FORTY-FOUR

WIZARD CLUTCHED A CHESTERFIELD BETWEEN BONEY fingers. Silent curlicues of smoke drifted up toward the ceiling. He'd forgotten his medication—thankfully his secretary had remembered. It was a little after noon. Noble and the Witwicky girl should be making their move on Bekir soon. If they found proof he had the scientist, Wizard could green light a quick reaction force and hopefully stop this madness before it started. If not... Wizard didn't like to think about that.

He took in a deep lungful of smoke and let it out through his nose. He was gazing at the wall of clippings and string, at a briefing on a Crimean outfit called the Bashmaki syndicate. They were, Wizard had thought, a relatively small-time operation based in the Crimea, Ukraine and, to a lesser extent, eastern Europe where they moved girls and guns. They were on his wall because they had ties to another organization called Global Security Solutions, owned by a shell company called First Initiative Holdings. GSS specialized in recruiting former soldiers from all over the world to work private security. They were a mercenary company owned and operated by First Initiative Holdings which was in turn owned by Otto Keiser, a German hedge fund billionaire who had recently tried to crash the US dollar by flooding the American economy with counterfeit currency.

Wizard traced the lines of red string from the Bashmaki crime syndicate to Global Security, to First Initiative Holdings, and finally to the glossy 8 x10 of Keiser, a fat, liver-spotted spider crouching at the center of his web.

Unfortunately, Wizard couldn't prove any of this, or he'd make the case for taking legal action, but with intelligence work, you often know more than you can prove.

There was a knock at the door and Director Armstrong stuck her head in.

"Any word yet?" she asked.

"Not yet," Wizard told her and then jabbed the glowing end of his Chesterfield at the wall. "Take a look at this."

"What am I looking at?"

"The Bashmaki crime syndicate has been on my wall for years," Wizard told her. "I knew that name sounded familiar. Now I know why. They've got connections to Global Security Solutions."

Armstrong closed her eyes and pinched the bridge of her nose between thumb and forefinger. "I was afraid of this."

"Afraid of what?"

"You're off chasing the bogyman again, Al."

"I'm following the evidence."

"What evidence?" Armstrong asked. "You've had a hard

on for this guy since I met you. He's a villain, I'll give you that, but he's not behind every plot."

"I never said he was behind every plot," Wizard croaked. "But he's behind this plot."

"How can you be so sure?"

Wizard waved an arm. "It's all right there in black and white."

"Right where?" Armstrong spread her arms to take in the wall. "Are you seeing the same thing I am? This is the work of a madman."

"That's part of his genius," Wizard said. "He's got so many front companies and shell corporations that it's impossible to trace anything back to him. On the surface he looks like a kindly old hedge fund manager, but you scratch the skin and you'll find rot, I guarantee. He keeps his nose clean so anyone who accuses him of foul play looks like a loon."

"Or you could be seeing connections where there are none," Armstrong said. "Look hard enough and you'll find connections between just about every criminal enterprise on the planet. That doesn't mean it's a conspiracy. Criminals all swim in the same pond, Al."

"It's him," Wizard told her. "He's behind this. I can feel it."

Armstrong let out a breath and shook her head. "Do me a favor and don't mention any of this to the president."

"He's back?"

She nodded. "And he's sided with the SecDef. As of now, your operation in Ukraine is being run by the Secretary of Defense."

"Stall them," Wizard said.

"I can't stall them, Al. This comes directly from the Commander in Chief. You know, your boss and mine? That guy. He wants all the files on our operation copied and sent by courier to the White House. And he wants it ten minutes ago. They've got a war room up and running and they want to know all their options."

"If we turn this over to the joint chiefs, they'll screw this whole thing up and you know it."

"It's out of my hands."

Wizard crushed his cigarette in an ashtray on his desk. "Give me an hour to gather up the paperwork."

"Now, Al."

Wizard picked up a stack of folders and loose papers, sorting through documents. He knew where everything was and could lay hands on it instantly, but said, "It's going to take me at least an hour to dig through all this, maybe more. That's the cost of being an absent-minded genius."

Armstrong crossed her arms over her breasts and her nostrils flared. "You've got an hour. And then I want those files on my desk."

"I'll do my best."

Soon as she was out of the room, Wizard unearthed the files, took a burn bag from the bottom drawer of his desk and stuffed the papers inside. He peeled the tape and sealed the bag.

# CHAPTER FORTY-FIVE

"I don't like it." Ezra had a cup of microwave noodles in one hand and a plastic fork in the other, but he wasn't particularly hungry. He stabbed his fork into the noodles and set the Styrofoam cup aside. "I don't like it at all. You're playing fast and loose, Noble."

"You heard Wizard." Noble stood with his back against the wall and his thumbs tucked in his pockets. Shaggy locks hung down in rakish waves that made him look like a cross between a rock and roll musician and a high school quarterback. He said, "Fast and loose is the order of the day."

Gwen lay on the bed. She had traded the red dress for corduroy trousers and a button down, but she was missing the usual wool sweater and her top couple buttons were open. Her glasses were lying on the bedside table. She said, "We haven't got much time, Ez. The EMP might already be on its way to a major city."

"Like I care if some Ukrainians want to blow up Moscow."

"You should," Noble said. "If Moscow gets hit, they'll use their ICBM arsenal on America. They'll think we initiated a first strike. It could lead to a global nuclear exchange."

"I still don't like it." Ezra crossed his arms over his chest. "You're putting Gwen's life in danger. She's no field operative. She isn't trained for this type of thing."

"Excuse me." Gwen's eye narrowed down to dangerous slits.

"You know I'm right," Ezra said.

"I've been to the Farm," Gwen reminded him. "I'm trained."

"You aren't, you know..."—Ezra waved a hand at Noble—"trained like him."

"I'm just as much a CIA agent as he is," Gwen said, an edge to her voice.

"Keep your voices down," Noble said. "We aren't in the third floor basement. We've got neighbors. And she's got all the training she needs. It's a simple meet and greet. We just need to get eyes on the redhead. Then we can run surveillance on him and see if he's got Lukyanenko."

"And if he does?"

"We call in a fast reaction force," Noble said.

"Maybe I should go instead," Ezra said.

Gwen made a disbelieving note in her throat. "Why would you go? What would you do? What's your cover?"

"Maybe I'm the second in command."

Gwen gave another snort.

Noble said, "That would never work."

"Why not?"

"Because I told Bekir I've got girls to sell," Noble said. "The Brit is going to want to see girls."

"And what if the pervert wants to sample the goods?"

Some of the color drained from Gwen's face.

Noble said, "I won't let that happen."

"How you going to stop it?" Ezra said.

"It's not going to come to that."

Gwen's shoulders had crept up around her ears. "You sure?"

"I'm sure," Noble told her. "You're going to be just fine. I promise."

Ezra said, "Is that what you told the last team you worked with?"

"Ez!" Gwen looked from Ezra to Noble, concern written all over her face.

Noble's eyes turned to cold dark slits and the muscles in his jaw bunched.

Gwen said, "That was uncalled for."

"But true," Ezra said. "People have a habit of dying around him. You want to be his next victim?"

"You're out of line!" Gwen said.

"It's okay." Noble scrubbed his palms on his pant legs and took a deep breath. "He's right. People have a tendency to die around me. I take the missions no one else wants because no one else can pull 'em off. There's an EMP out there powerful enough to destroy a nation. We've got good intel that suggests the Brit has Lukyanenko. We have to find out where he's being held. Millions of lives hang in the balance. We didn't ask for this situation. We drew the short straw but, like my mother always says, you play the hand that's dealt."

Ezra shook his head. "I'm against this."

"You don't have to like it," Noble told him. "You just have to do your part."

"Ezra please," Gwen said. "This may be our only chance to find Lukyanenko."

"Fine." Ezra grabbed his cup of noodles, slopping sauce onto the desktop. He stared hard at Noble. "If this goes bad, I'm holding you responsible."

Noble inclined his head. "Understood."

"What's the plan?" Gwen asked.

"Same as before," Noble told her. "But this time we'll have to be a little smarter about our listening devices. They'll search us and if they find a phone on speaker, we're blown."

"We haven't got time to find a stash," Ezra said.

"Give me your cell," Noble said to Gwen. "We'll take it apart and turn the microphone into a battery-operated receiver."

"You know how to do that?" Gwen asked, surprised.

Noble jimmied open Gwen's burner, removed the microphone and then liberated the backup lithium battery from a digital alarm clock next to the bed. Fifteen minutes later he had a makeshift listening device the size of a nickel.

Ezra downloaded a scanner onto his burner phone and paired it up with the tiny microphone. Noble stepped into the hall and whispered into the mic. When he came back, Ezra nodded. "It works but the signal's weak. She won't be able to put it in her pocket."

"They'd find it in her pocket," Noble said.

"Where are you going to hide it?" Ezra asked.

"We're going to tape it to her."

"Er... where exactly do you plan to tape it?" Gwen asked.

"Between your breasts."

Gwen flushed a deep crimson.

# CHAPTER FORTY-SIX

Noble pulled the hotrod into the carwash just after eight and found Bekir waiting for him. The fat man stood next to a blue panel van with one mismatched door. A pair of thugs flanked Bekir. They both had broad shoulders, thick necks and shaved heads.

Gwen's eyes got wide. "I don't like the look of that."

"They're just trying to intimidate us," Noble said.

"They're doing a good job."

"Remember what we talked about," he said. "Play coy and don't talk much."

She wet her lips with her tongue.

Noble swung the hotrod into an open spot and killed the engine. The sky was spitting little bits of ice that collected on the windshield wipers. He leaned over to Gwen, like he was giving her a quick peck on the lips, and whispered. "Keep breathing and we'll get through this."

She put a hand around the back of his neck, as if she were returning the kiss and said, "Promise me it will be okay."

"I promise."

They popped the doors and stepped out into the cold. A brisk wind threw Noble's long hair around his head in a crazy cloud and put spots of color in Gwen's cheeks. She had added a simple beige overcoat to her ensemble, but left it open to show the lines of the dress. They walked arm in arm to the van. Noble thrust his chin at the pair of body guards. "I come here in good faith and you bring muscle."

"Shut up and lift your arms," Bekir said.

Noble did as he was told and one of the goons patted him down. He bore the rough treatment in silence. The other man took his time searching Gwen, his hands roaming her body. She smacked her gum and tried to look nonchalant, but the bright pink roses in her cheeks turned a shade darker. When he finished, he stepped back and gave his boss a nod.

Bekir rolled open the door of the van. "Get in."

"Where are we going?"

"You want to see the redhead?"

Noble nodded.

"Get in."

"Not until I know where you're taking me."

One of the goons got in Noble's face. "Taking you someplace safe. Get in."

"Fine," Noble said. "She stays. I'll go."

"Both of you will go," Bekir said and produced a gun from his jacket pocket. He kept it low, partially shielded from view by his bulging gut.

Gwen's face was a white stone mask.

Noble gave her a tight smile. "Let's go for a ride, darling."

"That's more like it." Bekir stepped aside and motioned them to the open door with the barrel of the gun. Noble went first. Gwen climbed in beside him. The two heavies flanked them and Noble knew what came next. The goons reached beneath the seats and produced a pair of rough burlap sacks.

Bekir got behind the wheel, turned the key and the van farted once before roaring to life. The engine made an awful chunking noise that probably signaled a bad piston. Bekir backed out of the spot, ground the gears and then swung around the car wash. He said, "My employer likes his anonymity so you'll understand the need for the masks."

"Not very trusting," Noble said. "Is he?"

"No," Bekir agreed as he pulled out onto the street.

The last thing Noble saw was Ezra in the driver's seat of the Slavuta. The little guy was trying not to look suspicious, but his eyes were locked on the van, his face tight with concern. Noble tried to give a small, imperceptible nod to let Ezra know everything was okay, but the goon was already fitting the burlap sack down over his face and everything went dark.

## CHAPTER FORTY-SEVEN

As a rule, The White House Situation Room is far more average and unassuming than most people think. Hollywood movies generally depict the Situation Room as some kind of high-tech star chamber. Nothing could be further from the truth. In reality it's a fairly modest room; some would even call it cramped. The walls are simple beige wallpaper framed by dark wood. Leather chairs surround a table with a brass strip down the center which hides power and USB outlets. There's a large screen on one wall and the presidential seal on the other. Depending on which party is in power, the flag of the United States sometimes stands in one corner.

Today the screen was showing snapshots of Lukyanenko's notes sent over by Cook and Witwicky, along with a detailed diagram of what the finished device might look like as imagined by Harold Trasker, the CIA's EMP expert. Trasker had worked up CAD images of the device disguised as an automobile, a vending machine, and a large aquarium pump.

The Joint Chiefs were gathered around the table, along with the ashen-faced Secretary of State. The Director of National Intelligence had joined the group as well, along with the Secretary of the Treasury and the Head of Home-land Defense. A dozen aids and secretaries were also jammed into the room, making sure their respective bosses had water, coffee, and any relevant files. And, as Wizard suspected, the more brains they added to the mix, the less they accomplished.

The CIA's director of operations sat at the far end of the table, slumped in one of the leather office chairs, wishing he could light up. He reached several times for his pack, but stopped himself before he could pull them out. Smoking went over like a lead balloon with the weenies in the White House. Wizard remembered the days when this room was so full of smoke that you couldn't see the television screens. Back then it didn't matter because the screens were small with rounded corners, powered by flickering tubes, and you could never make out the details anyway. In those days they had made decisions based on human intel, not satellite feeds.

*God, how he missed the Cold War.*

"We can't take any action that might lead to a full-scale nuclear exchange," the acting Secretary of State was saying. Mrs. Ogden had obviously done her homework on EMPs. She looked more haggard than ever, with dark bags under her eyes.

"What if we're the target?" someone asked.

That was always the fear with a doomsday device on the open market.

"If we get hit with an EMP," the Secretary of Defense

said, "We might not be able to retaliate. Our ICMB silos are hardened against an electromagnetic attack, but only in theory. It's never been tested."

Armstrong was standing, leaning on the back of a chair. She looked to Trasker for confirmation. "Is that right?"

He nodded and drew their attention to the screen were Lukyanenko's notes had been translated into English. "Like the SecDef said, we harden our missile silos against EMP attacks but the measures put in place were never designed to protect against something like this. Lukyanenko's device is totally unique."

The Secretary of Defense said, "Which is why I think we need to seriously consider a first strike option. If we're going back to the Stone Ages, let's at least take our enemies with us."

"On who?" Armstrong said.

"Isn't it obvious?" he said. "The Russians."

"You don't know that for sure," Armstrong said.

"Clearly they learned about the Ukrainian's research and decided to put it to use."

"How do you know it isn't the Ukrainians?" Wizard asked. "Maybe they plan to use the device against Russia?"

"Why would they kidnap their own scientist?"

Wizard shrugged one boney shoulder. "Plausible deniability."

The Secretary of Defense snorted and shook his head. "You know as well as I do that's not what's going on here."

"All I know for sure is that Lukyanenko is missing, along with his research."

"That's not all we know." The acting Secretary of State reached for the collection of files in front of her.

Wizard's secretary had put together a dummy file with only the most basic facts on Jake Noble's mission in Ukraine. Armstrong had turned a brow up at the slim folder when Wizard handed it over, along with his excuse that he kept most of the relevant details in his head. She didn't buy his story, but had accepted the folder without a word.

Ogden scanned the handful of pages. "We've got good intel that suggests a Crimean syndicate may be involved. That would suggest to me this might be some kind of terrorist organization."

"And we haven't got any evidence the device, if there is one, will be used against the United States," Armstrong added. She was trying to throw some water on the fire. Any time the president's emergency cabinet met in the Situation Room to discuss a potentially world-ending disaster, there were always one or two war hawks who wanted to strike hard and strike fast at all perceived enemies. The thinking was, get your enemy before they get you. But in this case they didn't know who the enemy was. Tomorrow they might wake up to find out Kuala Lumpur had been hit with an EMP and the crisis would be over. Everybody could take a deep breath and get on with life. There was no way to know for sure, and Armstrong was not willing to nuke millions of people on a hunch, but ultimately it wasn't her decision to make. That belonged to the president.

Unfortunately, the Commander in Chief had yet to put in an appearance. He had his own crisis unfolding in the form of an upcoming election and another in a long line of never-ending impeachment investigations. But he had made it clear that he wanted a definite course of action from the emergency cabinet before the end of the day. That was easier said than done. Put a dozen people in a room and you can't get them all to agree on the color of the wallpaper, never mind what to do about an impending disaster of this magnitude.

"Look," said the Secretary of Defense, "the president wants action."

"Right now our best course of action is the collection of intelligence," Wizard said.

A vein throbbed in the SecDef's forehead. "You intelligence types always think the best thing to do is wait. We can't sit on our hands and wait. I took an oath to protect America from all threats. I can't sit by and wait for a lunatic with a bomb to knock out our power grid."

"I sympathize," Wizard said.

"Do you?"

He nodded. "Believe it or not, I don't want to see America plunged into the dark either. I'm old and I won't last long without my medication, but launching a full scale nuclear exchange won't save lives, it will destroy them."

The Director of National Intelligence, a man named Oliver McPherson, leaned forward, propped his elbows on the table and steepled his fingers. He was a former Army Staff Sergeant and Wheaton graduate who expected national intelligence to run on a 9 to 5 schedule and he didn't like being called away from his vacation. "How did this happen? How did the Ukrainians develop an experimental weapon without us knowing?"

He was already looking for someone to blame. Despite his Army background, McPherson was a politician and they were always pointing fingers. He leveled a hard stare at

Armstrong. "Isn't it your job to tell us what other countries are up to?"

"We know of a dozen brilliant minds scattered around the globe working on terrifying technology for various world governments and tinpot dictators," Armstrong said. "This is the first time one has been kidnapped."

Wizard felt his phone buzzing. No one was allowed to have a phone in the Situation Room but he wasn't willing to give up his only link to Noble. Besides, bureaucrats rarely ever surrendered their phones when they went into top secret meetings. They had a laissez faire attitude about security. It never occurred to them a foreign government might hack their phone and listen in. Wizard slipped the device from his pocket, keeping it below the table, and looked at the caller ID. It was the Cook kid calling in.

The DNI said, "Are we keeping you from something, Dulles?"

A dozen sets of eyes turned on him. McPherson had a nasty grin on his face, like a teacher who had just caught a troublesome student goofing off in class.

"It's my team in Kiev."

The smug look slipped from McPherson's face. "What have they got to report?"

"Let's find out." Wizard put the phone to his ear. "Talk to me, Cook."

"On speaker if you please," the SecDef said.

"Hold on, young man." He took the phone away from his ear and tried to figure out how to activate the speaker. A young aide finally reached over and did it for him. Wizard said, "Cook, you're on speaker with the Joint Chiefs."

They listened as Cook brought them up to speed. Faces

around the table turned grim when he told them both Noble and Witwicky had been forced into the back of a van at gunpoint.

When he finished, Wizard said, "Have you got eyes on the van?"

Cook's voice cracked. "I'm following at a distance."

"Keep following. Call us back when you have a location."

"What am I supposed to do if..."

Wizard ended the call before Cook could do any more damage.

Silence fell over the Situation Room. For several seconds nobody spoke. Noble was their best bet at tracking down Lukyanenko and now he was in the back of a van at gunpoint. McPherson finally said, "Sounds like you lost two agents."

"Not necessarily," Wizard told him.

"Did we all hear the same thing?" McPherson said. "Your lead investigator has just been taken hostage."

"Sometimes a good field officer has to willingly put himself in danger to get information," Wizard said. "It's all part of the job. Noble is trained for this type of thing."

The acting Secretary of State had a skeptical look on her face. "The guy on the phone didn't sound nearly so sure."

"Don't be fooled," Wizard told her. "Cook is one of our very best field officers."

McPherson's brow went up, along with Armstrong's.

"Let my people do their job," Wizard told the gathering. "If we find Lukyanenko, we might be able to stop this thing before it starts."

"And if we can't?" someone asked.

The Secretary of Defense said, "No offense, but it doesn't sound like your people have this under control. We have to give the president a definite course of action and I'm not going to tell him to wait and see. You've got three agents in a foreign country chasing after a crime syndicate, two of whom are now hostages. That doesn't inspire confidence. At the very least I think we need to scale up the alert levels for the military to DEFCON three."

"I agree," said General Moench. "This is moving quickly from an intelligence operation to a military one. There's a doomsday device on the loose. We have no idea who's got it or what they plan to do with it. We need to start acting like we're under attack."

"You're taking for granted the device even exists," Armstrong warned.

"We have to make that assumption," Moench said. "To do anything else is to invite disaster."

"It's settled then," said the Secretary of Defense. "We move to DEFCON three and I'm going to inform the president we have a very probable impending attack. I want a direct line to your people on the ground, Dulles."

Wizard held up the phone. "This is it."

# CHAPTER FORTY-EIGHT

THE SMELL OF BURLAP AND SWEAT FILLED NOBLE's lungs. Panic prowled the edges of his brain. His hands were loose fists in his lap and he felt every pothole. His eyes had adjusted and he could see through the rough weave, but only dim shapes and outlines. He could make out the bright red of Witwicky's dress and her pale thigh pressed against his own. He thought they were headed generally east, but they might just as easily be headed west. He tried to keep track of the turns. They had made a right out of the parking lot of the car wash, then a left and another left, then it felt like a right, or maybe it was a roundabout. It was hard to say, and because Noble wasn't familiar with Kiev, he had no idea where they might be going.

The van bumped through another deep divot, causing the heavies to bounce. Noble felt their weight lift off the bench seat and then settle back down. No one spoke. Bekir turned on the radio and a mutant mash up of hip-hop polka piped from the speakers. The musical fusion was enough to make Noble's ears bleed. He said, "Can we change the station?"

"Da," said Bekir. "What you want to hear?"

"American rock," one of the goons said. "Elvis Presley. The Beatles."

Bekir spun the dial and Noble listened intently as the transceiver moved along the bandwidth to see how many broadcast stations were within range. It would tell him whether they were still in Kiev, or if they'd left the city for the countryside.

There were plenty of stations within range, which put Noble's mind at ease, and Bekir fiddled with the dial until he found a rock song. The lyrics were Russian and seemed to be a sort of anti-establishment punk. It was only a slight improvement over the polka. Noble decided it would be just his luck to die with the Russian version of Rage Against the Machine stuck in his head.

He desperately tried to think of a way to communicate with Gwen. He couldn't whisper and he couldn't take her hand. That would look suspicious. He wanted her to be ready if he made a move, but had no way to warn her.

———

Ezra gripped the wheel of the Slavuta in one hand and the phone in the other. The van had crossed the Dnieper River, through the seedier neighborhoods of Kiev, then turned down an industrial lane headed towards the outskirts. Ezra locked eyes on the back of the van, seven car lengths ahead, and barked into the phone. "Hello? Wizard... er... I mean, Director Dulles? Can you hear me?"

Ezra peeled his eyes off the road long enough to peek at the screen. The call had ended. He tried calling back but it went straight to voicemail. Ezra dropped the phone in the passenger seat. The second phone was in the cup holder and a strange sort of folk R&B, like something you might hear in the back woods of Pennsylvania, was coming through the speaker. It sounded shrill and distorted, and interrupted by bursts of static. Ezra breathed a sigh of relief when Noble asked them to change the channel.

"Please," Ezra said to the empty SUV. "Anything but this."

There was a hiss of white noise and it took several tries to find a station, but the driver finally settled on something that sounded like eastern Euro trash punk. There was a lot of screaming and distorted electric guitars.

High rises and apartment blocks gave way to factories and processing plants, and Ezra was forced to ease up on the gas, allowing the beat-up van to pull ahead. He dropped back a hundred meters, then another fifty as the roads widened out.

His prominent Adam's apple bobbed up and down. He didn't know why they were headed to the wilds of the industrial sector and instinct told him it wasn't anything good. A cold fist closed around his windpipe and his knees knocked together beneath the steering wheel.

He thought about jamming the gas all the way to the floor, roaring up on the van and forcing the driver off the road. Part of him wanted to end this now. Ezra had the Makarov in his waistband. He imagined running the van into a ditch and then jumping out and using the gun on the driver and his two goons, but discarded that idea. It would be three on one.

"Have to wait," Ezra told himself. "Look for an opening. Remember your training."

He didn't want to think about what might happen to Gwen in one of these empty warehouses. The images made his heart hurt. Sweat ran down his face in greasy rivulets and his knuckles ached from clenching the wheel so hard. He realized his lips were pulled back from his teeth and forced himself to relax. But a few seconds later, unknown to Cook, his mouth had worked back into an ugly snarl.

"It's okay, Gwenny," he said to no one but himself. He was rocking back and forth in his seat now, his foot jumping against the pedal, causing the Slavuta to lurch. "It's okay. I'm not going to let anything bad happen to you."

# CHAPTER FORTY-NINE

Noble's guts were a bundle of electric eels. The sound of rubber on smooth blacktop had given way to the unmistakable rumble of cracked asphalt. The van jounced over divots and banged through potholes, as if Bekir was doing his level best to hit every rough patch in the road. Noble nearly bit off the tip of his tongue when they hit a particularly deep hole. His nerves were starting to fray. They had definitely left the city center and were headed someplace quiet, where no one would hear a gunshot.

It was a nasty thought and Noble didn't like his chances. He was essentially alone. Gwen wouldn't be any help in a fight. That made it three on one. His heart was knocking on the wall of his chest and a sheen of sweat formed on the back of his neck. He weighed his options as the van rumbled over rough roads, headed for the unknown. He thought about making a move, but by the time he jerked the bag off his head, the goons would have their guns out. Besides, a part of Noble's brain told him this might be a test. The Brit took his anonymity seriously and this might be his way of vetting potential business partners. Drive them out to the middle of the nowhere and sweat them a little, see how they held up under pressure.

Noble told himself to wait. Now was not the time to make a move, besides, one of the heavies was making moves of his own. Through the dim light penetrating his burlap, Noble watched a thick paw land on Gwen's knee and work its way up the inside of her thigh. Her hands curled into fists and her legs pressed together, but the big lug wasn't dissuaded. He groped the inside of her thigh until his hand was pushing up the hem of her dress.

Noble's heart squeezed painfully hard. Ezra's words echoed inside his skull like poison darts. Noble couldn't let the thug molest her. Gwen was delicate and that kind of hurt left a scar on a woman that would never heal. He racked his brain for some way to stop it before it went any further.

Before he could think of anything, Gwen solved the problem for him. One of her hands flew up in an arc and the flat hard sound of a slap filled the inside of the van, momentarily drowning out the music.

Gwen punctuated the slap with the Russian, "Svoloch'!"

The goon cursed and grabbed her hand. He was about to let her have one in return when Bekir said, "Lay off her, Luden. Wexler doesn't want them hurt."

———

Ezra let the rusty van slip further ahead and the audio from Gwen's microphone faded to garbled static filled with occasional snatches of Russian punk. They were rumbling over dusty roads, winding through what used to be a heavy industrial zone. Now it was a no man's land littered with derelict factories and abandoned mining operations. The area would make a great backdrop for a movie set in the zombie apocalypse. Ezra imagined undead stumbling along the deserted lanes.

He eased up on the gas until the van was just a dust plume rising in the distance. So far as Ezra could tell, they were the only two vehicles out here which would make spotting a tail easy. Ezra was loath to let the van get any further ahead but feared they would execute Gwen if they realized they were being followed, so he had no choice. Keeping Gwen safe meant letting the van out of his sight.

*You've still got the gun,* Ezra reminded himself.

He glanced at the tarnished black pistol and told himself not to panic. He couldn't help Gwen if he lost his head. He had to stay cool. He tried to remember his training —the CIA had taught him what to do in situations like this —but all he could think of was Gwen and what she must be feeling. Was she scared? Ezra's fingers clamped hard on the wheel. He rolled through the dusty streets, trying to watch everything at once. His eyes darted side to side, scoping out the narrow lanes between buildings, searching for any sign of danger. The van was fully lost from sight now. It had turned somewhere up ahead and the only thing Ezra heard through the audio was a loud clap that sounded suspiciously like a slap.

Who had been hit, he wondered? Was it Noble or Gwen? Were they hurt? His mind insisted he would hear a gunshot next but instead he heard a garbled burst of voices.

It was impossible to make out what they were saying, but it didn't sound like polite conversation.

Ezra took his foot off the gas and let the Slavuta coast while he palmed a slick of sweat from his forehead. They might hear a car coming so he decided to find someplace to park. His panic-stricken brain actually started searching for a parking space among the abandoned hulks. He realized that was a crazy thought and pulled the stolen Slavuta along a narrow alley running behind a row of garages housing dilapidated equipment. Most of the doors were open and Ezra could see inside. He thought about pulling the car into one of the open bays, but he might need to get out in a hurry, so he shifted into park in the middle of the lane. He almost switched off the engine but decided to leave it running.

He threw open the driver's side door and got a blast of cold air. The motor sounded incredibly loud in the empty stillness. He started to get out and then stopped to disable the overhead light. It was the one part of his field training that he could remember right now and felt vitally important. He grabbed both phones and the gun and took a few deep breaths. He had no idea what he was going to do, only that he couldn't let anything bad happen to Gwen.

*Have to find her first,* Ezra told himself. He plunged headlong into the industrial maze, phones in one hand and gun in the other.

# CHAPTER FIFTY

THE BRAKES SQUEALED AND THE ENGINE CUT OUT, cooling with a series of soft ticks. The side door rolled open, allowing a breath of cold air to wash over Noble. He allowed himself to be manhandled from the van and frog-marched across a gravel lot. He could see Gwen's feet and hear Bekir's the stertorous breathing. His soccer days were long past. He sounded like a winded buffalo laboring up a hill.

Noble was herded into a building. He felt concrete under his feet. Darkness made the burlap sack a shroud, blocking out all sight. His chest was tight and his legs felt like spring steel. The muscles in his back were tense and ready for action. It was a mental effort to keep his hands from curling into fists.

If Bekir's men were going to kill them, now would be the time. Noble kept expecting to feel the barrel of a gun against the back of his head. Would he hear the thunder clap? Or would it just be lights out? He licked dry lips, tried to swallow and ended up gulping instead.

"Nervous?" Bekir asked.

"Let's just say I don't like the hospitality so far," Noble spoke through the sack. His voice sounded strangely amplified in his own ears, like the burlap was catching the sound and echoing it back.

"You wanted to meet the Brit?" Umar asked.

"I've got girls if he wants to do business," Noble said, still playing his part. "I was told he was the man to see. What's with all the cloak and dagger?"

The burlap sack was snatched off. Noble blinked and found himself staring down the barrel of a .45 caliber pistol. He leaned back out of reflex, subconsciously trying to put as much distance between himself and the gun as possible, not that it would do him any good. A .45 caliber is a big bullet that would smash his skull like a baseball bat smacking an over ripe melon.

The man behind the gun was a six and a half foot ginger with a jaw carved from granite and shoulders that strained the seams of a tailored suit jacket. He pressed the Smith and Wesson forward until the cold barrel rested against Noble's forehead. "Cloak and dagger. Odd choice of words, wouldn't you say?"

"You must be Wexler," Noble said.

His nostrils flared and his finger tightened on the trigger. "How the hell does he know my name?"

Bekir stood off to one side, hands in his pocket. "I might have mentioned it."

Wexler gave a small shake of his head without taking his eyes off Noble. "Think you're pretty clever? I know a few things about you too. Your name is Jacob Noble and you're a field officer for the CIA."

Gwen's eyes got big. She said, "Jake..?"

"Stay calm," he heard himself say.

Noble tried to keep the surprise from his face. He'd never seen this giant redhead before in his life, of that he was certain. The guy looked like Opie on steroids. He would be a hard man to forget. But he knew Noble's name and who he worked for.

His first thought was another security flap. A senator on the Intelligence Committee had leaked vital details of Noble's recent mission to Iran. She was sitting in a jail cell right now, awaiting trial for treason. Maybe someone else on the Intelligence Select Committee was bent, or maybe Noble had crossed paths with this big bruiser in the past. In the end, it didn't matter. Wexler knew Noble worked for the CIA. Assuming Gwen's microphone was still functioning, Ezra would tell Wizard the op was blown, and Dulles would order a fast reaction team. Noble tried to do the mental calculations on a QRF. Where was the nearest carrier group? The Indian Ocean. It would take them at least an hour.

Noble dropped the Russian accent. "If you know I'm CIA then you know what will happen if you kill an intelligence officer. They'll hunt you down. There's no place you can run and no place you can hide where they won't find you."

Wexler grinned. "I don't scare that easy, Mr. Noble."

Umar Bekir shifted his feet. "I say we kill them now and be done with it."

The pair of thugs pulled guns and Noble tensed for action. A fat bead of sweat rolled down his cheek. He wasn't going to stand there and let them execute him. He'd throw himself at the nearest gunman and hopefully buy Gwen time to escape.

"Not so fast," Wexler said. "First I want a chat with Mr. Noble's lovely assistant."

"Me?" Gwen said. Her voice sounded high, on the edge of hysterics.

"That's right, lass." Wexler waved the gun at Noble. "I know all about Jake here, he's a former Green Beret and there's no way he knows anything about EMPs."

Wexler turned the gun on Gwen. "But you... You're no field officer. I'm guessing it was his job to find the bomb and your job to make sure it didn't go bang. Am I right?"

"Keep your teeth together," Noble said.

At a look from Wexler, one of the goons cuffed Noble on the back of the head with the butt of his pistol. Little lights popped in Noble's vision and his knees buckled. He hit the floor. Concrete sent a shockwave of pain racing up through his joints. His face pinched in pain. He groaned, massaged his left knee and tried to push himself back up, but the goon knocked him down again.

Wexler planted himself in front of Gwen, his nose an inch from hers. "I'm going to ask you some questions and you're going to answer honestly or I'm going to make Jake suffer. Understand?"

Gwen whimpered and her eyes flashed to Noble.

He shook his head.

Wexler said, "We do it the hard way then."

# CHAPTER FIFTY-ONE

Cook was getting closer. He could tell because the transmission was clearing up. Noble's voice came through the tiny speaker saying he didn't like the hospitality. His casual tone helped take some of the edge off and Ezra slowed his pace. Noble didn't sound like he was in any immediate danger. That was a good sign. Perhaps Bekir and his hired muscle had brought them out here for privacy. Plenty of criminals liked to meet in remote locations to avoid eavesdropping.

There was a rustle of fabric and Noble said, "You must be Wexler."

"Think you're pretty clever?" a British voice said. "I know a few things about you too. Your name is Jacob Noble and you're a field officer for the CIA."

Ezra's heart dropped right down through his stomach and landed somewhere around his ankles. He listened as Noble went back and forth with this new player. Then Bekir said, "I say we kill them now."

Ezra ran, feet pounding the broken concrete and air bursting from his lips in ragged gasps.

"Not so fast," the Brit was saying. He wanted to talk to Gwen before they killed anyone.

Ezra didn't stop. Didn't even slow down. He had spots of color in his cheeks and his tennis shoes scuffed on the pavement. He loped along an alley, peeking in through broken windows, searching for the van with the mismatched door. It had to be close.

"We do it the hard way then," the Brit said.

Gwen screamed and Ezra heard sounds of a scuffle. There were several hard smacks, like someone pounding on a side of beef, then a sharp crack and a grunt.

Noble was taking a beating.

Ezra found himself bouncing up and down on the balls of his feet. His legs had stopped but his brain was racing. The maze of buildings had him confused and running in circles. Even if he found them, he had no idea what he'd do. Then he remembered the phone.

Wizard answered on the fourth ring. "What's the situation, Cook?"

"They've got Gwen and Jake," Ezra said. His words came out a nervous jumble. "They've got Gwen and Jake and they're torturing them. They're gonna kill 'em. You need to send a rescue team right now!"

# CHAPTER FIFTY-TWO

THE TWO THUGS HELD NOBLE UP BY HIS ARMS WHILE Bekir slammed a meaty fist into his belly. The impacts sent a tidal wave of pain racing through his body. His knees sagged but the brutes kept him on his feet while their boss delivered three more rabbit punches. The last connected with Noble's solar plexus and the contents of his stomach came up in a stampede, headed for the exit. Noble doubled over and retched. His dinner splattered all over the bare stone floor.

"Please don't hurt him," Gwen said.

Wexler had a gun pressed to her head. Noble figured it was the first time, outside of training, she'd been held at gunpoint. It wasn't a pleasant experience. Gwen's lips trembled as she tried to form words. Most people can barely remember their own name while staring down a barrel.

Noble spat and shook his head. Sweat was dripping off his nose despite the cold. He said, "Keep your mouth shut."

"You keep *your* mouth shut," Wexler said with a withering look at Noble. He turned back to Gwen. "You know about electromagnetic technology? Am I right? That's why they sent you?"

Gwen started to shake her head. He grabbed her by the arm and shook her. "Don't lie to me, girly. It won't go well for Jake."

The big redhead snapped his fingers and Bekir rewarded Noble with two hard punches to the gut. He tried to contract his abs but it did no good. Bekir's knuckles slammed home with devastating force. It felt like a baseball launched from a pitching machine. Noble's vision blurred into a kaleidoscope of swimming lights. Sweat stung his eyes. He retched some more and would have puked again but there was nothing left in his stomach. He coughed up bile instead.

"So what are you?" Wexler asked. "A nuclear expert?"

Gwen shook her head.

"They didn't send you for your looks. What's your job?"

When she didn't answer, Noble got another punishing series of blows. Bekir finished with a shot to the cheek that rocked Noble's head back on his neck and left him semiconscious, moaning in pain. The room spun and he wasn't sure which way was up.

"Let him go," Gwen moaned.

"Not until you tell me what I want to know."

Gwen angled her head down, speaking toward her chest. "Okay, I'll tell you what you want to know, just don't hurt him anymore."

The ginger giant narrowed his eyes. "Did you check these two?"

Bekir nodded. "No guns."

"I know they're not carrying guns you imbecile," he said. "Did you check them for wires?"

Bekir opened his mouth and shut it.

Wexler grabbed Gwen's lapels and jerked the overcoat down over her shoulders. He patted it down and when he didn't find anything, tossed the coat and pointed to the dress.

Gwen clasped her arms against her chest and shook her head.

"Take off the dress!" he snapped.

Gwen stood there like a deer in headlights. Her shoulders inched up and her fingers knotted together. Her eyes, full of tears, went to Noble and she said, "Jake..."

"Don't panic," Noble told her and got another punch for his troubles.

Wexler reached for the shoulder straps and tried to push the dress down. He had to wrench her hands apart and he wasn't gentle about it, then forced the dress down around her ankles. She stood there, in panties and high heels, covering herself with her hands, while Wexler felt the material with his fingertips. He threw the shimmering red fabric down and pointed at her feet. "The shoes! Now!"

Gwen kicked off the heels while tears leaked down her cheeks in silent waves.

Noble ground his teeth together and fantasized about killing Wexler. He wanted to rip open the Brit's throat with his bare hands and watch him bleed, but flying into a rage would only get Gwen killed so he clamped his teeth together and tried not to think about what happened next.

Wexler went over the high heel shoes until he was satisfied there were no listening device hidden in the soles and turned his attention to Gwen. His eyes roamed her body and then he snatched her arm away from her chest. His mouth turned down in a frown. "Very old school."

Gwen let out a sob.

"Who's on the other end?" He ripped the small microphone away from her chest and stamped it under his heel.

Gwen didn't answer and Wexler gave her a hard smack. "Answer me."

"The United States Marines!" Gwen shouted. "And they're going to kill you."

Bekir cursed. "We have to get out of here. They'll be here any minute."

"Calm down," Wexler said. "If they had units in the area, we'd already be dead."

He reached inside his coat pocket, brough out a sheaf of papers and held them up. "You know what this is?"

She blinked and narrowed her eyes. "I can't see without my glasses."

"Play games with me and I'll blow his head off." Wexler pointed the gun at Noble. "These are Lukyanenko's notes. You know how to decipher them?"

Gwen hesitated.

He thumbed back the hammer on the pistol.

Gwen nodded.

"Excellent. You're just the person I've been looking for," he told her. "I've got a little job for you."

# CHAPTER FIFTY-THREE

WIZARD HAD HIS PHONE ON SPEAKER IN THE CENTER OF the table. A pair of White House AV techs hurried to tether the device to the room's audio system so the Joint Chiefs did not have to crowd around in an effort to hear. Cook was on the other end, talking so fast he tripped over his own words.

"They're torturing Noble," he was saying. "You have to do something. You need to get a quick response team here right away!"

Wizard shook a cigarette from his pack and lit up, ignoring a dirty look from the acting Secretary of State. He leaned forward, blew smoke and said, "Take a breath, son, and calm down. Everything is going to be fine. First thing's first. You need to get us a location."

"I have no idea where I am," Cook said in a voice edging toward hysteria. "Didn't you hear me? They're gonna kill Jake. We gotta do something."

"We need a location if we're going to get a team in there," Wizard said.

"They drove out to the middle of some abandoned

factory complex somewhere. I dunno. We're miles from the city. I dunno where we are."

General Moench covered the phone with one hand. "I thought you said this guy was one of your best. He sounds scared witless."

"Noble is the field operative," Armstrong said. "Cook is with the Intelligence Directorate."

"He's just a little rattled," Wizard said and signaled Moench to take his hand away.

The general drew back and Wizard said, "Cook, take a minute and get your bearings. We need to know where to send the rescue team."

"I dunno where I am!"

Wizard said, "That device in your hand will give you a pinpoint accurate location, son."

"Oh yeah!" Cook said and then, "One second."

They heard him take the phone away from his ear and a moment later he was back on. "Okay, we're in the Darnytskyi District outside Kiev. It's an old abandoned complex of some kind."

"Probably the old burn center," Wizard said. "The Russians started construction on a hospital to treat victims of the Chornobyl meltdown but never finished. It's been abandoned for years."

"You need to send somebody right away!"

"We're working on that part," Wizard told him and glanced at Armstrong. She had her head together with the SecDef, discussing their options. Wizard said, "Have you got eyes on Noble and Witwicky?"

"No," Cook moaned. "This place is huge."

"You're going to have to do better than that, son,"

Wizard said. "We need an exact building and you'll need to find some way to mark it for the rescue team."

Cook let out a few shallow breaths. "There's no way. This place is a maze."

"They're probably on the ground floor somewhere. Slow down, take your time, and use your senses."

"I keep getting turned around."

"Find some way to mark the places you've checked," Wizard said. "The only way we can rescue them is if you get us a location. It's all on you, son."

There was a pause while Cook collected himself. "Yeah, okay, yeah. I can do this."

While Cook walked the sprawling complex of industrial buildings, Armstrong and the Secretary of Defense started making phone calls. The closest quick reaction force was a team of Navy SEALS on a carrier group in the Indian Ocean and it would take them at least forty-five minutes. General Moench whispered this to the group.

Wizard's brows pinched. He took the cigarette from his mouth and breathed smoke. This was going from bad to worse. Noble was at the mercy of Crimean gangsters, along with one of the intelligence division's best analysts, and the nearest rescue team was an hour away. That didn't bode well.

"Oh my God," Cook said. "Oh no! No!"

Director Armstrong leaned forward, concern chiseled on the lines of her face. She said, "What's going on, Ezra. Talk to us."

"They found the microphone," Cook said. His voice was a high-pitched scree. "I lost the signal."

Armstrong turned to Admiral Cutter. "Get that rescue team in the air."

He had a phone to his ear and nodded. "They'll be airborne in ten minutes."

"That's not good enough," Armstrong said.

"I can't work miracles," Cutter said.

"My people are in immediate danger."

"They put themselves in the situation."

"Damn it, Admiral. These are human beings we're talking about."

"And I'm doing everything I can to help," he said. "But I can't break the laws of physics. Tell your man he needs to find the building and mark it. They'll be there in forty minutes."

Cook heard this last part and said, "Forty minutes! Gwen hasn't got forty minutes."

"One thing at a time," Wizard said. "Have you got eyes on Noble and Witwicky?"

"No," he moaned.

Armstrong leaned over the table and hit the mute button. "We haven't got forty minutes. The QRF is never going to make it in time."

"We can't tell him that," Wizard said through a cloud of smoke.

"What're you going to do?" The acting Secretary of State wanted to know.

"Not much we can do," Wizard admitted.

Ogden said, "We can't just let those people die."

Wizard shared a tense look with Armstrong. They both knew the score. Intelligence agents are forced to put themselves in dangerous situations and sometimes things break the wrong way. When it did, the cavalry was not coming over the hill to save the day. Wizard took a drag and unmuted the phone. "Cook, son, I need you to find the building where Noble and Witwicky are located and let me know when you do."

"And then what?"

"You've got a gun haven't you?"

"Yeah…"

"You'll have to rescue them."

"Wait, no. I can't… I don't… I'm not a field agent."

"You are now," Wizard told him.

# CHAPTER FIFTY-FOUR

GWEN COVERED HER SMALL BREASTS WITH ONE trembling arm. Goosebumps marked her bare flesh. Her cheeks burned with shame. The logical part of her brain wondered how she could be embarrassed at a time like this. She should focus on self-preservation, but the natural human instinct to cover herself from the eyes of strangers was overriding.

Bad as it was for Gwen, it had to be worse for Noble. Bekir had hammered his belly until Noble's knees gave out and the two men holding his arms were the only thing keeping him up. His head lolled to the side and a line of spittle ran from his open mouth. The big goon cocked his fist back for another punch and Noble was so out of it, he didn't even try to protect himself. He just hung there like a side of beef, hair dangling in front of his face.

"I'll tell you anything you want to know," Gwen said. "Just don't hurt him anymore."

The redhead shoved papers under Gwen's nose and

said, "You know how to interpret this? You understand the science?"

Noble's head went back and forth. He was warning her to stay silent and it got an immediate response from Bekir. The bruiser pummeled Noble's ribs.

Gwen heard herself saying, "Yes. I understand it."

"You just won the lottery," Wexler said. "Means you get to live a little while longer."

"What about Jake?"

Wexler said, "He's not so lucky I'm afraid."

Gwen let out a sob and rushed past the big redhead to wrap her arms around Noble. She had forgotten about her nakedness. She buried her face in his shoulders and wept. "I'm sorry, Jake. I'm so sorry."

"Not your fault," he mumbled. "Mine."

She held him in her arms and cried. "What should I do, Jake?"

"Stay alive."

She took his face in her hands and kissed him. "It can't end like this. It can't."

"Stay alive," Noble whispered. "The Company will find you."

"What about you?"

"My number's up," he said.

"Break those two love birds up," Wexler said. "We've got work to do."

"What should we do with him?" Bekir asked.

"Make sure they never find the body."

Gwen gave a high-pitched hysterical cry.

"And her?" Bekir asked.

"She's coming with me."

Bekir gave Noble a good hard slap to the face and the two heavies dragged him away. He didn't put up a fight. Gwen kept expecting him to do something. He was *supposed* to do something. He was the field officer. A former Green Beret. Gwen realized this whole time she had been waiting for Noble to pull some spectacular stunt and save them both, but he was human after all.

As the pair of thugs dragged Noble around the corner, his head came up a fraction, just enough to see his face, and Gwen thought he winked, but maybe it was a grimace. Then he was gone.

Wexler grabbed Gwen's arm and pulled her through the abandoned complex, past silent dark machinery, to the trunk of a black sedan. He used the clicker. The trunk latch popped open with a soft *clunk* and he pushed her in.

She tripped over the lip, landed with a solid thump, and then he was forcing her legs inside. Gwen didn't put up a fight. She knew she should, but she was too scared.

Wexler patted her bottom and said, "Keep quiet and I'll see that you aren't molested when we reach the islands. Make a fuss and I'll let the men do what they want with you. Understand?"

Gwen let out a sob and nodded.

The trunk lid came down, shutting out the light.

# CHAPTER FIFTY-FIVE

THEY DRAGGED NOBLE ALONG EMPTY LANES OF THE deserted hospital. The pair of brutes had hold of his arms and his toes scraped the dusty concrete while Bekir kept his pistol pointed at Noble's head. His heart was a racehorse inside his chest and his brain desperately searched for an opening.

They hauled him through an open door into what had once been a morgue. Abandoned gurneys stood empty and several of the freezer doors were missing, looted by teenagers ages ago. A graffiti artist had turned the room into a mad Picasso of lidless eyes and rude epitaphs.

"This will do," Bekir said. "It will be a while before anyone finds his body stuffed in one of these."

"On your knees," one of the goons said.

"I'll die on my feet." Noble made an effort to straighten up.

"I said on your knees." The thug kicked.

Noble's legs buckled and his knees smacked the dusty concrete. Electric spears raced up his spine and into his brain. He clamped his teeth together around a grunt of pain. He didn't want these clowns to hear him suffer. He wouldn't give them the satisfaction. He was about to die and he wanted to go out with some dignity. Fear formed an acid puddle in his belly that made him want to sick up. His hands clenched into fists.

Bekir pressed the gun against the back of Noble's head. He felt cold steel and smelled oil. His eyes squeezed shut. This was the end.

———

Ezra had the old Makarov pistol in one hand and the phone pressed against his ear. He was hurrying along the abandoned corridors, searching for any sign of Gwen or Noble.

He peeked through a grime-crusted window and saw the bulky outlines of dead equipment squatting in the shadows. "Where could they be..." Ezra muttered to himself.

"Cook," Wizard said into the phone. "How's it coming? Give us an update."

"I still haven't found them," Ezra said. His words came out in breathy little whispers, like a man who had just won a marathon trying to give an interview. "They gotta be close though. I'm almost certain."

"Almost only counts in horseshoes and hand grenades," Wizard told him. "You need to slow down and think, son."

"I am thinking," Ezra growled. But it was a lie. He was panicking and he knew it. He needed a system to mark off the places he'd already searched. He cast about for something to use as a marker and spotted a chunk of white stone in the weeds growing up through cracks in the weathered tile. He used it to put a big X on an open door, then ran to the next wing, marking walls as he went.

He was marking rooms one by one when he heard the unmistakable purr of an engine. The sound of the tires on the asphalt filtered through the busted windows and echoed along empty hallways. Cook paused. Was it Bekir and his men? If they were leaving it meant Gwen and Jake were already dead.

Ezra pushed that fear aside and kept marking rooms. He had to be sure. He was hurrying along a suite of operating theaters when he heard scuffing feet and turned at the sound. His throat clutched tight and his finger slipped onto the trigger. He crouched and waited, straining to hear, and caught muffled words.

Ezra took off at a silent run, his sneakers whispering over the carpet of dust. He rounded a corner and bounded down a hall in time to hear, "On your knees."

Noble's voice said, "I'll die on my feet."

"I said on your knees."

There was a muffled thump followed by a loud crack.

Ezra knew he had seconds to act. He was moving even before he knew what he meant to do. He sprinted the length of the hall and skidded to a halt in the open door to the morgue. His sneakers, one shoe untied, make a loud shriek on the old tiles. He spotted Noble in the middle of the room, down on his knees, fists clenched and his eyes closed. Bekir had a gun pressed to the back of Noble's head.

Ezra dropped the phone, raised the Makarov pistol in both hands, squeezed his eyes shut and pulled the trigger.

# CHAPTER FIFTY-SIX

Noble's world erupted into an avalanche of sound. His shoulders pulled up and his head sank, like a turtle crawling inside its shell. He heard the gunshots and waited for blackness, or a light at the end of the tunnel, maybe a choir of angels singing hallelujah. But none of that happened. He was still on his knees in the forgotten morgue, in an abandoned hospital on the outskirts of Kiev.

Bullets smacked the walls and went skipping over tiles. Bekir's thugs nearly jumped right out of their socks. One spun around, shouting a curse. The other reached for the pistol in his waistband.

Noble's mind raced to make sense of what had happened. It wasn't Bekir pulling the trigger and the bullets pinging off the dull metal cabinets weren't meant for him. His brain put all the pieces together in a flash. Cook had come to the rescue. The little guy actually did it. He'd come in guns blazing. He'd missed with every shot, but had bought Noble an opening.

Bekir, caught off guard, flinched and turned at the ear-piercing blasts.

Noble threw an elbow straight back and connected with Bekir's groin. The Crimean's face stretched in a comical O and he doubled over. Noble pushed off the floor, ramming the back of his head into Bekir's face with a hard, wet crunch. Bekir's nose mashed flat. Noble felt the bone break. Warm blood spurted over the back of Noble's head, drenching his collar. Bekir stumbled and Noble reached for the gun with both hands. He had to stay crouched to avoid bullets. Cook was still pulling the trigger, firing blind. The gun made a continuous whipcrack that felt like nails hammered into Noble's eardrums. He latched onto Bekir's wrist, slipped a finger into the trigger guard and used his weight to spin them both around.

One of the goons had his pistol pointed at Cook. His face worked into a snarl and his finger started to tighten on the trigger.

Noble, still wrestling Bekir, swung the gun up. The semi-automatic spit flame and the shot punched through the brute's neck, just above the shoulders. He was hammered off his feet. His body slammed against the metal lockers and his weapon slipped from nerveless fingers.

The second goon hesitated. He couldn't decide who was the bigger threat and his hesitation cost him.

Using his own body as a pivot, Noble wrestled Bekir around with a judo throw and hauled back on the trigger. Two bullets coughed from the gun. The first caught the goon in the belly and made his legs collapse. The second pierced his chest high on the left. He let out a strangled choking noise, spun and landed on his back. He still had the gun in his hand and was trying to use it but he had no strength left. The second bullet had ruptured something important and blood was leaking from his left side in shockingly red squirts that painted the morgue cabinets in ghastly sprays. His eyes were wide and staring. His mouth stretched in a silent scream.

Cook stood in the doorway, eyes closed and head turned to the side, finger still on the trigger. His face was a puckered fruit. The slide of the Makarov had locked back on an empty chamber and smoke drifted from the barrel.

Noble hit Bekir with an elbow to the face, wrenched the gun from his hand.

Cook opened his eyes, saw all three bad guys stretched out on the floor, and said, "Holy cow! I did it."

"Yeah," Noble said through a high-pitched ringing in his ears. "You got 'em."

Bekir started to crawl across the floor toward one of the fallen pistols.

"Don't even think about it." Noble caught him with a kick to the ribs that rolled him over onto his back.

Bekir let out a loud *oof!*

Noble pressed the gun barrel against Bekir's forehead. "Try anything and I'll end you."

# CHAPTER FIFTY-SEVEN

"Where's Gwen?" Ezra demanded.

"She's not here," Noble said.

"Where is she?" he asked, panic building in his voice.

"Wexler took her," Noble said.

The little guy turned on Bekir. "Where is he taking her?"

Bekir sneered. "I'll tell you nothing."

Now that the shooting was over, he had regained some of his confidence. He sat up with his back against the wall and wiped blood from his mouth with the back of one hand.

"We'll see about that." Noble grabbed the gangster by the shoulders, hauled him to his feet and slammed him against the wall of cabinets.

"I don't have to tell you anything," Bekir said. "You are Americans. I know how it works. You must follow the American rules."

Ezra started forward but Noble pushed him back. "You're going to tell us what we want to know."

"And why would I do that?"

"Because that was his girlfriend you helped kidnap," Noble said with a nod to Cook. "If you don't tell us where Wexler is taking her, I'm going to let my man Ezra go ballistic on you."

Bekir looked Ezra over and chuckled. "He is soft American. What can he do?"

Cook answered by smashing the butt of his gun down on Bekir's mouth several times in a row. Metal crunched on bone and blood squirted over the dusty tiles of the morgue. Bekir's knees collapsed. Ezra would have gone right on hitting him if Noble hadn't pushed him away. Ezra was red in the face and breathing heavy. He screamed, "Where is she!"

Bekir was on his knees now, one hand pooling with blood from his ruined mouth. He spit broken chips of teeth and muttered, "You will have to ask Wexler."

"Wexler has Lukyanenko?" Noble said.

Another nod.

"Why?" Noble said. "What's he got planned?"

"Who cares," Ezra said. "All I care about is saving Gwen."

"I don't know his plans," Bekir said through a mouth full of blood. "All I know is he paid the dancer to deliver the scientist."

Ezra pressed his pistol against Bekir's head, forcing his skull back against the graffitied metal cabinets. It was a hollow threat. His slide was still locked back on an empty chamber, but he said, "Where is he taking Gwen?"

"He's going to Boryspil airport south of Kiev," Bekir

muttered. "He has personal jet. Tail number zulu, lima, bravo, x-ray, seven, nine, nine. Where he goes beyond there, I do not know. Ask him yourself."

Cook pulled the trigger. There was a hollow click. His face was an ugly mask of hatred and a vein throbbed in his temple. He pulled the trigger again before realizing the gun was empty. He dropped it and scooped up one of the discarded weapons. This one wasn't empty.

Noble took a step to the side, clearing the line of fire, but said, "Don't do it, Cook."

Bekir pressed himself against the cabinets, closed his eyes and turned his head.

"Stay out of this Noble."

"You don't want this on your conscience, Ez."

Ezra stood for several long seconds, the gun pointed at Bekir's head. His eyes were wild and his teeth gnashed together.

"Let him go," Noble said.

"He'll talk," Ezra said. "He'll contact this Wexler guy. Tell him we're coming."

"No he won't," Noble said. "We won't let that happen."

"How?" Ezra asked. "The fast reaction team doesn't even know where we are."

Noble unlatched one of the cabinets and rolled open the stainless-steel gurney. "This ought to keep him until the QRF gets here."

Bekir took one look at the metal gurney and said, "I'm not getting in there."

"Have it your way," Noble said and turned to Ezra. "Ice him."

"Okay!" Bekir put both hands up and started toward the slab. "Okay, I'm getting in. Just don't kill me, okay."

"Face first," Noble said and forced the gangster into the cabinet. He rolled the table inside, threw the door shut with a bang and turned around to find Ezra's gun pointed at him.

# CHAPTER FIFTY-EIGHT

"What the hell is this?" Noble asked.

Cook stood with the gun aimed at Noble's forehead. Tears rolled down his cheeks and his mouth curled up in an ugly frown. "This is your fault!"

"Take it easy, Ez." Noble held his hands out to the sides, palms open.

"Don't call me that," he screeched. "Gwen calls me that."

"Okay, Ezra," Noble said. "Just take it easy okay?"

"Stop telling me what to do!" Ezra's face scrunched up and a fresh wave of tears burst from his sockets. He let out an animal growl, reared back with the pistol, and cracked Noble on the forehead. He didn't put his weight into it, not like he had with Bekir, but the butt of the gun bit Noble just above his left eyebrow. He staggered back and a hot spill of blood ran down his cheek.

Searing pain throbbed in Noble's forehead. He'd have a splitting headache in a few hours. He wiped blood from his forehead and straightened back up. "You want to shoot me, go ahead."

Ezra aimed the gun and took a few deep breaths. "You did this. You put Gwen in this situation."

Noble kept his hands out to the side and stepped forward, letting the barrel of the pistol rest against his chest. "You're right," he said. "This is my fault. I made the call. I put Gwen in harm's way. It's all on me. And I wouldn't blame you if you pulled that trigger, but right now I'm the best chance you have at getting her back."

"How?" Ezra said. "Huh? How're we going to do that? You heard him; Wexler is on his way to the airport right now. He's probably there already. They might already be in the air. How are we going to find her? She's gone! She's gone and it's your fault!"

"I'll find her," Noble said, keeping his voice calm. "I'll find her and I promise you, I'll do everything in my power to get her back."

Ezra was openly weeping now. "You promise? You promise you can get her back?"

"We'll do it together," Noble said.

Ezra hiccupped and wiped snot from his nose. "If anything bad happens to her..."

"I'll take whatever punishment you want to dish out."

"I'll kill you!" Ezra screeched. "I'll kill you if anything bad happens to her."

"And I won't stop you."

The gun finally went down to Ezra's side and he let out a painful moan. "I can't live if anything bad happens to her, Noble. I can't."

Noble took the gun from Ezra's trembling hand and stuffed it in his waistband. "Nothing bad is going to happen," Noble told him. "We're going to get her back. I promise."

# CHAPTER FIFTY-NINE

GWEN WAS CURLED UP IN THE TRUNK, AS FAR FROM the opening as possible. A plastic glow-in-the-dark tab with the words EMERGENCY RELEASE mocked her. She had pulled and pulled but nothing happened. At first her panic-stricken brain insisted she pull harder. She had gripped the tab in both hands, fingers pinched tight, and jerked until her forearms ached. But Wexler was one step ahead. He had disconnected the emergency release and all her efforts were in vain. After that Gwen pushed her back against the seats and cried in the dark.

She kept telling herself that she was a CIA officer, that she was trained to deal with situations just like this, but that was a load of bull. She was an analyst. Her field training at the Farm had been more like an adventure camp. She had done the drills, secure in the knowledge that she would never have to use those skills again. Now here she was, naked in the trunk of a car, wishing she had paid more attention.

Tears coalesced on her lashes and tumbled down over

her cheeks. She shivered, curled in on herself and waited for the ride to be over. She had to pee, but she held it. Being stripped and forced into a trunk was bad enough. Peeing herself would make the humiliation worse. Wexler would think she had pissed herself out of fear. And maybe some of it was fear, but the motion of the car over rough roads wasn't helping any.

She shut her eyes tight, turned her face to the floor of the trunk and cried. She kept hoping the car would screech to a halt, that there would be a brief exchange of gunfire and then the trunk would open and Noble would be smiling down at her. But the car kept driving, bumping over potholes until finally it rumbled onto blacktop—Gwen could hear the difference—and then they were on the highway. God only knows where. The drive seemed to take forever and the longer it went on, the more Gwen came to realize that Noble was not coming to save her, that he was in all likelihood dead.

That thought made her cry even harder.

She was still weeping when the engine downshifted. The car made several turns and then slowed even further. It was obvious they had reached some destination. Gwen thought she heard the roar of a jet engine overhead. Near an airport maybe? Then the car slowed right down to a crawl. It seemed to go on like that for a very long time, or maybe Gwen's sense of time was skewed, but finally the car braked to a stop.

This was it. They had reached their destination and whatever Wexler had in store. This might even be where he was keeping Lukyanenko. A surge of desperate energy welled up inside Gwen. If she was going to make an escape, now was the time. Wexler would have to open the trunk to get her out. That meant she had a small window of opportunity.

She scooched across the rough carpet until she was up against the opening and cranked her knees up to her chest, her feet ready to lash out, and braced her arms against the seats. She'd kick Wexler in the face the moment he opened the trunk, then hop out and make a run for it. They were probably someplace remote. Maybe someplace with trees. She would run to the tree line and lose him in the woods. Then it was just a matter of finding a phone and contacting Langley. Gwen had it all worked out in her head. Her heart was beating so hard it felt like it might explode inside her chest and every breath was a ragged gasp. She coiled her legs into springs, ready to explode.

The car door opened and she felt the sedan rock. She heard the chirp of the key fob and the trunk lid popped up an inch. Light slipped in around the opening. Then fingers grasped the lid.

Gwen took one last gulp of air and, as the trunk lid swung up, she pistoned both legs.

She missed completely. Instead of kicking him square in the face, she kicked air. Her legs and bottom burst from the trunk like a trick snake from a can. Her lower back smashed down on the lip, sending jolts of electricity racing up her spine. She pushed with her arms and wriggled her way out of the trunk in a desperate bid to escape. She came down in a crouch, like a naked savage, and then sprang to her feet. She made two whole strides.

Wexler stuck out a foot, caught her ankle, and sent Gwen sprawling. She landed flat on her belly. All the air went out of her lungs and her chin bounced off smooth concrete. Firecrackers exploded behind her eyes.

Gwen didn't know how long she laid there, but when the fog finally cleared, Wexler stood with a boot on her shoulders, pressing her into the cold floor. She coughed, gasped for air, and managed to whisper, "Please."

"Promise to behave?"

Gwen only nodded and he took his foot off her back.

She gulped air, pushed up from the ground and got her first look around. She was inside an airplane hangar. The sedan was parked across from a gleaming white jet with gold stripes. The fuselage door was open and the stairs were down, awaiting passengers. A cold wind blew in from the open hangar doors causing gooseflesh on Gwen's naked bottom.

Wexler held Gwen's dress in one hand. "Promise to be a good little lass, and you can have this back. Wouldn't that be nice?"

Gwen choked back tears and nodded.

He jerked his chin at the jet. "Get on the plane."

Gwen pushed to her feet, standing up slowly, trying her best to cover everything with only two hands, and walked in a humiliated crouch toward the jet. The pilot stood at the top of the stairs. He was a thin man with a balding head and pockmarked skin. He wasn't surprised by the sight of a naked woman climbing aboard. He ignored Gwen and spoke to Wexler. "We can lift off whenever you're ready."

"Good. Get us in the air."

Gwen moved halfway down the center aisle, stopped and turned. The interior was all beige calfskin and soft lights. It could seat eight with plenty of leg room. In a small voice she asked, "What are you going to do to me?"

"I'm not going to do anything to you." Wexler threw the dress at her. "You're my meal ticket, luv."

Gwen caught the fabric in both hands and hurried to pull it on over her head, letting the silky material slither down over her hips.

"But I have business partners who aren't so cultured and if you don't do exactly as I say, I'll let them have their way with you. Understood?"

The pilot brought the stairs up, secured the hatch and disappeared into the cabin.

Wexler took a seat and motioned for Gwen to sit across from him. "No need to make this unpleasant, luv."

She sat, knees together and her fists in her lap.

"Buckle up."

Her nostrils flared. "If we crash I'd rather not survive."

He produced a pistol. "I insist."

Gwen reached for her safety belt.

# CHAPTER SIXTY

THE SPEEDOMETER IN THE OLD SLAVUTA POINTED TO one hundred and thirty-seven kilometers an hour as Noble raced south along the M03. The engine gave out a steady clanking rhythm and the back end fishtailed slightly on the corners. Thankfully the M03 was mostly straight. Noble gripped the steering wheel in both hands and ignored the temperature gauge as it inched closer to the redline.

Cook was in the passenger seat, one hand clutching the dash and his foot pressing down on the floorboard, like he could make the vehicle go faster. The skin around his eyes was tight. He kept muttering to himself. It sounded like *Hang on, Gwen.*

He said, "Faster."

"Never let the enemy force you to move faster than you can think," Noble told him. It was an old Special Forces mantra. After a moment he added, "Or drive."

One of the phones was buzzing. Noble said, "Get that, will ya? I'm a little busy."

Ezra put it on speaker. Wizard came on the line. "Cook? How's it going, son?"

Ezra rattled off the events of the last half hour in a confusing jumble and Noble cut him off. "We're on our way to the airport."

"You're alive," Wizard said. "Good. What happened to the girl?"

"Taken by a guy called Wexler." Noble jerked the wheel and steered around a flatbed hauling timber. "I don't know if that's his real name or an alias. He's got Witwicky and they're headed to the airport."

Ezra was frantically waving at Noble from the passenger seat.

Noble dropped his voice and said, "What?"

Cook pointed to the phone and mouthed the words, *Joint Chiefs.*

Noble nodded understanding.

Wizard was saying, "What about Lukyanenko?"

"Lukyanenko can wait," Noble said. "Wexler has one of my people."

"Noble, this is the Secretary of Defense. I'm officially in charge of this operation. We'll get your friend back when and if we can. Right now, that scientist and his device are top priority. You need to locate Lukyanenko and find out if he's actually built an EMP."

Ezra's face turned red. "They're gonna kill her!"

Noble snatched the phone away. "We find Witwicky, we'll find Wexler, and that will lead us to Lukyanenko."

Ezra sat in the passenger seat fuming.

"Noble," Armstrong came on the line. "Can you give us a description of Wexler?"

"He's British. His accent is Yorkshire unless I miss my guess. He's six and a half foot tall, red hair, bulging shoulders, and a pug nose. Kind of looks like Opie on steroids." Noble dropped the phone into the center console and used the breakdown lane to pass a line of tractor trailers. "One other thing, he knows me. Knows my name. Seemed to know everything about me."

The Slavuta gave a loud fart from the tailpipe and the engine clanked.

Wizard said, "Are you telling us someone made book on you?"

"Possible," Noble said. "But I've never seen the guy before in my life."

"You certain?" Armstrong asked.

"You don't forget a face like that," Noble told her. "He's got danger written all over him. I wouldn't be surprised if he's former military and he's probably got a criminal record."

"Okay," Armstrong said. "We'll see if we can dig up anyone matching that description."

"Noble?" Wizard's scratchy voice came on the line. "Any idea why they would take Witwicky?"

Noble winced. He had been hoping to avoid the subject. He had several ideas and none of them were good. He said, "Wexler had Lukyanenko's research notes and wanted to know if Gwen understood the science."

"And did she?" Armstrong asked.

"I think so, yeah."

The Secretary of Defense asked, "If he's got Lukyanenko, why's he need anyone else?"

"I don't get paid to speculate, sir."

That was a lie, of course. Field officers speculate often. That's the only way to put the puzzle pieces together. You have to be able to think like the enemy. You theorize what he might be up to and then check your hunch, hoping it pays off. Sometimes you get lucky.

The secretary of Defense said, "If he needs someone who understands the science, he may no longer be in possession of Lukyanenko."

"Doesn't change anything," Noble said, but he knew what the SecDef was thinking. Without the bomb maker, Wexler would not be able to deploy the device. That made Gwen a lynch pin, which could be either good or bad.

They crested a rise in the rolling green landscape and saw a military checkpoint ahead.

Noble cursed.

# CHAPTER SIXTY-ONE

"No!" Ezra screamed. "No, this can't be happening."

"What's going on?" The SecDef said. "Talk to us."

"Road block," Noble told them.

"Police?"

"Military," Noble said.

With Russian troops massing along the border, and tension between the two countries heating up, Ukrainian military had erected random checkpoints along major highways.

"What are we gonna do?" Cook wanted to know.

The road block consisted of a BTR-4 armored personnel carrier with a mounted 30mm machine gun on top, a dozen troops, and an old Soviet-era jeep. A line of cars had queued. Drivers eased up to the yellow and white sawhorses, rolled down their windows, and flashed their IDs at bored soldiers.

"We're definitely not going to stop," Noble said.

Cook reached for his seat belt.

Noble twisted the wheel and steered off the road into the tall grass. Tires rumbled over uneven terrain and the engine changed pitch. A worrying whine came from under the hood. The needle immediately dropped to seventy-five, then sixty-five, then sixty. At that speed it was hard to keep the hatchback straight. Noble tightened his grip and fought to keep the bucking Slavuta under control.

"Noble?" The SecDef said. "What are you doing?"

"I can't stop for a roadblock," Noble said. "They'll want to know why two Americans are doing ninety in a stolen vehicle."

"Noble, you need to slow down and stop," the SecDef said.

"He can't stop," Wizard said.

"He must stop," the Secretary of Defense fired back. "If they get caught it'll be an international incident. Ukraine doesn't know we're running an op in their country. We need to stay under the radar."

"Wexler will be long gone by the time we get through this road block," Noble said.

"We're not stopping," Ezra whispered.

"Noble," the SecDef said leaning down into the microphone. "I'm ordering you to stop."

Wizard came on the line. "Jake, I'm ordering you to keep going."

"You aren't in charge," the SecDef said.

Armstrong interrupted. "Jake, this is Director Armstrong, do as the Secretary of Defense says."

"It's the wrong call," Noble said. They were flying over

open fields, the Slavuta jumping and throwing them around inside the cabin.

The troopers saw them veer off and two immediately ran for the olive-green jeep. A third piled in before the driver got the engine started.

"I agree," Armstrong said. "But it's his call to make. You need to stop."

"Sorry," Noble said. "Could you repeat that? I'm losing cell signal."

"Noble," Armstrong raised her voice. "You heard what I said. Stop the car immediately."

Noble motioned at the phone.

Ezra turned off the roaming. The signal immediately dropped. He said, "We are in so much trouble."

"Stay on mission," Noble told him.

They went shooting past the roadblock, the jeep close behind. Soldiers were yelling for them to pull over. One man aimed his rifle in the air and cracked off a warning shot.

"They're shooting at us."

"They're shooting into the air."

Cook twisted around in his seat. "Should I shoot back?"

"What?" Noble nearly lost control of the car. He was angling back toward the roadway and said, "Hell no! Do not shoot at them."

"What're you going to do?"

"Just hang on tight and promise you won't start shooting," Noble said.

He kept the pedal down and checked the rearview every few seconds. Once he was back on the road, he pushed the Slavuta up to eighty but the jeep was gaining fast.

One of the soldiers leaned out, braced his AK-74 rifle against his shoulder, took careful aim and squeezed off a shot. The bullet impacted the back bumper with a flat thwack, missing the tire by inches.

"Now they're shooting *at* us!" Cook yelled.

## CHAPTER SIXTY-TWO

THE SECRETARY OF DEFENSE SLAMMED A FIST DOWN on the table, causing coffee mugs to jump. He was red in the face and breathing heavy. "This is totally unacceptable. What kind of people have you got working for you?"

The last part was aimed at Armstrong.

"Believe it or not Noble is one of our best field officers," Armstrong said.

"Well that doesn't say much about the rest of the people you've got over there at Langley." The Secretary of Defense shook his head. "I want this guy brought in. He's totally off the reservation."

Wizard lit a cigarette off the end of another and said, "That would be a mistake."

"A mistake?" The SecDef's eyebrows climbed halfway up his forehead. "The mistake was putting him onto this in the first place. We need someone in the field we can trust, and Noble obviously isn't a team player."

"He's doing what he feels is best," Wizard said.

"Exactly," The Director of Homeland Security interjected. "He's doing what *he feels* is best. He's not paid to do what he thinks is best. He's supposed to do what we order him to do."

Armstrong crossed her arms and cupped her elbows. "That may be how you train your people in the DHS, but in the CIA we teach our people to think on their feet, to make strategic decisions in the field under pressure."

"Look where that got us," The director of Homeland Security said.

The Secretary of Defense pointed a finger at the phone and barked, "Get him back on the line. Tell him he is off this mission, effective immediately, and that if he ever makes it home in one piece, he'll likely be arrested for sedition. I'm going to throw the book at that guy."

"Hold on just a minute," General Moench said. "Noble is a former Green Beret. He's been trained, by us, to never leave a fallen comrade behind. One of his people is in danger, he's going to do everything he can to pull her bacon out of the frier. I'd do the same."

"That's not the point." The Secretary of Defense rounded on the Marine Corp General. "We have to think about the big picture. We're talking about the fate of a nation here. You're talking about one silly little girl who got herself kidnapped."

Moench looked like he was about to take a swing on the SecDef. "She put herself on the line following *our* orders, trying to find Lukyanenko and his EMP. We owe it to her to do everything we can to get her back."

"Are you even listening to yourself? You want to focus on a captured field officer instead of stopping an EMP attack? What if that bomb is headed for the United States?"

"I think Noble's right," Moench said. "Finding Wexler is our best bet to find Lukyanenko."

"Well you aren't in charge," the SecDef said. "I am and I'm pulling Noble's leash. He's finished. We're going to do this my way."

"And what do you suggest we do?" Armstrong asked.

The muscles at the corner of his jaw bunched and released. "What we should have done from the beginning. We open up lines of communication with the Russian and Ukrainian presidents. We let them know there is a terrorist group in possession of an EMP. Then we put troops at every airport and harbor, check everybody coming and going. If they try to bring an EMP into this country we'll catch them as they cross the border."

"What if they march it across the border from Mexico?" Moench asked.

"What if they fly it in from Canada?" someone else suggested.

"We'll deal with that when and if it happens," the Secretary of Defense said. "Right now I want someone reaching out to Russia and Ukraine. We need to let them know what's going on."

"That's a mistake," Wizard said in a quiet voice.

The SecDef wheeled to face him. "With all due respect, Mr. Dulles, you're paid to run covert ops, not dictate international policy. You're out of your depth."

"Dulles is right," Armstrong said. "Russia and Ukraine are on the verge of war. You tell them there's an EMP on the loose and each country will be certain the other has it and is ready to use it. You might start a nuclear exchange."

"Which might be exactly what these terrorists want,"

Wizard said. "Pop off an EMP in the heart of Saint Petersburg. The Russians will think the Ukrainians are responsible and launch their nuclear arsenal. America will be forced to enter the fray."

"That's why we need to contact them," the SecDef said. "Before something happens and everybody starts lobbing ICBMs at one another."

Wizard shook his head. "You're making a big mistake."

"It's my call," the SecDef said. "Get me an open line to Vladymir Petyn."

Wizard glanced at Armstrong. Her face was pulled tight and she gripped her elbows like she was afraid her arms might fly away. Her expression said everything Wizard was thinking. This had just gone from bad to worse.

The SecDef pointed again at the phone. "Get Noble on the phone. Tell him that he's off this mission and he's going to be answering some tough questions."

Wizard picked up the phone and pressed redial, but it went straight to voicemail.

# CHAPTER SIXTY-THREE

NOBLE HAD HIS FOOT GLUED TO THE FLOORBOARD. His brow knotted and his stomach was a bundle of high-tension wires. The Slavuta rattled like a tin can in an earthquake and the temperature gauge fondled the redline. Black clouds from the tailpipe washed over the soldiers in their jeep.

The Ukrainians had closed the distance. They were less than ten feet from the back bumper. One of the troopers winged another bullet off the back of the car, blowing out a tail light. Lead connected with a heavy splat and Ezra winced.

"We gotta do something," he said. He had never been shot at before and his eyes were wide with terror.

"Get your hand off that dash," Noble ordered.

Ezra did as he was told.

In the center console the phone was buzzing.

Noble mashed the brake pedal to the floor. Tires locked with a howl of rubber. The front bumper did a nosedive.

The back end humped in the air, throwing Noble against his safety belt.

The driver of the jeep tried to swerve but was too close. Bumpers met with a loud crunch of metal and buckling plastic. The stolen Slavuta was thrown forward. Noble, already locked against his belt, took the jolt and managed to keep the vehicle moving, more or less, in a straight line. The front end weaved back and forth across the roadway, but Noble quickly got it under control.

Behind them, the driver of the jeep went face first into the steering column. His nose broke with a sharp crunch and blood spurted over his lap in bright red waves. The passenger lost hold of his rifle and the automatic went clattering over the highway into a shallow runoff.

Ezra's expression changed from terror to jubilation as the jeep swerved and rolled to a stop. The driver was knocked senseless, holding his nose in both hands while fountains of blood poured over his camouflage top. By the time the soldiers regrouped and got the vehicle moving again, Noble and Ezra would be long gone. Ezra's face split into a smile.

Noble was back on the gas and the needle was climbing up past fifty. The Slavuta was rocking back and forth now, letting out earsplitting bangs every few minutes. Noble said, "We're going to have to ditch this car."

"Why?"

"Those soldiers are going to call this in. Thirty minutes from now Ukrainian military will be crawling all over the countryside looking for this claptrap."

"What about Gwen?"

"We'll ditch it as close to the airfield as possible," Noble said. "How much further?"

Ezra consulted an app on his phone. "Maybe ten miles? Hang a left up ahead."

Twenty minutes later they jogged up to a chain link fence overlooking a small airfield. Private airplanes were lined up along one side of the long black tarmac strip and half a dozen hangars crowded the base of the tower. A sleek white jet with gold trim was lifting off from the runway. Noble grabbed hold of the diamond-shaped openings in the chain link with one hand and squinted. The craft lifted into the sky with a flash from twin engines and was soon lost from sight.

Ezra said, "Did you get the tail number?"

Noble nodded but said nothing.

# CHAPTER SIXTY-FOUR

GWEN SAT IN THE WIDE LEATHER SEAT, HER KNEES clamped tight and her arms crossed over her chest, listening to the sound of the twin engines as the Gulfstream streaked through the sky, bound for the unknown. Her belly was twisted tight and her heart was a freight train. Her hands shook so hard she had to tuck them into her armpits. Goose-bumps dimpled her skin and, without her glasses, the world was a blur.

The whole time they were on the runway she kept expecting Jake, that larger than life figure, to show up on the tarmac and stop the Gulfstream from lifting off. But the jet had taxied onto the strip, the engines climbed to a rumble, and the craft went speeding down the blacktop. When she felt the tires lose contact with the hot top, Gwen realized she was on her own. Totally cut off. The plane was in the sky and there was nothing anyone could do about it, not even Jake Noble. She was at the mercy of the man sitting across from her.

He had watched the takeoff with the fascination of a

child, leaning over to look out the window, a smile on his face. When they reached cruising altitude he said, "I always love that bit. It reminds me of man's triumph over nature. Fascinating to think we're speeding above the earth's surface at over five hundred miles an hour, isn't it?"

It wasn't fascinating at all. It was a simple question of aerodynamics and air speed. Rather ordinary and predictable when you understood the laws of physics, but Gwen didn't bother to tell Wexler.

He unbuckled his belt and excused himself, going aft to the lavatory while Gwen sat, listening to the engines, her mind working at a fevered clip. The wild idea of racing to the bulkhead door and throwing it open occurred to her. The sudden change in pressure would suck her and her kidnapper out. They'd go plummeting through the atmosphere to their deaths. That would put an end to Wexler, but deep in her heart Gwen knew she would never kill herself. She had the undeniable human urge to go on living, to fight for every last second. So she discarded the idea of crashing the plane and racked her brains for another solution.

Perhaps she could force a landing? She leaned close to the window and squinted but couldn't make out the ground. Forcing a landing in the middle of the Atlantic wouldn't work, and she didn't know how to force a landing anyway, short of storming the cockpit.

Wexler returned with a pair of tumblers full of amber liquid and gently clinking ice. He offered one to Gwen and she shook her head. She could smell the strong odor of whisky.

"Suit yourself." He shrugged and relaxed into the

leather seat, sipping at one glass, then the other. "More for me."

"What do you want with me?"

"Ah!" He nestled one of his drinks in the cup holders and reached into a leather satchel, pulling out a thick sheaf of papers. "I need you to finish putting together my little toy."

He handed the papers over. Gwen squinted. Like most nearsighted children, she had gone to school without her specs on more than one occasion, and found that she could see the board when she screwed her eyes down to slits.

Wexler asked, "What's wrong?"

"I can't see without my glasses," Gwen told him.

"What kind of a spy wears glasses?"

"I'm not a spy," Gwen said. "I'm an analyst."

Wexler leaned forward, invading her personal space and dropped his voice. "You do understand the science, yes?"

Gwen shuffled pages, doing her best to pick out relevant details. It was hard work. Lukyanenko had an untidy scribble and Gwen's knowledge of Ukrainian was practically zero. Thankfully most of it was in the universal language of math. And still it made little sense, but telling Wexler might get her shot. Instead, she pretended to study the pages in detail. She was more interested in why Wexler needed her.

The answer came to her in a flash. She said, "Lukyanenko is dead."

"You're a quick study," he said.

She handed the papers back, or tried to. Wexler refused

to take them. Gwen said, "I won't do it. You'll have to kill me."

He laughed, slipped into the seat next to her and put a hand on her knee. His fingers trailed up the inside of her thigh. "I won't kill you. I'll do much, much worse."

Gwen tried to press her legs together but he sank his fingers into her flesh and wrenched her legs apart. His smell, a cheap cologne, invaded her nostrils and hot whisky breath tickled her ear. "Now do you understand the science? Or not?"

Gwen looked again at the stack of papers. Her hands trembled so hard that the pages shook like someone had opened a window on the airplane. She swallowed a lump in her throat and nodded.

# CHAPTER SIXTY-FIVE

Ezra shoved Noble. The young analyst clenched his fists. His mouth was an ugly scar and his prominent Adam's apple climbed his skinny neck like a monkey scaling a rope. He snarled through clenched teeth, "You did this!"

Noble nodded. "Yeah, it's my fault and if you want to beat me up again you can, but right now I'm still the best chance you have at getting her back." After a minute he added, "I might be your only chance. The SecDef isn't interested in saving Gwen and if you think Armstrong is going to prioritize one analyst over the lives of millions, you're in for a nasty surprise."

That wiped the anger from Ezra's face. His expression softened and he turned back to the fence, threading his fingers into the diamonds. "What do we do now?"

"Find out where that plane is headed," Noble told him.

"How do you plan on doing that?"

"Let Langley do the heavy lifting," Noble said. "Have you got the phone? The basement dwellers should have no trouble tracking the bird."

"What about Gwen?" Ezra asked as he pulled the cell from his pocket.

"One thing at a time." Noble took the device and dialed.

Wizard came on the line after just one ring. "Jake, you'd better have some good news for us. It's your butt on the line."

He quickly brought them up to speed. The head of DHS said his people would track the plane and a Marine corps general pointed out that a craft that size could carry enough fuel to reach Miami or Washington DC.

"What if they've got the bomb on board?" The SecDef asked.

A furious debate started. Noble winced. Scared people make bad decisions and if the Joint Chiefs thought there was a bomb in the air, headed toward DC, they might do something rash. Noble had to raise his voice. "Director Dulles, can you hear me?"

The talk quieted and Wizard came on the line. "I hear you, Jake."

"Find out where that Gulfstream is headed. Cook and I will be on the next plane out."

"I'm afraid that's out of the question," Wizard said.

"What are you talking about?"

The Secretary of Defense came on the line. "You're off this mission, Noble. I want both of you on the first plane to DC. You've got a lot of explaining to do."

"Wexler has one of our people, one of *my* people. I won't abandon her."

"Let us worry about Ms. Witwicky," the SecDef said. "She's our problem now. I want you and Mr. Cook on the next flight to Washington."

Noble gripped the phone a little tighter and turned his face up to the sky like he might still be able to see the plane. A few black birds wheeled in the empty gray expanse. He said, "I want to talk to Director Armstrong."

"I'm here, Noble."

"Director, we need to find that plane."

"We will," Armstrong told him. "But right now, you and Cook need to get back to DC."

"What about Gwen?" Ezra demanded.

"We're going to do everything we can to bring her home safe," Armstrong said. "But as of right now, you two are officially off this mission."

"This is bull crap," Noble said, "and you know it."

The Secretary of defense barked, "What did you say, mister? Keep running your mouth and I'm going to bring you up on charges."

Armstrong cut in. "Jake, I don't like it any more than you, but the SecDef is running this now. You and Cook need to come home."

Tears were running down Ezra's cheeks. On the tarmac, a single engine Cessna was lining up for takeoff. The propeller sped up and the flaps worked, then the little craft nosed forward on the runway.

When he didn't answer right away, Armstrong said, "Noble, you and Cook need to come back to Langley for a debrief. I want to hear you say it."

He lifted the phone. "We're on our way back to Langley for a debrief."

"Good," Armstrong said. "We'll expect you..."

But Noble didn't hear the rest. He pressed the disconnect button and pocketed the phone.

"We can't," Ezra said. "We can't! We've got to save Gwen."

"Right now we have to get out of here," Noble told him.

"Why?"

Noble nodded to a pair of Ukrainian military transports trundling up to the front gate of the airfield, likely hunting for two guys in a beat-up Slavuta who had run their road-block. Noble took Ezra's sleeve and they backed away from the chain link toward the tree line.

## CHAPTER SIXTY-SIX

Wizard watched the Situation Room dissolve into chaos. The Secretary of Defense had put in calls to the presidents of both Russia and Ukraine. The tension between the two countries was now at a boil, ready to spill over into open violence. Russia was convinced the Ukrainians had hatched a scheme to destroy Russia with a single stroke and Ukraine was certain the Russians had kidnapped their scientist and were about to use their own technology against them, a technology they insisted they had been developing in secret to protect themselves against an openly hostile neighbor. If the Secretary of Defense had been hoping to defuse the situation, he failed. His actions had the opposite effect. Now both countries were threatening to commit troops to a ground war and the SecDef was scrambling to repair the situation. He was on the phone with Russia while the Secretary of State talked to the Ukrainian president. The SecDef paced near the head of the table, one finger plugged in his ear while he tried to placate the Russian president. The Secretary of State was in the opposite corner, listening to the president of Ukraine with wide, frightened eyes. Neither looked like they were having much luck. Meanwhile, the Joint Chiefs argued over the best course of action. Some of them wanted to blow the Gulfstream out of the sky. Others insisted they had to wait until it was in American airspace before they could do anything. But that was all dependent on finding the craft, and so far they'd had no luck tracking it down. Still others wanted to send military and police units to every airport in the country. The president had been on the phone twice. Airforce Two would land in less than an hour and he wanted to know who had made such a hash of things. He was not a patient man and folks in the Situation Room whispered that someone was going to be fired. Most people were too busy trying to insulate themselves from the president's impending wrath to bother dealing with the looming crisis of an EMP attack somewhere in the world.

Wizard watched it all with a cigarette in one hand and ribbons of smoke drifting up toward the ceiling in lazy little curls. He ignored the din of panicked voices and searched his memory banks for something just out of reach. He took a long drag, held it, and let the smoke out through his nostrils. "Wexler."

"What's that, Al?" Armstrong took a break from all the shouting and turned to him.

Wizard blinked, unaware anyone was paying attention to him and said, "Wexler. I'm sure I've heard that name before."

"Do you know where?"

He shook his head, tapped his temple with two fingers

and said, "It's just not as fast at making connections as it used to be."

Armstrong said, "This is going to hell in a hand bucket."

Wizard nodded but didn't speak. He was too busy trying to remember where he'd heard that name. Right now, more than ever, he needed to be in his office back at Langley, surrounded by his notes. He was certain the answer was there somewhere. He was about to get up and excuse himself when Trasker blew in through the door and shook his head in defeat.

He'd been trying to track the plane, to no avail. The local airstrip said the flight was bound for Hapsburg, but that was a short flight, only a few hours and no matching planes had landed anywhere in Hapsburg or the surrounding cities. Trasker pushed his way over to Armstrong and Wizard, dropped his voice and said, "The plane isn't anywhere in Germany. That much I'm sure of. We're checking the neighboring countries one by one, hoping to get lucky."

"Don't bother with Europe," Wizard told him. "The pilot doesn't want to be tracked. If he logged Germany as their destination, you can bet they aren't anywhere in Europe. I'd start looking in South America."

"You think that bomb is head for America?" Armstrong asked.

Wizard nodded. "Now more than ever."

"What makes you so sure?"

"Something about that name," Wizard told her. "Like I said, I've heard it somewhere before."

A frown creased her face. "You aren't chasing the boogeyman, are you Al?"

"He's no boogeyman," Wizard said. "He's flesh and blood and he's hell-bent on destroying the United States."

Armstrong shook her head and turned to Trasker. "We need to know where that plane went."

He spread his hands in a helpless little gesture. "We're doing everything we can. There's no tracker, so there's no way to know where they're going until they land."

"Forget about where they're going," Wizard said. "The pilot had to log the flight into Ukraine. Find out where the plane flew in from. They're probably going back to the same place."

Armstrong said, "That's good thinking, Al."

Trasker slapped himself in the forehead. "Geez, I never even thought of that. The plane had to come from somewhere. I guess the stress is getting to me. Sorry. I..."

"Never mind the apologies." Wizard took Trasker by the elbow and drew the younger man aside. "Soon as you find out where that plane took off from, I want to know. Text me on my cell."

"Sir..?"

Wizard gave Trasker a hard stare. "Text me on my cell. Understood?"

Trasker nodded, then glanced around the room. "You want me to keep it hush hush?"

"Just give me a head start."

"How much of a head start, sir?"

"As much as possible," Wizard said.

Trasker nodded. "I'm on it."

# CHAPTER SIXTY-SEVEN

GWEN WOKE WITH A SCREAM DYING ON HER LIPS. There was a shriek of rubber and a hungry growl from the twin engines. The nose settled and the Gulfstream slowed, making Gwen feel like she was being pushed and pulled at the same time. She sat up in her seat, the stack of papers slithering off her lap onto the floor, and rubbed sleep from her eyes.

How long had she been asleep? She had no idea.

They had been in the air more than three hours when Wexler told her to get some rest. "You've got a busy day ahead, luv."

Gwen had snorted and shook her head at the idea of sleep. She was hurtling through the air in a tin can with a terrorist. She had sat there, squinting at Lukyanenko's spidery scrawl until sleep crept up like a thief. Next thing she knew the plane was on the tarmac, rolling to a stop.

Beyond the windows, the sun was setting which mean they'd gone west. It had been afternoon in Kiev and hours later the sun was now setting on the opposite side of the world. The lush tropical jungle told Gwen she was probably somewhere in South America. The airport was the kind of rough dirt strip used by drug smugglers. It certainly wasn't a municipal airport. She pressed her nose to the glass in an effort to get a better impression of the blurry details. Mostly she saw fuzzy outlines of palm trees and what might have been an old Quonset hut.

*Colombia maybe?*

"Cuba," Wexler said in response to her unspoken question.

"Then America is the target," Gwen said, more to herself.

"Of course."

"Why?"

The plane was rumbling over uneven dirt toward a large hanger. The engines cycling down made a low hum in the body of the craft.

"I'm in it for the money." Wexler sat down across from her and grinned. His face was a big blurry moon in Gwen's vision. She wanted to kick him, but that would get her nowhere.

"What money? she asked. "Who would pay you to set off an EMP? The Iranians? Iraq? Saudi Arabia? Who do you work for?"

He smiled. "Wouldn't you like to know."

"I'm going to die," Gwen said. The words felt strange coming out of her mouth. "You're going to kill me as soon as I finish the bomb. Why not tell me?"

"Let's just say he's a man with a vision of the future."

"A vision of the future where millions of innocent people die."

"No one's innocent."

"Is that how you justify it?" Gwen asked. "Is that how you justify the cold, calculated murder of people you've never even met?"

"I don't have to justify it." He shrugged. "When this is over, I'll be rich. That's all that matters."

"You're disgusting."

"I prefer to think of myself as a pragmatist," he said. "If I don't do this job for the old man, someone else will."

She crossed her arms. "All those deaths are inevitable so you might as well make some money?"

"Exactly." He nodded his head. "You ever read Theodore Roberts?"

Gwen frowned. "The self-help guru?"

"He's an expert in Neuro-linguistic programming," Wexler said. "Not some cheesy late-night self-help fraud."

"If you say so."

"I read a lot of Roberts's work," Wexler went on. "His book, *Become the Giant,* changed my life. In it he talks about focusing one hundred percent of your energies on achieving your goals. My goal has always been financial independence. Not just rich, mind you, real financial independence. The ability to live life on my terms, nobody telling me what to do. I spent the last ten years working toward that goal."

He spread his hands to take in the plane. "Now here I am. Days away from wealth most people can only dream of. You see? I focused all my attentions on achieving my dreams of success, and it worked. A few days from now, I'll be my own master. No one to tell me what to do. So what if a few people have to die? Those people were never going to amount to anything."

Gwen unfolded her arms, leaned across and slapped him. Her hand cracked across his face with a sharp *pop!*

Wexler exploded from his seat, grabbed her jaw in an iron grip, and pressed her head against the headrest. She felt her teeth creak under the pressure and the breath caught in her chest. Wexler leaned in close. "Do that again and you'll regret it. Understand?"

Gwen couldn't move her head. She tried to convey obedience through her eyes. Wexler held her a minute more and then the smile came back to his face. He took her by the arm and pulled her to her feet. "Time to go."

The plane had eased under the shade of the hangar and the pilot emerged from the cockpit to lower the stairs. Wexler pointed at the fallen papers. "You'll need those."

Gwen bent down to pick them up and felt Wexler's hand on her backside. He said, "Behave yourself and I won't have to find ways to motivate you. Is that clear?"

Gwen stepped away from his hand, straightened up and nodded.

# CHAPTER SIXTY-EIGHT

Wizard stood in the Rose Garden with a cigarette in hand, but wasn't smoking. The Chesterfield had burned out and a long elephant's trunk of limp ash hung from the butt. He was trying desperately to remember where he'd heard the name Wexler. He stood, staring out at the profusion of red blossoms, bullying his brain for the answers, but his brain refused to cooperate.

"Not as sharp as I used to be," Wizard told the sea of roses. Getting old was hell. He lifted the cigarette to his lips. The rope of ash broke up and drifted apart. Wizard glanced at the dead butt, frowned, and flicked the filter into the nearest shrub. A gardener saw and gave Wizard a nasty look.

A low beat announced the arrival of Marine One. The Sikorsky VH-92A swooped in low and fast, coming in from the south over a line of trees. It touched down on the lawn with a hard chuck of rotor blades and the scream of the collective. A Marine Corp Sergeant hurried across the lawn, head down, one hand clamping his white dress cap to his head. He stopped at the door of the chopper, took up his position and saluted as the stairs came whirring down.

The president emerged, straightened up and his eyes travelled across the lawn. His wife had recently made changes to the landscaping, an act that sent the opposition into fits of rage, proving the utter ignorance and childishness of the president's opponents. Always wrong but never in doubt, is how Wizard often thought of them. Not that it mattered. They never questioned themselves or their tactics. It wasn't important who was right or wrong, so long as they were winning.

Wizard meant to intercept the president before he could reach the situation room and be influenced by his Secretary of Defense, but Trasker came hurrying out a side door.

He was breathing heavy. "Found it!"

"Good man," Wizard said. "Where?"

"It took off from Bern," Trasker said, "but never returned. I checked. It was nowhere in the area. That got me thinking about where it might have been recently and I did some digging. Over the last six months, it's been in and out of Cuba on a pretty regular schedule."

"Where in Cuba?"

Trasker gave a helpless shrug. "Still working on that."

"Anyone else know about this yet?"

Trasker shook his head. "Just you and I."

"Keep it that way." Wizard took out his phone and tapped out a message.

# CHAPTER SIXTY-NINE

WEXLER PULLED BACK A DUSTY TARP TO REVEAL A doomsday machine held together by a crude metal frame with ugly welds. At its center was a large centrifugal housing and a riot of colorful wires. The EMP had been built into the cargo bay of an old converted Airbus A310. Sunlight filtered in through small, dirt-streaked windows and a pair of generators farted clouds of noxious diesel fumes. The exhaust, mixed together with shafts of light, made for a drowsy experience, like a catholic church full of incense.

Gwen circled the device slowly, taking in all the parts. She was repulsed and fascinated at the same time. It was crazy to think that something so ordinary and uninteresting could change the fate of the world, could destroy nations and redraw maps. It could kill millions and, if Gwen did as Wexler wished, would do just that, taking the lives of countless Americans, most of whom had no idea what the letters EMP stood for.

Sometime in the late nineties the pentagon and CIA

had both warned government officials about the dangers of an EMP attack. The CIA even went so far as to call an EMP attack the greatest threat to American national sovereignty. Analysts had determined that a country like China might never risk open war with America, but would gladly attempt to destroy American infrastructure with a high altitude nuclear explosion that would knock out the power and leave America defenseless. Of course, those warnings went unheeded by politicians who knew nothing of EMP technology and could not conceptualize an attack which didn't involve fire and explosions. The idea that an enemy could knock out the power without causing any damage was something they had never experienced and, like most people, they were victims of the normalcy bias; unable to imagine something for which they had no point of reference.

Gwen reached out, almost touched one of the crude metal girders, and drew her hand back. She swallowed hard. Her heart was thumping gently inside her chest. She wanted to snatch a hammer from the workbench and smash it, but that would never do. Wexler would shoot her dead the moment she gave even the smallest hint of wrecking his little toy.

"Magnificent," he said. "Isn't it?"

"It's terrible," Gwen muttered. Her body was wrapped in a layer of sweat that had soaked through her dress and left her hair a frizzy mess. Thankfully there were no mirrors in the old Airbus. She reached for the end of a dangling wire and followed it back to its origins; it seemed to be part of the trigger mechanism.

Some of Lukyanenko's notes were making more sense

now, but she'd need time to sort it all out. This was way beyond anything Gwen had ever dealt with before. Her brow pinched and her lips pressed together.

"Can you finish it?" Wexler asked.

When she didn't answer right away he said, "If you can't finish it, then you've only got one use to me and my men."

"I can put it together," Gwen said. "But I'm going to need water."

He looked at the device. "Why do you need water?"

"Because I haven't had anything to drink in nearly twelve hours," Gwen said. "I can't think if I'm dehydrated."

"Of course," said Wexler. "Where are my manners?"

"You haven't got any."

He stepped closer and dropped his voice. "I'll have water brought to you, but mind your tone, luv. One more remark like that and I might decide to come visit you tonight."

Gwen shuddered at the idea.

Wexler put a hand on the back of her neck and rubbed. "Finish the EMP, and nothing bad will happen to you." His hand turned to steel and his fingertips sank into her flesh. "Toy with me and I'll make your life a living hell. Do you understand?"

Gwen tried to nod, but the muscles in her neck were on fire. She said, "I understand."

"Good." He let her go. "How long will it take?"

"A couple of days," Gwen said with a look at the half-finished device. "Maybe longer."

Wexler shook his head. Sweat had beaded on his forehead and he looked half deranged in the spill of light coming from the windows. He said, "Not good enough."

"Are you in a hurry?"

"We've got a *dead*line," he said and stressed the word dead, leaving no doubt in Gwen's mind what he meant. Finish it or else.

"Get me some coffee and I'll finish it in two days," Gwen said. She was probably over promising. It would take her two days just to decipher Lukyanenko's notes, but Wexler could only kill her once.

*He's not going to kill you,* a nasty little voice at the back of her mind insisted. *He's going to do much, much worse.*

Wexler grinned. "Cream and sugar?"

"Please," Gwen said.

"Anything else?" Wexler asked.

"A pen, some paper, and a good Ukrainian dictionary."

"The pen and paper is no problem. The dictionary might take a little more time."

"I have to translate his notes if I'm going to make this thing work," Gwen said. "You decide how fast you want it."

There was a hard gleam of hateful intent in Wexler's eye but it evaporated almost immediately and he smiled. "One Ukrainian to English Dictionary, coming right up."

He turned and stalked down the loading ramp, leaving Gwen alone with the bomb. She picked up Lukyanenko's notes and ran a hand through the mousy curls on her head, wondering where to begin. Wondering *if* she should begin.

# CHAPTER SEVENTY

THE LIGHTS WERE OUT IN THE ECONOMY CLASS section and most of the passengers were sleeping, or trying to. The big jumbo 747 hit a pocket of turbulence and the fuselage rattled. Beyond the windows, the sky was a mottled purple canvas, shot with streaks of deepest night. Ezra checked his watch, a cheap Seiko with Wolverine on the face. The comic book character's claws were pointing to midnight Ukraine time. Wexler's Gulfstream had lifted off over thirteen hours ago. They were probably already on the ground in Cuba. What would they do to her? Why had they taken her? He passed a hand over his face and then mussed his unruly mop of black hair. "I can't get the images out of my mind."

"I'm thinking about it too," Noble whispered.

Ezra didn't have to elaborate. Gwen was a girl. Wexler was a man. The rest was self-explanatory. Ezra's heart ached just thinking about it. That kind of trauma could wreck a woman forever.

He gripped the arm rests and his knuckles turned white. "We're going to save her right?"

"We're going to try." Noble sat in the aisle seat, his chin sunk to his chest and his mouth a grim line.

"I can't lose her, Noble. I can't."

Noble turned to face him. "We'll save her or die trying."

"Do you think they..."

"Don't go down that road," Noble told him. "That won't get you where you need to go."

"I can't stop thinking about it."

"Think about our next move."

"Which is?"

"We need to do a surveillance detection route as soon as we land," he said. "And then hit a weapons cache."

"That'll take time," Ezra said and his volume started to climb in the quiet aircraft. A fat man in the next aisle over snorted and shifted in his sleep.

Noble made a calming gesture. "We have to make sure the Cubans haven't got a line on us. We can't do anything for Gwen sitting in a Cuban jail cell."

"Alright, fine," Ezra said. Jake was right, of course, but the SRD would eat up an hour or two. He said, "But do we really need to hit a cache? That could take most of the day."

"We'll need guns," Noble told him. "Wexler is bound to have heavies guarding his investment. We can't take them on empty handed."

"Can't you, like, kill them with your bare hands or something?"

"This isn't a movie," Noble said. "It doesn't work like that. Besides, we're not even sure where they're holding her, yet."

"I've been thinking about that," Ezra said. "Cuba's a pretty small island and they'll be drawing a lot of power to build something as complicated as an EMP. It's unlikely they'll be anywhere near the large cities. They'll be someplace rural."

"Most of Cuba is rural," Noble remarked.

"We could use satellite imagery to pin point hot spots," Ezra said.

"That's good thinking," Noble said. "Soon as we get clear of the airport, and we're sure we're not being followed, we'll float that idea to Wizard."

Ezra nodded and they lapsed into silence. After a minute he asked, "Do you think we're going to be fired?"

"I think we're *already* fired."

Ezra accepted that without comment.

Noble probed the side of his head where Ezra had hit him with the gun.

"Does it hurt?" Ezra asked.

"Not really." Noble said. "Physical pain is not so bad as the hurt you get when you lose someone."

"Someone like Sam Gunn?"

Noble nodded. "Someone like Gwen."

"Think we can pull this off?"

"It's a long shot."

Ezra considered that for a moment and then said, "If anything happens, and you have to make a choice between me or Gwen, you save Gwen. Okay?"

Noble inclined his head and said, "The same. If you have a chance to save her, you do it. Don't worry about me."

"I wouldn't think twice about it," Ezra said.

A half smile tugged at Noble's lips. He rested his head

against the seat cushion and let his eyelids slip shut. "Try to get some sleep. You're going to need it."

Ezra settled back, but sleep eluded him. He kept thinking about Gwen. He was head over heels in love with her and, even though she didn't love him back, he would sacrifice everything to save her. He wanted her to live a happy life, get married, have kids. If that meant sacrificing himself, he'd do it gladly.

# CHAPTER SEVENTY-ONE

THE SINGULAR GROUP CONTAINED WITHIN THE Situation Room grew, fragmented, and eventually spilled out of the secure room into other parts of the White House as the crisis dragged on. Small knots of pentagon personnel and presidential cabinet members huddled together in the corridors, or gathered around tables in the White House Mess, speaking in whispers.

Wizard sat in a stiff-backed armchair outside the door to a men's room with his phone to his ear. His secretary was on the other end.

"I don't know, Al," she said in a plaintive voice. "You know I can't make heads or tails of this web you've constructed."

"Take your time and *look*," Wizard told her. "It's got to be there. I know it is."

"If you know it's here," she said, "where is it?"

"Top left corner maybe." He had a cigarette between his lips, but it wasn't lit, and a zippo lighter in hand.

"Why don't you come here and do this yourself?"

"Because I'm stuck here."

"I don't know what to tell you, Al. I don't see any... Wait a minute. I think I found him. The picture is black and white so it's hard to be sure, but he might be a ginger. Yeah... He kind of does look like Opie. Bit of a pug nose."

"That's him," Wizard said. "What notes are connected to him?"

"Real name Wilbur Wexler. No wonder he goes by his last name. Former SAS," she said. "He's part of a private security firm..."

"Global Solutions," Wizard finished for her.

"You've heard of them obviously."

"Private contractors owned by one of Otto Keiser's shell companies. They employ former Special Forces from all over the globe."

"There is a handwritten note here that says Wexler is the head of Keiser's personal security detail."

"Of course." It was coming back to him now. Wexler was a British ne'er do well who had an aptitude for explosives. He'd been drummed out of the SAS and gone to work for Global Solutions after a stint as a demolition contractor. Just the sort of fellow you'd want to oversee an operation involving advanced weaponry. Wizard said, "That's our boy. I want you to do a complete work up on him. I want to know everywhere he's been the last six months and I need it ten minutes ago."

"Any other *miracles* you need while I'm at it?" she asked.

"A fresh pack," he told her. "I'm almost out."

"Suffer," she told him. She had been bullying him to quit for years, buying patches and chewing gum, none of which worked. "I'll be there as soon as I can."

Wizard rang off and stuffed the phone in his pocket.

Armstrong had stepped into the hall, laid eyes on Wizard and said, "More bad news."

"What now?" Wizard pushed to his feet with a creaking of old joints.

Armstrong cocked a thumb over her shoulder in the direction of the Situation Room. "We tracked the Gulfstream to a small airport in Cuba."

Wizard flicked his lighter, then touched flame to his Chesterfield and said, "Tell me something I don't know."

"You already knew about the plane?"

He nodded. "Trasker tracked it down over thirty minutes ago."

"Why wasn't I told about this?"

"Insulation," Wizard said. "First thing you'd have done was tell the Joint Chiefs."

Armstrong shook her head. "Remind me to reprimand Trasker and then give him a commendation. Anything else you want to fill me in on?"

"You first," Wizard said. "You never gave me the bad news."

Armstrong lowered her voice. "The SecDef has almost convinced the president to make a first strike."

"Against who?"

"Cuba."

Wizard's brows bunched together over the bridge of his hooked beak. "They can't do that. For the love of God, they'll start a full-scale nuclear exchange."

"I agree," said Armstrong. "But you know how impulsive the president can be. We need some cooler heads in there."

"Tell them we've got boots on the ground," Wizard said.

Armstrong's eyebrows went up. "You didn't?"

He nodded and checked his wristwatch. "Noble and Cook should be landing any minute now."

"You're way out on a limb here, Al."

"What other choice do we have? The SecDef will be lobbing ICBMs across the Atlantic by this time tomorrow if we let him. Like you said, we need cooler heads. Tell them we have people on the ground already in Cuba and that they are actively searching for the device. They're our people and they need time to work. That should give the president pause."

Armstrong thought it over and nodded. "I'll see what I can do, but now it's your turn. What else are you sitting on, Al?"

"I found Wexler. He's one of Otto Keiser's personal bully boys. Former SAS with a background in explosives. He's the one running the operation, which means Keiser is pulling the strings."

Armstrong shook her head. "It always comes back to Keiser with you."

"Believe what you like," Wizard said. "Noble said the guy's name is Wexler. Keiser's head of security is named Wexler. That might be a coincidence but..."

"You don't believe in coincidence."

Wizard tipped his head in the direction of the Situation Room. "We'd better get back in there before some dummy convinces the prez to break open the nuclear football."

She held up a finger. "I don't want you breathing a word about Keiser. Understood?"

Wizard mimicked locking his lips and throwing away the key.

# CHAPTER SEVENTY-TWO

"You ever done this before?" Ezra asked.

They were two miles outside Havana, in a scrapyard full of rusted out car bodies, dilapidated machinery, and busted small appliances. The smell of tacky grease and oxidation filled the warm subtropical air. The sun was hanging low in a clear blue sky, a large red fruit ready to drop. Sweat stood out on Noble's skin, turning it to a sticky shell. He poked his head around a tottering mountain of rusted metal bands that had once been attached to oak barrels. Now they were reduced to a crazy lump of Medusa hair in a forgotten dump on the outskirts of a shanty town south of Havana. He said, "Many times."

"Is it always this hard to find?" Ezra questioned. He had his phone out, trying to pinpoint their exact coordinates, but the GPS capabilities on the average smartphone are only accurate to within a few dozen meters. He shook his head. "It could be anywhere in this area and we're losing the light."

"Don't let the enemy force you to move faster than you

can think," Noble said as he scanned the mounds of castoff junk slowly turning to rust.

"What does that even mean?" Ezra asked. The panicky edge was creeping back into his voice. After leaving the airport, they had spent over three hours on the streets of Havana, winding their way through the city like tourists, doubling back and cutting down cramped alleys to be sure they were not followed. Ezra had spent the entire time pressuring Noble to pick up the pace. He wanted to get down to the business of rescuing Gwen. Noble couldn't fault his thinking, but they had to do it the right way. Sticking their heads into the proverbial lion's mouth wouldn't do Gwen any good. First they needed weapons and that meant locating one of twelve arms and equipment caches the Company kept scattered around Cuba.

"It means if you go too fast you'll make mistakes," Noble told him. "And mistakes get people killed."

"If we don't move fast Gwen is going to get killed."

"They won't kill her." Noble shook his head. "Not yet."

"How do you know that?"

"Because they need her," Noble said. "Why else would they take a CIA officer hostage?"

"I hadn't thought of that," Ezra said. He shifted a refrigerator circa 1930 to look behind it, then pulled the latch and peered inside.

"It won't be anyplace someone might stumble across it," Noble told him and then, "I've been thinking long and hard about it."

"Maybe they want her as a bargaining chip?" Ezra suggested.

Noble shook his head. "Wexler wanted to know if she understood the science behind the EMP."

Ezra grabbed Noble's elbow. "You think Lukyanenko's dead?"

Noble nodded. "Or escaped somehow, but my money is on dead, and now they need someone who can finish the bomb."

Ezra's eyebrows went up. He cursed.

"My thoughts exactly," Noble said. "But Gwen's a smart girl. She'll take her time. She knows we're looking for her. She'll try to run out the clock, give us time to find her."

"She probably thinks you're dead," Ezra said.

"But she knows you're still alive and that you'd never give up on her."

A determined frown creased his face. "Let's find this cache then."

"It has to be someplace where the locals won't stumble across it," Noble said, surveying piles of junk in the waning light. "Someplace where it's not going to get moved or destroyed by accident."

"There." Ezra pointed.

Noble followed Ezra's finger and spotted a low cinderblock construction on the edge of the scrapyard with the universal signage for toilets spray-painted on the weathered walls.

They wound their way through the mountains of junk and a breeze carried the smell of rotting offal baking in the harsh tropical sun. Ezra made a noise of disgust and covered his nose with one hand. "What a wonderful smell we've discovered."

"Han Solo," Noble said. "A New Hope."

Ezra's brows went up. "You've seen Star Wars?"

"I'm not *that* old."

"I just didn't think you were the type of guy who watched science fiction."

"I'm more of a Star Trek guy."

"Of course you are," Ezra said, but Noble knew he'd gone up a few notches in Ezra's estimation.

They poked around the outside of the brick outhouse and then stepped inside, first the men's side, then the women's. The smell was an overpowering mix of human feces and boiling maggots. Flies buzzed and looped around their heads. Using the flashlight on Ezra's phone, Noble found a thin chain attached to the underside of the crude hole cut in the stone floor. There was a rough metal hook drilled into the concrete lip and, from that, slimy metal links trailed away into darkness. It would be nearly impossible to find unless someone was willing to stick their head down in the hole.

Ezra dry heaved and covered his mouth. "Great hiding place. Certainly no chance anyone is going to find it by accident."

Noble nodded agreement. His face bunched up against the odor and his stomach threatened a mass revolt.

"Get it out of there quick," Ezra said. "I'm about to be sick."

"It's your first time. I should make you do it," Noble said, but covered his mouth with one hand and stuck the other down through the opening. He gave an exploratory pull and realized he was going to have to use both hands. The cache was buried beneath a decade or more of human waste. Fighting a rising tide of bile creeping up his esophagus, Noble took the chain in both hands and strained against it, praying the rusty links wouldn't snap. Slowly but surely, he pulled the cache up from the depths and after a few minutes of hauling hand over hand, a PVC capsule popped loose from the sludge with a wet sucking noise. Noble fell back against the wall, breathing heavy.

"If we get out of this alive," Noble said, "remind me to find the joker who buried this cache and pay him a little visit."

"I'll hold his arms while you beat him," Ezra said by way of agreement.

"Let's get out of here."

Dragging it by the chain, Noble left the bathroom and started across the scrapyard. They were halfway to the chain link gate when they heard the sound of a motor.

# CHAPTER SEVENTY-THREE

WEXLER RETURNED TWO HOURS LATER WITH TWO large bottles of water and a Ukrainian to English dictionary printed out on loose-leaf pages. He put the water bottles on the work table and then carefully placed the heavy stack of pages down next to it. "Best I could do on short notice."

Gwen picked up half the stack and inspected a page at random. It had been printed from a cheap printer, and in a hurry. Pages were askew with occasional gaps where the ink jet had missed a line or two and some pages showed fading ink where the printer had run low on toner.

In truth, Gwen no longer needed the dictionary. Two hours alone with the device was more than enough to figure out what had to be done. Lukyanenko had been nearly finished when he died. The electromagnetic field generator was already in place. Lukyanenko most likely hadn't connected the rest of the wiring because he feared an accidental discharge or because he was hoping beyond hope that someone would come to his rescue. The EMP was, more or less, ready to go. All she had to do was connect a few wires to the trigger mechanism and set the relays, then activate the central power supply unit and it would be finished. Then Wexler would have no more need for her. She trembled slightly as she replaced the pages so they would not get out of order.

"Good enough?" Wexler asked.

Gwen nodded.

He spread his hands and smiled. "I'll let you get to work then."

She picked up one of the water bottles and twisted off the top.

On his way down the ramp, he stopped and turned. "Oh, I nearly forgot. I promised my men if you haven't finished in the next six hours, they can have their way with you."

Ice cold fingers wrapped around her guts and gave a hard squeeze. She felt like her knees would give out. All she could think to say was, "You wouldn't."

Wexler smiled. "Try me."

With that he stepped off the ramp and trudged across the dirt runway to the rusty Quonset hut.

Gwen put the bottle down and turned to the device. She ran one hand over her mouth while she debated where to start. She had the basic idea of how it all worked, but knowing where to attach the leads, and actually doing it, were another matter entirely. This was not the sort of thing you wanted to rush, unless of course you wanted an electro-magnetic burst. The device going off accidentally probably wouldn't kill her, even standing right next to it, but it might disrupt her brainwaves and that could have serious long-term effects.

She went to work. Sweat seeped from every pore on her body and the red dress was a limp rag clinging to her wet torso. Her hair was a curly haystack atop her head and her fingers trembled, but she selected a flat head screwdriver, narrowed her eyes so she could see, and picked up the first bundle of leads.

She was hard at it when a friendly voice asked, "How is it coming?"

# CHAPTER SEVENTY-FOUR

Noble stopped, feet rooted to the dusty ground. One hand gripped the chain and his heart tripped quietly inside his chest at the sudden sound of a motor. A splash of headlights poked through the debris. Tires crunched in gravel. The last of the Sunlight was just a rumor on the horizon. Overhead, the sky was a mottled tapestry of blues and purples. Blood thirsty swarms of mosquitoes were out in force.

"What are we gonna do?" Ezra wanted to know. His voice was barely above a whisper and his eyes were large silver dollars in the gloaming light.

The vehicle weaved slowly through the mounds, coming steadily closer. Noble grabbed Ezra's sleeve and dodged behind a tottering pile of broken down appliances in time to avoid being caught in the spill of the high beams. A rusted out pickup pulled into view, stopping with a squeal of worn-out brakes. The driver shifted into park and the doors groaned open. Two men in dirt-stained chinos and threadbare shirts climbed out.

"What's that smell?" the passenger asked in Spanish.

"Smells like your wife's cooking."

"I'll remember that the next time you need to borrow money, Ricardo."

Ricardo left the engine running with the headlights on and circled the front bumper. "You still owe me fifty pesos from last week's poker game."

"What are you talking about? I paid you three days ago."

"I don't remember that," Ricardo said.

"Who bought lunch after work on Wednesday?"

Ricardo and his friend went on arguing about money as they pulled on heavy work gloves and made their way around the mountain of castoff appliances. Noble and Cook edged away, Noble playing out the chain as they went so as not to make any noise.

Ricardo and his buddy were less than thirty feet from the PVC capsule now and Ricardo waved a hand in front of his nose. "That's awful."

"Si," his buddy said. "Think it's a skunk?"

"Even skunks don't smell that bad," Ricardo said. "Smells like someone took a massive dump."

His buddy laughed and they turned their attention to the mound of broken refrigerators and busted stoves. Ricardo pulled out an old toaster oven, turned it over in his hands, frowned and tossed it aside.

Ezra caught Noble's eye and shrugged his shoulders up in question.

Noble hissed beneath his breath. "Scavengers. Probably looking for copper."

Ezra breathed a sigh of relief and whispered. "Let's get out of here."

Noble motioned to the capsule. It lay at the end of its chain less than twenty feet from where Ricardo and his poker buddy were digging through the refuse.

"Should we leave it?" Ezra hissed.

Noble didn't even entertain the notion. He wasn't going up against armed terrorists with nothing but his wits. He chewed the inside of one cheek in thought. There was no telling how long Ricardo and his buddy would spend sifting the piles and sooner or later one of them would stumble over the PVC pipe. Noble warned Ezra to silence, took the chain in both hands and began to pull.

He went slow, drawing in the chain link one inch at a time. The PVC, covered in sludge, scraped gently over dirt and gravel. Ricardo and his friend had found a halfway decent oven which they manhandled into the back of the pickup, helping to cover some of the noise, then they were back at the pile, talking bull and pawing through the collection of junk. The capsule was less than ten feet from Ricardo and Noble slowed down even more, teasing at the chain so as not to make noise. It was like trying to reel in a fish without disturbing the water.

The chain got stuck on a sharp rock and Ezra winced. Noble had to wait until Ricardo unearthed a salvageable television set before he was able to shake it loose. Ricardo's buddy helped heave the old set into the bed of the truck and then said, "Did you hear something?"

"Just my back popping. That thing must weigh a ton."

"I thought I heard something." He glanced around the scrapyard.

"Probably rats," Ricardo said. "Come on. I think I saw a refrigerator we can use."

They went back to work and Noble went back to pulling. He didn't know what these two locals would do if they found a couple of Americans with a PVC tube covered in human excrement, and didn't want to find out. Best case scenario, they'd want a bribe in exchange for their silence, and neither Noble nor Cook had a ready supply of cash. Worst-case scenario, they'd call the cops. So he reeled in his fish until it was within easy reach.

"What are you waiting for?" Ezra whispered. "Go on and grab it."

"Why don't you grab it?"

Ezra took a moment to consider the tube and then said, "You're the field officer."

Noble opened his mouth to respond and stopped short. Ricardo had got hold of something sharp and let out a hiss.

"Is it bad?" his buddy wanted to know.

"I've had worse."

"Better get it cleaned out. You don't want an infection."

"When we've got a full truckload," Ricardo said.

Noble let out a resigned breath and reached for the PVC. His hands closed around the cold wet ends, fingers pressing into soft slime, and the smell filled his lungs causing his stomach to revolt. He took a minute to be sure the contents of his belly didn't come rushing up. He'd smelled his share of rotting mess, first in the Special Forces and then in the CIA, but this was something altogether different. This was old and decomposing fecal matter baked to ripe perfection by the tropical sun. Noble had to close his eyes and fight his gullet. When he'd finally mastered himself, he slowly stood up, wincing at the sound of popping knees, and followed Ezra out of the scrapyard, going quickly but quietly, trying not to make any more noise than necessary.

# CHAPTER SEVENTY-FIVE

Gwen looked up. She had a flathead screwdriver in one hand and grease smeared on her forehead. She'd pulled her hair back in a loose ponytail. The sun was gone from the sky and the landscape beyond the plane was a dark smear. Bright work lamps lit the cargo bay, accompanied by the steady chug of the generators.

A man was coming up the loading ramp, carrying a plate of food. Without her glasses, Gwen had to squint. He was a tall Middle Eastern man with a beard and a scar on one cheek. He spoke English with a polite accent and placed the food offering on one of the work benches.

Gwen adjusted her grip on the screwdriver and set her mouth in a snarl.

He smiled. "I'm not here to hurt you. I'm only interested in the device. Are you nearly done?"

Gwen glanced once more at the screwdriver, trying to decide if she had the courage to plunge the tool into his chest and make a run for it. Her knuckles turned white on the handle.

He gave a rueful smile and shook his head. "You'd never make it. As I told Lukyanenko, we are surrounded by forty kilometers of dense jungle full of deadly snakes and venomous spiders. And you haven't any shoes."

Gwen looked down at her dirty feet, put the screwdriver on the bench, and reached for the plate. Dinner was black beans and runny eggs. Gwen hadn't eaten in over fourteen hours. She scooped beans with her fingers and spoke between bites. "Are you the one who killed him?"

His eyebrows went up and he shook his head. "Doctor Lukyanenko died of a heart attack. An oversight on our part, I must admit. We had no intention of harming him."

Gwen swallowed. "You just kidnapped him and forced him to build a bomb."

"A necessary evil."

"Why?" Gwen asked. "Because a dusty old religious tome tells you to?"

"Again, you have me mistaken," he said. "I'm not religious zealot. I have an altogether different motivation for destroying America."

"What's that?" Gwen asked.

He studied her for a long moment, then reached into his breast pocket and produced a photo which he placed on the work table. The edges were dented and the color was starting to fade. There were smudges where he'd spent long hours holding the picture between thumb and forefinger.

Gwen said, "Your wife and child?"

He nodded.

"How did they die?"

"I was an interpreter," he told her. "I worked for the American military in Afghanistan, helping to combat the

Taliban. I was just a young man when your war on terror started. I believed in the Americans. I supported their mission against Al Qaida. I helped uncover weapons caches and exposed troop movements. For most of my adult life, I was a warrior in the fight against radical Islam. The others," he waved at the Quonset hut, "still refer to me as The Interpreter, a moniker I received from your Special Forces."

"What happened?" Gwen asked.

He picked up the faded photograph and his eyes filled with pain.

"When the Americans pulled out of Afghanistan, my family and I were left behind. Abandoned." His voice turned hard. "For twenty years I helped the Americans fight my own countrymen and when I needed help, America abandoned me. My wife and my little girl were slaughtered by the Taliban. I was forced to watch while they were raped, tortured and then set on fire. Taliban fighters gave me this for my years of betrayal."

He ran a fingertip along the scar.

Gwen put the plate of food down, no longer hungry. "I'm very sorry."

He laid a hand on the device. "This will be my gift to America for their betrayal. Your countrymen will learn the price for their double-dealing."

"Is this what your wife and child would want?" Gwen asked.

The Interpreter hit her with a backhand slap that rocked her head to the side. She sat down hard, bit her tongue, and tasted hot copper pennies.

"How dare you," he hissed. "Do not speak to me of my wife and daughter. How should I know what they would want? They are dead. All I know is what I want. And I want America to pay for killing my family."

Gwen wiped a line of bright red blood from her lips and in a small voice said, "It won't bring them back."

"No," he agreed. "But it will silence their ghosts."

He indicated the EMP. "Now please, do not let me distract you from your work."

Then he was headed back down the loading ramp and across the tarmac towards the Quonset hangar. Gwen watched him go. He was just a blur by the time he reached the bottom of the ramp. She palmed more blood from her lip and then picked herself up off the ground and reached for the screwdriver. Once again, she was tempted to break instead of build, but that would do her no good. They would hurt her until she agreed to finish Lukyanenko's work, and she had a nasty feeling these men knew how to make life very unpleasant. She choked back a sob and bent back over the bomb.

# CHAPTER SEVENTY-SIX

WIZARD HAD HIS HEAD TOGETHER WITH ARMSTRONG and Trasker when his secretary arrived. They'd gathered outside the door to the situation room, talking in whispers. General Moench hung around on the outside of the circle. The Marine Corp general had become a de facto liaison between the intelligence services and the armed forces. The Joint Chiefs, with the exception of Moench, were in favor of a preemptive strike, against who they weren't sure, but they wanted to take the fight to the enemy before terrorists could pop off an EMP a thousand miles over Denver and shut the country down. "If we're going back to the Stone Ages", they reasoned, "might as well take our enemies with us". It was a desire that, thankfully, the president was not yet ready to indulge. Most of the generals were arguing for an attack on Cuba, if not nuclear, then a full-scale invasion. Unfortunately, the presidents of Russia and Ukraine were now part of the equation and Russia made it clear that an attack on Cuba would be tantamount to an attack on Russia. Meanwhile the Ukrainian president was urging America to attack both Cuba and Russia without delay.

"We may have to move forward with an assault on Cuba," Armstrong said. Her hair was coming loose from the plastic clip and a few strands framed her face. She had dark bags under her eyes and tight worry lines around her mouth.

Wizard shook his head. "You'd have another Bay of Pigs fiasco on your hands."

"What do you want to do, Al? Sit here and wait for the lights to go out?"

"Give Noble time to work."

General Moench said, "One man against a terror group?"

"Noble has gone up against worse and come out on top," Wizard said. "Don't underestimate the kid."

"That *kid* as you call him is going to be facing serious consequences if he ever makes it back to the States alive," Moench pointed out.

"I doubt that's factored into his thinking," Wizard said. "I'll deal with Noble when the time comes. Right now, we need to figure out what we're going to do about this bomb."

"We know it's in Cuba," Moench said. "I have to tell you, the longer this goes on, the more inclined I am to side with the other Joint Chiefs. We need to move against Cuba, if not a tactical strike, then a ground invasion."

"That's a mistake," Wizard said and shook his head. "Wexler and his people might be in Cuba, but that doesn't mean they're supported by the Cuban government. Putting boots on the ground would be an act of war."

"What do you call using an EMP?"

"An act of war," Wizard said, "but not necessarily perpetrated by Cuba."

Armstrong said, "Never thought I'd see the day when you'd defend Cuba."

"The times they are a-changin'."

"Did you just quote Bob Dylan?" Armstrong asked.

"Is that who sung it?"

"Never mind the folk music," Moench said. "We need to come up with a game plan or the President might take the advice of my colleagues and start firing ICBM's."

"Do you think a Marine force could secure the island?" Armstrong asked.

Moench nodded his head. "No doubt in my mind."

"How long?" Armstrong asked.

"A few hours."

"I'm afraid I don't share your optimistic appraisal," Wizard said. "We tried that once already. It didn't go so well."

Armstrong said, "That was the sixties, Al."

"We've come a long way since then," Moench added. "Besides, that was a bunch of Cuban nationals on a godforsaken stretch of beach surrounded by Castro's army. This is different. This would be the full strength of the United States Marines backed by American air support. We could own that whole island in less time than it takes to get your oil changed."

Wizard put his cigarette between his lips and drew in a lung full of smoke. "And if Wexler manages to slip through the net? It would be easy for one plane to make it out in all the confusion. What then?"

"I think you underestimate us," Moench said.

Armstrong said, "This may be our best bet, Al."

"It would start a war with Russia that we can't walk away from."

"We have to do something," Moench said. "Otherwise this thing is going nuclear, and no one wants that."

Wizard's secretary chose that moment to appear, a file folder clamped under one arm, trapped against her overly large bosom.

"I may have the answer." Wizard nodded to her. "What did you find out?"

She held the file out to Wizard but Armstrong intercepted it.

"Wexler's company, Global Security Solutions, has leased four different properties in Cuba. Flight logs show them coming and going fairly regularly over the last six months, with most of the activity in the last three weeks. The plane has flown in and out of Havana twenty-seven times."

"That's a lot of security work," Wizard said.

"That's what I thought."

Moench's eyebrows went up as he listened to the exchange. "You found Wexler?"

Wizard inclined his head. "He works for Otto Keiser."

"The billionaire investor?"

"One in the same."

"You think Keiser is behind this?"

Armstrong flashed Wizard a warning look.

"All I know for sure is that Wexler works for Global Security Solutions and GSS is owned by a subsidiary of Keiser's hedge fund."

"Then he might be a rogue agent," Moench suggested.

"He's *probably* a rogue agent," Armstrong said with an edge to her voice. She passed Wizard the file and turned to the secretary. "This is good work. Now instead of the whole island, we only need to check these locations."

Moench said. "That's a lot of ground to cover."

"We'll start with the most likely spot," Wizard said as he brought out his phone.

"Hold on just a minute, Al." Moench held up a hand. "I've played along with your lone ranger act for as long as I can. This isn't a one man show. We've got credible intelligence. We need to take it to the President."

"That means looping the SecDef in and he's already made a hash of this," Wizard said.

"Be that as it may, there's a chain of command and we're going to follow it."

Wizard turned to Armstrong.

"He's right, Al. We've got to play ball. It's the only way to keep the President from launching a ground invasion, or worse."

Wizard took the page with the list of locations leased by Global Security and handed the rest of the file back to Armstrong. "You kids go play diplomat. I'll get Noble and Cook working on finding the bomb."

Armstrong took the file but her eyes were chips of ice. "Thin ice, Al. Thin ice."

# CHAPTER SEVENTY-SEVEN

Noble twisted the cap off the PVC pipe and set it aside. They had dragged the cache a quarter mile to a shantytown outside Havana where they found a spigot attached to a row of cinderblock housing units with corrugated metal roofs. This was the side of Cuba the recent influx of tourists never got to see, the run-down rows of dilapidated structures slowly giving way to time and the elements, populated by the poor and the destitute. Someone coughed and a dog barked in the distance. A farting pickup, maybe Ricardo and his buddy returning from their salvaging trip, came rumbling up the rutted dirt lane to the little village. The last of the light had slunk from the sky like a scolded dog, leaving a black canvas overhead, pierced with stars and racing clouds. The wind was coming up, gusting in strong, sudden bursts, carrying with it the smell of salt and brine. Noble, a Florida native, knew what that meant. The tropical storm would bring horizontal rain and enough wind to take the shutters off the little shantytown. The locals knew it too. The storm had sent them racing for cover. They were hunkered down inside their homes, doors closed tight and oil lamps burning against the darkness. It gave Noble and Cook an opportunity to use the local water supply.

They had rinsed the PVC capsule and then Noble got the worst of the filth off himself before opening the cache. Inside they found two tightly rolled woolen blankets, a satellite phone, over ten grand in local currency, a small collection of easily concealable burst transmission microphones, four blank passports, and a pair of field glasses, but no guns. Noble reached his arm down to the bottom of the capsule—the watertight threads had kept the inside clean and dry—and pulled out a half dozen rations.

"No guns?" Ezra hissed.

Noble shook his head.

"How is that possible?" Ezra wanted to know.

"Whoever planted this cache didn't think guns would be necessary," Noble said. "Most field officers go their whole career without ever using a gun."

"Well, we need them," Ezra said. "We can't go up against these guys without guns."

"It's not ideal," Noble said.

"That's the understatement of the year."

Noble ripped open one of the rations. He hadn't eaten since they left Ukraine. He nibbled the end off what might have been a meat patty, or maybe it was supposed to be potato. Hard to tell. His mind was ticking over the problem. He'd had a cold hard knot in his belly ever since Gwen was taken and now it had spikes. He was on his own in Cuba, his only backup a computer jockey and he had no gun. Noble couldn't think of a worse situation if he tried. He spoke around a mouthful of food. "We'll have to improvise."

Ezra sat back on his haunches. His face was a mask of worry. "How can you eat at a time like this?"

Noble passed him a ration. "You'll need your strength."

Ezra opened his package, took a bite and said, "These things give me the worst gas."

"It's the sugar alcohol," Noble said. "Probably giving you an ulcer as well, but they're great for a quick burst of energy."

"I'm surprised you knew that," Ezra said and then, "You're smart for a..."

Noble finished for him. "A field agent?"

Cook shrugged a little sheepishly. "We used to think all you field guys were just big dumb jocks. No offense."

"I used to think all computer ninjas were a bunch of weenies," Noble said. "You proved me wrong. You and Gwen both."

"You mean that?" Ezra asked.

Noble nodded.

They finished their field rations and Ezra wiped his mouth with the back of one hand. "There's a good chance one or both of us is going to die tonight, huh?"

"Try not to think about that..."

Ezra shook his head. "It's not like that. I'm not scared. I'm just crunching the numbers in my head. Two of us, unarmed, against an unknown number of hostiles. They'll be on guard."

"Long odds," Noble admitted.

Ezra sucked his teeth.

"Remember your training and you'll get through it just fine," Noble said. It was a lie. Plenty of guys did everything right and still went home in body bags. More often than not it came down to luck. But why tell Ezra?

Cook hauled in some air and said, "If I don't make it..."

"You will," Noble interrupted.

"If I don't," Ezra persisted, "tell Gwen I love her."

"She already knows."

"Yeah," Ezra said and drew the word out. "And I know she doesn't feel the same about me, but still, I want you to tell her."

"Fair enough," Noble said. "If I die, I need you to look up my mother for me."

"What do you want me to say?"

"Tell her..." Noble stopped to think. There was a lot to sum up and he needed to pack it all into a few words or Ezra might forget. "Tell her that I believe."

"What's that supposed to mean?"

"She'll know what it means," Noble said. "Just don't forget."

"I won't," Ezra assured him.

Noble grabbed the cash along with the blank passports. The rest could stay. He said, "Now we just have to find Wexler."

"I still like my idea," Ezra said. "Look for hot spots."

His phone started to buzz and Noble winced. They both looked around, expecting heads to appear from windows at the sound of a phone, but the wind helped cover the electronic warble. Ezra thumbed the talk button and Wizard came on the line.

His voice was broken and shot through with static. "I might have a location for you."

# CHAPTER SEVENTY-EIGHT

It took Gwen just four hours to finish what Lukyanenko had started, though she had no watch and no way of knowing how long she'd been working. It was dark outside and felt like she'd worked through the night. Her internal clock was telling her it was close to morning. In fact it was not yet midnight, but Gwen was exhausted. Her dress was ripped and stained, and her hair was a tangled rat's nest. She had a large greasy smear on one cheek and her fingertips were black, but it was done. Once she'd studied Lukyanenko's device, it was all rather simple, an incredibly easy and elegant solution to a rather complicated problem. Gwen envied the mind that had come up with such an incredible piece of machinery. She wondered at the output. Would it be enough to knock out power to the entire United States? If the numbers on Lukyanenko's notes were any indication, the answer was a resounding yes. And he had packaged into a housing no bigger than the average sedan. Gwen padded on bare feet, careful not to step on any loose screws, around the EMP, trailing dirty fingertips along the housing.

She fetched a sigh. Now that it was done, Wexler had no more use for her.

*Should have thought of that before you got caught up solving the puzzle,* Gwen thought.

No matter, she told herself. Done is done. It wasn't like anyone was coming to save her.

She went over and dropped down onto the narrow canvas cot, the same cot on which Lukyanenko had spent his last days, and put her head in her hands. Tears came, streaking down her cheeks in silent rivers. She had been so excited at the prospect of working with Jake. It had seemed like one grand adventure. But her adventure had turned into a nightmare and now she had reached the end. She thought about all the things she'd miss out on; marriage, kids, family. She couldn't even say goodbye. That thought brought up another freshet of tears. Her nose was running now, leaving large wet drops of snot on the floor between her bare feet. Strangely enough, the person she wanted to see most before she died was Ezra.

*And just what do you suppose that means?*

The question put a temporary stop to the tears while she considered the implications. Then she heard feet in the gravel and the tears dried up completely, replaced by cold hard fear welling up in her throat until she could barely breathe.

Her CIA training told her she had to do something, anything. They were coming to kill her and this was probably her last chance to save herself. She imagined sprinting down the ramp and into the jungle. Instead she sat with her butt rooted to the cheap cot, her guts turning to ice, and her arms trembling like live wires.

Wexler came up the ramp and looked first at the EMP, then at her. The Interpreter was at his side. Wexler checked his watch. "That's got to be some kind of record."

"Hurray for me," Gwen said without much enthusiasm.

He waged a finger. "You're a glass half empty kind of girl. Other people would appreciate the magnitude of this moment. You are now a key part of the history which will change the world. Doesn't that count for something?"

"You're psychotic."

"Potato, pah-tah-toe." Wexler gave the EMP an affectionate pat, like a man petting a faithful dog. "Think of it. The whole of human history is going to change. America will no longer be the dominate super power. No more big brother, looking over the shoulder of other countries, forcing everybody to play nice."

"And you think that's a good thing?"

"You ever read Robert E. Howard?" Wexler asked.

"Is he a philosopher?" Gwen asked.

Wexler laughed and shook his head. "He created Conan the Barbarian."

"The kid's comic book character?" Gwen asked, feeling that this conversation had taken a rather absurd turn.

"He's not a comic book character," Wexler said with an edge to his voice. "The Conan stories are mature stories."

"If you say so."

A terrible grin tugged at the corners of his mouth, like a puppeteer pulling strings, but the smile didn't touch his eyes. They were lifeless orbs in a grinning skull. He said, "Howard claimed that a peaceful society was an historical abnormality, that barbarism was the natural state of mankind."

"Sounds like he was crazy," Gwen said.

Wexler's savage grin only widened. "Howard was right. Look at history. Periods of peace are short and never last. War and struggle is the natural way of man. We've been killing each other since the dawn of time and we'll go on killing each other until Earth spins right out of its orbit."

"I guess Robert E. Howard will be happy," Gwen said.

"Sadly he's dead," said Wexler. "He blew his own head off in 1936."

"Maybe you should take a page out of his book."

He laughed as if she had told a particularly good joke and then clapped his hands together, rubbed them, and turned his attention to the EMP. He pressed the power button on the small control panel and a timer appeared. Wexler fingered the keypad.

"Three short hours," he said, turning back to Gwen. "And then the world is going to change. It's great and terrible to think about, isn't it?"

"It's murder," Gwen told him. "Plain and simple."

"Tomato, toh-mah-toe."

Wexler put his back against the EMP, propped his elbows on the cage like a teenager lounging against a hotrod car. His smile never faltered. "You've got a choice to make, luv."

"Yeah?" Gwen said in a dejected tone. "What's that?"

She expected him to ask how she wanted to die. Bullet to the back of the noggin or knife across her throat. Instead he said, "In a few hours I'm going to be insanely rich. You can come with me to South America and live a life of luxury, or you can go with my friends here,"—Wexler cocked his head at the Arabs—"and witness the beginning of the new era."

# CHAPTER SEVENTY-NINE

Ezra plugged the addresses into his navigation app as Wizard read them off. Lightning flashed across the sky and thunder boomed in the distance, causing Ezra to flinch. Noble, having grown up in the tropics, didn't even seem to notice. The wind was picking up, promising one hell of a storm, and messing with the cell reception. They had to ask Wizard to repeat the second address three times and it was clear the old man was getting frustrated. Ezra pinned the different properties on his phone's map. One was smack in the middle of Havana, which they discarded. Wexler and his men would never work on an EMP in the heart of the city where someone might stumble across their operation. That left three addresses, all were miles apart.

"You need to recon those locales," Wizard said. "And, Jake, you need to do it fast. The Joint Chiefs are pushing for a first strike initiative. They reason it's better to take out our enemies before they get a chance to do the same to us."

"Easier said than done," Noble told him, looking at the

pins on Ezra's screen. "These locations are in opposite directions. It's going to take all night."

"You haven't got that long," Wizard told them. "The President wants a plan of action. Right now the Joint Chiefs are the only ones with anything solid. All I've got to offer is two field agents with no solid leads. The President's not going to sit on his hands and wait for America to be plunged into the dark. No politician wants that to be their legacy. They want action."

Noble said, "We need to narrow down our list of target sites."

"If you can think of a way to do that, I'm all ears."

"Use satellite imagery to check the heat signatures on these addresses," Noble said. "Building an EMP would require a large power output. The heat signature should be off the charts, and in a backward country like Cuba, that's going to stand out like a sore thumb on thermal."

"That's excellent thinking, Jake."

Ezra scowled.

Noble winked at him and said into the phone, "Thank you, sir. I do my best."

In the end it was a forty minute delay while Wizard sent the request back to Langley and the IMGINT people went to work on the satellite feeds over Cuba. Lightning continued to blaze hot forks across a black tapestry and thunder shook the tin roofs of the shantytown. The island seemed to be holding its breath in anticipation. Noble and Cook found a simple lean-to with a mangy dog cowering in one corner. They sheltered next to the mutt and Noble absently scratched the pup's head with one hand while they waited. The dog's eyebrows twitched with worry and it put one paw on Noble's leg, a doggo's way of saying thanks for keeping me company, pal. Noble opened another ration for the mutt.

Wizard finally came back on the line and said, "Your bet paid off. We've got one location, the one south and west of the sugar cane plantation, giving off all sorts of heat. IMGINT people say it looks like they've got two industrial-sized diesel-powered generators going round the clock."

"That's got to be the place," Noble said.

"Jake," Wizard said, "our people wanted me to let you know that there's a storm bearing down on you."

"Tell me something I don't know."

"It's a category two hurricane and it's going to slam Cuba within the hour."

Ezra groaned.

Noble just closed his eyes and took a deep breath.

"And Jake?"

"Yeah."

"Good luck, kid."

"Thanks," he said. "I'm going to need it."

Ezra hung up the phone, examined the map and said, "That's over twenty miles from here." Thunder peeled and he added, "And it's about to start pouring rain."

Noble pulled out the stack of Cuban currency. "Let's go see if Ricardo and his buddy want to sell their truck."

# CHAPTER EIGHTY

GWEN STOOD THERE IN HER SWEAT-STAINED DRESS, now a limp gray rag held up by spaghetti straps. One shoulder had fallen down and she pushed it absently back into place. Wexler was a giant red-headed monster, towering over her, a slavering troll out of some fever induced nightmare. He grinned at her and said, "What's it going to be, luv?"

Gwen thought her legs would collapse, that her knees would just come unglued and she'd go down on the floor in a howling, half-mad heap. She heard the words come out of her mouth and it was as if she was watching herself from the outside. "You want me to come with you?"

"You're cute, in a girl next door kind of way," he said. "And I'm about to be insanely rich. You'll want for nothing. We'll travel the world, go anywhere we want, live a life of luxury. What do you say?"

"You want me to come with you?" Gwen said again as if he'd asked her to eat a rat liver with a side of goat intestines and a glass of cat piss to wash it all down.

"You could do a lot worse," Wexler said. He was closer now. Gwen didn't know how it happened but he had closed the distance between them and he trailed his fingertips along the bare skin of her shoulder, sending an icy shudder walking up her spine, like someone had just walked right over her grave. She tried to imagine, as an academic exercise, herself with Wexler, tried to imagine his naked body on top of her, and her stomach twisted so violently that she fought back a hot copper surge climbing her throat.

She said, "Not if you were the last man on earth and I were the last women. You disgust me! You're a selfish, twisted, ignorant, murdering man child with a god complex. You need to be locked away in a padded cell somewhere. I'd give myself to a gangrenous leper before I'd give myself to you!"

He caught her by the arms and gave her a rough shake. Her head went back and forth on her neck like a bobble-head doll. Wexler growled. "Think again, luv. It's me or him." He jerked his head at The Interpreter. "And that's a one way trip."

Gwen had never been so terrified in all her life, forced to choose between this ogre of a man and a suicide bomber. Wexler meant life and where there was life there was hope, but Gwen could never give herself to a maniacal murdering sociopath, even if it meant buying herself a few more days, and that's all it would be. With her heart trip hammering painfully hard and her tummy full of battery acid, Gwen worked up her courage and spat in Wexler's face.

The spit landed on his cheek, ran down and dribbled off his chin.

He stopped, stunned, still holding her by the arms. He blinked slowly and he let her go, mopped his face with his sleeve, then he hit her with a backhand that echoed around the open cargo bay.

The blow took her by surprise. Pain exploded in her vision, a bright yellow firework inside her skull, and she felt the floor come up to meet her. She landed on her side, the dress riding up over her hips. A hundred angry bees were swarming over her cheek, stinging gleefully wild. She put a hand to her face, tried to open her mouth, and for a moment her jaw refused to work. *He broke my jaw,* she thought wildly, *he broke my jaw and I can't even open my mouth to scream!*

But the muscles finally hinged open and she let out a hitching sob. Her jaw wasn't broken but she'd have a large purple welt if she lived through the night, which she doubted.

Wexler took a step back and turned to The Interpreter. "Guess she's made her decision."

The Interpreter clasped Gwen by the arms and pulled her to her feet. One spaghetti strap fell over her shoulder and the material slithered down, revealing one white globe topped by a pink nipple. Gwen tried to fix it, but he had a hold on her arms and wouldn't let go.

"This is goodbye," Wexler said. He took her face in a large work-calloused hand and planted a kiss. His lips mashed up against hers, his teeth forcing her mouth open and his tongue darted out. Gwen struggled to get loose, tried to pull her head away, but the Interpreter held her fast while Wexler shoved his tongue, a sticky wet slug, down her throat. In desperation, Gwen bit down on his bottom lip and tasted a hot spill of blood.

Wexler gave a high-pitched scream, totally out of place for a man of his size. He reeled, cupping a hand over his bleeding mouth. Dribbles of bright red coursed down over his chin and landed on his shirt. Wide, dangerous eyes bored into Gwen with white-hot hate. His face turned into a mask of fury. His fist came up, large and clenched.

Gwen moved her head at the last second and saved herself from being knocked out cold. His knuckles glanced off the side off her forehead, just above her left eye, ringing a bell inside her skull that would still be ringing a week from now. Psychedelic lights danced in her vision and her knees really did give out this time. The Interpreter was the only thing keeping her on her feet. All the muscles in her body went limp and it was several seconds before she could get anything working. Sounds came from her throat but they were just simple sounds, drawn out vowels, like a child first learning to talk. Her eyes rolled back in her head and she nearly slipped into the black but came clawing back to consciousness with a heroic effort and, once she was back, she wondered why she had fought to hold onto wakefulness. The blackness had promised sweet release. There was only terror and pain up here. But she was awake and scared and there was nothing to do but survive the next few moments.

Wexler palmed blood from his chin and snarled, "Lock her up."

The Interpreter pulled her toward a luggage cage in the far corner of the cargo plane.

Wexler started shouting orders at the others. "I want this plane off the ground in fifteen minutes."

Beyond the open cargo bay door, the winds were picking up. Palm trees swayed in violent gusts and fronds went whipping through the air. A fork of lightning split the sky.

## CHAPTER EIGHTY-ONE

WEXLER PUT A HAND TO HIS LIP. HIS FINGERTIPS CAME away bloody. The girl had taken a real bite out of him. The salty smell of ocean and brine mingled together on a breeze that tugged at his collars. He turned his head to the side and spat a wad of pink into the tall weeds on the side of the dirt landing strip. Lightning flashed overhead. The small hairs on his forearms stood at attention. Wexler stomped to the open door of the twin engine Gulfstream and climbed the stairs.

The pilot said, "We need to go now if we're going to beat the storm."

"Get us in the air," Wexler told him.

The pilot reached for the controls that would raise the stairs but Wexler said, "I'll do that. You fly the plane. We need to clear the runway so they can take off."

The pilot disappeared into the cockpit and the engines came to life.

Wexler spared one last look at the hulking cargo plane before closing the hatch on the Gulfstream and settling down into one of the wide leather seats. The jet was already taxiing as Wexler took out his phone and placed a call. "It's done. The package will be in the air in fifteen minutes."

"Well done, my boy," Keiser said. "The money will be in your account before America ceases to exist. Have you got an exit strategy?"

"I'm on my way to Argentina right now," Wexler told him.

"Careful what you say on the phone," Keiser warned.

"What does it matter?" Wexler said. "The only people who can do anything about it are going to be sitting in the dark in..." He consulted a Longines timepiece strapped to his wrist. "Roughly three hours."

"At long last." Keiser was quiet for a moment and then said, "Still, we can't have any loose ends."

"I'm one step ahead of you," Wexler told him. "I've arranged for my pilot to have an unfortunate accident shortly after we land in Argentina."

"Good boy," Keiser said. "As a thank you for all your hard work, I've put an extra million into your account. We won't speak again. This is goodbye."

"It's been my pleasure, sir," Wexler said. "And if I may say so, I think of you like a father."

"Yes, well," said Keiser. "Thank you very much Wesley for your faithful service."

The line went dead and Wexler sat there gripping the phone. The bastard didn't even know his name. It was a bitter pill to swallow. He thought about going to Bern and putting a bomb on the old man's gas tank, blowing him to hell, but what was the point?

Wexler shook his head. No matter. He was rich. More

than rich, he was loaded. He never had to take another order again. From now on, he'd be giving the orders. He grinned as the Gulfstream lifted into the air with a hungry growl from the jet engines.

# CHAPTER EIGHTY-TWO

"WE CAN'T TAKE OFF IN THIS WEATHER," NASIR WAS saying.

"I don't care about weather," Khan fired back.

They were in the cargo bay; the loading door was still open and they'd strapped the EMP to the bulkhead to make sure it didn't shift during takeoff. Rain had started to fall. Large wet drops hammered the body of the aircraft. Thunder boomed and streaks of lightning flashed across the sky, momentarily illuminating the muddy ground beyond the open door.

"All this rain will turn the runway to mud. That's going to slow us down," Nasir said. "I'm not sure we can lift off. We have to wait."

Sahem stepped forward, fists clenched. "He's lost his nerve."

"I've lost nothing," Nasir fired back. "If we crash on takeoff then we will have sacrificed ourselves for nothing."

"Unbelieving dog," Sahem snarled.

"We must wait for the rain to clear, brothers, if we wish to be certain of success."

Khan pulled a handgun from the holster at his hip and pressed the barrel against Nasir's forehead. "If this plane is not in the air in the next ten minutes, you will die, brother. Do I make myself clear?"

Gwen gripped the metal bars of her cage and watched the interaction with bated breath. For one hopeful moment she was certain The Interpreter would kill the pilot in a fit of rage.

Nasir lifted his hands in surrender and backed away. "You're making a mistake."

"It is mine to make," Khan said. "Now get this plane in the air."

"It's on your head, brother."

Khan stuffed the gun back in the holster. "So be it."

Nasir went forward while Khan worked the controls for the cargo door. The motor came to life with a whine and the ramp slowly lifted out of the mud with a wet sucking sound. Gwen's last look at the outside world was cut off as the ramp sealed against the bulkhead with a hollow thump.

Khan turned to the device and smiled, glanced briefly at Gwen, then told Sahem, "Stay with the bomb. Make sure the white devil does not try anything. She has a crafty look about her."

Sahem nodded and Khan followed the pilot forward. The sound of the engines climbed several octaves and then the plane was moving, doing a wide turn to square up with the long muddy airstrip.

Gwen closed her eyes, rested her forehead against the cold bars and prayed the wheels stuck in the mud.

———————

The pickup died three hundred yards from the airfield with a loud clanking of gears. Rain streaked the windshield in heavy sheets. There was a harsh grinding, followed by a muffled bang and the truck rolled to a stop with thick white plumes of smoke wafting from the grill.

The glow of towering arc-sodiums rimmed the trees beyond a sugar cane plantation, artificial daylight bled into the dark sky, like glimpsing light from a baseball field across a quiet neighborhood. Noble knew they were close. He cursed and threw open his door. A spray of salty ocean air attacked his cheeks. The wind was picking up, causing the crophead to dance and sway. The large stadium lights caught the rain as it fell, turning drops into winking diamond spears.

"We're on foot from here," Noble said.

He and Ezra raced through a thick hedge of sugar cane, cutting straight across the field. The towering plants were ready for harvest and long blades of grass whipped at their faces, slicing unprotected skin. Noble ran with one arm up to keep the grass from cutting his cheeks. His breath came in ragged gasps and his feet felt like lead weights. He pumped his legs until his thigh muscles burned.

There was a sharp snap. Ezra let out a shriek and went down hard.

Noble skidded to a stop. "You okay?"

"I'll be fine." Ezra was on his side, struggling to rise. His face was pinched. He'd stuck his foot in a rabbit hole and twisted his ankle.

Noble grasped his hand and pulled him up. "Think you can walk on it?"

"I'm good," Ezra said, but screamed when he tried to put weight on it.

Noble pulled Ezra's arm over his shoulder and together they hobbled through the field into a thick stand of trees as fast as they were able. The ankle was swelling up like a softball and Ezra's face was pale, but he didn't voice any complaints, just limped along on his good leg with his teeth grinding together.

They were close enough to hear the low rumble of airplane engines. Ezra clung to Noble like a drowning man to a life preserver and they crashed through the underbrush, branches clawing at their faces, until they burst from the trees onto the edge of a rough landing strip cut from the forest. Noble was staring across at an Airbus A310 preparing for takeoff. The twin-engine wide-body had all of its running lights on and made a slow turn, squaring up with the hardpack. The runway was the kind of strip used by drug smugglers in the wilds of Colombia, just a long stretch of hard-packed earth cut from the jungle. A pair of weathered Quonset huts hunkered at one end of the runway, flanked on one side by empty fuel barrels.

"That's the plane, right?" Ezra panted. "That's got to be the plane. Right?"

"Who else would take off in the middle of a storm?" Noble said.

"How do we stop it?"

Noble hunkered at the tree line, deep in thought. Water dripped from his nose and chin. Thunder peeled and the flash that followed illuminated the body of the aircraft. Noble's fists clenched and his fingernails made half-moons in his palms. "*We* don't," Noble told him. "I do."

Ezra said, "I'm going with you."

"Ez, I have to get on the plane in order to stop it." Noble had to yell over thunder and pouring rain. "There's a good chance I won't be getting off."

Ezra grabbed a fistful of Noble's shirt. "I don't care."

"I can't run and carry you," Noble said.

Ezra pushed to his feet and set his weight on the injured ankle with a grim frown. "I'll be right behind you."

Noble chewed the inside of one cheek, then nodded. "First call Wizard and give him the tail number."

"In case we fail?" Ezra asked.

Noble nodded.

Ezra brought out his phone and tapped in the message, praying the text went through.

"Last chance to back out," Noble said.

"No way."

Noble offered his hand. Ezra shook it.

"Let's do this," Noble said.

They hurried across the open ground, Ezra limping the whole way, until they were under the wing of the craft. The big cargo jet started to pull forward as they reached the landing gear. Noble laced his fingers together, making a saddle for Ezra. The little guy stuck his good foot into Noble's hands without stopping to question, and Noble boosted him up. Ezra latched onto the strut and pulled himself up into the wheel well. Noble had to jog in order to keep up. Once Ezra was inside, Noble sprinted alongside the lumbering cargo jet as the big rubber tires picked up speed, throwing water and mud. For one terrible moment Noble thought he'd fall behind. He lunged and caught hold of the landing gear. His feet dragged along in the wet and he nearly lost a shoe, then he was pulling himself up, hand over hand, into the body of the craft.

# CHAPTER EIGHTY-THREE

"You can't shoot that plane down," Wizard said. He and Armstrong were in the Situation Room trying to talk the SecDef out of a missile strike on the cargo jet. A pair of F-18 Super Hornets had already scrambled from MacDill Air Force Base in Tampa Florida. One of the television screens showed Hurricane Cassie as it swept up through the Lesser Antilles toward the west coast of Florida. Another screen showed the president. He was giving a statement about the expected impact of the storm, promising relief to the citizens of Florida.

"The hell I can't," the Secretary of Defense said.

Armstrong said, "Three of my people are on that plane."

"There's a bomb on that plane capable of knocking out the entire power grid," he shot back.

"Let my people do their job," Armstrong argued.

"And just what in the hell do you expect me to tell the President if your people fail?" The SecDef had his fists on his hips. His normally well-kempt hair was a mess. He had stubble on his chin and worry lines around his eyes. "What if they fail? You want me to tell the President, sorry about the millions of people who are going to die. We thought the CIA's people could handle it."

"At least give them a chance," Wizard said. He was all out of cigarettes and needed a smoke badly.

"Is this the same Jake Noble who led the rescue team to save Fatemeh Madani?" The SecDef fixed Wizard with a hard stare. "I did my homework on this Noble character. He's a bit of a loose cannon. He got tossed out of the CIA's Special Operations Group a few years back and he was the only one who survived the mission into Iran. His entire team got wiped out. And you want to hang the fate of the nation on this guy?"

Wizard said, "The rescue mission was compromised by someone on the Intelligence Select committee. The fact that Noble survived is exactly why you should trust him. He lived when everybody else died. That kid finds a way to win even when the deck is stacked against him. And, I might add, he managed to save Fatemeh."

"Hardly a stellar recommendation," the SecDef said.

Armstrong held up a hand for peace. "At least give him a chance."

The SecDef turned to the television screen. The muscles at the corner of his jaw bunched tight. His eyes were hard slits. He said, "Noble has until that plane reaches the Keys and then we shoot it down. If we have to blow it up, I don't want it going down over land."

# CHAPTER EIGHTY-FOUR

Nasir buckled himself into the pilot seat and checked his dials. He had been through his pre-flight checklist twice already, but did it a third time, hoping the weather would slacken while he made the necessary safety inspections. He was not afraid to die, he had prepared himself for this day, but he *was* afraid to crash the plane on takeoff. And with rain coming down in horizontal sheets, a muddy runway, and a hoggish cargo jet, he was likely to do just that. The Airbus was aptly named, it was much like trying to fly a bus. The controls were slow and sluggish and getting the big fuel hog off the tarmac was a challenge under ideal circumstances. With foul weather, Nasir would consider himself lucky just to clear the trees. He wiped a bead of sweat from his forehead, cycled up the engines and curled shaking fingers around the stick, thinking he might be afraid to die after all.

The cockpit door banged open and Khan filled the frame. "What's taking so long?"

Nasir resisted the urge to snap at the traitorous Interpreter. The man had spent two decades working with the Americans against his own country, against his own people, and now he had a chance at paradise. It didn't seem fair to Nasir, but then no one ever said God was fair. He turned in his seat and spoke calmly. "If you'd rather fly the plane, you are welcome."

Khan's nostrils flared. He knew less about flying than he did about bombs, which is why they'd been forced to rely on the German banker and his hired thug. Khan said, "We're running out of time."

"Then you had better sit down and strap yourself in," Nasir told him. "It's going to be a bumpy take off."

"Just get us in the air," Khan muttered and closed the cockpit door.

Alone again, Nasir eased up on the throttles. He felt the big cargo jet start to slog through mud, slow at first, then picking up speed. The windscreen was a wet blur. Floodlights on the wing tips did nothing to illuminate the dark landscape. The plane hurtled down the hardpack runway—Nasir had to fight the controls to keep it from drifting side to side—toward the line of swaying palm trees in the distance. The engines climbed to a fevered pitch and the yoke shuddered as the tires raced along the muddy track. For one terrible moment Nasir felt the craft would slide right off the runway, but he pushed hard to starboard and the plane held course. He could feel the flaps fighting against the heavy downpour. The nose wanted to lift up, but mud was sucking at the tires, slowing him down and the line of trees was coming up fast. Nasir jammed the throttle all the way up. The jet engines gave a scream and the nose finally pulled free of the muck. Rain lashed the windscreen, obscuring his view, but Nasir made out the dancing line of treetops against the night sky coming up fast. Too fast. Sweat poured down his face in large wet drops and landed on his shirt. His feet shivered, making the pedals hard to control. The altimeter rose reluctantly. A line of jungle filled his vision. Nasir's mouth opened wide, ready for a scream, then the cargo jet was up and over and Nasir thought he heard tree tops scrape the underside of the fuselage. A minute later they were lifting into the air with their deadly cargo.

———·———

Noble's shoulders drew up around his ears as the tire took the head off a palm tree with a meaty snap. He and Ezra were crowded into the cramped compartment of the port side landing gear, clinging to the bulkhead while the jet hitched and lurched through the air, struggling for altitude. Wind and rain swirled up into the space with a hollow sound, like the lips of God blowing into the world's largest pop bottle. Rain stung Noble's unprotected skin and rushing wind turned his shaggy hair into a funnel. Ezra's face was a pale globe. His eyes were shut tight and his knuckles were white on the cross girder. His mouth moved but Noble couldn't hear what he said.

Hydraulic motors whirred to life and the landing gear folded up into the compartment, taking up most of the space, forcing Noble back against the fuselage. The hatch closed with a soft thump, sealing out the rain and cutting off the horrible rushing noise. The only light now came from a small red emergency bulb.

Ezra's face was lit by the lurid red glow. He spoke between breaths. "I thought we were finished."

"You and me both." It was another minute before Noble convinced his fingers to let go of the cross girder.

The sound of the storm was deafening against the body of the craft and they had to raise their voices to hear. Ezra said. "So how do we get out of here and into the plane?"

"I'm not sure exactly."

Ezra turned to him in the dark. "What do you mean?"

"I'm not familiar with this model aircraft," Noble admitted.

"That's just great," Ezra said. "We're stuck in the wheel well of a plane."

"Relax," Noble told him. "There has to be an access hatch in case the landing gear fails. We just have to find it."

Ezra took hold of Noble's shirt sleeve. "You can fly this plane, right Noble?"

"I know how to fly."

"But can you fly *this* plane?"

Noble shook his head. "I've never flown one of these before."

Ezra cursed.

"It's a lot like riding a bike," Noble said.

"That's not true at all," Ezra spluttered. "Being able to fly a single-engine Cessna doesn't qualify you to fly an F-14!"

"You're right," Noble said. "I was just trying to make you feel better."

"You failed!"

"But I did find the hatch." Noble pointed to a narrow trap door set in the ceiling directly above the large rubber tire covered in mud. To reach it they would have to shimmy over the landing gear itself.

"That's something at least," Ezra said and then his phone was ringing.

It was a moment before either man heard the electronic jingle over the rushing wind. Ezra had to cork a finger in his free ear and yell. "We're inside! ... They what? ... Tell them not to do that! We're inside the plane..."

He lost the signal and looked at up at Noble, who was already straddling the landing gear, working on the access hatch. He said, "I think they're going to shoot the plane down."

"When?"

"Not sure," Ezra admitted. "The reception was piss poor, but I think I heard something about shooting the keys. That make any sense to you?"

"Probably going to shoot us down as soon as we're over the Florida Keys," Noble said. "That doesn't give us a whole lot of time."

"How far from Cuba to the Keys?" Ezra asked.

"Maybe an hour," Noble said. "Depends on airspeed."

"You can bet these guys have the pedal to the metal," Ezra said. "Any luck with that hatch?"

Noble tripped the safety latch, shot the bolt and heaved. The iron hatch groaned open with a loud metallic shriek. A moment later, he and Ezra were scaling a short ladder, through a second safety hatch and into the body of the craft.

They came up in a narrow utility corridor lit by bare bulbs in wire cages. An open locker door thumped and a loose bolt rattled around on the floor. Noble put his back to the wall and looked.

Ezra huddled next to him, eyes wide and his mouth open in a grimace, favoring his good leg. Ragged breaths escaped his lips and his hands flexed convulsively, like the hands of an addict in bad need of a fix.

Noble pointed toward the rear of the craft. "The cargo bay is that way. That's probably where they're storing the bomb. Get back there and disarm the thing."

"I'm not sure I know how to do that."

"Pull wires," Noble told him. "Smash it with a hammer if you have to, just make sure you disable it."

"What if one of them is guarding it?"

"You'll have to take him out," Noble said. "Think you can handle it?"

Ezra worked a determined frown onto his face and nodded. "What are you going to do?"

Noble pointed the other way. "I'm going up front to take over the plane."

"Without a gun?"

"Improvise, adapt and overcome."

Ezra said, "Good luck, man."

"You too," Noble said.

"If you find Gwen..."

"I'll take care of her." Noble offered a fist and Ezra bumped it, then they were moving in opposite directions.

# CHAPTER EIGHTY-FIVE

A PAIR OF F-18 HORNETS HURTLED SOUTH AT MACH 1 into the heart of the storm. Both were armed with heat-seeking and sidewinder missiles. MacDonald Douglas jet engines plumed dark trails from glowing afterburners. The lead jet was piloted by Benjamin "Big Bopper" Krantz, a ten year Air Force vet with experience in air-to-air combat. His wing man was John "Ringo" Ramone. This was John's second combat mission. He was still new to the game and sweating through his flight suit. The two supersonic fighter jets climbed through cloud cover and leveled out at forty-thousand feet, cruising along in formation, watching their radars for any sign of the cargo plane. Neither pilot knew the deadly cargo carried by the plane. Their orders were to locate a craft with the tail number NC14176 and shoot it out of the sky.

Big Bopper got a sniff on his radar. Ringo had the small green blip a moment later. Krantz radioed in the contact and then both jets were descending down into the booming storm, using clouds as cover for their approach. A fork of lightning streaked dangerously close to Big Bopper but the veteran never even flinched. A strike could easily ignite the jet fuel or detonate one of the missiles fixed under wing, but Krantz worked the controls like a long-haul trucker rolling down I75 under ideal circumstances. The contact was coming up fast, moving south to north at two-hundred and ten knots.

"They're really hauling butt," he said into his radio.

Ringo agreed and command ordered them to cut the chatter.

The two flat gray fighter jets streaked through the storm, silent messengers of death, invisible beneath a thick layer of cloud.

———

Noble made his way forward, moving quietly through the mid-section of the aircraft, keeping his eyes peeled. He had no idea how many men Wexler had onboard. How many men would willingly go to their death? Noble bet it wasn't many.

Sweat was seeping from every pore on his body and his hair was a stringy, tangled mess. His breath came out in ragged gasps that sounded like bellows in his own ears. He was sure the enemies would hear him coming long before they saw him but he was powerless to do anything about it. Fight or flight had taken over, amping his system up to ten, and that meant his lungs were working overtime, supplying his limbs with oxygen and blood. His fingers were pins and needles.

He was alone, unarmed, on a plane filled with an

unknown number of terrorists on a suicide run. Noble had passed barrels of jet fuel lashed to the bulkheads and knew the EMP was only the first strike. The terrorists would use the cargo jet the same way the September 11th hijackers had used passenger planes. After the EMP went off and the aircraft lost power, the pilot could manually steer it into the Capital building or the White House. And this attack would make September 11th look like a bloody nose. This strike would cripple the entire nation, killing millions. Noble couldn't let that happen, even if it meant crashing the plane into the ocean.

His face fixed in a hard frown and his legs were tensed, ready for action as he slid silently along the access hall to a closed door separating the front of the aircraft from the storage areas. He put his shoulder to the bulkhead, trying in vain to control his breathing, and tested the latch. It was unlocked and Noble turned it slowly, taking care not to make any more noise than absolutely necessary.

The door opened with a small peel of the rubber gasket and Noble chanced a peek. Beyond were several rows of utilitarian seats with an aisle running up the middle. Past that was a small curtained section for flight attendants and after that would be the cockpit door. He stepped into the seating section, leaving the door open behind him, and started up the aisle, painfully aware of the fact that he had no weapon. He had just reached the back row of seats when the curtain swept aside. A Middle Eastern man with a thick black beard and a scar stepped through.

———

Ezra licked his lips. His mouth seemed impossibly dry, like someone had scrubbed his throat with steel wool. No matter how much he tried to work up some spit, his tongue remained stubbornly dry, a big fat sponge in his mouth, soaking up all the moisture and making it difficult to breathe. His ankle throbbed with every step. He hobbled along, using his hands against the fuselage to keep his balance.

The utility corridor had led him into a cramped chamber—did you call rooms on planes chambers?—filled with what looked like spare parts in case of some inflight emergency. Several seats were stacked against the wall by the door, along with a number of rubber gaskets and chests full of tools. Ezra slid one of the drawers open and selected the biggest wrench he could find, then angled himself through the cramped passage to the opposite door. He took a deep breath before pushing down on the latch, certain this door led into the rear of the craft.

He was looking into a wide open space with a hulking device on pallets secured by straps to the middle of the floor. The EMP looked like something cobbled together by a mad scientist, built into a large metal housing, wires every-where, with a complicated gyroscope at its center. But Ezra didn't spare a second glance at the EMP. Gwen was locked in a cage to one side, sitting with her back against the bulk-head and her knees drawn up to her chest. Her head was down and mousy brown hair hung around her shoulders like a frizzy hive. The dress, which had been red once upon a time, was now a dingy grey. She made small sniffing noises, like someone who had been crying hard but was all cried out.

Ezra's heart leapt up into his throat. "Gwen!"

Her head came up, her eyes wide. She saw Ezra and came halfway to her feet, pressing a finger over her lips. "Shhhh!"

A shot rang out.

# CHAPTER EIGHTY-SIX

Noble locked eyes with the Arab. They stood in the center aisle, facing each other from less than twenty meters. Outside the storm raged. Thunder boomed and the cargo plane hitched on a pocket of turbulence. The only light came from windows, streaked with rain. It was a dim half-light that made details impossible, but Noble could see the gun holstered at the man's hip.

"Who...?" the man began. His face went from confusion, to fear, to anger. "How did you get in...?"

Noble was the first to move. He was already diving behind the back row of seats when the Arab jerked the pistol. Noble threw himself down, landing on his shoulder and banging his knee. There was a thunderclap inside the cramped confines of the plane that felt like a ball-peen hammer against Noble's eardrums. It was followed by three more sharp, earsplitting blasts.

Bullets punched through empty seats, hissed over Noble's head, and drilled through the back wall with hard flat *whacks!* Shredded bits of upholstery rained down and stuffing filled the air like confetti. The sharp tang of spent gunpowder filled the cabin.

Someone was yelling. Noble could barely make out the words over the high-pitched dial tone in his ears.

"Khan? What's going on? Who is shooting?"

"An infidel is onboard. Lock the cabin door."

A moment later Noble heard a soft thump. Getting through that door would be a challenge, but it was a problem for later. Right now he had more pressing issues. Khan had a gun and wasn't afraid to use it. He either didn't know, or didn't care, that a bullet through the fuselage would cause a critical depressurization that might bring down the plane.

Noble scrambled on hands and knees to the far wall and pressed himself flat against the floor in the hopes of avoiding any more bullets. He tried to keep track of how many shots Khan had fired. Was it four or five? It was hard to keep accurate count in the middle of a fight. And what kind of pistol was he holding? Noble had gotten a brief, shadowed glimpse of what looked like an old model Beretta, which meant fifteen rounds. That left Khan with plenty of firepower.

Peeking beneath the seats, Noble caught sight of Khan's feet as he stalked quietly up the center aisle. Trying hard to control his breathing, Noble shimmied under a chair, worming his way up into the next row. It was a tight fit—the space between the floor and the bottom of the seat was barely enough to admit Noble's chest and shoulders—but he managed to wriggle through. He was making his way forward while Khan made his way back. Noble had crossed three rows when Khan came into view, holding the Beretta out in front of him, gripped in both hands like a man who knew his way around guns. His eyes were narrowed against the dark and he was watching the back row.

Noble lay on his back, hardly daring to breath, as Khan crept past. His body was frozen, muscles tense. The cargo jet hit another pocket of turbulence and Khan took a moment to steady himself, then he was moving again, arms extended out in front, searching for a target in the dark.

Soon as he was past, Noble scrambled up. His only chance was to close the distance and get control of the gun. He planted a foot on the seat cushion, grabbed the headrest and launched himself.

Khan heard movement and turned just as Noble was throwing himself through the air. The gun came up and Noble hit Khan with all one hundred and seventy pounds.

———

Ezra's shoulders hitched up around his ears at the bullwhip crack of a pistol. Exquisite pain blossomed in his left cheek. The force of it almost ripped him off his feet. It was an effort to keep moving. The side of his face was on fire, like someone had slammed his head against a glowing hot griddle. A warm wet slick appeared on his chest. He'd been shot, but he had to keep moving, keep fighting. Had to save Gwen.

In truth, the bullet had smacked off the doorframe, shattered into pieces and a fragment had sliced open Ezra's cheek. But he had no way of knowing that. His world shrank down to pain and adrenaline.

"Ohmigod!" Gwen was shouting. "Ezra, look out! Look out!"

The shooter was at the very back of the cargo area, kneeling on a prayer rug with his back to the door when Ezra had entered. Now he was on his feet, circling the EMP. Ezra ducked behind the device, ignoring the searing pain and blood, and chanced a peek.

The gunman lifted his weapon but he didn't fire.

Ezra sank back down, gripping the wrench in his fist, and scrambled around the EMP, keeping the device between him and the terrorist.

"Come out," the man said, "and I promise to make your death painless."

"No thanks," Ezra heard himself say. His voice was a hoarse croak. His tongue was dry and his face numb. He hurried along the length of the EMP and dodged around the corner to keep out of sight, leaving a trail of blood. It was like a game of tag between school children, one boy chasing the other around a large tree. They went one way, then the other.

"Come out," the man demanded. "This is pointless."

He lifted the pistol and fired a shot over the device that smacked against the bulkhead with a sharp metal splat.

Gwen shrieked, "Don't shoot! You'll rupture the fuse-lage and kill us all."

"I am dead already," the man yelled. "My brother has decreed that we give our lives for the cause. What does it matter if I die now or in twenty minutes?"

"You could help me stop it," Ezra said. "Don't let your

brother dictate your death. Let's work together and put an end to this."

The man, not much more than a boy really, laughed and shook his head. "You understand nothing. Come out now or I will kill the girl."

He turned the gun on Gwen.

She backed up until she was against the wall, her hands shielding her face. She whimpered, "Please don't."

"Come out!" he shrieked. "Now!"

Ezra hesitated.

"I'll kill her." He pushed the gun through the bars.

"Okay." Ezra put his left hand up over the EMP and opened his palm in surrender. "Alright. I'm coming out. Don't hurt her."

"Step around where I can see you."

"I'm coming out," Ezra assured him.

Gwen said, "Don't do it, Ez. He's going to shoot you."

"You shut up!" the man barked and then, "If you don't come out, right now, I will shoot her. Do you want to watch her die? *Do you?*" His voice had risen to a hysterical pitch.

"Don't hurt her," Ezra said. "I'm coming out."

He stepped at the edge of the EMP, covered only by the metal framework, and took a deep breath. He still clutched the wrench in his right hand. The terrorist was fifteen feet away, his arm stuck through the bars and the gun aimed at Gwen's chest. She hunkered against the wall, her face a mask of terror. The thick, cloying smell of fear mingled with the sour odor of sweat and grease. Ezra adjusted his grip on the wrench. He had just one chance. He put his left hand up, empty palm out, held the wrench down behind his right leg and eased out around the EMP.

"See?" he said. "I'm coming out. Just don't hurt her. Point the gun at me, okay?"

The young man tried to change his aim but that required him to pull his arm back through the bars. Ezra made his move.

## CHAPTER EIGHTY-SEVEN

Noble hit Khan like a wrecking ball. The impact drove them both against the door separating the passenger section from the rest of the plane and it burst open, spilling them into the narrow corridor. They tumbled. Noble came down on top. A moment later, they were fighting for control of the gun.

Khan's breath was hot in Noble's ear. The Arab twisted and bucked in a vain attempt to throw Noble off. Noble had both hands around the weapon. He bared his teeth and grunted with effort, hoping to rip the gun away. His pinkie finger caught in the trigger guard. He heard a snap and felt a sharp jolt of agony. A scream escaped his lips. The digit was a throbbing mass of hurt that made it hard to think, and even harder to fight. The sudden flash of pain shattered Noble's concentration and Khan connected with an elbow. Noble's head rocked back. He felt his lip split and tasted blood.

Khan wrenched the gun back and forth. It was an effort just to hang on. He was like a bulldog with his favorite chew toy. He let out a low growl from the back of his throat, hinged open his jaw, darted forward and chomped down on Noble's hand.

A bright lance of electric panic went racing up Noble's spine. He could feel Khan's teeth sink deeper into the skin. Noble slammed his head forward, going for a head butt, hitting Khan's ear instead, but it was enough to make him let go.

Sometimes winning a fight is about doing what the other guy won't. Noble needed to get the gun away from Khan and couldn't take it by force. The only way to make him let go was to short circuit the signal between his brain and his fingers. Noble reared back and brought his head down in another vicious arc. The top of his skull crushed Khan's nose flat. There was a hard crunch and a spill of hot red blood. The hit was enough to daze Noble, but he kept his grip on the gun. He heaved up twice more, each time coming down with more force. The crown of his head slammed into Khan's unprotected face, mashing Khan's nose, knocking out his front teeth, and breaking the left cheek bone with a dull pop.

The last impact left Noble dazed, feeling like the big cargo jet was doing barrel rolls, but Khan's grip on the gun relaxed and Noble yanked it free.

Just holding the gun took all his concentration. His pinkie finger looked like an overcooked hot dog sticking up at an odd angle. Noble scrambled off the Arab in an effort to get some distance and heard the cockpit door open.

———

Nasir focused on keeping the big cargo plane steady. The sky was a dark swirling vortex of wind and rain and flashing light. And in one of those flashes Nasir could have sworn he spied the dark silhouette of a jet racing through the clouds. But who would be flying through this mess? Other than the American military? Nasir had adjusted his course in an attempt to get another look, but the storm refused to cooperate and he hit a large thermal up draft forcing him to fight the stick and adjust the pitch for several seconds.

Through the closed door he could hear the sounds of the fight. Someone had stowed away aboard the plane and now it sounded like Khan was locked in a deadly struggle. Nasir fretted in silence for several seconds, trying to decide what to do. It was his job to fly the plane, but two against one made better odds. After some deliberation, Nasir set the autopilot, unbuckled himself and got up.

He unlocked the door, slipped through the small section for flight attendants, and swept back the curtain to find a man, an American, aiming a gun at The Interpreter.

"Khan!" Nasir shouted.

———

Benjamin "Big Bopper" Krantz spotted the lumbering cargo plane as it sped north. He and his wing man were streaking south at Mach 1 and the other craft had just been a brief outline against the dark sky. The storm was really rocking the old tub. The pilot must be crazy to fly in these conditions.

"Ringo," Krantz said. "Did you catch that?"

"Yep," Ringo said.

Krantz radioed the visual to command and then said, "Let's move in for a closer look."

The two F-18 Hornets throttled down and streaked around in a tight arc that brought them up behind the slower moving cargo craft. Krantz worked the controls until he had an angle on the tail section. He didn't really need to get the number—there was nobody else up here, nobody else was crazy enough to fly through the outskirts of a hurricane—but he did anyway and radioed the positive ID back to command.

They were less than five minutes from American airspace and another ten from the Florida Keys.

———

Ezra threw the wrench in an overhand arc that sent the heavy steel club hurtling end over end. The young Arab saw it and his eyes opened wide. He ducked his head and tried to twist out of the way, but his arm was still between the bars. His other hand came up to protect his face. He wasn't quick enough. The wrench clipped him on the side of the head with a good solid *thock* and his knees buckled.

Gwen sprang forward, reaching for the gun. Her face was pulled tight and her eyes wide. She almost had it, but he jerked his arm back through the bars at the very last moment.

# CHAPTER EIGHTY-EIGHT

"They've got eyes on target," an Air Force Colonel in the White House Situation Room announced. The mood was tense. Everyone had been waiting in silence for word from the pilots. No one even bothered to complain about Wizard's cigarette smoke anymore. In fact, two of the generals had lit up as well and now lazy halos of smoke pooled around the overhead lights. The Air Force Colonel covered the mouthpiece and told the room, "Our boys are in place and ready to take the shot. Just say the word."

All eyes turned to the SecDef. He said, "Where are they?"

The Colonel spoke into the phone. "Give us a sit rep. What's the current location on target?"

There was a slight delay as the people at MacDill spoke to the pilots and then relayed the information back to the White House. The Colonel said, "They'll be over the Keys in roughly five minutes."

Armstrong closed her eyes and let out a breath.

The SecDef leaned back in his chair. "That's it then. We have to take action."

Wizard tapped ash into an empty coffee cup. "We agreed to wait until they were over the Keys."

"They're close," one of the generals said.

"Close only counts in horseshoes and hand grenades."

The SecDef turned to Trasker. "If they set the device off now, how much damage would it do?"

"Hard to say," Trasker admitted. "Rough estimate; they'd knock out most of the southeastern seaboard."

"Washington?" the SecDef questioned.

Trasker ducked his head. "Possibly."

The SecDef shook his head. "We can't wait any longer."

"What about the Keys?" Wizard asked. "I thought that was our line in the sand."

"That's less than five minutes away."

"Give my people that five minutes," Wizard urged.

"I'm sorry, Al. I can't." He turned to the Airforce Colonel. "Take the shot."

"Don't do it," Wizard said. "You shoot that plane down and you're condemning two of my people, maybe three, to death."

The Colonel hesitated, caught between the Secretary of Defense and the Deputy Director of Operations for the CIA.

The SecDef leaned forward. "Take the shot. That's an order."

"Tommy," Wizard spoke in a calm voice, "I'm asking you not to do that."

Colonel Tom Erlinger looked from Wizard to the

SecDef and said, "Maybe we should give them a few more minutes."

"We don't even know if his people are still alive," one of the generals argued.

"And we're running out of time to act," the Secretary of State added.

"Don't do it, Tommy," Wizard said.

The SecDef pointed a shaking finger at Wizard. "I want you out of here." The finger pivoted to Erlinger. "And you order those pilots to bring down that plane, or you'll be court martialed. Is that clear?"

Tommy Erlinger spared an apologetic look at Wizard. "Sorry, Al."

The SecDef swiveled to face a Secret Service agent stationed near the door. "I want Deputy Director Dulles removed."

The buzz cut in a suit started forward.

Wizard held his ground.

The agent motioned for him to get up and, when Wizard refused, the agent reached for his weapon.

Wizard blew smoke. "You'll be dead before it clears the holster, young man."

"Al!" Armstrong put herself between the two men and said, "I need you to leave, Al."

He held her gaze for a moment, crushed out his cigarette and stood up.

Tommy Erlinger licked his lips, lifted the phone and said, "Take the shot."

———

Ezra's heart climbed his throat and his legs pistoned, carrying him across the open space. His mouth opened and his arms pumped for more speed. He was screaming as he bore down on the dazed terrorist.

The young Arab pushed to his feet, his back against the bars, and the gun came up in one smooth arc.

"Ezra!" Gwen shouted. "Look out! He's gonna shoot." Her hands flew up to her mouth and her eyes bulged.

Ezra took a running leap, threw his leg out in a flying side kick, and sailed through the air, a high-pitched "*Haii-iyaaaa!*" coming up from his throat.

The gun thundered but the shot went low while Ezra's kick, a perfect flying side kick which he'd never been able to perform in karate class, connected with the terrorist's jaw. There was a muffled pop. The man's head cracked back against the bars, his eyes rolled up, his knees came unglued and he sank down into a heap. The gun slipped from nerveless fingers.

Ezra went to the floor. He was back up just as fast. His body felt light as a feather. His arms and legs were wild things, acting on their own. His mind was in overdrive. Events seemed to happen in slow motion. He jumped up from the floor and delivered a flat-bladed karate chop to the terrorist's neck, aiming for the bundle of nerves in the throat. He chopped once, twice, three times. Punctuating each strike with an energetic "Haiya! Haiya! Haiya!" His face was pulled tight in a crazy grimace, part fear, part excitement.

The young Arab pitched over on his side, his jaw broken in two different places and the blood flow to his brain temporarily interrupted. Ezra, in his fear-induced flight of strength, had in fact caused minor paralysis and brain damage which would affect the man for life, but Ezra didn't know it at the time. All he knew was that he needed to put this terrorist out of commission and stop the bomb, so he karate chopped until the Arab lay unconscious at his feet, then looked around for the gun, but Gwen had already reached through the bars and got hold of it.

"You did it," Gwen cried, her face beaming with joy. "You did it, Ez! You beat him."

"I beat him," Ezra said more to himself, as if he were confirming this information to his brain. "I sure did. I beat him."

Gwen reached through the bars, grabbed him by the collar and pulled him in for a kiss. Their lips met and, for several seconds, it was all Ezra could think about. He was kissing Gwen! He had dreamed of this day since they first met. It was like Christmas, his birthday, and New Years all rolled up into one. It was winning the lottery and finding out you didn't even have to pay taxes on the money. It was everything he'd ever dreamed, soft and wet and eager. Ezra wanted that moment to go on forever but his brain insisted he had more important matters, bigger fish to fry, and he reached a hand through the bars to gently separate them. It was the hardest thing he'd ever had to do.

He said, "Plenty of time for that later. Right now, I need you to help me disable this bomb."

"It's okay," Gwen told him.

"We've got to shut this thing down," Ezra said with a look at the timer. "It's going to pop off in less than forty minutes."

"He's got the keys," Gwen said, nodding at the unconscious terrorist. "Get me out of this cage."

Ezra patted the man down and found the keys. When he unlocked the door, Gwen threw herself at him, smothering him in kisses. He felt the softness of her lips and the press of her breasts. She wrapped him up in her arms, still holding onto the gun. She stopped long enough to whisper, "Look what they did to your face. You poor thing."

Then she was kissing him again. It was a heady experience, but Ezra pushed her back. "Later, okay? We've gotta stop this bomb."

She said, "No need to worry about that. We need to bandage your cheek."

"How can you say that?"

Ezra started to turn toward the device, but Gwen caught him and pulled him back. "I already disabled it," she said. "I attached the timer to a relay loop. It's totally safe."

Ezra's mouth fell open. "You tricked them?"

"You didn't think I'd actually finish an EMP that I knew was going to be used against the United States, did you?"

Ezra drew in some air and shook his head. "Clever girl."

They kissed again and this time Ezra wasn't sure how long it went on. She pressed up against him and he pulled her tight, only peeling open one eye to occasionally check on the unconscious terrorist at their feet.

When they finally pulled apart, Ezra turned back to the EMP. "You're sure it's safe?"

In answer, she went to the device and jabbed the detonate button with her fingertip. The clock turned to zero and nothing happened.

"That's one problem solved," Ezra told her.

"What's the other?"

"I think the military is going to shoot the plane down."

Her eyebrows went all the way up her forehead and tried to crawl into her hairline. "Why didn't you say so before?"

"I was preoccupied."

She grabbed his hand and hauled him toward the door.

# CHAPTER EIGHTY-NINE

Noble heard the shout and turned. He didn't know if the pilot had a gun but wasn't taking any chances. A man in shadow is a dangerous man. So Noble pinned the front sight on the silhouette in the curtained doorframe and eased back on the trigger. The Beretta boomed in the small space and shell casings went spinning through the air. All three rounds found their mark. One entered just below the pilot's collarbone, dead center, driving him back through the curtain. The other two shots took him low in the belly. He made a small yelping noise, like a dog that just got its tail caught under a rocking chair, and went stumbling toward the cockpit.

Noble started down the aisle. He meant to rush the cockpit before the pilot could lock the door, but Khan grasped hold of his leg in a last-ditch effort to carry out his villainous mission. His fingers sank into Noble's calf and his bloody mouth opened in a snarl.

Noble twisted round, jammed the barrel against Khan's head and jerked the trigger. The thunderclap took the back of Abdul's head off in a pulpy red splatter of gore that pasted itself against the fuselage. His fingers relaxed and Noble pulled his leg free.

————

Nasir, bleeding profusely, stumbled back to the cockpit. He was aware only of the fact that he'd been shot, multiple times, and was dying. There was no hope for him, so he commended his soul to Allah, and bullied his legs into carrying him the last few steps to the cockpit where the autopilot was engaged in an epic battle with tropical storm-force winds throwing the cargo plane around like a child's toy. He left a dark bloody slick every step of the way and wondered that his body could have so much blood. Even more surprising was the fact he could have lost so much and still be on his feet. It was on his hands, on his chest, and freshets were piping up from his throat and pouring out his mouth. His strength wouldn't last long. He could feel himself dying, a pocket watch in bad need of winding, his internal gears grinding to a slow and inexorable halt.

He made it through the doorframe, turned and slammed the door shut, then locked it. A small knowing smile appeared on his pale face. Whatever else happened, the auto pilot would carry this plane over the United States and the EMP would plunge the Americans into darkness. The resulting chaos would kill many millions. Nasir nodded to himself. He could die knowing he'd done his part. He tried to reach the pilot's seat but the last of his strength gave out and he went to the floor. The smile vanished, replaced by a grim mask of horror at what he glimpsed on the other side, then the light winked out of his eyes.

———

Noble hit the cockpit door seconds after it closed. He slammed up against the sturdy frame with a curse, rebounded, and threw himself against it again in an effort to break it down, but his shoulder came away sore and the door stood solid, mocking him.

Ezra and Gwen appeared a moment later, stepping over the body of The Interpreter. Ezra had a blood-soaked rag pressed against his cheek and he was limping heavily. Despite the bloody wound, he looked like a guy who just found a briefcase full of cash. Gwen held a gun in one hand. Her other hand was firmly entwined with Ezra's.

Noble drew a sharp breath at the bib of blood on Ezra's chest. "You okay?"

"Think so," Ezra croaked. "You?"

Noble nodded and turned to Gwen. "Thank God you're alive."

"Thanks to Ezra as well." She flashed him a smile. It was like watching the head cheerleader beaming up at the star quarterback. She gave his hand a little squeeze and said, "He saved me."

"The bomb?"

"Taken care of," Ezra told him.

"You're sure?"

Ezra nodded. "Gwen fixed it before the plane even lifted off."

Noble opened his mouth to ask how she'd managed that

but realized it was unimportant. He said, "We've got to get this cockpit door open and use the radio to let the White House know we're in control of this plane or they're going to shoot us out of the sky. Any ideas?"

Gwen and Ezra only looked at each other and shook their heads. Ezra said, "After September eleventh those things were reinforced with Kevlar and titanium crossbars. If it's locked from the inside, there's no way you're getting in."

Noble turned back to the door and ran a hand along the joints, searching for any weakness in the design. "That's not what I want to hear."

"It's the truth," Gwen said. "These doors are, for all intents and purposes, impossible to break open."

Noble shook his head. "I refuse to accept that."

"We could try shooting our way through," Ezra said, "but we'd probably end up destroying the controls in the process."

"Think," Noble growled. "There's got to be a way."

"The locks are electronic." Gwen looked around for some place to put the gun now that she no longer needed it, settled for dropping it in a seat and then turned to Ezra. "The locks are electronic!"

"Yeah," he said. "So?"

"Don't you see? If we reset the computers, the lock will automatically release."

"How you going to do that from outside the cockpit?" Noble asked.

"We don't have to be inside the cockpit to reset the computers," Gwen said.

Ezra snapped his fingers. "The forward avionics bay."

"Exactly," Gwen said.

"That's brilliant," Noble agreed. "But will you know which switches to throw when you get down there?"

Ezra nodded. "I think so."

"Don't waste time standing here talking to me."

The pair of computer ninjas hurried back down the aisle, looking for the first available hatch. They found one beneath Khan's lifeless body. They heaved the corpse aside and Ezra pulled open the small access door.

———

Benjamin Krantz put one hand to his helmet as the order to fire came over his headset. He got a burst of static in his ear and, more to buy time than because of any real fear he had misheard, he asked command to repeat the last order.

Command came back loud and clear with the order to shoot down the cargo plane a second time.

Big Bopper nodded. "Acknowledged."

In reality, he was covering his own butt. The flight logs were all recorded and admissible. If something went wrong, the Big Bopper would claim he was simply following orders. Not that he had any hang-ups about shooting an aircraft out of the sky. He had three confirmed kills in combat missions, but this was the first time he'd ever shot a plane down in American airspace and he wanted to make sure nothing came rolling back on him. He confirmed the order, then throttled back, allowing the cargo plane to pull ahead. He wanted plenty of space when he fired. Planes that break apart in midair throw off a lot of debris and Krantz didn't want a bit of tail section to clip his wings. He eased into position, got a lock on the craft, then armed his sidewinders.

———

It had to be twenty degrees cooler in the underside of the craft. Ezra shivered as he hurried along the series of tight catwalks to the forward avionics bay. Sweat poured from every pore on his body, ran down his forehead and seeped into his collar. Gwen was still clutching his hand, tight on his heels. They reached the bank of computer terminals powering the airplane and a red bulb in a wire cage gave just enough light to see.

"Which one is it?" Gwen asked.

There were two racks with blinking LEDs and each system bank was labeled with a number. Gwen found an operations binder chained to the terminals and they paged through laminated sheets in search of the computer that controlled the cockpit door. Gwen gave a leap, nearly knocking her head on the low ceiling when she found it. She jabbed at the page and said, "D-14! It's D-14."

"Got it," Ezra said. "You tell Noble."

He was already scanning the row of hardware when Gwen sprinted back through the passage to the open hatch. Ezra had just thrown the switch, shorting out the computer when she yelled up, "Jake, it should be open."

———

Noble grasped the latch and twisted. The door popped open and a second later he was stumbling over Nasir's body in an effort to reach the pilot's seat. The dead man had set the plane to autopilot which solved half of Noble's problems for him. He snatched up the headset, fitted them onto and started dialing through emergency frequencies.

"Mayday, mayday. This is unchartered flight NC14176. My name is Jacob Noble, I'm an American intelligence officer. I've commandeered this craft and I'm in need of assistance. Mayday, mayday. Does anyone read me?"

He repeated the message on three different channels before trying to reach the Miami Dade international control tower.

———

Benjamin "Big Bopper" Krantz had his thumb on the missile release. The target was locked in the guidance system. The sidewinder was armed and ready, and would explode on impact. He was just about to toggle the release when Ringo came over the headset.

"Big Bopper, I'm picking up an emergency broadcast. I think it's coming from the cargo jet."

Big Bopper took his thumb off the trigger. "Say again, Ringo."

"Got an emergency broadcast from the cargo jet," Ringo told him. "Guy claiming to be an American intelligence officer is saying he's now in control of the craft. He's asking for assistance."

Krantz locked and disarmed his missile guidance system before radioing in to command for further instructions.

# CHAPTER NINETY

WIZARD WAS IN THE HALL OUTSIDE THE SITUATION Room. He stood with his back to the wall, staring at the closed door like he could see through the wood at what was happening on the other side. His hands were hooked in the pockets of his slim black suit jacket and his face was fixed in a vulture frown. His eyes were cold hard chips of ice beneath scraggly salt and pepper brows.

Those unruly brows twitched when the door opened and Armstrong emerged. He knew right away it was good news. Her face was glowing. She said, "We just got word. Noble's in control of the plane. He's disabled the EMP. Cook and Witwicky are both alive and well, but in need of medical attention."

She crossed the hall, took Wizard's skeletal hand in both of her own and pumped it. "Noble did it, Al."

The barest hint of a smile turned up one side of Wizard's mouth. He nodded and let Armstrong wring his hand. The knot in his belly let go a little and he said, "That kid has the Devils' own luck."

"We're directing them into Mac Dill," Armstrong said. "I'm on the first flight down to meet them. Are you coming with me?"

Wizard inclined his head. "What about the SecDef?"

"Let him stew," Armstrong said. "Our people won this round. That's going to give us a lot of leverage. He won't be able to bring charges against you or Noble, not after you saved America from an EMP attack."

Wizard knew better. The Secretary of Defense was a politician and they held grudges. He said, "You have a cigarette?"

"No." Armstrong reached in her jacket and produced two slim cigars. "But I've got these."

They snipped the ends and lit up as they made their way through the White House, smiling at sour-faced political aides offended by the smoke.

# CHAPTER NINETY-ONE

Noble was slumped in a hard plastic seat next to Cook's hospital bed. The little guy hadn't just sprained his ankle, he'd fractured it. The pain must have been unbearable. His foot was now in a hard plastic boot and his face was covered in bandages. A bullet fragment had taken a nasty chunk out of his cheek. The doctors had tried to schedule a skin graft to fix the worst of the damage, but Ezra shook his head and said he'd live with the scar.

Noble had a broken pinkie finger. The doctor said it was a nice clean break and should heal in a month or two. A stiff metal brace was keeping the broken digit in place. The rest of Noble's injuries were scrapes and bruises. His back felt like someone had worked him over with a baseball bat and his neck was tight, but a few days of rest and some pain killers would put him back on his feet.

Morning sun filtered through the window of Ezra's private room. The hurricane had turned north and west, hammering the Texas coast, leaving Florida unscathed. The only sound was the soft, steady beep of Ezra's heart rate and oxygen monitors.

They sat in silence for a few minutes and then Noble said, "You did good, Ez."

"Thanks Jake."

"I mean it," Noble told him. "I never would have thought to access the avionics bay. I'd have beat my shoulder against that door until the plane went down in a ball of fire. You and Gwen saved us all."

Ezra said, "I never would have been on that plane without your help."

Noble reached across, shook Ezra's hand and they lapsed back into an easy silence, pain killers lulling both men toward sleep.

Gwen arrived dressed in aqua green hospital scrubs, with her hair pulled back in a ponytail, wearing a pair of second-hand specs that a nurse had liberated from the lost and found. Her face lit up at the sight of them.

"There they are!" Gwen threw her arms wide and hurried over to embrace them both. She wrapped one arm around Noble's neck and the other around Ezra. Noble had to lean sideways into the hug or be pulled right off his chair.

"My brave, beautiful, stupid boys!" Gwen said.

"Stupid?" Noble questioned.

"You never should have gotten on that plane," Gwen said and then added, "but I'm glad you did."

Tears were standing in her eyes when she finally let go. "I owe you both so much," she said. "You saved my life."

"It was mostly Jake," Ezra said, eyes downcast.

Gwen put one finger under Ezra's chin and turned his face up to hers. "Don't be so modest, hero."

He started to speak and she planted a kiss on his lips.

"All three of you are going to receive commendations," a familiar voice said.

Armstrong and Wizard stood in the doorframe. The Director said, "You saved millions of Americans."

"Congratulations are in order." Wizard closed the door to keep the conversation private. "Any chance Wexler admitted who he was working for?"

Gwen shook her head. "Whoever it is has pretty deep pockets."

"What about the third terrorist?" Ezra asked. "The one I knocked out in the cargo hold?"

Wizard tapped a cigarette out of his pack and lit up. "He only knows he was working for Wexler, and it was trouble getting that much out of him. He's got partial brain damage. Talking is difficult. He's going to spend the rest of his life in a diaper."

Noble said, "You already know who Wexler works for."

Wizard blew smoke and waved it away. "Too bad we can't prove it."

"We know who's responsible," Armstrong said. "That's the important thing, and we'll be keeping an eye on him. In the meantime, you three are going to get some rest. Doctor's orders."

"Did they ever find Lukyanenko?" Gwen asked. She was sitting on the side of Ezra's bed, holding his hand.

"Found him buried in a shallow grave right next to his wife," Wizard said. "A few meters from the private airfield."

"Poor guy," Ezra said.

"And the bomb?" Noble asked.

"Our people are reverse engineering it as we speak," Armstrong said.

Noble thought about that and said, "It's a lot of power for any one country to wield."

"And nobody knows we have it," Gwen said.

"Nobody is going to know," Armstrong told them. "You'll all be signing a strict non-disclosure agreement."

A humorless smile turned up one side of Noble's face. "You come to congratulate us, or make sure we didn't talk?"

Armstrong and Wizard exchanged a look. Armstrong said, "A little of both. Enjoy the next few days. You're expected back at Langley for a debrief by the end of the week."

# CHAPTER NINETY-TWO

SOMETHING HAD GONE WRONG. THE ARABS screwed up.

Wexler sat on the settee in a quarter-million dollar hacienda in Paraguay, a ceiling fan slowly spinning overhead, flipping through news channels on a big screen TV. The air was sweetly scented by a riot of oleanders growing wild in the garden outside his window. It was almost noon. Every channel should be covering America's mysterious blackout. Wexler opened a laptop, went to YouTube and found nothing.

Something had gone wrong. And it was Wexler's butt on the line.

He thought of the Old Man and an icy snake slithered up his spine. What would he do when he found out?

Wexler got up and went to the window, gazing past the brightly lit garden bursting white with oleanders to the gated entry. He told himself to relax. There was no way Keiser could find him. The pilot was dead and no one knew about Wexler's hacienda.

*No way for the Old Man to find me here.*

He took a calming breath, scrubbed the back of his neck and turned away from the window. That's when he heard the creak of floorboards in the hall. He tensed. His hands hooked into claws. He started for the cabinet on the side of the room where he'd stashed a Sig pistol, but he wasn't fast enough.

Four heavily armed men, dressed in black fatigues, spilled into the room. They carried MP5 submachine guns fitted with sound suppressors and their faces were covered by black ski masks. They were on Wexler before he went two whole steps. He was thrown to the ground, man-handled onto his stomach and his wrists were zip-tied behind his back.

"Keiser would like a word," one of them said.


The End.

# CAN'T WAIT FOR MORE JAKE NOBLE?

Sign up for the Jake Noble Fan Club and get, SIDE JOBS: Volume 1, The Heist for FREE! This story is available exclusively to my mailing list.

https://williammillerauthor.com/fan-club/

## DID YOU ENJOY THE BOOK?

Please take a moment to leave a review on Amazon. Readers depend on reviews when choosing what to read next and authors depend on them to sell books. An honest review is like leaving your waiter a hundred dollar tip. The best part is, it doesn't cost you a dime!

## ABOUT THE AUTHOR

I was born and raised in sunny Saint Petersburg, FL on a steady diet of action movies and fantasy novels. After 9/11, I left a career in photography to join the United States Army. Since then, I have travelled the world and done everything from teaching English in China to driving a fork-lift. I studied creative writing at Eckerd College and wrote four hard-boiled mysteries for Delight Games before releasing the first Jake Noble book. When not writing, I can be found indoor rock climbing, playing the guitar, and haunting smoke-filled jazz clubs in downtown Saint Pete. I'm currently at work on another Jake Noble thriller. You can follow me on my website WilliamMillerAuthor.com

facebook.com/authorwillmiller

twitter.com/man_author

instagram.com/wmiller314

## ALSO BY WILLIAM MILLER

**The Jake Noble Series in Chronological Order:**

Noble Man

Noble Vengeance

Noble Intent

Noble Sanction

Noble Asset

**The Mackenzie and Cole Series:**

The Devil His Due

Skin in the Game - forthcoming

**Crafting Fiction:**

Volume 1 - Hardboiled Outlines

Made in the USA
Las Vegas, NV
16 February 2023

67665720R00236